Anita Loos Rediscovered

Anita Loos Rediscovered

Film Treatments and Fiction

Anita Loos

Edited and Annotated by
Cari Beauchamp and Mary Anita Loos

UNIVERSITY OF CALIFORNIA PRESS

Berkeley   Los Angeles   London

University of California Press
Berkeley and Los Angeles, California

University of California Press, Ltd.
London, England

Library of Congress Cataloging-in-Publication Data

Loos, Anita, 1893–1981.
   Anita Loos rediscovered : film treatments and fiction
 / edited and annotated by Cari Beauchamp and Mary
 Anita Loos.
     p. cm.
   Includes bibliographical references and index.
   ISBN 0-520-22894-4 (alk. paper)
   I. Beauchamp, Cari.   II. Loos, Mary Anita, 1911–
   III. Title.

PS3523.O557A6   2003

813'. 52—dc21   2003003883

Manufactured in the United States of America

12 11 10 09 08 07 06 05 04 03
10 9 8 7 6 5 4 3 2 1

The paper used in this publication is both acid-free and totally
chlorine-free (TCF). It meets the minimum requirements of
ANSI/NISO Z39.48-1992 (R 1997) *(Permanence of Paper)*.♾

To the wit and wisdom of my beloved Aunt Anita.

Mary Anita Loos

The richest lives, like the best films,
are true works of collaboration—
To the wonderful women, past and present,
who have collaborated to make my life so rich.

Cari Beauchamp

CONTENTS

FOREWORD

Memory is not necessarily truth—it is a constant civil war. If there is anyone who could have written the history of writing for the screen, it was Anita Loos. Yet doing so had not seemed important at the time.

She began selling random stories to various companies to help pay the family rent, and eventually she procured a studio job with D. W. Griffith as a so-called story editor. (She bought many of her own scenarios, thus doubling her income. But, after all, hers were the best.)

She grew up with the newborn movie industry that led her into her great success with subtitles and on to feature films and early talkies. She moved to the big canvas of the golden years of studios such as Famous Players–Lasky (later known as Paramount), Metro-Goldwyn-Mayer, and Twentieth Century Fox. Her great success with her brilliant novel, *Gentlemen Prefer Blondes,* shot her like a comet into the world of celebrities and international society. Later, as a craftsperson of stage plays, she became a star maker and a biographer of talent. During the years she traveled in Europe and headquartered in New York, she continued writing by hand. Her humor spilled out of her writing to create laughter for the world, in spite of the secret sadness of her lonely life.

Anita was a woman who in her work and with friends hid her sadness about her marriage to a man who always clung to her talent, a man who ostensibly had married her to be her collaborator when, in fact, she did all the work. He had numerous affairs. He also squandered her enormous fortune from *Gentlemen Prefer Blondes,* lost everything in the stock market, and left her with a loneliness she tried to forget with her ever-moving pen while he retired on a large annuity.

As her close relative I was privy, in her middle and elder years, to the heartbreak that was hidden from most of the world. She told me, "As you get older, choose younger friends." She sighed. "It gets lonely."

Her laughter and her ability to listen as well as to express her unique humor made her a memorable companion. Her constant desire to do the best, to look the best, and to be a part of whatever life she had to face made her exceptional—as a person, as a talent, and as my beloved Aunt Anita.

Mary Anita Loos

Introduction

Anita Loos is perhaps best known today for informing the world that "gentlemen prefer blondes" and that "diamonds are a girl's best friend." Yet she did so much more than that. As early as 1917 her work was compared favorably with O. Henry's,[1] and for more than three decades she was one of Hollywood's most respected and prolific screenwriters. Anita was also an accomplished novelist, a short-story writer, and a much-in-demand New York playwright. Her full-page obituary in the *New York Times* in 1981 attests to the longevity of her celebrity status, but hard work went into that glamorous façade: Anita wrote almost every day for more than seventy of her ninety-four years.

Anita Loos Rediscovered is a showcase for the breadth and depth of Anita's talent. Anita left behind a treasure trove of previously unpublished material, and her niece, Mary Anita, and I combed through it for a sampling that would include varieties of form and styles to demonstrate the many different ways Anita told her stories. We also wanted to illuminate how writing for the screen matured over the years. These comedies, romances, and melodramas span five decades, beginning with the tales written from her home and sent off to New York to become silent films through one-act plays, magazine short stories, and treatments for "talkies." To complement Anita's stories, we have added Mary Anita's

remembrances of her aunt and my summaries of the times and circumstances during which Anita was writing. It is our hope that our three
voices in combination will reveal a more complete Anita Loos—her constantly evolving talent, as well as her complex, caring, and at times
conflicted personal life.

Anita began writing for the movies when they were still shown in
nickelodeons and between vaudeville acts; she was still working when
Cinerama was introduced. She was a high-perched participant in moviemaking from the time films were made on empty lots, through the as-
sembly lines of studios the size of a small city, and then through the
breakup of that same studio system. During her incredible career Anita
Loos knew all the Hollywood greats and worked with most of them.
Her first script was directed by D. W. Griffith in 1912 and starred Mary
Pickford; forty years later Anita was collaborating with Colette on *Gigi*
and discovering Audrey Hepburn to play the role on the New York
stage. In between, Anita created the athletic comic characters that made
Douglas Fairbanks a star and wrote romances for Marion Davies and
Constance Talmadge. Anita saw a halo of stardom around Jean Harlow
and pushed her career by writing most of her wisecracking characters;
three decades later she saw that same glow around Carol Channing and
successfully lobbied to have her play Lorelei Lee in the Broadway musical version of *Gentlemen Prefer Blondes*. Metro-Goldwyn-Mayer production chief Irving Thalberg knew he could count on Anita for unique
dialogue laced with double entendres, Clark Gable depended on her for
advice on roles, and director George Cukor insisted she be by his side
on the set.

Anita moved to New York in the mid-1940s and based herself there
for the rest of her life. She arrived in her new guise as a Broadway playwright having penned *Happy Birthday* for Helen Hayes and went on to
write more than a half dozen other successful plays. She also turned out
the novellas *Gentlemen Marry Brunettes, No Mother to Guide Her,* and *A
Mouse Is Born;* the nonfiction tomes *Twice Over Lightly,* cowritten with
Helen Hayes, *The Talmadge Girls,* the autobiographic *A Girl like I,* and

Kiss Hollywood Good-bye; and the fabulous coffee-table book of photographs and vignettes, *A Cast of Thousands.* Throughout her life Anita was always a much-sought-after guest on the international social circuit.

Anita Loos characterized herself as carefree and elfin, a writer who dashed off her stories without an ounce of angst. She said that screenwriting was so fun she "would have done it for nothing" and that once the plot was thought up, "it was a breeze."[2] She was much more complex, disciplined, and talented than she gave herself credit for, publicly or privately. The truth is she rose at five o'clock almost every morning to start writing and often found herself in "black despair" over a plotline. She agonized over every word and what the reaction to her stories would be. Carol Channing testifies to the care Anita gave to her work, as well as to her sense of style. "She worked long and hard at her writing. I still have a silver pen that has her chew marks on it. Everyone has heard of writers who chew on their pencils, but a silver pen? Only Anita!"[3]

As seriously as Anita took her work, her friends and family were of equal importance in her life. Charlie Chaplin, Aldous Huxley, H. G. Wells, Wilson Mizner, and H. L Mencken all sought her out and remained her close friends for years. She enjoyed the company of women as well, including beautiful ones like Paulette Goddard and Marion Davies. What was important to Anita was that they didn't take themselves too seriously and possessed a fine-tuned sense of humor. She had little tolerance for women like Mary Pickford or the so-called wits of the Algonquin Round Table because she thought they believed their own press clippings. Her address book was a "Who's Who" of Hollywood, but her interests and friends spanned the globe. To intrigue Anita for any length of time, you had to be smart, accomplished, and, most of all, you had to make her laugh. In contrast to her immortalized heroine Lorelei, Anita would always prefer a laugh to tangible rewards.

Although there were only a select few whose opinions Anita truly valued, how others perceived her was important to her. She cared passionately about being chic and dieted whenever she was a pound or two above what she considered overweight (anything over 101) on her four-foot, eleven-inch frame. She was an advocate of daily massages and tried to squeeze in a trip to a European spa every year. For exercise she took long walks or practiced ballet almost every day. She always dressed in the height of fashion and prided herself on the fact she was one of the first to bob her hair in the 1920s.

She was a self-educated student all her life. As a young woman Anita spent hours in the library devouring philosophers like Voltaire and Spinoza. She taught herself French and made a point of reading the East Coast newspapers to keep up on fashions and theatrical news so that when she went to New York, as of course she eventually did, she would feel at home. But Anita admitted to her niece that when she was alone in a city, she would occasionally write in her diary items such as "go to library" so she could tell herself she was busy. She put much thought and effort into appearing carefree.

One of Anita's secrets was that she was a great listener. With Mizner or Mencken she would sit quietly, hanging on their every word, and get off the occasional zinger. (*Gentlemen Prefer Blondes* was her written response to Mencken's melting in the presence of a ditsy blonde.) With others she was quite the raconteur.

In spite of her tiny size Anita could be very intimidating. As her friend Leo Lerman observed at her memorial service in 1981, "She was absolutely enormous within that tininess." Karl Brown, who first met Anita when he was Billy Bitzer's assistant cameraman working with D. W. Griffith, recalled Anita as "one of the brainiest young women alive" and "filled with more wit and wisdom than anyone I ever encountered." Brown was so taken by her constant repartee and the fact she was "so quick on the trigger, so fast on the comeback" that he finally asked her how she did it. Anita "answered, in a low conspiratorial undertone out of the side of her mouth, 'As long as I can hang on to my copy of Voltaire, there's nobody going to catch me without a snappy comeback.'"[4] This was vintage Anita. Her bons mots were her armor, yet by not accepting the credit for her wit, she felt safe in the knowledge that if the gag backfired, she had Voltaire to blame.

The more I learned to appreciate Anita's talents and the more I learned about her personal life, the more frustrated I became with her for presenting to the world this picture of a passive fun lover just along for the ride. I understood in a way and laughed as I read her version of her antics, but as I studied her scripts, plays, and books and what others said about her, I knew she was so much more than a devil-may-care gamine. This little woman who made light of her own accomplishments was a giant talent and a caring person who suffered in silence over more than one broken heart.

If she didn't appreciate herself as much as I thought she should have, I wanted others to appreciate her. Then, when Mary Anita, Anita's niece and namesake, shared Anita's papers with me while I was researching my book on Frances Marion and her friends, I knew I had to come back for more. Not only was Mary Anita a total delight herself, but Anita had clearly left material that cried out to be seen by more eyes than mine and a few select researchers.

With the encouragement of Eric Smoodin of the University of California Press, Mary Anita and I culled through the hundreds of pages of material Anita had left to her niece. Mary Anita obviously knew her aunt from a very unique perspective and enthralled me with her tales as I read through Anita's scenarios, plays, vignettes, treatments, and appointment notations. Together we selected a sampling of Anita's works to spotlight the wide variety of her styles and formats over the decades. Even when sorely tempted to "edit" (the phrase "nigger band" in *All Men Are Equal* jumps to mind), we have left her writings as we found them, without any changes.

Finally, a note on how this book should be read: there is no single way to read it. Of course you can be a traditionalist and go from page one onward, but each of the stories, treatments, and plays stands on its own. We should also add that we visualize this volume as an addition to Anita's other books—both her novels and autobiographies—not as a replacement. It is designed to supplement, not substitute. We have in fact tried not to repeat the stories that have been told in those other volumes, and we encourage the reader to go to Anita's other works—especially *Gentlemen Prefer Blondes* and *A Cast of Thousands*—either again or for the first time.

Personally, I find Anita Loos is even more inspiring as a person, and her talent all the more awesome, when we know the full, three-dimensional story. Of course, she must have had an inkling of hope for that recognition, or she wouldn't have carefully kept and stored her writings. It is a pleasure and a privilege to play a small part in rediscovering Anita Loos.

Cari Beauchamp

*Anita Loos and Her Stories
from San Diego, 1888–1915*

Corinne Anita Loos was born in April 1888, at her maternal grandparents' home in Etna, a small town in the shadows of Northern California's Mount Shasta. Her parents had met ten years earlier, when the charming, good-looking R. Beers Loos came strolling into town. Minnie Smith, the daughter of a successful cattle rancher, could not believe her good fortune.

R. Beers (as he was commonly known) was a firm believer in his own tales of greener pastures, and he could always be counted on to find something new and more interesting around the next corner, be it editing tabloid newspapers, managing vaudeville theaters, or some other surefire scheme. Minnie might have had a few doubts and may have let out a sigh or two of resignation, but they moved to San Francisco in 1892 with four-year-old Anita, her older brother, Clifford, and her younger sister, Gladys.

Anita adapted immediately and would always consider San Francisco her hometown. She idolized her father and adored tagging along with him and his plethora of friends to the saloons of the Barbary Coast, where lunch was free when you bought a beer for a nickel. R. Beers put his daughters on the stage at an early age to help pay the rent, and Anita's being the center of attention obviously pleased her father. Anita translated the applause she received into assurance that she was special and different from other children. At a very early age she found her forte— she had a talent to amuse.

When Anita's maternal grandfather left the family an inheritance, Minnie bought the house of her dreams in San Francisco's marina district. Although he had always shown R. Beers respect, Grandfather Smith must have known his son-in-law's penchant for running through money because he also created a trust for Clifford's medical school tuition at Stanford. Sure enough, the tabloid paper that R. Beers was positive he could turn around soon floundered, and he had to admit to Minnie there was no money left. But she had set her course, and with another sigh she sold her beloved San Francisco home, and the family moved to San Diego.

Minnie seems to have known who and what her husband was and accepted most of his shenanigans without complaint, including his so-called fishing trips, when he and his friends trekked to a nearby town for long weekends of debauchery and then stopped by the local fish market to pick up their "catch" before coming home. It was during one such absence that eight-year-old Gladys awoke with acute appendicitis. An emergency operation on the kitchen table failed to revive her, and by the time R. Beers returned, Gladys was dead and buried. This time Minnie spared no one; she told ten-year-old Anita where her father had been, and when the sobbing and repentant R. Beers asked what he could do, Minnie told him never to mention Gladys's name again. He never did.

Anita rarely told that story; the one she repeated more often was about a wistful beauty who came calling one day when Anita and her mother were home alone. The woman announced the purpose of her visit: to ask Minnie to divorce her husband so he would be free to marry her. Minnie graciously invited the woman in for tea and calmly informed the visitor that she was hardly the first to make that request, but since her husband had yet to ask her for a divorce, he would not be getting one.

Anita usually ended the tale by concluding her mother was either a fool or an earthbound angel. Anita never really did make up her mind. She continued to worship her father in spite of or because of the fact that he was a scalawag, and all her life she would find herself attracted to scoundrels. She longed to grow up to be just like her father; instead, she would, in many ways, retrace her mother's path.

At a time when little was expected, let alone accepted, of women, Anita found solace and nourishment at the local library and gave full credit for her education to the industrialist Andrew Carnegie, who had endowed it. She read a variety of philosophers along with the society pages of the New York newspapers. It is difficult to say which of these two influenced her most, but in the process she became a stylish, well-read wit.

It was during the time her father was managing a San Diego theater that Anita watched the one-reel films screened between the live acts. She quickly discerned a difference in their quality; the ones labeled *Biograph* were almost always superior. Copying the address off the labels on the film cans, she sent off several story ideas to 11 E. 14th Street, New York, N.Y., and to her everlasting joy and pride, back came the following reply:

October 1, 1912

Dear Madam:

We enclose our check for $25.00 in full payment of your moving picture scenario entitled "The New York Hat."

Kindly have two persons witness your signature after executing the enclosed assignment and return it promptly to us in the enclosed stamped and addressed envelope.

Yours very truly,
Biograph Company[1]

The New York Hat gave a struggling painter named Lionel Barrymore his first starring role in pictures. It also featured Lillian Gish and her sister, Dorothy, as extras and was the last film Mary Pickford made for D. W. Griffith before she was lured away for twice the salary by another studio. And for Anita Loos it was the first of over fifty stories she would sell over the next two years from her home in San Diego.

As Anita retold the story in later years, she got younger with each version, and some printed reports have her starting her professional writing career at the age of twelve. In reality Anita Loos was twenty-four years old when she sold her first story in 1912.

There were no great movie palaces in the early teens. Moviegoing was still primarily a working-class pastime and was looked down upon by self-respecting theatergoers, to say nothing of theater actors. Nickelodeons, vaudeville houses, and even buildings that were used by day for other businesses (such as mortuaries) were where most movies were screened in those early years. Within a decade thousands of movie theaters would dot the American landscape, but in the early teens the business was still in its infancy. Copyrighting of films also began in 1912, and although onscreen credits were spotty at best, it is through copyright records at the Library of Congress that we know that women wrote almost half of all films made over the next ten years. Many women would soon be hired to write for film companies and specific stars, but in those early days most of them began just as Anita Loos did, writing from their homes and sending in their stories.

Filmmaking was concentrated on the East Coast with dozens of small production companies laced throughout New York and New Jersey. Hundreds of other bands of filmmakers traversed the country making the movies that were an idea one week, in front of the camera the next, and in theaters within a month. Yet as free-for-all as moviemaking was at this point, one director was acknowledged as the leader and innovator: David Wark Griffith.

When Anita sold him her first story in 1912, Griffith was still two and a half years away from releasing his epic that would revolutionize American films, *The Birth of a Nation*. He had been directing since 1908 and, with his cameraman Billy Bitzer, had experimented with innovations that made him famous within the burgeoning industry. As historian Kevin Brownlow has noted, if Griffith can't be credited with inventing the fade-out or the close-up, "he used these devices with intelligence, sometimes with genius."[2]

The initial letters Anita received were signed with the impersonal "Biograph Company," but she soon was carrying on her correspondence with L. E. (better known as "Doc") Dougherty, the head of Biograph's story department. He was often specific about what the company was looking for, requesting "snappy comedies" and "melodramas with punch, someone in danger and others to the rescue."[3] When Griffith left Biograph in late 1913 to direct under the banner of Mutual Productions, Anita sold stories to both companies.

Anita's lifelong devotion to Griffith originated with her first sale, and his interest in her—at least by mail—remained constant. After selling him more than twenty stories in one year alone, she received a letter at 2915 F Street in San Diego in October of 1913: "I am directed by Griffith to advise you that he is . . . especially anxious to have me secure from you some of your excellent motion picture stories," Frank Woods wrote. "This company [Mutual] is prepared to pay the highest prices for work of this kind."

"The highest price" at the time was fifty dollars, more often twenty-five or thirty-five dollars, but two or three checks a month was heady pay. *The Highbrow,* a half-reeler, paid her only fifteen dollars, but *The School of Acting* was turned into a popular farce that brought her fifty dollars.

After several hours of writing each morning, Anita devoted time to cultivating an active social life. The Hotel Del Coronado was already a famous winter resort that drew the rich from all over the country, and its sprawling beachfront and gingerbread edifice topped with red tile had fascinated Anita since the family first arrived in San Diego. When her father became editor of the *Tent City Weekly,* the local newspaper named for the area of low-cost bungalows adjacent to the grand hotel, Anita spent several seasons using "the Del" as a laboratory for experimenting with personal relationships and discerning how she fit in.

Playing on the beach in wool bathing suits so heavy she would have drowned if she had gone into the ocean, she examined the upper classes at close proximity, and any deference to money alone was quickly dismissed. She found the majority of the leisure classes severely "lacking in vitality" and without enough imagination to waste their time creatively. She had a series of rich boyfriends, including the heir to a Detroit fortune and the son of a United States senator, but the thought of living in Michigan or Washington failed to inspire her. She was forced to admit, much to her own bemusement and partial disappointment, that as soon as she was able to manipulate a man, he bored her to tears. Finding herself unable to stick around long enough to take a man for anything monetary, Anita realized she was a failure as a gold digger and concluded she would "always pass up a diamond for a laugh."[4]

When she told two of the objects of her flirtations that she sold stories for the screen, the first man didn't believe her, and the other was disconcerted, at best, and a bit intimidated. As a result her opinion of men in general, and rich ones in particular, went down another few notches. Anita realized her accomplishments were perceived as a threat, made a mental note of the lesson, and for the time being kept her writing to herself. She also began a lifelong habit of publicly making light of her own work.

But in Hollywood her work was respected, and women were being welcomed into the industry. They were thriving not just as actresses but as producers, directors, and writers. Later in life Anita would infer she had to hide the fact that she was a woman, but all her surviving letters from this time are signed with her full name, and the letters she received are addressed "Dear Madam" or "My dear Miss Loos."

When Doc Dougherty wrote Anita in January of 1914 that he was coming to Los Angeles and "would like to have a personal interview" with her, she couldn't have been more excited. Although her mother was less than thrilled, Minnie agreed to accompany her daughter on the several-hour train ride up the coast. When they arrived at the makeshift studio, Griffith was in the middle of filming *Judith of Bethulia,* and Minnie Loos was so convinced it was the den of iniquity incarnate that she insisted on returning Anita post haste to San Diego.

Anita was not quite five feet tall and looked much younger than her twenty-six years, but she had already proven herself capable of supporting herself. Yet the times, and her own temperament, mandated her acquiescence to her mother's demand.

Anita knew she *had* to return to Hollywood, so she began plotting "escape by an archaic method that belonged back in the generation of my poor helpless mother."[5] Through it all Anita continued to send off her stories, and the stream of praise, acceptances, release forms, and checks that came in return gave her a confidence that set her firmly on her course.

What follows are examples of the stories Anita wrote and sold from her San Diego home that were turned into films between 1912 and 1915. Anita's stories stood out because of their succinct arc, often with a satiric spin. *The School for Acting* is a canvas for every emotion and *Plagiarism* and *The Man Who Looked Up* illustrate her use of twists of fate in everyday situations. All of them have happy endings, of course, but most important, all are written to *move*—almost every sentence in *Jane Wins Out* is a visual description of action. *A Ride with Billy* is particularly fun because it provides a synopsis and a cast of characters followed by a scene-by-scene breakdown.

Most of Anita's scenarios were three to five typed pages told as stories. That was perfect for a director like Griffith, who rarely used scripts; rather he would gather his company of actors, instruct them how to dress, tell them the emotions and actions he expected from their characters, and then order the cameras to roll. The films themselves were usually one or two reels (from ten to twenty minutes) and were typical of the two or three a week Griffith turned out to play in vaudeville houses or the movie theaters that were beginning to boom all over the country.

Cari Beauchamp

The School of Acting

Burlesque

Professor Bunk runs a school of acting. He has ten or twelve pupils whom he lines up in a row. On some large cards, about two feet square, he has printed in big type the names of the different emotions; such as "Anger", "Jealousy", "Love", "Hope", etc. One by one he flashes the cards in front of his pupils and they oblige by portraying the emotion. When he flashes the card reading "Love" they all sink to their knees and put their hands on their hearts; when he flashes the "Anger" card, they all jump up quick and gnash their teeth; when he shows up the "Jealousy" card, they all draw daggers and go for each other. Murder is just evaded by the Professor quickly flashing up the "Hope" card.

After the professor has gone through the cards slowly once, he goes through them again in double quick time and the pride of the school, Stella Watts, gets so mixed up that she sprains her temperament. After Stella is brought to, the professor collects ten dollars from each pupil and the lesson is over.

Now there are two pupils in the school, Algernon and Chester, who are in love with Stella and are hated rivals. They wait for her after the lesson is over and when Stella comes out, Algernon has a shade the best of her attentions. He and Stella go off together and Chester swears "Revenge."

The Bunk School of Acting is getting ready for a performance of "Romeo and Juliet." Of course, the Professor picks Stella for Juliet. The choice of Romeos stands between Algernon and Chester. Bunk looks them over from several different angles and finally chooses Algernon. Stella shows delight at the choice and Chester swears more revenge.

The day of the performance is at hand. Just before the show starts Chester sneaks into the theatre with an armload of the professor's "cards." He hides them in the wings and finds a hiding place for himself near them.

The show has progressed as far as the balcony scene. Stella and Algernon are working up to the climax and have reached the point where Romeo spots Juliet on the balcony. Romeo is just starting to confess his love when Chester, standing in the wings right before Algernon, grabs one of the Professor's cards reading "Anger" and holds it up so that it stares Algernon full in the face. Algernon struggles hard to tell his love, but how can he with that "Anger" card before him? His training has been too complete; he commences to rave and gnash his teeth in front of the surprised Juliet.

The audience is startled. Juliet doesn't know what to do. Just then Chester changes the card to one reading "Rage." Algernon grabs his dagger out, rages about the stage and bites a piece out of one of the wings. Then that archvillain Chester flashes up a card reading "MURDER!!" Algernon stares at it and is hypnotized. He makes a dash for the house of Capulet, grabs Juliet off the balcony by the hair and is just ready to start something when Chester rushes out from the wings and saves Stella. The house is in an uproar. The curtain is lowered. Bunk rushes back stage. The entire company is ready to throw Algernon out into the alley. He begs for just a moment, then he goes to the wings, gets the fatal cards and explains. Everybody turns on Chester and he is justly kicked out. Somebody grabs up a card reading "Love." Stella and Algernon look at it and fall into each other's arms.

THE END

The Highbrow

Comedy Drama

Laura Alden, while a child at school, is a serious little thing much given to reading. For this reason she is shunned by the other children who almost fear her. One day she is walking home from school, alone as usual, when a little boy leaves a gay party of children and comes over to talk to her. Delighted at the attention, Laura smiles up at him and they walk along together. Just then one of the little girls runs up, grabs the boy by the arm and, saying "Don't play with her. She doesn't like boys, she likes books," drags him away laughing. And Laura goes on alone, as usual.

Laura grows up and becomes the governess in a wealthy family, in which there are two grown girls beside the children whom Laura teaches. The house is always full of young people but Laura is as much alone as ever. Whenever she enters a room, the laughter dies down and the young people treat her with a sort of fearsome respect. Naturally she takes more and more to her books for companionship.

One day the girls have planned a picnic party and Laura watches them start off from her window. Finally one of the young men turns, shouts to the others, "I'm going back to ask Miss Alden" and runs into the house. Laura is so delighted she can scarcely believe what she has heard. She hastily arranges her hair at the mirror and waits in delight for the knock at her door. Just as the man reaches her door, however, one of the daughters of the house runs after and stops him. "Don't bother her", she says. "She hates men. She's such a highbrow!" So they turn and leave and Laura, who has heard them through the door, bursts into tears.

Time goes on and Laura becomes literally the "highbrow" of popular conception; an old maid immersed in her books. Even her love for the little children she teaches has been smothered by their fear of her. One day one of them becomes ill and Laura goes to the kitchen to prepare a special dish for her. While she is there Fate sends down the road Tony Antonio, a prosperous young Italian vendor of plants and flowers. Tony is illiterate, light hearted, devil-may-care; everything that Laura is not. He comes to the back door and, taking Laura for a servant, starts to talk to her. He pays her some extravagant compliments and Laura, too stupefied to move, hears him out. As a parting shot he steals a kiss, throws her a rose and tells her that he will be back soon. Highly outraged, Laura goes to her room and cries. She throws the rose down in contempt, picks up a book and starts to read, but it gradually slips through her fingers to the floor and she takes up the rose again.

Laura vows to herself that she will not see her strange admirer when he comes back but one day while she is sitting in a window, Tony throws pebbles against it from the garden, beckons to her and all of her pent up womanhood comes to the surface. She hesitates but a moment, then goes to the kitchen, slips on a servant's apron and meets him in the garden.

Her romance makes a different woman of Laura; the children seem suddenly to lose their fear of her and she learns for the first time what it is to be like other girls. In the meantime Tony provides himself with a ring and prepares to ask Laura to be his wife. He calls at the back door one day, asks to see Miss Alden and is shown by an astonished servant up to the schoolroom. Laura is at the blackboard explaining a problem in geometry. Tony stands stupefied in the doorway for some time before she sees him and when she does turn she reads in his face the same look of fearsome respect that men have always shown her; the look one gives a "highbrow." Mumbling some kind of an excuse, Tony says goodbye and goes. Laura watches after him, sees the romance leave her life, smiles a sort of a grim little smile and goes on with the geometry.

A year goes by and Laura has settled safely back into the rut when one day a servant announces there is a man to see her. Laura walks into the library and there sits Tony, all dressed up, and in his hand a paper which he shows her. It is a diploma stating that Tony Antonio has graduated from a night school course. "I am a highbrow too," says Tony and he takes her in his arms.

Plagiarism
Melodramatic Comedy

"Frank Jordan," a woman writer, decides to travel incognito into the mountain districts in search of new material. Being unused to the wild country into which she is going, she carries far too much money with her for safety. The money is seen by a member of a gang of thieves while Frank is making a purchase in a general store and he hurries on up the road to put his gang on the lookout for her. The storekeeper warns Frank to be careful where she goes but Frank says she is not afraid and she starts up the mountain trail on horseback.

The Forresters' House, a so-called "inn," is the hang out place of the gang of gamblers and thieves. A thunder storm comes up and Frank, exhausted, welcomes the Forresters' House as a place of refuge. Of course, she is more than welcomed by the thieves who make her very comfortable.

Rider Kennedy, naturalist and writer of fiction, leaves his little hut in the woods and is caught out in the storm. Night has fallen and Kennedy whips up his horse and hurries toward home.

At the Forresters' House a small glass of wine is doped and the old "Mother" of the gang offers it to Frank. Frank thanks her, takes a bit of the wine and notices a peculiar taste. Then, for the first time, her suspicions are aroused and she becomes terrified. She stealthily pours out the wine and creeps over to her door to see what chances there are to escape. In the next room she sees the men throwing dice for her. Faint with terror, she staggers into the room, gives the men her money and begs to go. They take the money, laugh at her and thinking that the doped wine will soon take effect, throw her into a corner. Then the gambling goes on. Frank pretends sleep.

The path takes Rider Kennedy past the Forresters' House and he sees what has happened through the window. Stealthily he rides until his horse is directly under the window. Taking out his pistol, he smashes the glass with one blow and gets the drop on the gamblers. Then he tells Frank to come to the window. She staggers over toward him, he grabs her out of the window, onto his horse and the two are off. One of the men rushes out, raises his gun and is just about to fire when the lightning strikes a tree and fells it directly behind Kennedy's horse so that the tree receives the bullet intended for Kennedy.

Kennedy takes Frank to a friendly farmhouse, puts her into the care of the farmer's wife and leaves, telling the farm people not to reveal his identity to the girl. Frank has a sentimental and warm regard for the man who saved her but, thinking that he must be an ignorant farmer or miner, she decides that she had best forget him. In the days that follow Kennedy often finds himself thinking of the girl but, believing that his life lies in his work, he tries to forget her.

The adventure has been an inspiration to both writers and both, during the following months, then weave it into stories and send them to different magazines. Both stories are accepted. Kennedy's comes out in the March "McClures" and Frank's in the April "Red Book." Frank is accused of plagiarism and a literary scandal follows. Kennedy's publishers ask him to sue this other writer and Kennedy, thinking the writer to be a man, does so. Kennedy does not know who "Frank Jordan" is until she is called to the stand. Then he recognizes the girl of his adventure. The whole thing is laughingly explained and, after the case is dismissed, Kennedy asks Frank if she will collaborate with him on the remainder of his life's work.

The Man Who Looked Up

David Provost had for five years been the idol of the American stage. That he was not the "pet" of New York society was to his own credit. A cultured, polished gentleman, equally indifferent to success or failure and asking nothing of life except that it should not bore him too much, he had been raised to public adoration through no efforts of his own. People said that he had no heart. Women especially laid this charge at his door. It was said that he never looked directly at a woman; that in speaking to them he kept his gaze toward the floor. If David Provost never looked at a woman it was probably because they had long since ceased to interest him; he had seen much of the world and it took something in the nature of a surprise to attract his notice, in women as in other things. And, it might be added here, that no matter how inscrutable or varying women are to the average mortal, to a man like David Provost they level themselves into a deadly similarity.

On the woman subject Provost was particularly reticent. He had once been heard to remark to his Japanese valet, just after having gone through his day's mail, that there weren't more than ten good women in the world. Of course, that was a broad statement. Everything in the universe is relative. Perhaps, from the view of a Provost, there aren't more than ten good women in the world. But I know of a cross eyed stable keeper who has been trying to get someone who would have him for the past ten years and he swears that all women are saints. Of course, we will take the stable keeper's view.

The week that Provost opened in repertoire in New York, Fate decreed that Molly Evans should come to town from Jersey with $1.35 and her diploma from the domestic science class of the Union High School. Molly had on a new pink gingham dress and it was so stunning that she could not help but grin all the way up Broadway. Little did she dream that one day she would ride up Broadway in a limousine and with an ermine coat on. Molly did her best to suppress her grin when she went into the employment office. The diploma, however, did not make quite the flutter that she had thought it would, "highbrow" cooks being in disrepute among the profession, but she landed a job and it was a good one, with plenty to do. To think that she had the entire welfare of a family of three in her hands filled Molly with pride. And to the family, she was a "jewel." She did all of the cooking and took charge of the baby while its mother was out; that is to say, she took entire charge of the baby. She loved it so that the baby seemed to realize that Molly ought to have been its mother. Things would have gone splendidly if the baby's father hadn't begun to realize it too and Molly had to go.

She went back to the employment office with eighty cents and started to wait for another family to take care of. Time dragged slowly on but the job did not show up. Two days went by and took twenty cents room rent and twenty-five cents board. Molly began to worry. She sat patiently on the bench and spent the time staring at the only bit of bright color in the dingy establishment, a lithograph of David Provost. She would speculate on how it would feel to be wealthy and famous like he was. She remembered how she had once made a "hit" reciting at a school entertainment and it had been very pleasant. Everyone had said that she would be fine on the stage. Molly gazed at the lithograph until she knew every dot in it. Still the job did not come and Saturday found her with not a penny in her purse, the pink dress all rumpled and the grin gone. By noon she decided that she might feel better in the fresh air, so she wavered up toward Broadway.

About this time the Great God of Luck saw her and decided to give the little Irish girl a chance to be wealthy and famous.

Molly got as far as 43rd street and decided that she would sit down and cry a little. So she picked out a clean spot on the curb, took out her handkerchief and went to it; not loudly, only just enough to make her feel better. Out of a building came a big man in a heavy overcoat, together with another man. They stumbled over Molly and the big man noticed her tears. He stopped and asked her about them.

"I'm entirely out of a job," sobbed Molly. She stood up and straightened out the pink dress. The big man nudged the other man.

"Gee, what a type!" he whispered.

"I don't suppose you know of a job," said Molly. Her pride and spirit were quite broken, so she forgot to mention the diploma.

"I believe I'll send her over to Provost," said the big man to his friend. Then he turned to Molly and asked her if she knew where the Amsterdam Theatre was. Molly didn't, so he pointed it out, scribbled some words on a card and sent her off.

Theatres were out of Molly's line but she bravely made her way through a crowd of women and girls waiting at the stage door; one day's strip of the perpetual line that waited on Provost "concerning an engagement." Molly's card proved to be magical for the door opened to her whereas others waited in vain.

David Provost sat at his table making up. He had been drinking hard for a month. His hand shook so that he could hardly apply the black to his eyes and he was in an awful humor. It pleased people to say that he would not last long at the pace he was going. Provost knew it and he did not care. He had seen everything and life had nothing new to offer. Molly's card was brought to him. He took it up and read its message; it said—Dave—Here is a perfect type I picked up—she looks like a wonder to me. Give her a trial. Sam.

"Another woman," he said to the Japanese. "Ye gods, will they never leave me alone!" Then he took another drink and ordered the woman to be brought in.

Molly walked in. Provost bowed with perfect grace but as he did not look up she made no move to speak.

"Well," said Provost and his voice was gallant but not nice.

"I came to see about a job," said Molly.

Provost grabbed a manuscript off his table and handed it over to her.

"Let's hear how you read," he said.

Molly took the book.

"I don't see what that has to do with it," she said.

"How am I to know whether you can act if I don't hear you read?"

First Molly's grin came to life, then she giggled and then she laughed out loud. Provost kept on with his make up, his eyes still lowered. He had met her kind before; there had been women who dared to laugh in his presence.

Molly controlled herself.

"I don't want to be an actress," she said. "I want to be a cook."

David Provost looked squarely at Molly Evans.

"You don't want to be an actress?" he said.

"No."

"You want to be a cook?"

"Yes."

He looked very long at her and then he said very kindly,

"Where is your mother?"

"I have no mother," answered Molly.

"Where is your home?"

"I have no home."

"Will you marry me?" said David Provost.

THE END

By Way of France

Two Reel Melodrama

Marie Renaud, a French girl of gentle birth, arrives in New York to make her living. Speaking no word of English, she is met by French friends at the boat and taken to their home. Soon after, she receives an offer of a position as governess from a family in Philadelphia. Marie is glad to accept the Westons' offer and she immediately prepares to leave. Her friends place her on the train and, as an additional safeguard, give her the following note to show to anyone who might wish to help her: "Mlle. Renaud speaks no English. She is to meet a Mr. Weston at Philadelphia. Any assistance given Mlle. Renaud will be appreciated." Placing the girl in the conductor's care, her friends leave her.

On the train is Fanny Slade, a woman to whom any fresh, unsophisticated girl is legitimate prey. Fanny makes friendly advances to the girl and, finding that she speaks no English, she plans an easy campaign. Marie has shown Fanny her note and the woman gets off the train at a station above Philadelphia and phones to an accomplice to meet the girl immediately she alights and introduce himself as Weston. The accomplice meets Marie and hurries her away in a motorcar while the real Mr. Weston waits in vain and goes home without his governess.

The accomplice, Harry, takes Marie to Fanny's place which is the rendezvous of all the crooks in Philadelphia. The girl is weary from her journey and, when she is shown to a room, she welcomes the chance to lie down and rest before meeting the family. Several hours later she is awakened by the sound of quarreling and singing. Somewhat startled she goes to her door and finds it locked! Now thoroughly alarmed, she looks through the keyhole and sees Fanny, Harry and a crowd of disreputable friends drinking and quarreling over a card game. Marie looks about for means of escape and finds that her window opens onto a blind wall. Presently Fanny enters, offers her a drink, takes her few little articles of jewelry and leaves, locking the door after her.

Faint with fear, Marie waits by the keyhole until everyone has left the next room except two men who are too drunk to notice anything. Then she stacks chairs against the doors and climbs through the trapdoor into the next room. Knowing that the least sound will bring Fanny and her crowd back, Marie stealthily looks for a means of escape. The window opens onto the street but it is too high to climb from. Desperate, Marie finally finds a pencil and, writing on a scrap of paper "au secours! au secours!" she looks about for some heavy object to carry her appeal safely to the street. She finally finds a small-framed picture of Fanny and, wrapping her note about it, she throws it into an empty auto that stands by the curb. Hearing Fanny returning, Marie quickly unlocks her door with the key which remains in the lock, enters her room and prays that her cry for help will reach someone who knows French.

Marie's appeal falls into the automobile of young Frank Tanner. He finds it there when he returns and puzzles his head over the photograph and the strange words on the paper. He is just about to put it aside when a friend comes along and he shows the friend the paper and asks him if he knows what the words mean. The man knows no more French than Frank does, so Frank puts the paper in his pocket, throws the photograph into the pocket on the door of the machine and, forgetting all about the affair, he drives away.

As a last resort Marie stacks all the furniture in her room against her door and successfully barricades it. Later, Harry and Fanny try to get in and have to resort to battering in the door. They make so much noise however that a policeman arrives and tells them to quit the noise so Fanny gives orders for everyone to let the girl alone and starve her out. All this time Frank Tanner is going nonchalantly about town enjoying himself and, every once in awhile, running across the paper in his pocket and wondering what it says.

Days go by and Marie becomes weaker and weaker from hunger and fear. Believing that her only chance for aid has gone astray, she has given up hope. In the meantime, Frank Tanner goes into a bookstore to buy a magazine when his notice is attracted by a stack of French dictionaries. They bring to his mind the almost forgotten incident of the strange words and he fishes through his pockets for the paper. He looks up the word "secours" and finds that it is a call for help!!! Immediately excited, he jumps in his machine and speeds to the police station. Telling his story, he shows the note and photograph and the police recognize Fanny Slade. A machine is loaded with police and Fanny's place is raided. Frank finds Marie, hears her story through an interpreter and, as he is a friend of the Westons, he takes her to them.

Later Frank calls to see how Marie is and he finds that being thanked by a pretty French girl with tears in her eyes is a very exhilarating experience. About the first thing he does on leaving is to hunt up a French teacher. After several weeks of earnest application, Frank is able, with the aid of a dictionary, to tell Marie "Je t'aime."

Jane Wins Out

Old farmer Higgins is the meanest man in California.

His daughter Jane comes home from boarding school with a city beau and the old man won't even let the boyfriend in the door. Farmer Higgins grabs Jane in and tells her that she has to marry a farmer.

The next day he puts an ad in the Higginsville Herald saying that he will hold a competition on his farm and the man doing the most work in the first week of the season will be given his daughter's hand.

One morning Jane looks out the window and sees the front yard filled with farm hands. The old man hires them all and they head out to the fields to work.

Jane doesn't know what to do but she writes a note to her city beau Jim and tells him to hurry up, disguise himself and enter the competition. Jim has never done a day's work in his life but he bravely agrees.

Then Jane gets a brilliant idea. None of the hands have seen her yet. She goes to her room, puts on a false putty nose, paints eyebrows clear across her face and fixes her mouth so that it looks as though it reaches from ear to ear.

Careful that her father doesn't see her, Jane takes a jug of cider and starts off for the field to give the hands a treat. She goes to one after the other and [the] poor men nearly faint at the sight of her. But Jane acts real kittenish and lets on that she is in love with each one separately. One by one the men jump over the fence and take to the road at high speed. When the old man comes out to the field, no one is left but Jim and he is working industriously.

The week ends and the old man has to give Jane to Jim in spite of his so so work. Every one of the old hands show up at the wedding to see poor Jim get stung and when the beautiful Jane shows up, they all fall over backwards.

A Ride with Billy

Comedy

SYNOPSIS

Marie and Amy are poor girls who work in a factory. Amy is hard working and unselfish while Marie shirks and spends all of her money on clothes. One day the girls are introduced to Billy the factory owner's son and Marie, crowding Amy entirely into the background, monopolizes him. Soon after, Marie receives a note from Billy asking her to take a ride with him. Marie proceeds to bankrupt the family buying motor apparel for the occasion. She provides herself with the motor coat, bonnet, goggles and a veil. The day of the ride arrives and—Billy drives up with a horse and buggy!! Marie, in her motor togs, looks the horse and buggy over in disdain and, with her nose in the air, marches back into the house. Billy does not know what to make of her action. Then, happening to see Amy he asks if she would like to go. Amy is delighted and they drive off. Down the road they come to a big seven passenger car with a mechanic working on it and an old farmer standing by. Billy gets out of the buggy, asks if his car is fixed and is assured that it is. Then he returns the buggy to the farmer, thanking and paying him for the loan of it and orders the astounded Amy into the big machine. When Billy drives Amy home in the big touring car Marie nearly dies of vexation. Of course, Billy marries Amy and Marie gets her just deserts.

Cast

Amy O'Neil	Billy
Marie O'Neil	Mr. O'Neil
Mrs. O'Neil	A Farmer
A Mechanic	

1. O'Neils' kitchen—Amy is wrapping up lunch at table—Marie stands at mirror admiring herself—enter Mrs. O'Neil—Amy grabs hat from table and puts it carelessly on her head—picks up lunch—kisses mother goodbye—waits for Marie who is still primping in front of glass—Marie, without kissing her mother, slowly joins Amy and they leave.

2. Exterior O'Neil cottage—Amy and Marie come out—Amy walks behind with bundle of lunch while Marie struts on ahead.

3. Employees' entrance at factory—Amy and Marie arrive—they meet boy friend with Billy—friend introduces Billy to the girls—Marie pushes Amy aside and proceeds to flirt with Billy—they talk for a moment—the boys go on—the girls enter the factory.

Leader—The girls meet their employer's son.

4. Employees' entrance at factory—employees come out, among them Amy and Marie—Billy is waiting—he joins the girls—they walk on.

5. Exterior O'Neils' cottage—Amy, Marie and Billy come down street—he says goodbye to them at gate—he goes on—the girls enter the house, Marie smiling after him.

6. O'Neils' kitchen, later—Amy and Mrs. O'Neil are busy getting dinner—Marie sits in chair reading novel—enter Mr. O'Neil with hod—he sets it in corner—Marie looks up, sees it and changes her chair so that it is out of her line of vision—Mrs. O'Neil, Mr. O'Neil and Amy sit down

to table—Marie yawns, stretches and leisurely takes her place—a knock at the door—Amy answers—receives a letter for Marie—takes it to her—the whole family all stand around—Marie leisurely opens letter and reads:—"My Dear Miss. O'Neil, May I take you for a ride Sunday afternoon? Billy Jones."—the whole family is pleased with Marie's invitation.

Leader—Billy asks Marie to take a ride.

7.   Marie's room—Marie is disgustedly going over her wardrobe.

Leader—Marie decides that she has nothing to wear for a motor ride.

8.   Parlor at O'Neils'—Mr. O'Neil is on couch smoking corn cob pipe—Amy and Mrs. O'Neil are darning stockings—enter Marie in ill humor—she declares that she has nothing to wear on Sunday—the family try to tell her that she looks nice in anything—Marie sulks—father pulls out his pockets to show that he is broke—Mrs. O'Neil shakes her head sadly—Marie goes to mantle—takes up vase and shakes money out of it—the family looks up, frightened—Mrs. O'Neil cries out that that is the rent money—Marie begins to cry—Mr. O'Neil pats her on the back and tells her that she may take the money.

Leader—Marie takes the rent money to buy motor togs.

9.   Exterior O'Neils' cottage—Marie comes out, dressed for shopping—goes down street.

10.   Exterior dry goods store—Marie enters.

11.   Exterior dry goods store—Marie comes out with big bundle—goes down street.

12.   Exterior O'Neil cottage—Marie comes down street with bundle—enters house.

13.   Marie's room—Marie is showing Amy her purchases—she unwraps motor coat—motor bonnet—goggles—veil—Amy looks on in delight.

14.   Marie's room, Sunday afternoon—Marie stands before mirror arrayed in motor togs.

15.   Exterior O'Neils' cottage—Billy drives up with horse and buggy—gets out—rings bell.

16. Parlor at O'Neils'—Amy shows Billy into parlor—enter Marie in motor togs—Marie and Billy start out—Amy follows them.

17. Exterior O'Neils'—Marie, Billy and Amy come out—Marie goes to curb and looks about for auto—Billy invites her to enter buggy—Marie steps back in surprise—disdainfully looks horse and buggy over—glares at Billy—enters house with her nose in the air—Billy looks after her in disgust—turns to Amy—asks if she would like to go—Amy gets in delightedly—they drive off.

18. Road—Big auto stalled in road—mechanic working on it—farmer standing by—Bill and Amy drive up—Billy gets out—examines car—is assured by mechanic that [it] is all right now—Billy helps Amy out of buggy—Amy is astounded—Billy delivers horse and buggy to farmer and pays him for their use—Billy helps Amy into car—they drive off.

Leader—Billy delivers the buggy to the farmer who lent it to him when his car became stalled.

19. In Billy's auto—Billy and Amy are happily riding along.

20. Exterior O'Neils' cottage—Billy drives Amy up in machine—he helps her out—they stand talking.

21. O'Neils' parlor—Marie sits pouting—she hears machine—jumps up—looks out window.

22. Exterior O'Neils' cottage—Billy and Amy stand happily talking by machine.

23. Marie at the window—close view of Marie at sight of Billy's car.

24. Gate at O'Neils—Billy and Amy bid each other good-bye—they shake hands—Amy goes in—Billy looks after her—gets in machine and drives off.

25. Exterior O'Neils' later—it is after Amy's and Billy's wedding—they come out followed by the wedding guests who throw rice, etc.—Billy and Amy enter machine and drive off amid cheers of friends.

Hollywood Success
and International Fame, 1915–1930

Anita's plan to escape her parents' roof and rules was, of course, marriage. "In looking over the field, I separated the men from the boys and purposely chose a boy." Her intended was Frank Pallma, the son of the band conductor for the outdoor concerts at the Hotel Del Coronado, a fun-loving young man only a few inches taller than she was. Anita claimed she tried to back out of "the larcenous arrangement" at the last moment, but her mother wouldn't budge because "I've already ordered the cake."[1]

When Anita retold the story in later years, she said her marriage lasted all of one awful night in a bungalow at the Del Coronado. She claimed she awoke the next morning, sent the groom off to San Diego by ferry to buy her hairpins, packed her few belongings, and ran home to her parents. In reality her marriage to Frank lasted several months. However, when she did return home, her mother's attitude was primarily one of relief. Now that her daughter had been respectably deflowered, Minnie Loos saw no reason to further impede Anita's moving to Los Angeles.

Still, Minnie insisted on chaperoning Anita, and after checking into the Hollywood Hotel, they found Griffith at his new Triangle studio. The great director welcomed Anita back, regarding the fact that she had been married and had left her husband as a sign of maturity. Griffith was now in partnership with Thomas Ince and Mack Sennett, and, with a long list of stars such as Mae Marsh, the Gish sisters, and Constance and Norma Talmadge under contract, the studio needed writers. Anita jumped at the offer of a full-time position and was only a bit discouraged to find that she wouldn't be working directly with Griffith. He was in the middle of building the sets for what would become *Intolerance,* and Frank Woods, the script department supervisor everyone called "Daddy," kept her busy writing original stories.

It had only been five years since Al Christie had arrived by train from New York and created the first Hollywood studio out of an abandoned roadhouse; two years later, Cecil B. DeMille arrived and took over a barn. Now the demand for films was skyrocketing as more and more small towns built actual movie theaters, and moviegoing, which only a few years before had been looked down on, was becoming accepted as a legitimate form of entertainment. If a moment has to be pinpointed when the shift in mass thinking occurred, it would have to be the release of D. W. Griffith's *The Birth of a Nation* in 1915. One- and two-reel films would continue being made into the 1920s, but this two-hour epic proved it was possible to present theater caliber performances and draw huge audiences from all classes.

Not that filmmaking itself was yet an acceptable profession. A large part of the reason that women and immigrants flourished in the movies is that filmmaking was not seen as a respectable business. Few saw it as a business at all; it had yet to attract serious investors, and most films were financed with the profits of the last one. Hollywood Boulevard was still a dirt road, and signs reading "No dogs or actors" were commonly hung on the fences of boarding houses. Alphonso Bell, whose great expanse of property would become known as Bel Air, kept his vow "not to sell one acre of my land to actors or Jews" for another decade.[2] However, the hoteliers and restaurateurs, who had talked of not allowing movie people in their establishments, were soon too busy counting their money to be discerning. By 1918 filmmaking was the biggest business in the Los Angeles area.

Anita couldn't have cared less about the social acceptance of her chosen occupation; she knew she was where she belonged. And soon she was working alongside Griffith when he chose her to help title *Intolerance*. Griffith tended to use title cards in his films to explain time and place and depended on the actors to emote the action, whether drama or comedy, but with *Intolerance* he allowed Anita a new freedom that resulted in wry titles such as: "Women who cease to attract men often turn to reform as a second choice." Best of all for Anita, titling *Intolerance* meant finally going to New York for the premiere. She had spent so many years reading about the great city, she was almost instantly at home.

Back in Hollywood, she set herself up in her own apartment, but her parents now ensconced themselves as residents at the Hollywood Hotel. At the studio she was introduced to a recent hire, John Emerson, a former Broadway actor turned director. Their first joint effort allegedly created a credit line that would be a source of lifelong embarrassment to Anita: "*Macbeth,* directed by John Emerson and written by William Shakespeare and Anita Loos." In search of his next scenario Emerson went to the studio files and found some of the stories Anita had written that had never been filmed. In several instances Griffith had bought them because he found the humor amusing but failed to see how the laughs could be translated to the screen. Emerson was given the go-ahead to film one called *His Picture in the Papers,* starring another new arrival, Douglas Fairbanks, a New York stage actor lured before the cameras by large sums of money. The sizzle was in witty title cards, an anathema to Griffith, who adamantly believed audiences didn't come to the movies to read; but *His Picture in the Papers* was such a huge hit that Emerson, Loos, and Fairbanks became a team. The clever titles underscored Fairbanks's charisma and energy, and the combination created a new kind of male star in films like *Wild and Woolly; In Again, Out Again;* and *The Americano.* Kevin Brownlow credits Fairbanks's *American Aristocracy* (written by Anita) as the film that inspired him to become a historian and film collector. Emerson took to adding his name as cowriter to Anita's scripts, but Anita didn't complain. Instead she joked that her stories for Fairbanks were hardly written at all—rather she simply had to come up with things for the actor to jump over or leap from because his acting was less important than his athletic prowess.

This is not to underestimate the success of his films. Fairbanks became one of the three most popular stars in America, along with Mary Pickford and Charlie Chaplin. Together, the threesome sold millions of dollars of liberty bonds, and the mobs of fans who turned out to greet them had never been seen in this country before.

It was as Doug's scenario writer that Anita became friends with Frances Marion, Mary Pickford's exclusive writer. Doug and Mary were both married to others when they fell in love in 1917, and who better to serve as their "beards" than their writers? Frances and Mary would ride horses together in Laurel Canyon and then meet up with Doug, who, as prearranged, was out riding with Anita. Doug and Mary went off together, usually to his brother's house nearby, and Frances and Anita would ride together or just talk for an hour or two until they reunited with their employers.

Anita and Frances shared a variety of sensibilities, including their belief in their own good fortune at being highly paid participants in the movie business and their mixed emotions about Mary and Doug's relationship. Frances's loyalty was to Mary; she saw Doug as an insecure male grabbing onto Mary's coattails to promote himself. Anita's loyalty was to Doug, whom she thought was an affable, fun-loving rascal; if not the brightest of men, he was certainly clever, and she found Mary to be a bit of a prima donna.

Frances's and Anita's similar outlooks extended to their conclusions that their early marriages were merely "youthful indiscretions" that served to get them away from home in a socially acceptable manner. Anita might have been a little more content with her work than Frances and Frances a little more comfortable in her own skin than Anita, but the two women were both disciplined workers in a Hollywood loaded with diversions, and their friendship flourished.

While working with Fairbanks, Emerson and Anita cultivated the press, and they were played up as the brains behind Fairbanks's success. Emerson hired his own publicity agent, a rarity at that time, and although Anita claimed to be appalled by the practice, she posed for the pictures of the two of them that appeared almost as regularly as those of the movie stars. A six-part series in *Photoplay* under their byline was the last straw for Fairbanks, who had tired of seeing himself billed with Emerson and Loos as equals in a "triple alliance."[3]

To avoid the "Were they fired or did they quit?" dilemma, John Emerson said he had medical problems that required East Coast specialists. In the first of what would be a series of physical ailments that seemed to flare up whenever things were not going to his liking, Emerson announced he was going to New York. Anita, in love with the director fourteen years her senior who acted blithely indifferent to her, went with him.

The trades were soon headlining the deal Anita and Emerson signed with Paramount to write and direct films in New York. Under the banner "John Emerson–Anita Loos Productions" their names appeared above or just under the title on films like *Oh, You Women!; Getting Mary Married; Let's Get a Divorce;* and *The Isles of Conquest* for stars like Marion Davies, Billie Burke, and Norma Talmadge. They also turned out two books, *How to Write Photoplays* and *Breaking into the Movies,* under their names, but it must be presumed Emerson hired a ghostwriter as the styles of these two books are very different from that of anything else Anita ever wrote. John Emerson thought all was well with his little world, and he explained the situation succinctly to Anita: he just wasn't the marrying kind. Born in Sandusky, Ohio, in 1874, Emerson was the son of an Episcopalian minister, and he himself had trained for the ministry before discovering the New York stage at the turn of the century. His acting claim to fame was costarring with Minnie Maddern Fisk for two seasons before turning to managing theaters for the Shuberts and Charles Frohman. He had left a wife in Ohio, but she had tired of waiting and divorced him by the time he met Anita.

At first Anita was happy to appear understanding. After all, she herself had left an early, brief marriage, and it all seemed so sophisticated. She was proud to be seen with the tall, good-looking man who might wander in the evening but was always back at her side the next day at the studio. However, Anita soon grew weary of pretending she didn't care and turned to her friends for advice. The Talmadge sisters counseled that if she really wanted to land Emerson, she had to pretend one more time and make it good. She had to find someone else to be the object of her affection and play it up in front of Emerson.

And in case that wasn't enough, Anita left the Algonquin, where he could easily keep his eyes on her, and moved into a house on Long Island with Frances Marion. When it appeared that other men were indeed interested in Anita, it finally occurred to Emerson he might actually lose her. Whether it was love or fear of having to find a new production partner, Anita's strategy worked. Emerson proposed.

Emerson had come to some fame in New York as a leader in the Actors' Equity strike that resulted in chorus girls finally getting their tights paid for by producers and in actors being paid for their time in rehearsal, yet many friends had doubts about his relationship with Anita. Frances Marion was one of the few, however, willing to tell Anita to her face that she thought Emerson had "a constipated brain" and was using her. Still, Frances agreed to stand beside Anita when she married Emerson in June of 1919. The wedding took place in front of twenty friends at the home of Norma Talmadge and her husband Joe Schenck. Joe gave the bride and groom a European honeymoon as a wedding present, but they were soon back at work at his studio in New York.[4]

Schenck produced his wife's films, but it seemed he had married the entire Talmadge family instead of just Norma. Peg, the mother of the three glamorous daughters, had a heart of gold but knew a meal ticket when she saw one. Seeking to get some space between his bride and her family, Joe appealed to Anita to make Norma's blonde sister Constance a popular success as well. Constance had appeared in films before, but it was Anita's stories like *The Virtuous Vamp* that shot Constance to stardom. (Schenck was so grateful that he gave Anita a $50,000 bonus.) The third and least photogenic of the Talmadge sisters, Natalie, married the rising comedian filming on the third floor of Schenck's studio, Buster Keaton. Although they now could all afford individual mansions, Peg stayed close to her girls.

Emerson and Anita were successful professionally; in between films they also wrote several Broadway plays, including *The Whole Town's Talk-ing* and *The Fall of Eve*. But it was with the publication of *Gentlemen Prefer Blondes* in 1925 that Anita Loos hit a nerve with the public that resounds to this day. The novel is a classic of American fiction and has been reprinted in dozens of languages, and the deliciously guileless gold digger Lorelei Lee has been personified on the stage and screen several times over.

Anita claimed she wrote her tome in response to being appalled by her pal H. L. Mencken's fascination with an empty-headed blonde. In-stead of being insulted, Mencken was delighted and urged her to pub-lish it, praising Anita as the first writer to make fun of sex.

In her retellings Anita sounds as if none of it required any effort: she dashed the story off during a train ride; it was Mencken who decided it must be published; Henry Sell serialized it in his *Harper's Bazaar* (with drawings by Ralph Barton); and yet another friend volunteered to have it printed privately so she could give the novella as gifts at Christmas. The fact that it immediately became a best-seller and went through twenty printings in a matter of months came as a complete shock to her. At least that was how Anita summarized it.

Most of the novel's development may well have happened that way. We know that in the course of serializing the story of Lorelei's conquests *Harper's Bazaar* doubled its circulation and attracted advertisers who had never been interested in the magazine before. Perhaps the most difficult aspect of Anita's version to swallow is that the initial story was just dashed off; after all, we know the care she put into everything else she wrote. In the end she was proud of *Gentlemen Prefer Blondes,* as well she should have been, and appreciated the fact it brought her critical and popular acclaim, as well as initiating valued friendships with people she esteemed like Aldous Huxley and H. G. Wells.

Gentlemen Prefer Blondes encapsulated the extremes of the Roaring Twenties: the stock market was booming, Broadway was bustling, and there were nothing but "Blue Skies" ahead. It lampooned morals at the moment they were up for grabs and threw a satiric eye on chorus girls' receiving diamonds and flower boxes the size of coffins from ultra rich older men who may have been successful in business but were severely lacking in romance.

On whom Lorelei Lee was based has long been a subject of conjecture. Many assume it was Peggy Hopkins Joyce, the real-life gold digger extraordinaire of the times. Anita occasionally mentioned Peg Talmadge as her inspiration—the unattractive but oh-so-practical mother of the Talmadge girls. Peg was a classic amoral wit who justified many things in life just as Lorelei did. In other ways Anita used her own experiences in *Gentlemen Prefer Blondes;* in her own life she couldn't pull off being a gold digger, but she had watched them firsthand, and in her heart she admired them.

The bottom line is that *Gentlemen Prefer Blondes* shot Anita into a new stratosphere of fame and made a fortune that dramatically changed the pattern of her life and that of her husband. Emerson started living in the style to which he wished to become accustomed, and, in this case at least, Anita went along for the ride.

Now they were regular participants in the society calendar: in January they were off to Palm Beach for "The Season," staying with the architect Addison Mizner, going to races, lunching at the Beach Club, and walking the golf courses. In April it was back to New York for several months of Broadway plays. (Anita always kept up with the movies as well, seeing two or three a week and noting her judgments in her appointment books.)

Anita and Emerson made pilgrimages to Europe each summer. In Paris she visited the salons of Mainbacher and Patou for the latest fashions and began her lifelong affection for spending several weeks each year at a spa in Germany or Italy, taking what she called the "obesity cure" (arriving weighing 103 pounds and leaving weighing 96). They lived the most rarified of lifestyles, and at times they were presumptuous to the point of audacity. Bennett Cerf, who eventually became head of Random House, remembered sailing from New York to England as a fellow passenger of the Emersons on the *Aquitania* in the mid-1920s.

The threesome got to talking one night and realized none of them had made London hotel reservations and that they were arriving at the time the city would be packed because of the Derby. Cerf was getting concerned, but Emerson just waved his hand and said, "Leave it to me." He wired an agent to get them reservations and meet them at the station, but when they arrived in London, the agent nervously informed them he had failed in his quest. However, he did know of a certain lord, currently in Scotland, who maintained a suite at the Savoy, and Emerson took it from there. They loaded Anita's twenty suitcases into several cabs and took off for the Savoy. Emerson, who of course had never met the lord in question, marched up to the desk and proceeded to get more and more agitated that everything was not ready for them as his lordship had assured them it would be. The manager ended up apologizing profusely and ushered them into a two-bedroom, two-bath suite with a huge living room and a view of the Tower of London and Westminster Abbey.

Anita not only went along with all this, but as soon as she took one look at the dazzling surroundings, she announced, "We've got to have a party." As Cerf recalled, they seemed to know everyone in London, and the next night more than one hundred people, including Tallulah Bankhead, floated into "their" suite. They stayed for a week, renting a Rolls Royce for a side trip to Stratford-on-Avon and generally living as high a life as it was possible to do. To Anita and Emerson it all seemed natural, properly irreverent, and, most of all, fun.[5]

Yet *Gentlemen Prefer Blondes* also brought Anita a new spate of publicity, and this time most of the photographs gracing *Vanity Fair, Vogue,* and the movie magazines were of her alone, sans Emerson. Her comings and goings were given the same treatment as movie stars' activities. Even Anita's father got in on the deal by selling *Photoplay* a long article on his daughter, subtitled "Sensational Expose of Miss Loos' Early Life by the Father Who Prefers Brunettes." There was actually little sensational about it, altogether a rosy picture of Anita's rise to stardom painted with a rather broad brush. Only at the end of the article did R. Beers mention Emerson: "I am very fond of my son-in-law—his clothes fit me perfectly."[6]

At this stage in their relationship Anita's father was one of the few giving Emerson even backhanded compliments. His ludicrously audacious manner and his frankly insulting treatment of Anita appalled most of her friends. When company gathered around the dinner table, Emerson would suddenly demand Anita change seats with him because he was in a draft. She called him "Mr. E.," and he referred to her, publicly and in private, as "Bug" or "Buggie."

With Anita getting all the attention, Emerson reacted by claiming illness. He decided that it was necessary for him to sit on an inflatable donut, and he took it with him everywhere. There they were on opening night, both dressed to the nines, and Emerson would walk down the theater aisle with Anita on one arm and the donut on the other. Next he convinced himself that he had a serious throat malady and, to assure the spotlight, refused to talk, writing on a handheld blackboard to communicate. Entire trips were taken to find new cures, difficult at best for a nonexistent ailment. Finally, a European doctor confronted Anita with Emerson's hypochondria and suggested a possible solution: put her husband under anesthesia, severely scratch his throat so he would feel some pain, and then present him with a jar of nodes and claim they had been removed from his throat. It was so absurd that it worked. With a tangible sign that his illness had been real, Emerson regained his old love of life, albeit temporarily.

They returned to New York where he decided they should have separate apartments, with her income covering the cost of both residences. Anita consoled herself by purchasing her first mink coat (since Emerson wasn't at her side to criticize the expenditure) and tried to make the best of the situation. She rarely even hinted to friends or family that her husband was not the great man she once imagined him to be. Like her mother before her, Anita gave a sigh of resignation and followed her husband's path.

Between 1915 and 1926, screenwriting changed dramatically, evolving from a few summary pages into scenarios up to one hundred pages long.

Throughout those years Anita continued to write short stories as well as story ideas, treatments, and full scripts.

What follows is a sampling of her work that covers that period, all very different from the biting satire of *Gentlemen Prefer Blondes*.

The Heart That Has Truly Loved is a time-traveling, melodramatic magazine story in which Anita plays with dialogue and story structure in a very different way than her film scenarios required. It is a gentle, sweet story, without any of her usual satiric comments on society and is laced with her self-taught familiarity with classic literature and various philosophers.

A Play for Mr. Fairbanks was never filmed. Who knows what happened? Although there is some physical action for the Fairbanks character, the physical demands were no greater than those required of other characters, and that was unusual in a Fairbanks film. Kevin Brownlow calls *A Play for Mr. Fairbanks* "a joy to read. It has all the zip of the best Fairbanks pictures. I can just see it with Jewel Carmen (or maybe Bessie Love). What a shame it never got made."[7]

All Men Are Equal is a one-act play, written, perhaps, to be performed in one of the playhouses that thrived in Los Angeles at the time. It is Anita's pre-*Babbitt* commentary on mainstream America, with a few pontificating jabs at "career women" in particular, most men in general, and parental influence on their children's direction in life. The play's final speech advises the heroine to "run away to your happiness; to your happy work," and one cannot help but wonder if Anita wrote it wishing that that is what her mother had said to her after their first trip to Hollywood instead of insisting she return to San Diego and marry Frank Pallma.

Where Does Annie Belong? is a draft treatment for a feature-length film. Titles, as well as descriptions of settings and actions and camera movement suggestions, appear intermittently. It was written at the height of the anti-German hysteria that was whipped up with the active assistance of the film industry. Ads actually urged audiences to "Come and Hiss the Kaiser." While *Where Does Annie Belong?* shows the growing sophistication of scenario writing, it is probably the least subtle of

Anita's writings. At times the treatment is almost a throwback to the evil, mustached landlord of vaudeville, and it even includes blatant character names such as the "futuristic artist Art D. Stroyer." Yet despite its patriotic bookends, *Where Does Annie Belong?* is at heart a classic love story, with Anita's unique take on class and foibles riddled throughout. As usual, there are a few elements of her own life thrown in, such as the fact she, like Annie, designed her own clothes from pictures in sophisticated magazines and was always very conscious of where she belonged.

Anita wrote "The Moving Pictures of Blinkville" as a newspaper short story that was then reprinted in the *Moving Picture News* in late 1919. In it Anita pokes fun at her chosen profession, as well as at the audiences that were clamoring to see the movies, no matter what the quality. She was in New York with Emerson by this time, writing sophisticated comedies for the likes of Constance Talmadge and Marion Davies, and "The Moving Pictures of Blinkville" is a prime example of her outward attitude toward her work: the business was for suckers, nothing to take seriously, but if someone was going to pay her good money to be in the middle of it, she was happy to go along for the ride.

Cari Beauchamp

The Heart That Has Truly Loved

Sometimes Nature inserts into the fall of the year a day that is half spring-like in its freshness; a day so steeped in a quavering golden haze that it seems to portend new life and fresh hope instead of being a foreboding of winter. On a day like that the rays of an October sun glanced into the window of a room on East Fourteenth Street, and lit up a spot on the dingy matting so that it fairly dazzled the eyes of the near-sighted young man who sat reading at a table in the corner. The sunlight thrilled the young man, yet he did not get up and go out into it as a thoughtless youth might have done under the circumstances; he merely gazed at it for a moment, sighed deeply, and then went back to his book, from which he was learning that Knowledge is a synthetic judgment a priori.

The young man was Alonzo Kimberly. His mother must have had a prophetic vision of his appearance at twenty-four when she named him that, for he was everything that an Alonzo should be. His face was pale and esthetic, his black hair curled just a bit and was too long, and he had worn horn-rimmed spectacles for reasons of hygiene long before they were resurrected by Fashion as a briefly lasting fad.

Alonzo had spent all of his boyhood and youth among books and everything that books can do for a person, they had done for Alonzo. In return for his attention, they had given him a gently inquiring mind that found interest in everything, and an almost superhuman sympathy with mankind. That is what books do for one who lives among them in love. Those who go to them with the mere desire for instruction are always paid for their mercenary interest by having their souls sapped dry of every drop of human feeling. Well has the great Frenchman said; "Do not read as the children read, to be amused; nor as ambitious people read, to gain instruction. No! Read to live!"

Alonzo had lived a full dozen lives among his books, so that here, at the very threshold of youth, he looked out upon a world from which all the gilt of illusion had been rubbed. He knew life! And yet he found the world a good place to be in, in spite of the fact that he was never to be deliciously fooled by the illusions of romance that Nature devises for the young in order that they may be tricked into carrying on her work of replenishing the race.

The majority of the roomers in the house on East Fourteenth Street were school teachers, and among those ladies Alonzo passed for the veriest rake; all on account of his having tried to amuse a number of them whom he found sitting bored and listless on the front steps one sweltering June evening. He had been spending the afternoon in translating Horace, and he thought that just the thing to put some "pep" into their poor, tired lives would be to read them his translation of a certain ode; which he did and after which they excused themselves rapidly, one by one, and scurried into the house blushing. Now the ode was very mild, for Horace, and in addition, it was splendid hot weather literature. To read it was not immodest; to blush at it was, and showed the moral inferiority of the female mind. Alonzo was no searcher after classic dirt, as superficial readers of the classics are. The episode only went to prove again that his love of books had made him all too human, while the schoolma'ams' mere desire for instruction had turned them into hopeless prigs. It was just such misunderstandings as this that had driven Alonzo back and farther back among his books until now, not even a quavering October sun could lure him for more than a few seconds from his volume of Kant.

As Alonzo read on he was annoyed by a light tapping at the window as if a twig were being blown against it by a rising gust of wind. Then he noticed with some impatience that a cloud had settled over the sun so that the bright spot on the floor was more than half blotted out. The temporary shadow annoyed him, as such things will, for his eyes had grown accustomed to the light. The shadow kept fluttering, fluttering on the floor until, with an impatient exclamation, he rose to change the position of his chair. Then he looked down at the obstruction to his bit of sunshine and saw, for the first time, that it was the perfectly formed shadow of a woman's hand! It startled him; he stepped back, gazed at it a moment fascinated, rubbed his hand over his eyes and learned that his hand was ice cold and his forehead damp. From the floor his glance wandered to the window and he stepped back, another pace, this time in real alarm. There, at the side of the window was a woman's hand in a white glove, beckoning to him to come out! Always distrustful of his faulty eyesight, he looked again. Yes, clearly it was beckoning to him! Gradually he came to his senses and smiled. The whole affair was palpably a clumsy flirtation gotten up by one of the girls in the neighborhood. It was characteristic of Alonzo that he should try to figure the whole thing out mentally and without personal investigation. Having settled the matter in his mind, or having at least tried to believe that he had, his fastidious attention fixed itself once more on his book.

Among every other thing in life, Alonzo had speculated on the relations of the sexes, and out of his scientific investigations and deep study of history, philosophy, and biography there had shaped in his mind the belief that the sentimental relationship which we commonly call love has never, in the history of mankind, been proven to exist in any single case over a limited period of time. Always, after the great flush of passion, comes the aftermath; days so full of bitter, active regret or so full of deadly, passive disillusionment, that no ecstasy the heights of passion had ever reached could compensate for their restless sorrow or leaden dullness. As the first axiom in his theory of life this gentle, lovable soul, barely on the threshold of manhood, had written; "Love does not last." Lucky and safe the man who so early forms his conclusions on that subject and can so guide his footsteps far from the devious pathway of passion.

Alonzo did not look up again but he thought he still heard the gentle tapping and presently he was aware that the hand was again at the window. The silly creature, whoever she might be, did not mean to be overlooked. Perhaps a few moments conversation would bring the episode to a close and allow him to continue his study in peace. He went to the window and opened it, meaning to conduct the whole thing gently so as not to hurt her feelings.

"Well, bless your heart!" he commenced briskly and he touched the hand which crumpled under his touch into two thicknesses of white kid with nothing between! Then there wafted in to him the strongest odor of benzene. Alonzo was too much the philosopher to be surprised at the fact that a now briskly blowing October wind and a newly cleaned white kid glove which had caught on the ivy vine beside his window should have been able to play such havoc with his senses. He was only intensely relieved. He leaned out and looked over onto the adjoining window sill; sure enough, the white glove's mate was safely perched there. He stood at the window for a moment and looked out into the street. There was a compelling élan in the autumn air that he breathed deeply and thankfully into his lungs. It was good to be alive a day like that!

To return the glove was the next thing. Alonzo examined it and wondered to which one of the galaxy of nondescript females in the house it belonged. It was very tiny; he had never given any woman he had seen about the place the credit of so attractive a feature as the hand must be that went into that glove. Then he remembered that he had heard someone moving about that morning in the adjoining room and that there had been a "For Rent" sign in the window for some time past. Apparently a new roomer. He started for the door, stopped, paused, thought a moment and then went back to his table and selected with care a heavy looking volume from among his books, to carry along as a sort of mental chaperone. He did not wish to frighten this new female, who would probably think him a common type on flirtation bent.

So he presented himself at the next door as a busy man whose studies had been rudely broken into by his neighbor's carelessness with her day's cleaning. He enjoyed the deception of appearing stern and, as he stood there, the sweet, resigned smile that was characteristic of him in moments of amusement played over his gentle face. There is a smile, half tender and half bitter, that we only find in those lonely ones who have raised themselves above the vanities of life and so can smile only "at" and not "with" the world.

"Come in!" called a fresh voice.

Alonzo straightened his face and opened the door.

Seated on the floor in the middle of the room was a delicious little blond, busily engaged in sewing some lace onto some white cloth. She showed surprise at seeing Alonzo and started to rise, but he motioned her back into her position on the floor with an imperious wave of his hand.

"Is this your glove?" he asked sternly.

"Oh," gasped the girl, and Alonzo learned what a white glove meant to her by the rapid dash she made to the window to see if the other one was safe. He noticed that her room, despite the fact that it was furnished exactly like his, seemed fuller and warmer and more complete.

"It was nice of you to bother with my glove," she said when she came back from the window.

"Don't mention it," answered Alonzo soberly, "It has only disturbed my studies for a moment." He was bound to play out the game.

"I am sorry; I know what that means," said the little blond, "especially if you were studying *that* book."

"Locke on the Human Understanding," he answered, "is a great comfort," and he fingered the volume lovingly.

"Yes," said the blond, "But why then are you carrying around the *Decameron?*"

Alonzo looked quickly at the title on his book. In his concern about returning the glove, he had absent-mindedly picked up the wickedest, most frivolous, entertaining and lovable volume that this dreary old world has ever supplied copy for.

The game was off. Alonzo simply screeched and the little blond sat down on the floor and rocked back and forth in an ecstasy of laughter.

"Oh, oh, oh," she cried, "What kind of a trick are you trying to play on me?"

Then he explained the reason why he had brought along the supposed volume of Locke. She listened to his story, which was well punctuated by their laughter.

"I think you reached out and stole it," she asserted, and what was the use to deny it? The lie was more believable than the truth.

She asked him to sit down, which he did, and in no time at all he learned that her name was Marie Dupont and that she was in New York from Canada to study singing, that her dainty little head was stored with the wisdom that a combination of ambition and poverty always breeds, but that she also had something which is greater than any book learning or creative wit; good common sense. Her company was a revelation to the young student of law and philosophy. He had always thought that there might be a woman like this some place, but in his world none had ever appeared. The girls he knew were uniformly sensuous, lacking in humor and abnormally eager for love.

Alonzo explained something of his studies and ambitions to finish his law course by the end of the year. Time flew quickly and before either of them realized, a far-off clock sounded six hours. Marie Dupont jumped up from her chair where she sat sewing all the while.

"You will have to go," she said. "I am off on a dinner engagement in half an hour."

Something like a chill went through Alonzo's breast; a dinner engagement probably meant a man. He rose and held out his hand in which the white glove still rested. As she took it a muffled "Oh" escaped her lips.

"What is it?" he asked with concern.

"My glove."

On the wrist of it was his own clumsy thumb mark deeply printed in ink. A long and profuse apology followed, after which Alonzo found himself alone in the hallway.

He entered his room from which the spot of sunlight on the floor had long since departed, and that was probably the reason why it looked colder and barer and dingier than he had ever noticed it before.

That evening Marie Dupont seemed rather distrait to the man who took her to dinner and showed an inordinate interest in a black smudge on her glove.

That night Alonzo took a brisk walk along the Hudson and, in the darkness and gathering fog, he reasoned with himself concerning the girl he had met that afternoon.

"This woman only goes to prove my theory that love is to be avoided," he argued. "To fall in love with a creature like she is would inevitably bring about a greater calamity than my nature could bear. To fall out of love with her would be unbearable. To have her fall out of love with me would be Hell. To become mutually indifferent would be dumb agony. And love does not last. That I have proven beyond refutation. Love does not last!" And so he walked and thought until well into the morning.

They met the next day on the stairway, he on his way to the office of the lawyer with whom he was reading law, she on her way to her lesson. She looked very fresh and charming. He asked her if she had enjoyed her dinner of the night before.

"As much as I ever enjoy a dinner that is merely dinner," she answered. Then she looked up at him frankly and added, "I had much rather have continued talking with you."

Alonzo had conquered in his long struggle with himself through the night. From the heights of his knowledge he looked down on her with a fatherly smile.

"Well," he said briskly, "bless your heart!"

Marie Dupont started. What sort of a youth was this who was blessing her heart in so fatherly a manner when he could boast of but four meager years of seniority? It rather hurt her and she parted from him at the doorway with a stiffly murmured good morning.

More than a week went by before they met again. During that time Alonzo nursed a mighty unrest in his soul and the fact that his knowledge enabled him to analyze it as the mere fleeting desire of the male of the human species for the female did not mitigate the condition as much as it should have. He could only thank his luck that he knew enough to call it what it was and to keep out of the alluring trap that Nature had now set for him.

However, often and often as he sat at his table trying to study, he found himself listening to catch the faint sound of her footsteps as she moved about her room. He wondered why he never heard her singing; people who study singing always have to practice. This worried him for three whole days until, by matching up the times he heard her leaving and returning, he figured that she went away regularly each day, evidently to practice. A thoughtful and considerate trait in her nature! Presently he began to worry about this. The poor child was inconveniencing herself in order to keep from disturbing the other roomers, chiefly himself, on account of the adjacency of their rooms. This was too bad as he felt sure that her voice would not annoy him. Then he got to wondering about her voice; it must be of a singularly sweet timbre. Three more days went by and he could stand it no longer. He could not study, he could not sleep, he could not even eat for thinking about this fellow creature's sacrifice. He waited until the evening of that third day, when he put on his best coat, combed his hair neatly at his bit of broken mirror and presented himself at her door, not to visit; merely to tell her that her voice would not annoy him if she wished to practice in her room.

Marie Dupont was unaffectedly glad to see him. If he had hurt her by his condescension in blessing her heart at their last meeting, she showed no resentment now. She sat and sewed after showing him to a chair; her thrifty little fingers were never idle.

She told him she would never think of singing in the house; there were places, halls, uptown provided just for saving people that agony. So that was settled!

That led to a discussion of her voice, which led to Alonzo hinting that he would like to hear her sing.

"Would you?" she asked, pleased.

"Yes," he answered, and he gripped his chair. Now he was to hear her sing!

Later in life Alonzo Kimberly knew what it was to be lonely and sad and bitter, but his memory never failed him in one sweet recollection; the picture of the girl, Marie Dupont, who sat singing at dusk by a window that looked out upon the straggling lights of East Fourteenth street in New York. Her voice was wonderfully soft, very pure and very clear. People in the street below stopped to listen.

> "The heart that has truly loved never forgets,
> But as truly loves on to its close
> As the sunflower turns to her God when he sets
> The same face that she turned when he rose."

And the song was over! The people in the street below moved on.

"Did you like it?" she asked.

Alonzo swallowed a lump in his throat.

"It is a quaint melody," he answered. "I always liked that song. Of course the words are rather extravagant in sentiment."

"Oh, of course," echoed Marie. She would have agreed with him in anything.

"We, who understand, can take such sentiments with a grain of salt. However, it is all very sweet."

She looked up at him rather wonderingly and he saw that she was as yet too young and inexperienced to accept the truths of life, which he had mastered.

． ． ．

All through the fall and winter their friendship grew, but it remained friendship and nothing more. If he had had a less deep and tender regard for her he might have allowed himself to wander into the bypaths of sentiment; it would have been an alluring adventure with so sweet a companion. Or, if he had been wealthy and so could have provided for her in luxury all the days of her life, he might even have broached the subject of marriage. But to ask Marie Dupont to share a grinding poverty for the few years of love that were all he might offer her; that was too much! So they walked together, dined together, planned their separate futures together, and one day Alonzo brought up the subject that had been forced into so prominent a place in his mind; the subject of love and the sexes. He thought so much of her that he wished her, too, to know life as it was. Nor was he wrong in his judgment as to her sterling good sense. She was growing to know the world and to lose her illusions, although as yet she had not acquired a foundation of sound philosophy to fall back upon.

"I supposed there were a few cases in history of lasting love," she mused. "How about Dante and Beatrice?"

"That was a poetic illusion on Dante's part. It endured because he never even kissed Beatrice. If he had possessed her, the affair would soon have been over. At any rate it didn't prevent him marrying and having several children."

"And Paolo and Francesca?"

"They offer no proof, because they were both killed in the first flush of their passion."

"Abelard and Heloise?"

"He never loved her sincerely. He treated her like a cad."

"You are good to tell me so much of life and truth," she went on. "Another who knew as much as you do might have made love to me just for the amusement of it. Now I will always trust you, because you have told me the truth."

She looked up at him with tears welling into her eyes, and he took the little blond head into his hands and said,

"Bless your heart!"

And so Marie Dupont was initiated into his belief about love and she, too, learned the inexorable law of the pendulum by which Nature so makes it that if we taste great pleasure we must go to the other extreme of great pain, and there is no escaping.

The next thing these two were aware of was that spring was upon them. Alonzo knew that with the springtime there would come a mightier struggle with his youth than he had ever had, but he had finished his examinations and was soon to return home, where he would have the struggle for a living.

Marie had grown very solemn and sweet. She was a different girl from the light-hearted little creature he had discovered sitting on the floor that day in October. He tried to make himself believe that she had improved under his guidance; in truth she had doubled her knowledge of the world, she had gained a great poise and womanliness and her character rested upon more firm a foundation. But she had grown very pale and delicate in appearance and that annoyed him more than he liked to admit. He tried to find comfort in the fact that she promised him that she, too, would go away some place into the country before the heat of summer should be upon New York.

With the coming of April it was time to say good-bye. A busy, useful life opened out for Alonzo. And, as for Marie, he fondly planned that the future might hold a successful career for her and that some day she might marry some good man who would be able to take care of her always in luxury.

The last meeting took place in her room, the same room in which they first had met. Supper was sent up to them and, after supper they were to say good-bye. She was not to see him to the station because she did not want to come back through the streets alone after he was gone. The supper progressed without much enthusiasm.

"You should eat more, Marie," said Alonzo. "You need to eat to put color into your cheeks."

Marie smiled wanly. She was very reminiscent and sad. She watched her friend eat, not even making a pretense at trying to herself.

"From October to April!" she mused, "We have known each other that long!"

Alonzo stopped eating and looked across at her drawn little face.

"Are you glad, Marie," he said, "that we have not allowed ourselves to fall in love with each other?"

"Of course I'm glad, Alonzo," she answered. "You have been so wonderfully kind to me. To warn me against the sorrows of life as you have! I didn't think so at first, but now I know that one is very wise to save himself from those things; to raise thyself above earthly love, hope, pity, fear and vain regret! You have been very kind to me."

"You are a wonderful little woman," he said tenderly.

He looked down in his plate and said nothing. She rose, walked around the table and put her hand on his head.

"Don't worry about that, my friend," she said. "I really believe as you do. And this pain now is nothing to what the great humiliation of disillusionment would be. I could not trust myself to say to you now, 'I will always love you.' How could I ask you to swear to me that you would always love me? Now we can have an eternal friendship that will do us both great honor. You were right. We have chosen the right course, my friend. I am content."

He jumped up.

"Marie!" he cried. He took both her hands in his and kissed them once, the only time he had ever kissed her. Then they stood in silence for a while, until it was time for him to go.

At the threshold she stopped him.

"Once again, before you go," she asked, "say to me, 'Bless your heart.'"

He put his hands on her shoulders.

"Bless your heart!" he murmured.

"When you say, 'Bless your heart,'" she said, "I wouldn't care if the world came to an end."

"Bless your heart," he repeated huskily.

The next instant he was gone.

. . .

Five hours later there was a loud rapping at her door. Marie had been lying on the sofa crying softly ever since Alonzo had gone. She jumped up, rubbed her eyes and opened the door on Alonzo.

"I've come back," he said. "I've got a plan." He was out of breath and she motioned him to a chair.

"Alonzo!" was all she could gasp.

"Listen to me, Marie," he said, "and talk this over sensibly with me."

"I couldn't go away. I love you and I can't get along without you—for awhile at least. I tried hard to go away. I didn't want to ask you to give up your best years to me when I can offer you so little."

"Oh, don't say that," she begged. "You have so much to offer!"

"Then listen, Marie. You are without illusions and so am I. Why can't we go into this like sensible, thinking beings, for as long as it lasts and then take things rationally when it ends?"

"And you think the game is worth the candle?"

"If we take things reasonably, why not?"

"And when it does end, Alonzo?"

"We will talk that over sensibly, just as we are talking over the beginning, sensibly. There will always be truth between us, at least, and reason. If it is you that falls out of love first, all I need is the word from you that will send me packing. If it is me, I shall not hesitate to tell you the truth. And always, always we will be sensible about it."

"There may be bitter regrets, Alonzo."

"I will be brave enough to meet them. Could you be?"

"I could try."

"And the first time you realize that the thrill has gone out of our relationship, then you are to say to me, 'The time is up.' I will do the same."

"I will do that."

Alonzo came over and took her into his arms. He looked down into her upturned face and allowed all the tenderness he had so long struggled against to show in his eyes.

"To think that we two believed that we could beat this out of us!" he said.

She smiled up at him.

"And, when it is all over, Alonzo, at least we can say that it was good while it lasted!"

. . .

They were married, Alonzo insisting on the legal ceremony, and into a small town in western New York he brought his bride. They were very poor. Little Marie's busy fingers worked twice as hard as they had ever worked before, and she had no time at all to spend on her wonderful voice. But they were happy, because they were two fine and noble natures in whom respect for themselves and for each other evenly balanced their love. And, over and above everything, they were always, always sensible. As to their compact, well,—now we come to the most sensible part of their story.

. . .

It was Marie who was leaving Alonzo. They sat on the porch of the little cottage where they had been so happy together, and he was as gallant and gentle to her now as he had been the day he led her there a bride.

Marie sighed.

"I didn't think—I should be the first to leave!"

Alonzo looked down at her and then turned his face away. There were tears in his eyes that he didn't want her to see.

"You will be all alone!" she mused.

"Don't think of me," he said bravely.

They sat in silence a long, long time. Then there wafted to them the faint sound of distant music. It was a street organ. Nearer and nearer it drew; the tune it was playing gradually became discernible and its raucous tones louder and louder and more insistent.

> "The heart that has truly loved never forgets,
> But as truly loves on to its close
> As the sunflower turns to her God when he sets,
> The same face that she turned when he rose."

. . .

The music faded out in the distance.

Alonzo's breaking heart could stand no more. He hid his head in his hands and sobbed like a child.

"You are making it very hard for me, Alonzo," she said gently.

Gradually he became calmer.

"I'll not be long now," she continued, "Is there anything more you wish to say?"

He put his hand on her head as if in benediction.

"Bless your heart!" he murmured.

A big touring car whirled around the corner and came to a stop in front of the house. Out of it there jumped a handsome, dark, strong-featured chap; the very opposite of the lean, intellectual Alonzo.

Marie clutched Alonzo's hand.

"I am going now," she said, and then in a whisper hardly heard above the throbbing of Alonzo's heart, "Good-bye."

Alonzo turned deadly white.

The young man was swinging up the path.

Alonzo called to him.

"Doctor! Doctor!" he cried.

The young man rushed to Marie's side. He took her hand in his; then he turned to Alonzo.

"She is gone," he announced.

Alonzo sank in a heap on the threshold.

The doctor looked down at the woman's face.

"I never saw a face so young in death," he said.

Alonzo raised his head, white with the cares of eighty-four years.

"She was only eighty," he sobbed.

THE END

Play for Mr. Fairbanks

Martin Goodbody, the "Parsons"   Douglas Fairbanks
Billy Hepp, his sporty college chum
Maggie, poor girl in tenement
Teddy, her young brother
Father Ignatius, Chaplain
   of St. Anne's Orphanage
Gregg, Social Gangster (Heavy)

PROLOGUE

Billy Hepp and Martin Goodbody have been chums all through their college life, despite the fact that they are of entirely different natures. Billy is a sport and has spent his life in more or less riotous living. Martin, on the other hand, is a serious youth studying for the ministry. He spends most of his time with books, being of the typical bookish type with horn-rimmed spectacles and absent-minded mannerisms. Martin has only one vice; he always carries a little striped paper bag of peppermint lozenges in his pocket, eating them and passing them around to his friends. Aside from this one habit, he leads an exemplary life. Martin often remonstrates with Billy when he comes home drunk to the room they share together and Billy is always promising to reform.

One day during the last week of their college life, Billy comes in with his ice skates and asks Martin to go skating with him. Martin refuses to skate but he takes his book and accompanies his friend, sitting on a bench near the pond while his friend practices stunts on the ice. Martin studies diligently, absolutely impervious to distractions. Several pretty girls try to flirt with him and a squad of kids make him a target for snowballs, but Martin sticks to his book. Presently he hears a scream and sees with terror that Billy has gone through the ice some little distance out into the pond. The skaters all run away from him, fearing thin ice and Billy is left struggling in the water. By the time that Martin reaches him, Billy has become unconscious. Without hesitation Martin jumps into the hole and holds his chum up. Aid is a long time in coming, owing to the state of confusion among the other skaters and the two boys are pulled out just in time.

A week later the two boys have to part to take up their separate ways in life. They feel very serious over the parting, after having gone through so much together, and Martin suggests that they make a solemn vow of lifelong friendship, swearing that if either of them ever is in trouble or needs help, that the other shall come at his call, no matter where they each may be. The vow is solemnly taken and the chums part, Martin begging Billy to lead a godly life in the future. As Martin watches Billy depart on the train, he sheds a tear, eats a peppermint and fades out.

Several years go by and [we] find Martin preaching to a little congregation in Pike's Junction, Maine. Thoroughly settled in his rut, Martin is even more innocent and unworldly than ever. He is worshipped by his congregation. The female members shower him with attentions, which, however are taken absolutely impersonally by Martin. He has been presented with enough embroidered slippers to sink a ship.

Meantime Billy, in New York, has been going the pace that kills. He is surrounded by a gang of parasites and confidence men that has been

living off him for months and he is a regular hanger-on at all the cafes
and gambling houses in New York. He is just on the verge of the D.T.'s.
One morning about 6 o'clock he is careening home in his automobile,
drunk, when he runs over a little boy who is crossing the street. The boy's
sister, a girl of seventeen, happens to cross the curb. She grabs her brother
and rushes into the house with him, intent only on seeing how badly he
is hurt. Billy takes the address of the house, a tenement, and hurries home.
The shock has been too much for him, added to his near approach to
D.T.'s and he keels over on making the house. The doctor is sent for.
Then, in his remorse over killing the boy (as he believes) and also over
the terrible life he has been leading, his thoughts travel back to his old
chum who was so upright and good and he orders a servant to telegraph
him to come at once; that he is dying. When Martin reaches his bedside,
he is very low. He has a lawyer there and, in the presence of Martin he
draws up a deed, deeding his entire fortune of $75,000 to Martin on con-
dition that he remain in New York and spend the rest of his life in undoing the wrongs that he (Billy) has done while on earth. One of the parasites (Gregg) happens to be in the next room listening and the idea of
the innocent country minister with all that money to spend on charities
sounds good to him. Billy, expecting death any moment, tells of the child
he killed and gives Martin the address at which to look for him and make
matters right with the family. (Gregg takes the address down carefully
on his cuff.) Billy scarcely gets the deed signed before he lapses into un-
consciousness.

Gregg rushes out and telephones into the gang's headquarters telling
them what a pie is in store for them. He goes back to Billy's later and
runs into the doctor who is just leaving. Gregg pulls a long face and asks
how his dear friend is and whether there is not some faint hope of recovering. "Recover?" says the doctor, "Why you couldn't kill him with
an axe. He'll be alright in a week, he's merely raving with the willies."
Sadly Gregg goes home to break the news to the gang that their hopes
are blasted. The gang, including the principal female member, Katie the
Kid, are drinking to the health of their victim when Gregg enters and

tells the sad news. "Is the deed all made out?" asks Hophead Henry. "Sure," answers Gregg. "Suppose we send the minister back to his church over Sunday, kidnap Billy, run him up the river and hide him, and let the minister think he has died and been shipped to the family plot in Frisco. Then we gets in and trims the minister at our ease." The plot is immediately put into execution. Martin consents to leave his friend and attend to his home duties and, while he is in Pike's Junction, news comes of the death. The gang hide Billy in a cottage up in the country, where he is kept a prisoner, locked in the cellar. He is still more or less delirious.

The next week Martin starts out with his $75,000, to right the wrongs of his dead friend. The gang looks him over as he steps off the train, the easiest mark in New York. As Hophead Henry says, "It is almost a shame to take the money."

Now the little boy whom Billy ran over lives with his sister, Maggie O'Neil, in an east side tenement. The two have always been the greatest of chums (this to be shown earlier in the picture) and together they have made great plans for the future. Maggie remembers having seen the country once when a child and her brother is never tired of hearing her tell about it. She always ends her story with "some day we'll go and see it together." Maggie is slangy, Irish and full of pluck. The boy is not really badly hurt and, as Maggie has a little money saved up to pay the doctor, she feels that they are both very lucky. The gang, knowing that Martin will look up the injured boy the first thing, goes to the tenement, rents Maggie's room over her head by paying extra for it, and plants a hard faced woman in it, with a monkey faced little demon of a boy who is to play the cripple. Maggie and her brother leave, little knowing why they were turned out.

Martin gets up early in the morning and starts out. He is not used to the tipping system and is astounded at the way in which New Yorkers demand money for every little service. The lower order of grafters have gotten wise to his presence and the sidewalk outside the house is lined with beggars. Martin hands money right and left, looking more and more astonished at the awful state of things in New York. He is bound direct for the tenement house to look up the injured child and, once outside the door, he grabs a handful of bills from his pocket to be ready for the demand. The woman is waiting for him in the hall and she steers him into her room and shows him the child. Martin gives him a peppermint and the little angel immediately takes a slingshot from his pocket and hits him in the eye with it. The woman makes a terrific demand for the money and Martin writes out a check and hands it over.

In the meantime Maggie has discovered that she left her one treasure at the old room, a geranium plant in a tin can. She comes back for it, accompanied by her brother who hobbles along on crutches. She knocks at the door and the woman answers. When the woman sees who it is she slams the door quick. This gets Maggie's Irish up and she starts to bang at the door. A fight ensues between the woman and her kid on one side and Maggie and her brother on the other; in the melee the angel child of the grafters forgets that he is wounded and kicks Martin in the shins. Maggie finally breaks in and the truth is out, the grafter's kid beating it down the street at very high speed for so injured a party. Maggie gets the check away from the woman before she beats it also and leaves Maggie and the minister alone. The minister sees Maggie to her new home, helping the boy as he hobbles along on his crutches. At Maggie's new home Martin offers her the money. For the first time since he has arrived in New York his money is refused. Martin can hardly believe his eyes. Maggie makes some tea for him and he proceeds to tell his story. Maggie sees right away the precarious position the poor innocent fellow is up against. They part very friendly, Martin asking Maggie for help in his life's work.

The gang, in the meantime, is quite disconcerted over the failure of their first attempt. They are wrangling together in their headquarters when Katie the Kid gets disgusted with them and decides to do a little work on her own hook and for herself. She takes a photograph of herself, marks on the back of it "To Billy, from his little Elsie," sneaks up to Billy's house, where Martin now lives, and slips the photo in the desk,

unseen by anyone. Later Martin comes in and runs across it. It aston-
ishes him greatly and he is greatly shocked, so he eats a peppermint.

On Sunday Martin takes Maggie to see the squirrels in Central Park.
They are very happy, Martin has fallen in love for the first and last time
in his life. They part on Maggie's doorstep and Martin goes home walking on air. When he arrives he finds a note reading, "Billy, have just got
into town. For God's sake come to me. Elsie." The address is added. Martin starts immediately to go to this girl who evidentally [*sic*] does not yet
know of Billy's death when, all of a sudden, something stops him. He is
beginning to be a little suspicious. So he phones Maggie and takes her
with him. As they walk through the slums Martin comes very near to
proposing, but he is always so scared when he gets anywhere near the
question that he eats a peppermint and remains silent. Together he and
Maggie enter a very poor tenement and find the number of the room
given by Elsie. They are invited to enter by "Elsie" (who is, of course,
Katie the Kid) all dolled up like a poor innocent country girl. She asks
anxiously for Billy and when told that he is dead she says "My God, and
I wear no wedding ring" and faints with her arms about Martin's neck.
Martin thinks of his oath, "to spend his life undoing the sins of his friend"
and he sees only one course open to him; to marry the poor girl. He turns
to Maggie and she nods her assent; that is the only thing to do. The wedding is set for the next week, and after Martin and Maggie have left Katie
the Kid lights a cigarette and congratulates herself on putting one over
on her pals.

But Katie's pals have not been idle. Their headquarters is a very respectable looking house in the residence quarter which, until it was
pulled some time back, was a very profitable gambling place. Gregg decides to rig the place up as an orphans' home, go to Martin as a philan-
thropist and say that the home is not going to be able to run unless it has
immediate endowment. The gang put a big placard over the door reading "St. Anne's Orphans' Home" and Gregg starts out for Martin. He
finds him and lays the sad tale before him, telling how the orphans will
have to be run out into the cold unless they get an endowment. Martin

thinks the matter over and tells Gregg he will let him know later what he decides.

Now, unknown to the crooks, there is a genuine "St. Anne's Orphans' Home" in New York; a little ramshackle place that is run by an old retired priest. After Gregg has gone Martin gets to thinking about the orphans and feels so sorry for them that he is astonished at his cold heartedness in turning the kind man away. So he looks up the address of "St. Anne's" in the telephone book, calls it up and, of course, gets the genuine old priest. Martin asks is there anything particular that the orphans are in need of and the priest tells him that they will soon need hats. Now Martin never bought any feminine headgear in his life but he walks boldly into the first store he runs across, which happens to be Seigle Coopers. Martin is met by a dizzy blond saleslady who so overawes him that he can hardly speak. She asks what he wants and he manages to tell her that he would like to look at some hats that would be becoming to an orphan. The result is that he takes everything the saleslady shoves at him and leaves with a fine lot of Paris creations which comes to $700. Martin arrives at the genuine St. Anne's, meets the old priest and they get to talking. Martin sees right away that there is something wrong, as the priest never heard of the man named Gregg. Martin deals out the millinery, which completely demoralizes the poor little orphans, and he goes home thinking deeply.

Now it so happens that Billy, in his prison up in the country, has been fed on bread and water and, getting no booze at all, he has recovered completely. There is a young girl living on the adjoining farm who discovers him through the cellar window one day and, although too frightened to say anything about her discovery (and perhaps enjoying the romance of it) starts to bring Billy cake, pie, buttermilk etc., which she wraps in newspapers. Billy, who is crazy with worry, finds in one of the newspapers one day the announcement of Martin's engagement together with a picture of the bride, whom he recognizes as the notorious Katie the Kid. He realizes that a gang of grafters have gotten hold of his friend and are probably getting his money. When he reads in another paper (gotten the same way) that Martin is going to give $50,000 to an Orphans' home he nearly faints.

Billy begins to dig himself out of the cellar.

The day after Martin visited the real orphans' home, Gregg comes after him in an auto to go visit the phony home. Martin is beginning to wise up. He goes along, saying nothing. The gang is crazy to get their clutches on the money before Katie the Kid marries him. Martin goes to the phony home, which is planted full of newsboys, looks it over and just about sizes things up right. He has wised up at last. But, if he was nice to Gregg before, he is doubly so now. He calls him "brother", compliments him on his charity and finally ends by stating that, if they can get $10,000 placed in the bank in escrow for St. Anne's Home, he will donate $50,000. Gregg is somewhat taken aback by this but he doesn't lose heart.

After Martin has gone the crooks scurry around and see if they can possibly raise the $10,000. Some of them object to risking the money but, as Gregg assures them, the St. Anne's Home is a phony. Gregg puts in nearly $5,000; all of his earnings from gambling. One of the gang steals and hocks Katie the Kid's diamonds. The crooks put in every nickel they have and at last are able to put the escrow papers into Martin's hands. He then calls up his friend, the old priest, and tells him he has $10,000 more for the orphans.

Martin is spending his last days with Maggie. They are very sad. The little brother and Martin have grown to be great chums and Martin tells him about how different the country is from New York. "Are you ever going back?" asks the boy. "No," answers Martin and Maggie bursts into tears and leaves the room. That night they say good-bye, Maggie crying as though her heart would break. The next day is the wedding. When Martin gets home he takes his picture of Billy, looks at it for a long time and almost regrets his friendship [with] the wicked ruiner of young girls.

Billy, up in the country, digs out of his cellar and starts for New York, riding the rails.

The next morning Gregg calls Martin up and asks if he has his check ready. Martin tells him that he will give it to him after his wedding, which occurs at noon. Gregg and his gang decide to be Johnny on the spot immediately after the ceremony. Martin then calls up the old priest and tells him to be there.

Along about 11:30, Gregg gets a wire from his pals in the country saying that Billy has escaped and has long been on his way to New York. They realize that it is imperative that they get Martin's check before Billy shows up. Gregg and his pals get in autos and race to the wedding. They arrive just as the knot is about to be tied. They enter the house (the wedding takes place at Martin's house) and are no sooner in than a lookout stationed at the door signals that Billy is coming down the street with blood in his eyes. Without more ado the gang kidnap the bridegroom, rush him out the side entrance, into a machine and off to the gang's headquarters.

Billy enters the house and learns what has happened. He telephones the police. Katie the Kid, sore at the rest of the gang for upsetting the wedding, tells the police where they can find them.

Up at the Gang's headquarters the gang attempt to get Martin's money at the point of a gun. They are desperate, knowing that the police will soon be after them. Martin struggles with them.

The police, accompanied by Billy and the old priest, race toward the gang's house, knowing that they may not stop short of murdering the poor minister. When they arrive and break in the door, they find Martin sitting on a stack of disabled grafters eating a peppermint. As the grafters are being led off, Martin waves their escrow papers in their faces. They sneer, saying that the home was a phony. Then Martin brings up the old priest, explains that there is really a St. Anne's home in New York and that their money goes to it. The crooks are led off, utterly squelched.

Then Martin calmly turns and tells Billy to give his check for $50,000 to the priest. At first Billy remonstrates but Martin says, "So, that is the kind of repentance you make, is it?" Billy, like a good fellow, turns over the check.

Martin calls for Maggie and tells her that he is going to the country and that he wants to take her as his wife. Maggie falls into his arms. At the first sermon he preaches after his return, Billy and the country girl, now married, sit on a front pew together with Maggie and the little boy.

All Men Are Equal

An Act

CHARACTERS

ESSAE.

MR. WARREN,
 ESSAE'S FATHER.

BRILL.

MAYOR LINDSEY,
 A SELF MADE MAN.

ALTBERG,
 A JEWEL WORKER.

TIME: The present

PLACE: A city in the United States

SCENE: Living room in the house of Mr. Warren, a well to do American. Mr. Warren sits reading a newspaper. Essae enters, rather nervous in manner.

ESSAE: Did you want to see me papa?

MR. WARREN: (putting down newspaper) Oh yes. Did your mother speak to you about—about Lindsey before she left?

ESSAE: Why, I think she said something.

MR. WARREN: He has been to me quite frankly and, of course this will be a big thing for you. The mayor of a big city like Wellington, you know! It isn't every girl that has a chance like that. He is waiting down stairs and, if you wish, you may give him his answer now.

ESSAE: I—I suppose it will be yes papa. He is a good man and of course I will have everything. But I don't want to be in a hurry. Please don't let him make me be in a hurry!

MR. WARREN: You are a sensible little girl. Lindsey is a fine man, a self made man, one of nature's noblemen. I'll send him up.

ESSAE: (starting to stop him) Oh, wait a moment! (relenting) All right.

(Mr. Warren exits. Essae goes to the window and looks out; she appears worried. Brill enters into the room. He is a handsome man of about thirty five years. His manners and expression show traces of a large experience in the world and a deep sympathy with humanity. Essae turns, sees him and starts.)

BRILL: I beg your pardon, Miss Essae, but the maid told me that I might come right up.

ESSAE: I am so glad to see you. Oh, Mr. Brill, I'm so nervous and upset. I am waiting here for Mr. Lindsey. Papa is sending him up.

BRILL: I'll go immediately.

ESSAE: (pleadingly) No, please don't! You don't know how you can save me! (regaining possession of herself) I didn't mean that, but—

BRILL: I understand. It is hard for a fastidious girl to fall in love sometimes, isn't it?

ESSAE: You understand how it is, don't you?

BRILL: (looking at her tenderly) Yes.

ESSAE: I think that I am rather old fashioned. The girls I
know, why, they just seem to take to this sort of thing
and really enjoy it. The men never fluster them a bit.
But with me, I always feel like running away. They all
say I am old fashioned.

BRILL: Not old fashioned, Miss Essae. On the contrary I
believe that you are way ahead of the time. Americans
as a rule have not yet learned to be fastidious.

ESSAE: I wish that I were clever enough to understand all that
you say to me.

BRILL: I am glad that you are not. Most American women are
clever and it is a great fault in them.

ESSAE: You think it is a fault then to be clever? I am so glad of
that because I have tried so hard to be clever and can't.

BRILL: The only quality that a woman can handle with grace,
little girl, is her womanhood; her femininity. She is
tremendously awkward when she tries anything
heavier and women were not made to be awkward.

ESSAE: I am glad to hear that. Sometimes I have been almost
jealous of clever girls with careers ahead of them.

BRILL: Yes; careers so far ahead of them that they never even
see what they are.

ESSAE: What do you mean?

BRILL: Some years ago, in this country, there was a very clever
girl; a wonderful girl. She would have made a great
woman lawyer. But she happened to have been born
before the days of careers for women and so there was
no way open to her. She never even had a chance! And
so, she married a poor man and lived all her life in a
cabin in the forest.

ESSAE: Oh, too bad!

BRILL: Her name was Nancy Hanks.

ESSAE: The mother of Lincoln!

BRILL: And she never had a career!

ESSAE: Oh, I think I understand.

BRILL: The trouble with clever women of today is that they all think their cleverness was given to them for their own use. As soon as a woman finds out that God has lent her a propensity to do a certain thing well, she selfishly rushes off on a career and refuses to be a mother. Where are our great men of the future coming from? No man of genius can be born of a fool. And this great Democracy of ours is rapidly reaching a period where only fools are having babies.

(Enter Lindsey. He is a husky type of man, aged twenty seven.)

LINDSEY: (looking from Essae to Brill and back to Essae again) I understood that you were alone.

BRILL: I am just leaving.

ESSAE: Please don't go.

BRILL: I must. Good day Miss Essae. Good day Mr. Lindsey.

ESSAE: Will you wait downstairs? I wish to see you before you go.

BRILL: With pleasure. (Exits.)

LINDSEY: Essae, I don't like that fellow with his confounded polite airs. Seems to think that he's a little better than anyone else. Some day he'll wake up to the fact that he's living in America where everybody's equal.

ESSAE: Mr. Brill is a very clever man.

LINDSEY: Well, that don't make him any better than common folks. I'm a common man, I am, and I'm not ashamed of it. I've risen through my own efforts and I'm not going to let any snide book worm take airs with me. Why, I have more influence in this country than ten like him can ever hope to have.

ESSAE: (half to herself) Perhaps that is what's the matter.

LINDSEY: WHAT!

ESSAE: Please don't be angry. It frightens me to see you so angry.

LINDSEY: Well, I didn't come up here to be mad or jealous. You know what I came for Essae.

ESSAE: Yes.

LINDSEY: I'm a plain man and proud of it. There's no frills about me. You'll be a plain man's wife and have everything that money can buy. What do you say?

ESSAE: I thank you, Ned.

LINDSEY: Will you, little kid?

ESSAE: (half frightened) Yes.

(Lindsey grabs her impulsively and kisses her.)

ESSAE: (breaking away) Oh!

LINDSEY: Why, you aren't scared, are you. Lord! Seems hardly possible. What's the matter?

ESSAE: I—I suppose I'm old fashioned.

LINDSEY: That's all right. You'll get over it. Come, let's make up. (he kisses her lightly) We'll have a fine time together, baby. (holding her in his arms) And the night of the wedding I'll give the biggest party and ragfest this town has ever seen. I'll bring a nigger band clean from Baltimore! Little kid, do you know, I hold this city in the palm of my hand and on that night I'm going to turn it upside down.

(Enter maid.)

MAID: There is a gentleman downstairs who wishes to see you Mr. Lindsey.

LINDSEY: Show him up. (exit maid) It's a jeweler who has been working on something for you. You're going to be surprised!

(Enter Altberg. He is a young Pole with a fine and spiritual face.)

ALTBERG: How do you do. The piece is quite finished sir.

LINDSEY: Well, let's see it.

(Altberg tenderly unwraps a box which is done up in tissue paper. He opens the box and hands it to Essae.)

ESSAE: (looking at the ring in the box) Oh, how beautiful!

LINDSEY: The only stone of its size in town.

ALTBERG: The stone is very beautiful, sir.

ESSAE: But I was looking at the setting.

ALTBERG: Oh, thank you miss!

ESSAE: You made it?

ALTBERG: (looking tenderly at the ring) My own design.

ESSAE: It is exquisite.

LINDSEY: But look at the size of the stone, dear.

ESSAE: Are all those little angels carved by hand?

ALTBERG: Yes, miss.

ESSAE: Why, you ought to be celebrated!

ALTBERG: Oh, it is nothing. I am only glad to get the chance to do something fine. You see, the public wants mostly common settings. I had a hard time to get

Mr. Lindsey to let me use my own design on this.

LINDSEY: I was afraid it would interfere with the size of the stone. Don't know but it does.

(Essae and Altberg exchange a quick, sympathetic look.)

ESSAE: Ned, will you run down and call Mr. Brill? I want him to see it.

LINDSEY: H'm. All right. (He exits.)

(Essae and Altberg stand with their heads together looking at the ring.)

ESSAE: It is beautiful. This little figure here is all grace.

ALTBERG: I am glad that you fancy it.

ESSAE: Oh, I want more than to fancy it. I want to appreciate it!

ALTBERG: (quickly) I believe you do. (assuming an air of depreciation) Oh, really, it is nothing. An artist always takes his work too seriously.

(Enter Lindsey and Brill.)

ESSAE: Oh, Mr. Brill, meet Mr. Altberg. And see my ring.

(Lindsey greets Altberg and looks at the ring.)

BRILL: It is indeed beautiful. Whose workmanship?

LINDSEY: (disgusted) Good Lord man, you're looking at one of the biggest diamonds in the country! And then asking about the workmanship!

ESSAE: It is this gentleman's design.

BRILL: (examining the ring) I believe that Cellini did nothing more exquisite.

ALTBERG: Oh, sir, I am very glad to meet somebody who appreciates the pains I took with it. It is so seldom that I get a good commission and when I do I put my whole soul into it. Oh, if I could only work as I want to, with gold and silver and bronze! If people only wanted *fine* things!!

BRILL: This country will never need artists, my boy, until an aristocracy rises above the people to direct their taste. Not until Art has the reverence of a public that is guided by finer ideals than a public can make for itself. Then perhaps, you may know the blessed peace and inspiration of patronage.

LINDSEY: I wish you would stop chewing the rag over your crazy theories. We're all men and we're all equal. That's the plan that this country is built on and it suits me.

ALTBERG: I must be going. I am glad that you like the ring.

ESSAE: Thank you so much. Good-bye.

ALTBERG: Good day. (He exits.)

LINDSEY: Say, who gave you the ring, me or the jeweler?

ESSAE: You, of course.

LINDSEY: Well he seems to be getting all the credit. Will you see me down to the door, Essae, I've got to be going.

ESSAE: Certainly.

LINDSEY: Good-bye Brill. You knew that Essae and I are engaged?

BRILL: I guess. Congratulations.

LINDSEY: Thanks. Come on Essae. (Essae and Lindsey exit.)

(Brill stands looking out after Essae. He is disturbed in his reverie by the entrance of Warren.)

MR. WARREN: H'm, you still here?

BRILL: I was just congratulating Mr. Lindsey.

MR. WARREN: Yes, Essae's a lucky girl. This will be the making of her. She always has been a finicky little thing; a bit too—well—too fastidious. This will do her good. Get her out into the world; make her take to life like other girls. Do you know, sometimes I've been most afraid that Essae would be an old maid. She is rather that temperament.

BRILL: Nonsense. Essae is the most lovable little woman I know of, and the most feminine.

MR. WARREN: That's just it. She's too feminine. The men don't take to those kind nowadays. They like the good pal kind of a girl, one who is just as quick to get into mischief as they are. The men like to be run after. All the women do it. Why, even me, at my age—h'm. I don't believe Essae would have had a chance if it hadn't been for my taking things in hand and looking out for her.

BRILL: Perhaps she has never been in love.

MR. WARREN: Nonsense. Girls fall in and out of love ten times a day.

BRILL: I don't mean that. I mean love; real love. A woman only loves once, no matter how shallow or changeable her nature may be. A woman like Essae realizes this and can accept nothing but the real thing. The mistake that most women make is that they are so anxious for marriage that they cannot wait for love. Nine times out of ten a girl is not so much in love with her lover as she is with her trousseau.

MR. WARREN: How is a parent to know when a girl has found the right one? A fool woman always swears that her present lover is the only one she could ever care for.

BRILL: We should guard our girls from cheap things so that they shrink from them instinctively. From cheap music, cheap literature, cheap dancing, cheap ideals and cheap love. Those things are for the common herd, not for us whose taste should be aristocratic.

MR. WARREN: Common herd! Aristocratic! Bosh, man, we're living in America.

BRILL: Yes, that is our only excuse for being what we are.

MR. WARREN: Well, I don't claim that we are any too good at that. (taking up the newspaper) Did you read today's evidence in the Allen case? I don't know what the young women of this country are coming to. But our societies are doing noble work. Saving and reforming dozens of girls every day.

BRILL: That is very nice of them, but, Mr. Warren, can't they find something more profitable to spend their time and money on?

MR. WARREN: More profitable! Good God, man, can you think of anything more profitable than saving the souls of the young girls of the country? I myself have put hundreds into the cause.

BRILL: I think it rather impertinent business, myself. How do you know that they want to be saved? Most of them that I know prefer not to be. Why should society be so constantly worked up over this class of little creatures who have but followed the inevitable course of their type? Why, their poor, paltry little souls, even after they are saved, aren't worth a nickel a dozen.

MR. WARREN: Brill, I am astounded!

BRILL: America is continually concerned with the worst element it contains; its lower classes. They and their vulgar affairs are all that we think about; our government funds are spent on trying to reform and exalt them; we are morbid on the subject. I met a man today, a jewel worker, a master! If one half the money and attention were given this artist that is given to save the soul of any unmoral creature of the streets, this country might boast another Cellini.

MR. WARREN: Brill—I'm—I'm astounded!! I don't know what a Cellini is but this country seems to be getting along very well without it.

BRILL: You are right. This country has no need of a Cellini.

MR. WARREN: By God, Brill, I should think you would stop trying to argue with me. You always have to own up that I'm right.

(Enter Essae.)

ESSAE: Oh, papa, see my ring.

MR. WARREN: H'm. Look at the size of that stone! Must have cost a young fortune. Are you happy, little girl?

ESSAE: (looking straight ahead) I was never so happy in my life!

MR. WARREN: That's right. Well, I've got to be getting down town. So long, Brill. Don't try to put any of your fool ideas into Essae's head because she hasn't got the brains that I have to prove you're wrong. Good-bye, Essae. (he exits.)

ESSAE: (to Brill) I wish that you would talk to me. I like to talk to you because you tell me about real things and other people only gossip and talk nonsense.

BRILL: What shall we talk about, little lady?

ESSAE: Let's talk about love.

BRILL: Why that subject?

ESSAE: Because I would like to know if you think as I do about it. I have been thinking about it a lot just now.

BRILL: (looking at her keenly) Do you want me to talk about you—and Lindsey?

ESSAE: (starting) I wasn't thinking of him.

BRILL: Who then?

ESSAE: (confused) Very well, then, talk about Mr. Lindsey. I want to get this thing straight in my head. Do you think that he loves me?

BRILL: That is for you to judge, little girl. Love is a passion. There is very little passion in our lives. Men's and women's thoughts have become too paltry, too scattered to produce passion. It is given to very few to love greatly: great masterpieces of love are like great masterpieces of art, very rare. Every man tries to love just as every man, sometime in his life, tries to write poetry. But that does not signify that he does love or that he does write poetry. It takes keen living and culture to produce passion. Those things we do not have in this country.

ESSAE: (bursting into tears) Oh, I can't marry that man; I can't.

BRILL: Poor little woman!

ESSAE: All the time since he has been gone I have been thinking—thinking. I couldn't be with him alone. I couldn't be alone with him.

BRILL: (goes to her and pats her gently on the shoulder) There, there!

(Essae rests her head on his breast, still sobbing.)

ESSAE: Can—can love come to one in just a second?

BRILL: (holding her tenderly) It does not take long.

ESSAE: Am I being wicked?

BRILL: No, little woman.

ESSAE: I never understood till now. I used to shrink from it, but now I know. I want everything. And I want to give—everything.

BRILL: Poor little waking soul.

ESSAE: You understand. You understand.

BRILL: I wonder if I do?

ESSAE: Oh, you do, you do! You know so much. You see so clearly. Comfort me please. Tell me that this is right.

BRILL: It is the only thing in the world that is right.

ESSAE: What you said about passion—it is all true. It has come to me—that great thing that comes to so few.

BRILL: I believe it, little modern woman with the soul of a Franceska.

(There is a noise of an argument off stage. It comes closer and closer until Altberg's voice can be distinguished.)

ALTBERG: (outside) I tell you I must see your mistress.

(Essae leaves Brill's arms as though waking from a dream. Altberg rushes in. He is wildly excited.)

ESSAE: (rushing to Altberg) Oh, thank God! I knew that you would come back!

ALTBERG: (taking her in his arms) I understood.

ESSAE: I knew you would! I knew you would!

ALTBERG: I couldn't leave without seeing you again. The moment I first looked at you, I knew—I knew. And when you praised my work, Good God, it put ambitions into me that fairly burned. I can WORK now! Look.

When I went back to my shop there was a man waiting
for me, a strange looking fellow who chanced to see
me working on the ring one day. He talked to me and
I saw that he understood life. Today he was waiting for
me. He is the Archduke Paul of Moravia. He wants to
take me home with him. He starts tomorrow. I am to
have a little shop in the palace. And gold and silver
and bronze to work with!! But I couldn't go until
I had seen you again. I can't go unless you will go
with me.

ESSAE: I will! I will!

ALTBERG: My darling, how we two will live!

ESSAE: (a moment in his arms, then turns to Brill) Oh, Mr.
Brill, we entirely forgot you. You will help us, won't
you? I shall go away now—now before I have to see
any of them again. We will be married. Explain things
to papa. I shall come back to say goodbye if he wishes.

ALTBERG: That will be kind of you, sir. Make things as easy
as possible for him and—and Mr. Lindsey. It will be
hard for both of them. I know I don't deserve her.
I'm only a poor artist—

BRILL: There, there! Don't say that. Run away to your happiness; to your happy work. You will indeed love; in an
atmosphere where living and loving is possible. I will
arrange things with your father and Mr. Lindsey,
Essae. And, if they complain about the man you have
chosen—I have but to remind them that they are
living in a free country where all men are equal.

CURTAIN.

Where Does Annie Belong?

In August of 1914, there is wandering through Northern France an artist, accompanied by his daughter, a girl of twelve. We first see the two of them trudging down a country road, the artist with his pack of materials over his shoulder, and the little girl running along at his side, both very happy.

Now, with the title, we introduce their noonday meal. The artist pauses in his sketching and takes from his pocket a handkerchief, from which he unwraps some black bread and cheese. He calls to the little girl who is playing with some flowers and they sit together and start their luncheon. The little girl snuggles up beside him, caresses him and says, "Don't we have good times together, Daddy?"

The artist smiles down at her and asks, "Do you know why we are happy?" The child shakes her head, and the artist begins to philosophize.

"We are happy because we are where we belong," and he motions with his hands to the green fields about them.

The child asks him if he was always happy, and the artist shakes his head and says, "Where I came from people thought only of money and social position. So I left them to go to the place where I belonged. I found it, you see, many years ago, and so we are very happy."

The child is very attentive, and seeing that he is making a strong impression, the father follows up his little philosophical talk with the admonition, "If you find out where you belong, my dear, then you will always be happy."

Now, with a title, say that forty-eight hours later this beautiful country was caught in a cyclone of hate and destruction and terror. We now show a portion of a road near a Belgian town with the peasants fleeing in terror. We then show the artist and the little girl; the little girl is crying and the artist is trying to cheer her up, saying "Be brave, my child, we are Americans. We are not afraid."

About this time, an automobile loaded with a Burgomaster and his family and valuables breaks down on the road and the artist stops in his flight to help them. The Burgomaster says to him, "Ah, Monsieur, you must not stop to help us, you have your own lives to save." And the artist assures them that he is safe because he and his daughter are American citizens.

A party of Germans on horseback are almost upon them when at last the automobile gets started. The Burgomaster offers to take the artist and little Annie into the already overloaded car, but the artist refuses, saying, "Hurry away, my friends, we are safe."

The Germans, outraged at the escape of their prey, ride up upon the artist and the child and the leader orders the artist's arrest.

"You make a mistake. I am an American citizen," says the artist. "You can't arrest me."

"You have given help to the enemy. American citizen or not, the penalty is death." (Hisses from the audience.)

The leader orders the artist to be led up against a tree and shot. The child frantically clings to him, but the artist is brave. He takes the child's head in his hands and says, "If you escape these beasts, find your way back to America. That is where you belong now." He starts to kiss her and the Germans tear him from her and lead him to the tree, while the leader shoves the child out of the way and throws her to the ground.

The father is shot, and as the child runs to him, the Germans snatch the body and throw it in the river that is near the road. The child falls down on the ground weeping, and we fade out.

Now, we come to the family of Jean Vuyts, a Belgian farmer, who is fleeing with his wife and fourteen children towards the seacoast. Jean has stopped to water his horses and the children are swarming all over the wagon, inside and out. Little Annie sees them and walks towards them in a dazed manner. She is cringing beside the wagon unnoticed when Jean, having finished watering his horses, starts to pile the kids back into the wagon and without noticing, piles Annie in too. The wagon goes on its way and we fade out.

At last, on board a ship for the Promised Land, Jean Vuyts stops to count his offspring. The scene is in the steerage of a boat which Jean has reached after a wild, hurried voyage. His family is huddled about him and for the first time he has a chance to count them. He does so, and to his great amazement, counts fifteen. He goes over them once more carefully and says, in Belgian, "Ah ha, there is something rotten in Denmark." He then scans each child's face carefully, until he comes to one which is tightly covered with a shawl. He orders the shawl removed and Annie, scared to death, holds it tighter across her face. Finally, he manages to wrench it away, disclosing a totally unknown child. Mrs. Vuyts starts in to rave, saying, "As if we don't have enough already," but old Vuyts tries to calm her down.

"It's one more mouth to feed," she says.

"Ah," says Vuyts, "It's two more hands to work." And so Annie bums her passage to the Promised Land; the land where she belongs.

AFTER A YEAR IN AMERICA, SPENT IN TRYING TO BELONG
TO THE VUYTS FAMILY, THIS IS WHAT HAPPENED TO ANNIE.

We now show the kitchen of the Vuyts tenement, Annie just finishing scrubbing the floor. She is entirely worn out, and just as she gets the last bit done, in walks old Vuyts from his day's work, looking like a burlesque of Oom Paul. Up jumps Annie, tired as she is, and grabs the big easy chair and moves it towards the stove for him. About this time, Mrs. Vuyts appears in the doorway and watches unseen. Vuyts sits down, puts up his feet and poor, tired Annie takes off his shoes. We then cut to Mrs. Vuyts with business of biting fingernails.

Annie then lights old Vuyts' pipe and by this time Mrs. Vuyts can stand no more. She storms into the room and says, "You dirty hussy. It is not for nothing go I to ze movies and zeese Theda Bara vampires. Out of my house dis instant."

Poor Annie, utterly dumbfounded, has to pack up her rags and leave, not knowing what she was fired for, when she was trying to make everybody happy.

She wanders down the street totally forlorn and broken hearted, until she happens to pass a picture show, in front of which is a grand lithograph of a woman labeled "the Vampire." Annie stops and reads the title, thinks for a moment, and says to herself "why, that's what she called me," and perking up considerably, struts down the street.

AFTER SEVERAL MORE UNSUCCESSFUL ATTEMPTS
TO FIND HER PLACE IN LIFE, ANNIE GETS A JOB OF TENDING
THE MOTHERLESS CHILDREN OF ISIDOR KOZINSKY.

Now we show the secondhand clothing store (exterior) of Isidor Kozinsky, and Annie sitting in the doorway, attending to the Kozinsky kid. The kid has been drinking its milk and refuses to take the remainder. Annie, who is always hungry, starts in to drink it herself, when a stray cat comes up and meows at her feet. She gives the milk to the cat. Kozinsky sees this from the window and hurries out in rage, saying, "Schumelaka! You think I am Sam Goldfish that I should feed stray cats. I report you to Mr. Hoover."

Annie tries to plead for the cat, but Kozinsky gets angrier and angrier and finally fires her.

TITLE: ONE NIGHT IN LATE OCTOBER.

Annie stands on a street corner in Greenwich Village at a weird looking sign which reads "The Vermilion Hound." Annie is awe stricken at this sign which is the only light in the whole street. Finally, she crawls into the archway of this Greenwich Village restaurant and goes to sleep and we fade out.

THE NEXT MORNING.

The cook and the proprietor of the Vermilion Hound, who is a fat good natured Swede, goes to get the morning paper when in rolls Annie, bumping her head and waking up. The cook is dumbfounded and asks where in the name of Yon Yonson she came from. She struggles to her feet and tells him that she has been all over the world trying to find where she belongs and that maybe it is here. He takes her into the kitchen and gives her some food and tells her that she can stay and help around for her room and board. Annie is tickled to pieces and starts right in to help clean up.

NOW WITH A TITLE WE TAKE UP THE OTHER THREAD
OF OUR STORY INTRODUCING GERALDINE VANERPOL
WHOSE HIGH-STRUNG SOUL IS WEDDED TO HER ART.

We now show Geraldine in her boudoir on Fifth Avenue copying Nell Brinkly drawings with the aid of tracing paper. Geraldine's mother comes in, looks at her in astonishment and says, "Aren't you dressed for the ball yet?" Geraldine wrings her hands, rolls her eyes in anguish and says, "Oh, why will you seek to cage me in a gilded ballroom, when my soul is seeking freedom of expression?"

Her mother picks up the picture she is tracing and says, "I don't see much freedom of expression in that." Geraldine starts to pace up and down the room saying, "Will nobody understand me?"

TITLE: DOWNSTAIRS IN THE RECEPTION ROOM IS WARREN
BROOKS, THE YOUNG MILLIONAIRE WHO IS IN LOVE WITH
GERALDINE AND HAS COME TO TAKE HER TO THE BALL.

He paces up and down looking at his watch, for it is very late. Finally, Geraldine dashes into the room, still raving over her artistic soul and tells Warren that she is through with society and its frivolities; that if she has to go to another ball, she will scream; that her soul must have the freedom of Bohemia, where people will know and understand her.

Her mother comes in at this time, greatly distressed, and Mother and Warren try to calm her as we fade out.

IT IS LATER, AND ANNIE HAS BEEN INITIATED

INTO THE MYSTERIES OF THE ARTISTIC LIFE.

We now show the dining room of the Vermilion Hound. It is filled with long-haired men and short-haired women, and fairly reeks with soul-freedom, garlic, cheese and Dago Red. Annie, waiting on tables, wanders around through the maze, utterly bewildered. She stops by the table of Ivor E. Bean, the great poet, who believes in free verse, free love and free liquor.

Ivor is spouting some of his latest verse, which Annie listens to critically, and then she goes over to a corner and says to herself, "Gee, I wonder if this is where I belong."

TITLE STATING GERALDINE

HAS BECOME A GREENWICH VILLAGER.

Geraldine and Warren now enter the Vermilion Hound. Warren is making fun of the Villagers in a good-natured manner and Geraldine on her dignity.

Geraldine and Warren sit at the table with Ivor E. Bean, at whose shrine Geraldine worships. Geraldine and Ivor are soon lost in an artistic oblivion, while Warren struggles to keep his disgust from becoming too evident.

Warren begins to ask who several of the people are, and as they are pointed out to him, we show several "close-ups." One of them is of Harry

Bush, the great philosophic mystic. Warren points over to a wild-eyed female and asks, "Who is she?"

"That's Hedda Bone, the great writer."

"What does she write?"

"She is addressing envelopes now," says Geraldine, "but she has a great future."

Warren looks around for a waiter to get a drink to steady his shattered nerves and at this moment Annie looks through the little glass window that is in the swinging door which divides the kitchen from the dining room and sees this wonderful man.

Into her mind comes some of Ivor's poetry and she whispers to herself, "My soul mate."

She stands intently looking at this man, until the waiter dashes in, opening the door in her face and she does a Charlie Chaplin backwards. She follows the waiter and says, "What did HE order?"

The waiter looks in amazement and says, "Who?"

"HIM," says Annie. The waiter, exasperated, starts on his way, but Annie grabs him by the hand and points out of the window to Warren.

"Oh, that bird," says the waiter. "He ordered a Manhattan." And he goes over to tell the fellow who mixes the drinks at the little bar. Annie follows, and starts to help the bartender by cleaning glasses, etc., and when the drinks are ready to go out, she grabs the cherry bottle and puts an extra cherry in the Manhattan cocktail. Then, as the waiter starts to carry the tray away, she runs after him, and puts in yet another cherry. She then takes her place at the little window and stares at Warren Brooks.

Warren gets his cocktail, and is surprised to see three cherries in it. He laughingly takes them out and feeds them to Geraldine, while Annie nearly dies of anguish and jealousy as she stands at the window.

NOW WITH A TITLE, WE BRING GERALDINE
AND WARREN TO GERALDINE'S STUDIO
IN MACDOUGAL'S ALLEY.

Warren pleads with Geraldine to give up the sham life she is leading, and to let him marry her and give her a real home. Geraldine, however, is obdurate and says, "No, this is where I belong."

Warren leaves disheartened and goes sadly home.

The last thing we see of Annie that night, she is washing up the dishes and dreaming of such a wonderful man. In her reverie, she grabs a wet plate and hugs it to her chest. Then, getting all wet, she suddenly comes to, and finds herself in the kitchen. Going on with her dish washing, she sighs to herself, "If I could only belong to him."

TITLE SAYING THAT EVERY NIGHT FOR WEEKS,
THE FOLLOWING LITTLE SCENE REPEATS ITSELF.

We then show a short scene of Warren and Geraldine at a table in the Vermilion Hound, and Annie in the kitchen with her nose pressed against the window, watching Warren.

ANNIE GETS HER FIRST LOOK-IN AT A
GREENWICH VILLAGE STUDIO WHEN SHE IS ENGAGED
TO CLEAN UP IN PREPARATION FOR THE GREAT
FUTURIST PAINTER ART D. STROYER'S EXHIBITION.

We now show Art D. Stroyer's studio, decorated with wild, weird paintings that only their master could love.

Annie is scrubbing up the floor with a small scrub brush and tidying up the room.

Now, Warren has promised to meet Geraldine at this exhibition, and in his impatience, he arrives early and enters the studio before any one else has arrived. Even Mr. Stroyer himself is out somewhere. Annie nearly dies of delight when she sees her hero actually coming into the room where she is. Warren starts to go about and look at the pictures, shaking his head in despair over them. Finally, he notices Annie, who is standing awe stricken and says, "Hello, kiddie, where do you come from?"

With a great effort, Annie manages to gasp out that she is cleaning up and looks up at him like a sick fish.

Warren starts to talk to her in a kidding way, and looking at her scrub brush, says "You're quite some artist with the brush yourself," at which Annie says, "Oh thank you, sir," very flattered.

Finally, Warren points to the worst of the pictures with his cane, and says, "Do you think you could paint a picture like that?" Annie says, "Oh, sure!" Warren laughs and says, "By George, I think you could."

Warren looks over to one corner of the studio and sees an empty canvas, and a fiendish idea enters his brain. He goes and gets the canvas, puts it on the easel and says to Annie, "I'll give you ten dollars if you paint me a picture like that."

At this Annie gets scared, but she needs only a little encouragement from Warren to make a stab at it. She starts in to use one of the artist's brushes, when Warren stops her and says, "I think you can do that kind of art better with your scrub brush." He picks up the scrub brush and dips it in the paint and gives it to Annie. She starts in gingerly to dab at the canvas, but as he encourages her, she gets more bold and commences to just fling the paint around, getting a good part of it on herself. The two of them are so interested and amused that they forget all about the expected guests when they hear a crowd of them in the hall. Annie gets a terrible fright, but Warren tells her to hide quickly behind a screen. He then takes the canvas and puts it over in a corner, with the picture towards the wall and greets the Villagers who enter to look at the exhibition of Art D. Stroyer.

Geraldine soon shows up, looking more freakish than usual, as she has now bobbed her hair. When the studio is at last well filled, Warren steps to the middle of the room and says, "Ladies and gentlemen, I have a surprise for you. It has been my privilege to introduce to you the discoverer of a new art. I have here her latest masterpiece, entitled "The Eurhythmic Writhings of a Sinning Soul." Warren then gets the canvas and turns it towards the breathless audience. They simply go wild over it, and while they are in the heights of ecstasy, Warren goes to the screen, puts it aside, leads Annie out into the studio and says, "Ladies and Gentlemen, Mademoiselle Scrubrushki, the discoverer of a new art."

The Villagers fairly fall at her feet and Ivor E. Bean kneels at once, kisses her hand and composes a sonnet.

Annie is so overcome with joy that she just accepts it all and says nothing. Her eyes follow Warren where ever he goes, and escaping at last into a corner, she clasps her hands and says, "This is where I belong."

As the Villagers are busy examining the picture, Annie runs back to her kitchen and tells the cook that she has painted a great picture and got ten dollars for it. The cook, thinking that somebody has merely given her the money, laughs at her and tells her she had better hurry up with the dishes and to put her money someplace where she won't lose it.

A TITLE STATING THAT ANNIE DECIDES TO SPEND HER
TEN DOLLARS IN MAKING HERSELF A COSTUME FOR THE
VAMPIRES' BALL THE NEXT EVENING AT WEBSTER HALL.

We then show Annie sitting in the kitchen madly sewing on a gown, with a copy of "Vogue" in front of her, in which is a picture of the dress she thinks she is reproducing. The fat cook is working about the kitchen, and once in a while stops to pat her shoulders.

ANOTHER TITLE SAYING THAT
AT LAST THE TIME FOR THE BALL ARRIVES.

Annie is in the kitchen dressed in her ball dress and parading up and down in front of the cook, who is lost in admiration. The cook finally looks over toward the sink and sees a bunch of carrots. He goes over and cuts the top off with a knife and taking them to Annie, he places them against her waist and looks in admiration at them, this being his contribution to Annie's Vogue creation.

As the parting word, he tells her, "Be sure to be back by half-past one, because there will be a lot of dirty dishes tonight." Annie says that she will and hurries out the back door to go to the ball.

Annie sneaks in to the Webster Hall just about half scared stiff and is standing quietly in a corner when Ivor E. Bean spots her, and throwing his arms in the air, he cries, "Ah, Mademoiselle Scrubrushki, your presence makes our ball a complete success." And with that he goes over, takes her hand and she walks down through the crowd like the Queen of England.

Annie is, in fact, the belle of the ball, being the latest nut to make a hit in the Village, and she is everywhere crowded by men who rave over her art, her beauty and her soul.

At length, Warren and Geraldine arrive, and Warren is surprised and delighted to see his little partner in the joke. Being surrounded by men, and having Warren single her out for attention, completely turns Annie's head, and she thinks that Warren is dead in love with her.

The awarding of prizes for the most daring and original costume at last takes place, and Annie is given the first prize. This is almost too much. She nearly faints with joy.

To cap the climax, Warren comes and asks her for a dance. As he does that, she says to herself, "Now I know he is my soul mate."

It so happens that at this time, Geraldine is carrying on a mild flirtation in a side room with Ivor E. Bean. As Warren dances around the room with Annie, who is in her seventh heaven, they pass this room and Warren, looking in, sees Geraldine in Ivor's arms. Without a word he stops immediately and goes into this room, leaving Annie flat. Dumbfounded, Annie follows after, like a little dog.

Dashing into the room, Warren orders Geraldine to come with him at once, as he has the privileges of a fiancé to take her away from this place. Geraldine starts in to say that he doesn't own her soul—she must have freedom, and that Warren does not understand her. By this time, quite a little crowd has gathered. As Geraldine loves a scene, she is talking her loudest in order to create one. Warren, overcome with rage, says,

"I understand you better than you understand yourself. I, at least, do not allow myself to be fooled by this sham Bohemia." He looks about in rage, and his eyes light on Annie, who is watching the scene wide-eyed. He goes over and grabs her by the wrist and dragging her to the center of the room says, "No, you 'lovers of art,' I'm going to show you how much you know about Art. This wonderful woman that you have all been groveling to is nothing but a little gutter snipe, a common slavey, whom I hired as a joke to use her scrub brush on a piece of your canvas."

At this the Villagers stand back rather abashed while poor little Annie falls from the height of ecstasy to the lowest depths of despair.

Warren finally casts her aside, unthinkingly, and orders Geraldine to let him take her home.

Geraldine slowly rises and allows Warren to lead her out, and poor little Annie, left alone with all her glory stripped from her, goes unsteadily down the street and to her place in the kitchen of the Vermilion Hound.

Annie goes to work, but her heart is broken, and she murmurs to herself, "I didn't belong there after all."

SEVERAL DREARY WEEKS GO BY AND NO MORE
DOES ANNIE SEE HER SOUL MATE AT THE VERMILION HOUND.

Scene of Annie working listlessly.

One day we see Geraldine writing a note to Warren, saying "So glad you are back. You can see me tonight at the Vermilion Hound at eight o'clock."

TITLE — AT THE VERMILION HOUND AT EIGHT O'CLOCK.

We now see Annie going drearily about her work, with all of her heart gone out of her. Finally, she goes to the little window and looks at the place where Warren used to sit. Now there is sitting in it a man in uniform, an officer, of the United States Army, and as he turns his face she sees that it is Warren. "He is going to war," she murmurs to herself in despair.

Late that night, she decides to go and see Warren and say goodbye to him before he goes away to the awful thing from which he may never return. She gets his address from the phone book.

Annie, too, has decided to set out again in the world, as she knows now that she does not belong in Greenwich Village where she was for two days so supremely happy. She does up her few poor little rags in a bundle, leaves a note for the Swedish cook who was kind to her, and starts out, stopping on her way at a florist's to buy a bouquet of flowers for her hero.

NOW, WITH A TITLE, BRING HER TO WARREN'S APARTMENT.

Annie tries to push by the butler who blocks her entrance and tells her that Mr. Brooks is not receiving at this hour. Warren, who is in the library reading, overhears the argument and, coming into the hall, is dumbfounded to see little Annie. He greets her kindly, although very much surprised, and asks her into the library.

She tells him that she is about to start on her journey to find out where she belongs, and has come to say goodbye.

"Why, what do mean, my child?" he asks. "Well, you see," answers Annie, "I have gone all over the world trying to find where I belong, but no one ever wants me. I thought that you wanted me, and those others wanted me when I painted the beautiful picture. You made me terribly happy then, but I guess it was a mistake after all."

"Why, you poor kid," says Warren, and for the first time he begins to realize how cruel his use of Annie in his little joke on the Villagers was. Annie stands looking up at him, and in her nervousness, pulls her bouquet all to pieces.

"Well, I guess I had better go," she says. "I know a place down in Hogan's Alley where I can get a job and maybe somebody there will want me. But, oh, Sir, I did want to be an artist like my Daddy was."

"Was your father an artist?" he asks.

She answers "Yes" and he questions her about her name and finds that her father belonged to a fine old New York family.

At the end of his questioning, Annie says, "Here is a bouquet I brought you. I guess I better go."

"Wait a minute," says Warren. "Suppose you just let me find a place where you belong." He then gives her a card with an address on it and tells her to call there the next morning. After she leaves, he phones his lawyer and tells him that he is sending a child to him whom he wishes taken care of, and given an education. That he is liable to be called away at any moment, and that he leaves her entirely in his charge, and that he wants her to have the best of care and a thorough course in art.

AFTER THE ALLIED NATIONS ARE VICTORIOUS.

Warren comes home from the war. The first thing he does is to call on Geraldine at her studio, where he finds that she is Mrs. Ivor E. Bean and that she and her husband have started a Nature Cult and are flitting about the studio dressed only in rhythm rags.

Warren makes his escape, thanking his lucky stars that he didn't marry Geraldine. He drops in at the Club that night and picks up a copy of "Life." Running through it, he sees a little sketch entitled "Unrequited Love," in which a little urchin is presenting a scraggly bouquet of flowers to a grand looking man in uniform. The scene is, in fact, an exact replica of his scene with little Annie when they parted. Highly amused, he looks at the signature and sees that it was indeed drawn by Annie Schuyler. He phones to his lawyer and gets her address. The next day he calls at Annie's studio, where he finds a very pretty and charming young girl, quite different from the little Annie of the Vermilion Hound.

He is embarrassed at first, but presently they both begin to laugh.

"Do you know what I thought you'd look like?" he asks.

"No," says Annie.

He starts to describe, and we dissolve into a scene of Annie looking like a typical Greenwich Village frump, with bobbed hair, a queer dress, big black horn-rimmed glasses, and painting at an easel. The scene dissolves out and we find Anne and Warren still laughing.

Warren looks about the studio, and says, "Well, so at last, you have found where you belong. Are you happy?"

Annie smiles for a moment, then shakes her head "No."

Warren, surprised, says, "Why, what's the matter?"

And Annie answers, "I have not yet been able to draw the thing I want most."

"What is it you can't draw?" looking around at the different sketches on the walls.

"The man I love," answers Annie, as she turns away with an embarrassed smile.

Of course it is up to Warren to take the cue and come through with a proposal.

TITLE — WHERE ANNIE BELONGED.

We see two arms enfolding Annie and fade out.

The Moving Pictures
of Blinkville

Curley slouched luxuriously over two chairs and the desk of the Palace's little two by four box office. Somewhere from the dim interior of the theater came sounds of the musical struggle with which Al, the piano player, was teaching Miss Flossie Fuggybrain the new illustrated songs. The ballad was a pathetic thing in which somebody promised to meet someone when the something bloomed again and Flossie was having a terrible time with its delicate and intricate melody. Just outside the box office door Williams, the manager, was cursing loudly over the new bunch of films the Los Angeles agency had just sent down. But through all the surrounding tumult Curley, unhampered by any ornate or superfluous clothing, lay in blissful and picturesque indolence.

He was really a handsome fellow, but that did not count much, as he did not know it himself and he was generally too dirty or engaged in too ludicrous an occupation for others to see it. Also, to the persons with whom he associated, the ideal of beauty was embodied in a "college soot," loud hatband and diamond horseshoe. His hair, from which he took his name, was as fine a shock as that which adorns the Apollo Belvidere; his skin, tanned through a long career of street fairs, was healthy and full of color, and his dreamy brown eyes were the sort that poets rave about. His body was graceful and slender. Evidently "glomming," the professional name for his occupation, did not seriously interfere with his health.

Presently the manager stuck his head in the door.

"What, you still here?" he asked. "Soon as rehearsal is over, we're going to lock up."

"Go ahead," said Curley. "Maybe it'll keep the flies outa here."

The manager looked discouraged. Curley had been out of a job for two weeks, during which time he had calmly taken possession of the Palace as sleeping quarters and its manager as a bank on which to draw for meals. The manager was a good fellow, but his patience was gradually giving out. For the last few days conversation between the two had consisted chiefly of a series of hints to vacate from Williams and graceful evasions of the same by Curley.

The manager fumbled around among the papers on his desk: that is, among as many of them as were not pinned down by Curley's feet.

"Gee," he said, "but business is rotten. Getting worse and worse every day. We can't keep open much longer unless somethin' turns up. Here the blame film agency has sent me an old reel of the Hudson-Fulton celebration that has already been shown at the other house. How'm I going to hold up under that kind of treatment?"

Curley did not offer an answer. He followed the manager with his eyes as he puttered around the little office. Finally he went out, slamming the box office door as he did so. Curley heard him exit up the hole that led to the picture operator's box and tell him to lock up when he left. Then Flossie giggled. Al laughed, the manager grumbled a little more as they left the theater and all was silent. Curley remained in peace until he heard Frank, the picture operator, climbing down his little ladder.

"Oh, Frank," he called.

That individual put his head in the door and asked "What?"

"Say," said Curley leisurely. "Williams is a fine fellow, ain't he?"

"Aw, rats," said Frank. "I'm in a hurry," and he started to go.

"Wait a minute," called Curley. "I was just thinkin' I'd like to do something for him. He's been a fine fellow to me."

"Well," said Frank in disgust. "Spit it out."

"Would it be hard to get a picture machine down outa the box?"

Frank's face took on the slightest tinge of interest.

"It would be dead easy," he said, "but we couldn't sell it and if we did they'd git us before we got to Old Town."

"Well, Lord love us," answered Curley in sheer astonishment. "If you ain't so darn crooked you can't even believe in the pure motives of a honorable guy like me."

"Aw, come off it," said the other. "What's your idea?"

"Well, could you git it down, that's the question?"

"Sure," said Frank, "and there's the old machine I could pass through the hole in a minute."

"Well," said Curley, and he roused himself for the first time that day, "you just pass 'er down. We're going to do some special advertizin' for this here joint that will put that other honkey tonk outa business. I thought up the idea just now an' it's a peach. We take the machine out in front, I stand there an' turn the little old crank, all the boobs think we're takin' moving pictures and the house'll be jammed, just from the talk that'll get around."

"That's all right," said Frank in disgust, "but any idiot knows that machine ain't a movin' picture camera."

"Frank," answered the ingenious inventor of the idea, "compared to the rube in this town an idiot would be a college professor, so we're perfectly safe. You haul 'er down."

Frank hesitated but a second and then fell into the wild scheme.

With much effort they lowered the old moving picture machine down through the hold in the floor of the operator's box. Curley went to the saloon next door and borrowed a table on which to set it. He placed the table in the shallow lobby just in front of the ticket window and under a huge sign which read "Moving Pictures." Curley even persuaded the now enthusiastic Frank to spend a quarter on a piece of black cloth with which to cover the machine camera fashion. Finally all was ready and Curley mounted the table.

"There's only one thing," he said to Frank as last instructions. "If any one asks you are we takin' movin' pictures, don't tell them we are. We ain't going to do any lying about this. We don't need to. Just keep mum, that's all."

As several pedestrians went by, Curley mysteriously and scientifically shifted and adjusted the machine. Then he paused and looked eagerly up and down the street as though watching for picturesque material to come into view. Finally two little girls came in sight and quick as a flash, Curley ducked under his black flannel and grabbed the crank. By this time about ten people had stopped to watch the proceedings. As the little girls came into the bogus camera's imaginary focus, Curley slowly turned the crank. The girls stopped, made as if to turn back, giggled and finally walked kittenishly past the "camera."

An old man approached Frank.

"Be you taking moving pictures?" he asked.

"Naw," said Frank, "we're shooting spitballs at Haley's comet."

Curley came out from under his black cloth, and posing with one hand on his hip, gazed eagerly up and down for new material. The crowd grew and he became more and more mysterious and formidable. Finally a policeman attracted by the mob showed up in the distance and Frank for the first time began to look nervous and worried, but Curley never turned a hair. As the policeman charged down upon the crowd, Curley called his assistant and whispered something into his ear. Frank made his way through the throng and stopped the policeman and whispered to him. The latter straightened up, looked important, finally crossed into the middle of the street and took up a haughty position in front of the "camera." Once again Curley ducked beneath the black cloth and turned the crank. Then he came out again and whispered to Frank who again conferred with the policeman who then went further into the street, and paced back and forth, chest out and club swinging, the very picture of manliness and valor. Curley "took" him again. The ordeal over, the officer bowed imperiously to Curley and unheeding the throng, which was now seriously interfering with traffic, went on his way.

Before Curley's day's work was done the news of it had spread all over town, the mayor, six councilmen, two policemen, two doctors and the oldest inhabitant had all "chanced" to pass that way and condescended to pose. Moses Levi had even hurriedly had a clothing advertisement painted which he made little Moses carry back and forth in front of the phony camera for an hour.

When Williams showed up at 2:30 for the matinee he could hardly get to the door of his theater and the rumors he heard as he made his way through the throng sickened his soul with apprehension. Curley, with an important air and an angelically innocent face, was just packing the machine inside.

"Good heavens," said Williams, once safely in the theater, "what have you two idiots been doing?"

"You better get busy selling tickets to the crowd we brang," said Curley and the manager hurried into the box office for the eager populace was actually pounding on the ticket window for admittance.

For the first time in its unsteady career, the Palace played to capacity business and not half the people attracted by the crowd could be accommodated. Williams went after Curley, blood in his eye.

"You've got me in a fine scrape," he stormed at the ingenious youth. "Yes, chances are I'll have to blow this town."

Curley was surprised and shocked as, the picture of injured innocence, he asked why.

"Why?" said Williams. "Why, every blooming idiot in that theater has asked me when we're going to show the moving pictures we took this afternoon and as soon as they get onto being bunked they'll lynch me, that's why. Someone is already saying they are fakes and I'll have to skip town when the pictures don't come through, that's all. That darn old fool of a mayor has ordered fifty seats for the night we show 'em and that idiot policeman has bothered the life out of me about it already.

Says he wants his wife's family to come up from Oceanside for the event."

Curley looked grieved and thoughtful.

"Say," he said, "ain't you got some old parade film you could ring in on 'em. They'd never know the difference."

The manager, too disgusted to answer, turned on his heel and walked away, but an idea to Curley meant action and he did not intend that his well meant help to the manager should go astray.

After the matinee, he and Frank went over the film of a parade of the Hudson-Fulton celebration which was booked for the next week. The picture was almost hopelessly metropolitan, but by long and labored work at scratching and clouding the film the effect was produced that the most keen eyed observer would fail to understand. The scene projected on the curtain was not a picture—it was a series of blurs and blotches, with here and there a human form indicated amid the surging storm of scratches. Williams, on the theory that he might as well be dead as the way he was, finally decided to let Frank run the film as "Scenes of Blinkville."

The night of the exhibition was advertised and the excitement it caused gave Williams another attack of cold feet. He finally decided to sell out the house, pocket the money, stay in front during the performance and when the worst happened, take to the woods. A suspicious looking stranger who had been hanging around all day did not add any to his courage. Of all the theater force, only Curley remained calm and debonair.

The house was packed and, as the show proceeded, Williams paced the lobby. When the fateful film at last arrived on the program he was too unnerved even to glance in the door at what was sure to be his ruin. Finally a mighty roar came from within and, quaking with fear, he made for the street and oblivion. He was just slinking around the corner into a dark alley when the suspicious stranger tapped him on the shoulder. Williams nearly fainted.

"Say," said the stranger, "do you own this house?"

"Yes," Williams managed to gasp weakly.

"Well," said the stranger, "I've been looking the place over for a couple of days and seeing your packed houses. How much would you sell for?"

"What?"

"I'll give you four thousand for it just as it stands."

Williams was too flabbergasted to speak. Just then, Curley turned the corner.

"Hey, Williams!" he called. "The crowd wants you to come up and make a speech. The picture just set 'em daffy and the mayor wants to thank you for your enterprise."

Dumbly Williams allowed himself to be led back by Curley and the stranger. The crowd was surging from the theater. The mayor came forward and grasped his hand.

"Mr. Williams," he said. "I—in fact we all—want to thank you. Your photographic efforts—ahem—were perhaps a little clouded and indistinct, but it gives you—ah—all the more honor for undertaking the—er—enterprise of having the pictures made under the great difficulties of light and development which your esteemed photographer has just explained to me." He nodded to Curley and Curley nodded back with a smile. "I did not understand his technical terms," the mayor continued, "but I can realize the difficulty under which he worked."

Williams bowed idiotically.

"And," the mayor lowered his voice, "I have just made arrangements to purchase the film for $500 after you are through with it. I shall send it back for exhibition in my home town in Ohio. I trust you will not make other disposal of it as I have placed a deposit with your photographer."

When at last they were alone, Williams fell on Curley's neck.

"Curley," he said, "to think that I ever abused you and you've went and made my everlasting fortune."

Curley looked at the fifty dollars which the manager put into his brown palm.

"Gee," he said. "I won't have to go back to glomming for a year!"

My First Memories of Aunt Anita

Mary Anita Loos

The first social event I remember attending with my Aunt Anita was her wedding, in 1915 at the Hotel Del Coronado in San Diego. I was five years old, and, as the only child of her adored only brother, it was a command performance for me. What I remember best is my beloved grandpa, R. Beers Loos, done up with a white winged collar and fancy cravat, picking me up at our little cottage in Tent City, the area set up next to the hotel to house hundreds at cheaper rates. Grandpa and our housekeeper, Dicey, got me into my best white dress just as my nose decided to start bleeding. He cleaned me up and rushed us up the road to the fancy hotel, deposited me with Grandma, and, in great disgust over her choice of a husband, walked Anita down the aisle.

Skimming through the scrapbook my grandfather devotedly kept, I find a newspaper clipping describing the event as a "Tom Thumb wedding" because Anita was only four foot eleven inches tall, and her groom, Frank Pallma, was only one inch taller.

Frank was a minor composer and the son of the bandleader at the Del Coronado; and, of course, none of us knew that the wedding was all part of Anita's plot to get to Hollywood. Within the next six months Anita left Frank and headed north.

I saw little of my Aunt Anita during my growing-up years. Since my father was the house doctor at the Del Coronado Hotel and had a flourishing practice in San Diego, it was a good life, but I remember the excitement of visiting Anita in Hollywood in 1916.

My parents, grandparents, and I took the train to Los Angeles, and although we were there to see Anita, the big draw was the studio where she worked and where the great D. W. Griffith was in the process of filming *Intolerance*. He had built a set so massive it created its own skyline, and the dramatic, elegantly draped scaffolding near the corner of Vine and Hollywood Boulevard was the showcase of its time.

Pretty girls were stationed precariously on edifices supposedly reminiscent of ancient Babylon. My grandmother gasped, "Those ladies are half naked." As a doctor, my father's concern focused on the trauma that would result if any of them fell. And Grandpa just smiled and said, "They sure got some good looking girls." But the only immediate result of our gawking was that we were told to get out of the way. And Grandma's vociferous warnings about the city of sin lasted all the way home.

Two years later my dad went off to war, and my mother's father, O. T. Johnson, a wealthy early citizen of Los Angeles, wanted her closer to him; so we moved there, but Aunt Anita had already moved on. After titling *Intolerance* for Griffith and literally creating a new genre of film for Douglas Fairbanks, she went to New York, where many films were still made. There she discovered, among other things, the exclusive gown shops that were her delight. When Anita was a child, her Aunt Nina had sent her elegant handed-down frocks from Europe, and now it was my turn to be the recipient of Anita's New York finds.

From my grandparents I learned the family history, usually delivered in little fragments, but as I look back and piece the bits of information together, it helps explain the path Anita took, as well as her fixation on the general enchantment associated with blondes.

It seems that Grandma had a beautiful blonde sister, Nina, who was inclined to get into trouble with the local boys. Before she was "finished" in Etna, her parents sent her to a young ladies' finishing school in San Francisco, but on the train she met a handsome con man named Horace Robinson. His interest may well have been piqued by Nina's mentioning that her father was a gold rush success story and owner of a large cattle ranch, but however it happened, Horace managed to borrow ten dollars for immediate expenses and a marriage license, and he and Nina eloped.

Her father's heart was broken, but Nina took off for Europe with her new husband; and faded newspaper photographs of the beautiful blonde and the handsome, well-dressed dude show what a dashing pair they made. They were a high-flying international couple, selling newly printed Marconi stocks, and they shared their good fortune with Nina's sister, Minnie, and her little girl Anita back home. Horace bought little Anita a tiny chip of a diamond in a child's ring, and I can't help but think that that ring planted in Anita's fertile imagination the notion that "diamonds last forever." Packages of outmoded elegance arrived from foreign ports, and Anita had a good chance to examine the elegant Patou gowns before her mother cut and sewed them into more practical garments. Of course, in later years Nina no longer had either her own beauty or the handsome Mr. Robinson, "but at least," said Anita to me, "Nina was always dressed to the nines in Paris born garments."

This made perfect sense to Anita since her one obsessive, expensive, and lifelong fling was with elegant clothes; and, at least for a brief while, I was the beneficiary.

One dress I remember particularly well was a product of Anita's Bohemian days. On a blue sheath she had fashioned little circles of multicolored yarn, each with enough ribs to sustain a penny. I thought it was the grandest thing and wore it often, even as I continued to grow. One day Grandpa stopped me cold.

"I think it is time to give that dress up. You look like the three B's in it."

"What's that?" I asked.

"Bosom, bottom, and belly."

I was enraged, but he was right. I was too big to ever wear Aunt Anita's treasured finery again; but Anita must have known it too, for she began sending me other kinds of treasures like a beautiful book on Paris, an elegant kidskin purse with a shoulder strap, Coty cologne, and, from England, golf clubs in a grand leather bag, which I never used. However, I do remember waving around finely embroidered handkerchiefs she sent me and feeling very sophisticated when my "it floats" Ivory was replaced with fragrant *savons*.

I wondered about those faraway shores and longed to see them myself, but most of all I wanted to see my Aunt Anita again. I read her letters, of course, but now she had become so famous that I could also read about her in movie magazines. They reported her travels and the plays she saw, complete with pictures of her new windblown bob after she had shed the long hair I had brushed in San Diego and given up the towering hats I had thought were so grand.

Anita based herself in New York, writing films for Marion Davies and Constance and Norma Talmadge for several years, and then a phenomenon occurred.

On a train one day Anita began to think about the fact that blondes seemed to attract much more attention than brunettes. She was devoted to the witty author H. L. Mencken, who at the time was interested in a young blonde. Anita suddenly realized that although this girl was her age, and although my aunt was just as pretty and a great deal smarter, somehow or another, the blonde attracted more attention and eventually ended up with more diamonds than her brunette counterparts did. In the long train hours from New York to Hollywood she wrote the nucleus of what was to be *Gentlemen Prefer Blondes*.

Even though publicity has suggested that it was an overnight smash, this is not quite true, according to old newspapers in my possession. After a while she sent *Blondes* to Mencken, the editor of *Smart Set*. He wrote,

"Young woman, you've done the unforgivable. You've made fun of sex!" The dean of Broadway critics, George Jean Nathan, rejected it too, but later he admitted, "We were fools."

Cosmopolitan bought the story but didn't print it, and then Henry Sell, who was a great friend of Anita's and editor of *Harper's Bazaar*, bought it because he needed something for the noted caricaturist Ralph Barton, whom he had under contract, to illustrate.

Sell suggested she expand the story (which at the time ended with Lorelei and Dorothy getting on a boat to Europe), and the diary-style story was serialized in *Harper's Bazaar*. Within months circulation had doubled, and *Gentlemen Prefer Blondes* had been praised by intellectuals and the public alike. When the stories were issued together in book form, the book sold "like bathtub gin" and rocketed through forty-five printings. Eventually it was translated into thirteen languages (including Chinese), and in 1926 it became a smash hit on Broadway, in 1928 a Paramount movie, in 1950 a musical starring Carol Channing, and in 1953 a violently expensive and showy portrait of Marilyn Monroe and Jane Russell that hardly reflected the biting wit of the original story, but the film made a fortune.

Gentlemen Prefer Blondes is still in print, and Lorelei flourishes in summer stock. And Anita's sequel, *Gentlemen Marry Brunettes*, directly intersected my own life when my then husband Richard Sale and I paid Anita thirty thousand dollars and produced it as a film in 1955.

I was still a young teenager when Anita and I were reunited in 1927. The now world-renowned author of the best-selling *Gentlemen Prefer Blondes* was coming "home" because her book was being made into a film.

Dad and I went to the train station to meet her, and I will never forget how elegant she looked stepping out with all her fancy French Vuitton luggage and her fancy new husband, John Emerson (whose clothes were at least as elegant as hers). And there waiting for them was a tremendous limousine, complete with two crystal vases for orchids at the sides of the backseats and a very elegant liveried chauffeur. I hugged

Anita, who now was much shorter than me, and asked, "Where did the car come from?"

Anita laughed and said, "This is hard to explain to a kid," so, of course, I listened all the harder. "It seems that the movie star Gloria Swanson gave it to the Schencks as a Christmas present after a good movie. That's the way they do things in Hollywood."

Well, I was a student at the Hollywood School for Girls and often visited my grandparents at the Hollywood Hotel, but I had never heard anything like that before.

Anita and her husband were also settling into the Hollywood Hotel for the duration of their film, so my mother allowed me to visit often and even to spend the night once in a while. I helped Anita unpack and gasped over the beautiful clothes and, most of all, the shoes. There was one gold pair with lacings that ended in faux diamonds that enthralled me, and I couldn't help but notice when I held those tiny shoes in my hands, several inches of my fingers were still visible.

I soaked it all in, and several observations were immediate: there was a big difference between Grandpa's catalog-bought Sears Roebuck wardrobe, which I had thought so grand, and Emerson's Bond Street tailor-made suits. Also, Emerson's high style of conversation was borrowed Broadway wit and differed strikingly from R. Beers's Keystone-type wisecracks.

And although it was clear Aunt Anita adored him, I took an immediate dislike to this man Emerson. First of all, he told me I reminded him of his first wife and took to calling me Betty. Why did he have to mention her in front of Anita? I watched as he ordered my petite Anita to fetch him pills and get him a shawl à la Abe Lincoln. And I listened as he took bows for her book and script of *Gentlemen Prefer Blondes*. I was appalled, but Anita, with her well-kept figure, Paris clothes, and adoring friends, seemed on top of the world.

From one of those friends, Ruth Dubonnet, I learned Emerson was a hypochondriac and that he and Anita slept in different rooms. She rose at dawn to write, and he slept late. After a comfortable late breakfast in bed Emerson read what she had written, added a few commas, and then took half credit for all her work.

My feelings must have been obvious, and Emerson disliked me from the start as well. He was not interested in an interfering teenager tagging along watching his moves, yet Anita seemed to be able to turn a blind eye when he said he was exhausted and went off to "rest" for several days at a time at the Coronado Hotel. I detected a pattern that these periods of exhaustion usually immediately followed an "interview" with an attractive blonde, but as much as I resented his escapades, they gave me time to be alone with Anita.

She and I would stroll down Hollywood Boulevard together, and I felt all elbows and knuckles around that petite fashion plate with her Parisian sophistication. But she was sensitive to my awkwardness, and one day she kindly said, "I think we better do a little work on your eyebrows. I'll bring some tweezers out, but we won't tell anyone else." That was just one of her many kindnesses to me, small and large, that made her such a special aunt.

Anita was joined in Hollywood by her friend the famous photographer Cecil Beaton. He had risen to fame photographing the Royals and English society, but he left it behind for a contract with *Vogue* magazine. Beaton was in heaven photographing Joan Crawford, Dolores Del Rio, Tallulah Bankhead, and Johnny Weismuller—instead of princes he was shooting stars. Beaton also took my portrait, which I have to this day; however, my grandfather, with his usual pragmatism, cut the picture to fit a frame he already had and, in the process, removed Cecil's signature.

Anita took Beaton with her to William Randolph Hearst's San Simeon, which I am sure was the highlight of his visit, but to me the high point was when he played a very important role in my life: my first official "date."

The occasion was the gala party for the premiere of the film *Gentlemen Prefer Blondes,* and my mother bought me my first evening gown from the current grand dame designer of Beverly Hills, Bess Schlank.

It was a beautiful long, layered tulle with a billowing skirt edged in pale pink taffeta.

It was a great success. Even Anita was pleased and proud, and I was thrilled to join her, Cecil, and Emerson in being chauffeured the entire two blocks between the Hollywood Hotel and the Roosevelt Hotel.

The other glamorous guests included Irving Berlin and his new bride, Ellen Mackey. Irving asked me to dance, but with the first steps I realized he was no match for my height. As he twirled me around, he stepped on a layer of my tulle, which in turn twirled around our feet as more and more of it ripped off. The only thing to do was pull off the rest, and Irving laughingly whirled it around our heads like a banner. We sat down to applause, not just from Anita's table but the entire room.

"You were great," Anita assured me. "What an act. I'll have to use it sometime."

As I sat down, I was comforted again by a pat on the back from the new Mrs. Berlin, and I actually thought all would be well. But when I looked at Anita again, I saw a look of concern and realized she was wondering how my mother would react to the destruction of my dress.

All hell did break loose when I got home, but it had been a wonderful night.

Anita would reenter my life once I was an adult, and her constant desire to do the best, to look the best, and to be a part of whatever life she had to face made her an exceptional person and an exceptional aunt. We stayed close, visited often, and took a variety of trips together—but more on that later.

Return to Hollywood, 1931–1944

Even when the world was thrown into the depths of the Great Depression, the rarefied existence Anita and Emerson led continued unabated. Anita's diaries for October of 1929 reflect no economic concerns; she spent that month in London and Paris, dining with friends like Cecil Beaton, H. G. Wells, and celebrity party-giver Elsa Maxwell and her partner, Dickie Gordon.

The bubble finally burst for the Emersons at the end of 1931; what hadn't been lost in the market, Mr. E. had methodically been putting into now worthless foreign bonds. When he announced, "One of us will have to go to work," Anita knew full well which one he meant. Almost relieved, she happily packed for California to accept a contract offer from Metro-Goldwyn-Mayer.[1]

The Hollywood Anita returned to was far different from the one she had left only a few years before. The "talkie" revolution required a different kind of writing, and even the physical layout of the town had changed. Ironically, sound meant silence when it came to filming, and huge sound stages rose to create literal skylines at the studios. Metro-Goldwyn-Mayer, in Culver City, was still fairly isolated, but Hollywood had been thoroughly paved. The conversion to sound also meant huge infusions of money to pay for all the changes, and that meant banks and Wall Street were involved to a degree unfathomable a decade before. Movies had become big business.

For writers, pressure mounted to be productive, but sound also gave them a new freedom. Silent films had put a premium on actions and emotions that could be pantomimed; now not only did dialogue allow subtlety and zing, but sound effects, as slight as doors slamming, water rippling, and bells ringing, added depth to their stories.

Gentlemen Prefer Blondes had proved Anita could write witty dialogue, and that was why Irving Thalberg, MGM's production chief, decided she was just the person he needed to quickly fix the script for *Red-Headed Woman.*

Anita arrived in Los Angeles in mid-December 1931. First, she dined with her parents; her brother, Clifford; and her niece, Mary. The next morning she was in Thalberg's office, discussing the script.

Red-Headed Woman was a novel by Katherine Brush, first serialized in the *Saturday Evening Post* and bought by the MGM story department before they knew how it ended. It turned out to be an absolutely straight melodrama of Lillian Andrews, a conniving "Midwest sexpot" from the wrong side of the tracks who sets her sights on her happily married boss as her vehicle to rise in society. Katherine Brush was known as "the wicked lady novelist," and although it meant walking a censorship tightrope, a well-publicized story was such a leg up at the box office, it was assumed to be worth the effort.[2]

The first writer assigned to adapt *Red-Headed Woman* was F. Scott Fitzgerald, but Thalberg found that "Scott tried to turn the silly book into a tone poem."[3] Thalberg ordered Fitzgerald released from his contract and, with time running out, turned in desperation to Anita. The production had been announced to ride the wave of popularity the story had enjoyed in serialization, and the publicity department was busy promoting a search for the actress to bring Lil "Red" Andrews to the screen. Clara Bow, Joan Crawford, Barbara Stanwick, and even Garbo had been mentioned in the press as possibilities. So many tests were reported being made that the sixty-year-old comedienne Marie Dressler mugged for photographers wearing a red wig, underscoring the point that *every* MGM actress was being considered.

Thalberg knew that for the film to be a success, Lil Andrews had to be a caricature more than a character, and he had his eye on Jean Harlow to play the role. Anita, like just about everyone else who knew her, enjoyed Jean enormously but thought the actress "looked about sixteen and her baby-face seemed utterly incongruous against the flaming wig."[4]

When Anita and Irving met with Harlow, she told them a few stories from her own life that assured them the actress had the right attitude to make the audience laugh with her, rather than at her, as she sashays her way up a string of men, each richer and older than the one before.

Thalberg was responsible for producing almost a film a week at MGM. He delegated the actual line production process to one of a handful of supervisors, men who would be called producers today. Only after Thalberg himself had assigned the writer, approved the script, and often decided most of the casting was a director assigned from the stable of those under contract.

The first inkling Irving and Anita had that everyone didn't share their sense of humor about *Red-Headed Woman* was when the assigned director, Jack Conway, reported back after reading the script: "Look folks, if you are trying to be funny, I'm here to report that a girl like that almost broke up my home once and believe me it was no joke." They convinced him it could be entertaining, but Irving assigned Anita to stay on the set to "keep reminding you that the picture's a comedy."[5]

With this, Anita became one of the privileged few writers who saw their films through production (after all, they were being paid to write). Thalberg's faith in Anita was returned with an adoration of him that would never waver. He respected writers, and they knew they had his confidence and his ear. Later in life she looked back and said, "The directors were dunces you know. That they ever made anything good was due to Irving Thalberg. He handed them scripts that were practically foolproof."[6]

For *Red-Headed Woman* Anita massaged what could have been a banal soap opera into a script riddled with double entendres and clever one-liners, and she and Irving were sure they had a hit on their hands. She particularly liked the sequence where Harlow tells her girlfriend Jane, played by Una Merkel, "I'm in love and I'm going to be married," quickly and pertly clarifying that she is going to marry the octogenarian "Coal King" and is in love with his chauffeur, played by a very young Charles Boyer.

Thalberg was a big believer in sneak previews and didn't stint on reshooting if he thought it would improve the picture. The preview for *Red-Headed Woman* revealed that it took the audience way too long to get a handle on Lil's attitude toward life and love, and then came word from the Hays Office: *Red-Headed Woman* would never be approved. Thalberg had been in communication with Will Hays's office, the Motion Picture Producers and Distributors Association (MPPDA), about the story since the previous fall, and MGM had been assured that "we read the synopsis of the *Red-Headed Woman* and with proper treatment it could be produced without offending the code or official censors."[7]

But synopses were just that, and when he saw the film, the Hays Office representative insisted on changes if it was to be released. Thalberg responded that the representative was "100% wrong" but agreed to make it clearer that MGM's intention was to "play the picture as a road burlesque."[8] To accomplish this and to help audiences immediately identify the type of woman "Red" was, Irving told Anita she had to write a scene so blatant it would appease both the audiences and the Hays Office. She went back to her yellow pad and wrote a classic sequence (and a plug for herself in the process).

In close-up Harlow smiles knowingly at her own reflection in a hand mirror and rhetorically asks, "So gentlemen prefer blondes, do they?" The camera then cuts immediately to a scene in a store's dressing room. "Red" holds out her skirt, sashays in front of a window, and inquires sweetly of the saleslady, "Can you see through this?" When the offscreen female voice responds, "I'm afraid so," Jean breaks into a devastating grin and says, "I'll wear it then."

In less than sixty seconds we know who and what "Red" is, and the next preview left the audience howling. The Hays Office representative asserted that "the changes make all the difference in the world" and added, "May I take this opportunity to congratulate you on the very fine job you have done."[9]

The picture was an immediate hit. Charles Boyer had heard he was going to be released and, assuming his brief Hollywood career was going nowhere, was making plans to return to France. But as soon as *Red-Headed Woman* opened, Boyer was inundated with fan letters, and MGM quickly put him under a lucrative, long-term contract.

Enough people saw *Red-Headed Woman* as farce to fill theaters to capacity, but enough others, particularly in the South, saw it as "heavy sex."[10] They began complaining loudly and vociferously both to the Hays Office and to local governments with a renewed demand for official censorship. Women's organizations, with the Catholic Church close behind, made the MPPDA's approval of *Red-Headed Woman* into their case in point that Hays had failed the public. Within a year reasonable forces within the MPPDA were replaced by Joseph Breen and a new production code that would rule Hollywood for the next twenty years.

But the ramifications of the changes to come were yet to be played out, and Anita felt immediately at home at MGM. Living in Los Angeles again for the first time in twelve years, she was happily reunited with her family, and for intrigue in her personal life she turned to her old friend, the raconteur gambler and now part owner of the Brown Derby restaurant, Wilson Mizner. Mizner was one of the handful of men, like Mencken before and Aldous Huxley later, who inspired Anita intellectually—she was pleased to be their partner in crimes of the mind, but a part of her always longed to be their lover as well. Instead, she settled for being treated more as a pet and played the role of witty, adoring gamine.

And then, to complicate matters, Anita's real-life husband returned to her doorstep, announcing after only a few months alone in New York that he was coming to join her. Anita could no longer even pretend Emerson had been a loyal husband; when she was packing to move out of the New York home he had lost through his poor investments, she found the bills for women's clothes and jewelry she had never seen, as well as love letters from several of his girlfriends. Still, she was resigned to supporting him and knew she had to find something constructive to keep him occupied. She went to Irving Thalberg, who pointed out the obvious: there was absolutely no reason for MGM to hire Emerson. In desperation Anita asked Thalberg to just split her salary between the two of them. The workaholic head of production resisted at first, but she was so insistent that he agreed, but only after informing her, "You are even more of a masochist than I am."[11]

The fact that Emerson was dependent on Anita seems to have been an open secret and fodder for public discussion. Sam Goldwyn was credited with the malapropism "John Emerson lives off the sweat of his frau."[12] Anita went so far as to call herself her husband's "pimp," and many of her surviving notebooks play with the concept as potential subject matter; yet in reading them one is left with the feeling that Anita was trying to sort out her own thoughts more than she was searching for fresh material.

When Anita finished *Red-Headed Woman,* she was immediately assigned to work on the dialogue for *Blondie of the Follies.* Frances Marion had drafted a script from her own original story *Three Blondes,* written specifically for Marion Davies, but Frances was under doctor's orders to rest in bed for a month because of exhaustion. Shooting was scheduled to start in six weeks when Anita was handed the script. One of her first calls came from Marion Davies's "protector" and producer, William Randolph Hearst. Anita had worked (and played) with Davies and Hearst a decade before in New York, but those carefree days seemed to be behind them as far as Hearst was concerned. He was now taking Davies seriously as an actress and had very specific (and idiosyncratic) ideas on how she was to be presented on the screen. At their first meeting over the *Blondie of the Follies* script Hearst cautioned Anita to "curb your inclination to humor," and Anita's initial enthusiasm for the project quickly waned.[13]

When Frances Marion returned to work, Anita happily returned the script to her, but group conferences on the ongoing struggle to produce a solid story that Hearst would approve show that Anita continued as part of the creative team. She was kept on *Blondie of the Follies* to spice up the dialogue and to develop a secondary character for Jimmy Durante to play. (Comics like Durante were a weak spot for Thalberg. He loved Durante, the Marx Brothers, and Buster Keaton, and put them all under contract, but he often had trouble finding the right properties for them.)

Durante's role in *Blondie* was a constantly evolving one: at one point he was to play the rich older man that director Eddie Goulding described as "a real chicken hawk—a Joe Kennedy type." That was too much of a stretch, so Durante was then considered for the role of Marion Davies's shiftless brother-in-law. Anita went with the flow and wrote character descriptions as instructed; the paragraph she came up with for Durante as the brother-in-law is a classic that reflects her cynicism about relationships in general and men in particular:

> Pete's life has been ruined by his making the *Believe it or Not* column as the man who can whistle through his nose. . . . He keeps an enormous scrapbook full of clippings, all of which are exactly alike, but from [different] newspapers all over the country. This scrapbook he calls "his publicity" and fondly believes it is going to lead him to fame. Pete has a basic theory of life: men were supposed to be supported by women. When he married his wife she had a good job but marriage ruined her. "That's just the way with women," says Pete, "As soon as they hook a guy, they start deteriorating."[14]

Anita continued to ride the often angst-filled waves of assignments, but she found some solace in feeling at home in her bungalow at MGM. She put her name on the line in support of ending Prohibition and was in attendance at the first large gathering in April of 1933 of what would become the Writers Guild. She saw a variety of friends and went often to premieres and films, as well as symphony performances and long dinners and walks with pals.

One of her best friends was also her writing "partner," Robert Hopkins. "Hoppy" was unique in that he rarely ever put pen to paper. An iconoclastic holdover from the silent era, he was the studio's one and only "gag man" who talked out his ideas in one-liners that were often unrepeatable in mixed company. Yet Anita quickly came to depend on him as a sounding board for talking over story ideas and plot structure.

Anita worked constantly, with varying degrees of passion, but in 1936 she went to work on an original story with Hoppy that she cared deeply about. *San Francisco* was her homage to what she considered her hometown and to Wilson Mizner, who had recently passed away. In Blackie Norton Anita created her ultimate romantic hero: the Barbary Coast devil-may-care tough guy with the heart of gold, meltable only by the right woman. Who better to play him than Clark Gable, Anita thought, but she had to be persuaded that Jeanette MacDonald could play his love interest. Adding Spencer Tracy as the priest who is Blackie's best friend and conscience rounded out the cast, and Anita, pleased with the script, happily headed to the set to begin filming.

Clark Gable was a little disconcerted to find himself paired with Mac-Donald in *San Francisco,* but Anita laughed that the acrimony between the two stars helped their characterizations because through most of the story theirs was a love/hate relationship. However, Anita was in no joking mood over the director, Woody Van Dyke, who had picked up the nickname "One take Woody" because of his quick and often careless approach to directing. Anita stayed on the set to try, as she jotted in her notebook, to "put some sense into his gin soaked brain."[15]

San Francisco was filmed entirely on the lot with intricate movable slanted platforms creating the earthquake. For the scene with dozens of citizens running in terror Van Dyke told several extras just to pick up one of the other actors as if they were carrying an injured victim. Anita, standing nearby, found herself whisked up into camera range by an extra looking for the lightest load.

She fought for retakes and even tried to get Van Dyke replaced by Emerson, but in the end she was pleased with the result. So was MGM when *San Francisco* picked up several Academy Award nominations, including Best Picture and Best Original Story. In the nominations, Emerson was named as one of the film's producers, and Anita, in a burst of he-needs-the-credit-more-than-I-do sympathy, gave Hopkins sole story credit.

Anita was one of MGM's highest paid writers at $2,000 a week. Not only did she occasionally do double duty as the equivalent of a line producer, but she was expected to produce original stories and to doctor other writers' scripts, often without credit and usually without anyone but Thalberg knowing about it.

Irving Thalberg's death at the age of thirty-seven shook all of Hollywood, but the MGM writers who had come to depend on him for protection and respect were particularly devastated. On September 16, 1938, Anita attended Thalberg's funeral and that evening dined with her parents, her brother, and her niece to quietly celebrate her mother's seventy-seventh birthday.

Anita scrawled "unable to work" in her appointment book for a week following Thalberg's death, and when she did pick up her pen again, it was to work on *Saratoga,* an original horse racing story she had started the previous spring. Bernie Hyman had been the story's supervisor, but now he was the sole producer.

When Thalberg was alive, Anita found that she might have to wait all day to see him, but then "in 10 minutes, all the problems were solved." Hyman, on the other hand, seemed incapable of making a decision, let alone sticking to one. He solicited everyone's opinions on scripts, often in front of Anita, and when he "asked an office girl her opinion of the script, I blew up."

After months of rewrites, with occasional input from her "collaborator," Robert Hopkins, Anita finished the script, and *Saratoga* went before the cameras the next spring. The film would star two of her favorites, Jean Harlow and Clark Gable. Anita was exhausted, but she still wasn't finished. She was called to the set because Bernie kept changing his mind about what he wanted, and even the affable Hoppy gave him a dressing down over how his indecision was making a mess of the film.

Anita wasn't thrilled with the director, Jack Conway, either, but after three weeks of shooting, filming came to a halt with the news of Jean Harlow's sudden death from kidney failure on June 7, 1937. After the funeral Hyman asked Anita to evaluate *Saratoga*'s possible future, and she told him she thought it could be salvaged. She was at work smoothing over the scenes yet to be filmed when Hyman announced his latest idea: Harlow would star in the first half of the picture and then the actress Rita Johnson would play the same role for the second half. Anita's and Hoppy's response: "We all but fainted."

Once again Anita tried to put some sense into Hyman, and once again he saw the light. Jean Harlow is the only female star of *Saratoga,* even though another actress is seen in silhouette in several scenes including the rather abrupt ending.

Anita was worn out from the fighting and the tension. She was used to pouring her heart and soul into writing, but the gap between her own sensibilities and Hollywood's priorities was growing. She had no respect for Hyman or his judgment, and when *Saratoga* was a box office smash, she noted that it was a happy ending only for Louis B. Mayer. She found herself so depressed she wrote in her appointment book, "I wish I was with Jean at Forest Lawn."

Instead of quitting outright, as she desperately wanted to do, she took two weeks off and boarded a train for New York. She basked in the joys of the city that always refreshed her, seeing plays and dining with her friends Marge and Eddy Duchin and then heading up to Nyack with Ruth Gordon to visit Helen Hayes and Charlie MacArthur.

Emerson had stayed behind and busied himself getting her out of MGM and into a new contract with producer Sam Goldwyn. So tired and fed up she didn't care, Anita returned to duly report to Goldwyn, who assigned her to write a cowboy romance for Gary Cooper. Cooper was fine, but she found Goldwyn "impossible to work for." He called to tell her he "loved every word" and then the next day announced, "[I]t stinks." Her frustration grew as her script was handed back and forth (often behind her back) to other writers including Dorothy Parker and Leo McCarey. In turn Anita was told to rewrite Parker's script of a *Ziegfeld Follies* clone called *Goldwyn Follies.* Anita chafed under the lack of continuity but channeled her anger into her diary by calling Goldwyn "the most vile slimy loathsome mouse I ever dirtied myself by contracting [*sic*]."

Now Anita found herself wondering why she had left MGM in the first place. She seriously considered just picking up and moving to New York, but she stayed put because of her growing concern over Emerson's behavior. He was becoming increasingly erratic—riddled with angst one moment, giddy over nothing the next. Even her chauffeur and house-keeper were concerned. One morning Emerson actually started to choke her, threatening to kill "my little Bug" because he was so worried about her. George, their driver, came to her rescue, and her brother, Clifford, talked Emerson into voluntarily checking himself into Las Encinas San-itarium that evening.

After a sleepless night Anita went to the bank to discover her Gold-wyn contract in Emerson's safe deposit box. She had never thought to actually read it, and now she found she was being paid only half her usual salary and that Emerson had taken the signing bonus of over $100,000 and bought annuities payable only to himself.

Numbed by the double cross, Anita headed straight for Las Encinas. She looked at Emerson with new eyes and knew he was "completely in-sane." He was an extreme manic-depressive, and now, full of remorse, he cried in fear that he would be sent to San Quentin for what he had done to her. If there was any question in Anita's mind about what to do next, it was answered by the doctor, who told her flatly, "You must never live under the same roof with Mr. Emerson again."

Emerson would live most of the rest of his nineteen years at the ele-gant sanitarium, and Anita consoled herself that the annuities he had stolen from her would pay for his care.

With her savings gone again and facing her fiftieth birthday, Anita went to see her old nemesis Bernie Hyman and told him everything that had happened, personally and professionally. A few days later Mayer's number-two man, Eddie Mannix, called to ask her to come back to MGM for a guaranteed two years. Anita in turn asked her agent Phil Berg to get her out of the deal with Goldwyn. Instead, Sam raised her salary to $2,250 a week. Anita ended what she would declare "the worst year ever" over a Christmas dinner of Chinese food with a few friends, still under contract to Goldwyn and still writing the Cooper script.

Sam Goldwyn finally released Anita in February of 1938 (and got his revenge by leaving her name off *The Cowboy and the Lady,* the Gary Cooper story she had slaved over for a year). After a trip to San Francisco and a long weekend with Marion Davies and W. R. Hearst at San Simeon, Anita was happy to report back to MGM.

It was great to be back with Hoppy, but soon she was also back in conferences with Bernie Hyman, who still changed his mind with the wind. She worked alternately on major treatments for original stories called *Alaska* and *The Great Canadian,* depending on Hyman's whim. Anita longed for direction and assurance; instead, she found fear and indecision.

Her mother passed away after a brief illness in early October 1938, but within weeks a new life came into Anita's world. Her dear friend Marge Duchin had died the year before, days after giving birth to a son, Peter. The child's lungs were so frail that he had been under twenty-four-hour care since birth, and the assumption was that he would not survive. Friends urged Eddy Duchin to return to his whirlwind schedule of band appearances; assuming work was the best medicine to assuage his already deep grief. Marge's best friend from school, Marie Harriman, volunteered, along with her husband Averell, to care for Peter at their Long Island estate, but it was soon decided that young Peter would have a better chance of flourishing if he lived in a warm, dry climate. Anita and Marie were also friends, and they had grown even closer with the loss of Marge. Anita was happy to do what she could, so she headed to Palm Springs to find a suitable house for the child and his nurse. Averell Harriman was already involved in government and would eventually become America's ambassador to the USSR and governor of New York, but he was also head of Union Pacific Railroad, which had been founded by his father. Peter, now a little more than a year old, and his highly trained pediatric nurse, Rita Chisholm, were placed in a specially constructed private car that would take them on their train ride across the country. Anita was there at the station with an ambulance to meet them, and after Peter had spent several weeks in the hospital, she helped move them to their new desert home.

Maternal is hardly the first word that would come to mind to describe Anita, but she had loved Marge deeply and was devastated by her loss, for Eddy and Peter as well as for herself. Anita charted Peter's medical progress diligently and was thrilled when he was well enough to join her at her beach house for visits. With the help of Peter's nurse, "Chissie," and Anita, whom he called "Neetsie," the child's health improved steadily.

Sundays, Anita's one official day off from the studio, were now dedicated to an early morning trip to Palm Springs to check on Peter and then a late afternoon return via Pasadena to spend time with Emerson, who one week would be full of cheer, the next quiet and low. She also dined regularly with her father, whose drinking was causing her concern. She also spent time alone with her niece Mary Anita, who often stayed at the beach house on weekends.

Anita saw films several nights a week and dined occasionally with friends like Ernst Lubitsch, Salka Viertel, Mercedes de Acosta, Cole and Linda Porter, Aldous and Marie Huxley, and Paulette Goddard and Charlie Chaplin. Most weeknights, however, she stayed home alone, feeling low and churning out the pages.

Anita played with a film treatment called *Flame over New York,* about the *Hindenberg* disaster, and another called *Coney Island.* She wanted to put Clark Gable and Mae West together on the screen, and when she met with West, Anita discovered her to be "delightful, intelligent and nice," but nothing came of the idea.

In early 1939 Anita was at work on *Alaska* when she got the call that her friend George Cukor had been abruptly fired as director of *Gone with the Wind.* They spent that afternoon together at his house discussing their growing misery and bemoaning the current MGM regime. Yet within a month they were both in producer Hunt Stromberg's office discussing a project that excited all of them.

Both Scott Fitzgerald and Jane Murfin had adapted scripts from Clare Boothe's play *The Women* when Stromberg handed it to Anita. Shooting was scheduled to begin in a month, with Cukor directing and half a dozen of MGM's biggest actresses (several of whom had tested for the role of Scarlett O'Hara) leading the ensemble cast.

Hunt Stromberg was an MGM veteran who had trained for years under Thalberg, and Anita grew so close to him so quickly that she started referring to him as "Stromsie." Hoppy thought she was "carrying a torch" for Stromberg and she didn't deny it, but whatever the case, Anita was back in her element working with two men she respected. And she was the perfect choice to tweak the almost one hundred lines or phrases from the play that the Hays Office had deemed unacceptable. Deleting the disallowed word *virgin* and replacing it with "a frozen asset" and loading up on double entendres, Anita's script glided right past the censors.

She heightened the bitchy wit while diluting the mean-spiritedness, and along the way Anita massaged a restructuring that resulted in the creation of a classic. Reading the play and the script side by side is a revelation, a veritable textbook example of the subtlety of arc, character development, and dialogue.

Cukor insisted that Anita be at his side on the set throughout the shooting, as well as during the previews. She even worked with the publicity department, writing and editing the trailers. This was just like the old Thalberg days when she saw a project through from beginning to end, but *The Women* turned out to be an aberration.

She was next assigned to spice up the script for *Another Thin Man,* the third in the successful William Powell/Myrna Loy series, and then to write a new story for Joan Crawford, *Susan and God.*

Anita had agonized over the war news from Europe for the past two years and was almost relieved when Pearl Harbor forced America to enter the war. She jumped into supporting the war effort, but on the home front Anita was coming to the unavoidable conclusion that screenwriting had changed for good. Her friend Frances Marion, also still at MGM, said it had become like "writing in the sand with the wind blowing." Anita looked back and decided, "As long as Thalberg was alive, I adored the movies"; working with Irving had been "like a love affair," with "just as many thrills and none of the drawbacks."[16] If Irving had assigned you something, it was going to be made, and once he approved a script, it was close to chiseled in stone. Now nothing was sacred.

Writing wasn't the only thing that had changed at MGM. Thalberg had produced forty-five films a year, with half a dozen supervisors; in 1943 it took forty producers to make the same number of films. Louis B. Mayer was running the studio by committee, the bureaucracy was mushrooming, and the constant failure of studio executives to stand by decisions was frustrating almost everyone.

Travel of any sort was always a release for Anita, and she enjoyed spending a month in early 1942 in Washington, D.C., and Des Moines, Iowa, researching the Women's Army Auxiliary Corps (WAAC) for her film treatment *Women in Uniform*. But back at the studio Anita concluded that in having worked with both Griffith and Thalberg, "I had two pieces of great luck and I knew I couldn't have any more," and set her mind on finding a way out.[17]

Over the next year and a half she turned out four scripts for MGM: *They Met in Bombay,* starring Clark Gable and Rosalind Russell; *When Ladies Meet,* for Joan Crawford and Robert Taylor; *Blossoms in the Dust,* starring Greer Garson and Walter Pidgeon; and *I Married an Angel,* starring Jeanette MacDonald and Nelson Eddy.

Several years before, Anita had worked on restructuring *Gentlemen Prefer Blondes* for a Broadway revival, but it had not gone beyond the preview stages. Now her thoughts turned to New York again as a way out of Hollywood. When, in early 1943, her old friend Lionel Barrymore suggested an idea for a play about the last empress of China, which would star his sister Ethel, Anita picked up her pen in earnest. She completed the dry comedy—about the culture clashes between the empress and the American dentist she imports to design her false teeth—in six months, and Lionel was "thrilled with it";[18] but then Hollywood, which hadn't been interested in Ethel Barrymore for over a decade, called her with the script for *None but the Lonely Heart,* and Ethel grabbed it. (Barrymore went on to win the Best Supporting Actress Oscar for her performance.)

Miserable as she was at times, Anita thought she had put up a good front as she juggled producers, so she was shocked to be told in the middle of what was a typical production meeting in August of 1943 that MGM was not renewing her contract. When the studio publicly made it sound like it was her idea, she was even more saddened and depressed over how it was handled. And she was more determined than ever to get to New York.

While she was at MGM, Anita was either working on a particular assignment or creating story ideas and proposed treatments. Studio chief Louis B. Mayer was credited as saying, "MGM has more stars than the heavens," and treatments were often written with specific stars in mind.

Winkie Boy is an example of the short-story treatment form, this one designed to showcase up-and-coming female contract players. Anita's frustration with Hollywood underlies this satiric cautionary tale. Anita herself had a passion for small dogs, Pomeranians in particular. When she writes of Maxine's altering her life around the dog's wants and whims, Anita is describing herself. She was known to hire sitters to be with her dogs when she was out and to work with a flashlight under her sheets because her dog, who slept with her, of course, barked when she turned on the bedside lamp.

Anita's treatment for Buster Keaton and Jimmy Durante is such a potential visual delight that it is particularly disappointing that the story never went beyond the written page. One can only imagine what those two could have created with Anita's story, which in some ways was a throwback to the physical comedies she had written in the teens for Douglas Fairbanks. Durante and Keaton had been featured together earlier in 1932 in *The Passionate Plumber* and were in the middle of filming the Prohibition comedy *What, No Beer?* when Anita wrote out her ideas. Un-

fortunately, alcohol was taking its toll on Keaton's real life at that moment, and Louis B. Mayer released Keaton from his MGM contract
shortly after *What, No Beer?* finished shooting in late 1932.

Anita wrote *Evelina* for Jeanette MacDonald, who was a particular
favorite of Louis B. Mayer's. He was always on the lookout for vehicles
to spotlight what he considered MacDonald's multiple talents, and
Anita's note that her treatment was written to "show every facet of our
star's capabilities" may well have been written specifically to him. Anita
respected Jeanette's talents, but the actress took herself a little too seriously to be a good friend of Anita's. Anita's not-so-hidden agenda in writing the treatment of *Evelina* was to create a situation in which she could
work with her friend Cole Porter, whom she had in mind to do the music. Yet what is also obvious, in hindsight, is that Mayer's tendency to put
women he adored on a pedestal of purity, at least publicly, would have
never allowed him to cast MacDonald as a woman who had lived with
a man to whom she wasn't married.

Women in Uniform was one of the last full treatments Anita wrote before leaving MGM, and it is a reminder of how long she had been writing movies; she had written *Oh, You Women!* about soldiers returning
home from the First World War in 1919.

Women in Uniform is a story very much of its time—women are
"girls," the style of the uniform is of utmost importance, and patriotism
is at an all-time high. The purpose of the story is clearly to increase enlistment in the WAACs and to increase respect for women in the armed
services.

Women in Uniform is an example of Anita's work in which the male
characters are relatively guileless and less sophisticated than their female
counterparts, who tend toward scheming and underhanded motives and
behavior. Without delving into the psychology of Anita's own self-worth
or her opinion of her sex, there is no debating one similarity between
Anita and her protagonist: Anita cared deeply about the war, and, at least
by the end of the story, so does her heroine.

The copy of *Women in Uniform* in Anita's files is laced with handwritten corrections and additions that are then typed into the next variation. What is reprinted here is the most complete and corrected version, and the first-draft nature of the treatment is reflected by her notes on the need to flesh out certain themes and a few spelling errors. Still, the story is infused with costume descriptions, camera moves, and detailed set decorating ideas for rooms, buildings, and landscapes. Given that the entire work was done between the sixth and twelfth of August 1942, it is a remarkably developed story.

Cari Beauchamp

Winkie Boy

Three girls were lolling over the lunch counter at Schwab's Drug Store romancing, as girls do, about security.

"Isn't it funny," said Ruth, "that even if you dreamed of landing Gable, you'd want to feel it was on a thousand acre ranch near Tucson?"

"That's true!" spoke up Inez. "But when a guy dreams of romance, he doesn't require any more territory than a couch."

As Ruth and Inez reacted philosophically, the third girl, Maxine, spoke up.

"Men know that money isn't everything," she said.

The two other girls treated Maxie to a look which was more of resignation than disgust.

"I suppose the casting director on your last job told you that!" commented Ruthie.

"I can't even *remember* my last job," said Maxie grinning, and her air of amused resignation brought up what seemed to be an issue between the three.

"You can kid all you want," spoke up Ruthie, "but you can't go on forever getting your vitamins out of a bag of peanuts."

"What I'd like to know," Inez asked of Maxie, "is what good it's doing you to spend all your dough on dramatic lessons when you never contact the guys that hand out jobs?"

Maxie looked bored and said nothing. But Ruth, taking a swig of Coke, suddenly reacted as if it had contained an idea.

"What Maxie needs," she spoke up, "is a dog! Before I got my 'in' at Warner Brothers," she went on to explain, "I used to come in here with the landlady's Spaniel. And that dog picked up assistant directors like a dream."

"I'd never train a dog to live on peanuts!" commented Maxie with another grin.

"If it's any kind of dog," remarked Ruth, "it can go out and hustle for itself."

"Why don't *you* two get a couple of dogs?" asked Maxie. "I don't see you landing any term contracts anywhere."

"We don't need dogs," answered Ruthie. "We get around."

"If we can't clip off careers for ourselves," spoke up Inez, "we deserve to marry chiropractors."

This declaration brought on a pause, and looking off toward the magazine rack near the entrance, Maxie spotted one of Ruth's admirers.

"There's one of those assistant directors you specialize in," she remarked to her friend.

As Ruthie hailed the humble yet necessary young man, her face lit up like Garson looking at Pidgeon, and she greeted him with commensurate sincerity. Bob (that being his name) sauntered over to join them.

"What are you doing tonight, girls?" he asked genially.

"Celebrating my birthday," answered Ruth, doing a little rapid calculation.

Inez and Maxie exchanged grins. As a spot for extemporaneous shopping, Schwab's Drug Store stands supreme in all of Hollywood and contains everything from baked sea bass to Guerlain's Jasmin.

"Birthday!" exclaimed Bob. "Why didn't you let me know? Shove those Cokes away, girls," he continued, climbing onto a stool, "I'm buying champagne."

"Wait a moment," spoke up Ruthie before he could give the order to the drug clerk. "This is no time in the world's history to be buying wine. I'd rather have a dog." With which she shot a significant glance at Maxie.

"What kind of a dog?" asked Bob.

"A peanut hound," spoke up Maxie, grinning.

"Shut up," said Ruthie, fearful her beneficiary-to-be might throw a spike into the project. "A dog is what I want," she reiterated, "and let's go get it."

So the four of them repaired to Bob's roadster and thence to a pet shop on Hollywood Boulevard.

As Maxie's proverbial bad luck would have it, a woman had just come in from her kennels in the San Fernando Valley with a Pomeranian, and it was this small, orange colored puff of concentric fuzz that instantly caught Maxie's eye. Seeing that the dog was being bought for her, Ruthie joined Maxine in a contemplation of its points.

"What's its name?" she asked the kennel woman.

"Winkie Boy," was the reply, spoken fondly.

Ruthie treated the woman to a searching glance. It didn't seem possible that anyone so redolent of concentrated dog smells could deal in nomenclature that was so coy.

"Winkie Boy!" repeated Maxine lovingly. She bent down to pet him, at which Winkie Boy growled, feinted and then bit her on the ankle (which was as high as he could reach).

Masochistic, as always, Maxie began making excuses for him.

"He couldn't hurt anybody!" she exclaimed and to prove it, picked him up and held him boldly to her face. Knowing that his twelve inches of indignation were futile, Winkie Boy did not struggle, but flattened his ears tight against his head, turned his miserable eyes as far from Maxie as they could reach, and let out a long, protracted mumble.

"He'll never love anybody but his owner," remarked the dog woman with pride. "Pomeranians are a one-man breed."

"That's just what we don't want," spoke up Ruthie in alarm.

"We want a dog that goes for men," put in Inez. "Something on the order of a retriever."

But Bob threw his weight in for Winkie.

"You'd be crazy getting a retriever," he said. "Where would you keep him in that two by four hall bedroom?"

"A Pomeranian is a wonderful watch dog," his mistress now boasted. "He won't let anybody come near you!"

Ruthie regarded Winkie's four and a half pounds of snarling animosity with distaste.

"Take him away," she cried in mock alarm. "He stinks!"

"It isn't him you smell," protested his owner with super-salesmanship. "It's me."

This being indubitably the case, and seeing that Maxie wouldn't even look at another animal, Ruth had to cease her protests.

As the kennel woman turned Winkie Boy over, she gave instructions on how to treat him.

"The main thing to remember about Pomeranians," she said, "is that they don't know they're dogs. They get awfully hurt when you don't behave as if they're human."

Posing as his new owner, Ruthie promised to remember, Winkie Boy was paid for, removed, flat eared with anguish, from his ex-mistress and time marched on.

The two girls hadn't seen Maxie for about a week, when after five days of rallying around Errol Flynn as the King of France, they relinquished their pointed hats and dresses covered with fleur-de-lis, and left the studio to look her up.

They could hear Winkie Boy barking long before they turned into the driveway to the garage over which Dennie rented a room. Winkie Boy would hardly let them into it. He had developed a technique that was extremely effective of striking straight at the toes where they emerged from the open type shoes worn by the women of this unhappy decade.

Maxie, who had been studying a Portuguese lesson from her phonograph, announced that her conquest of Winkie Boy had been achieved. She picked him up and holding him to her face, stated he knew that he belonged to her and had grown to love her.

An expression of dream-like sublimity came into Winkie Boy's eyes and he started to lick her cheek.

"Look at that," remarked Ruthie in awe. "She's gazing at him like the Sistine Madonna."

"He sure goes for Max Factor's Suntan Number Two!"

"Picked up any pay checks since we saw you last?" Ruthie now demanded with a note of accusation.

Maxie admitted that she hadn't.

"I had to stay home with Winkie Boy," she explained, "so he'd get to know me. Anyway," she added, "I had a lot of lessons to do."

Inez and Ruthie exchanged glances. Everything about Maxie's activities irked her friends. She had too many of the earmarks of the perpetual student to be viewed without alarm. Hollywood is full of girls who spend their time and money taking various assorted lessons, and are at it long after their faces have passed all hope of photogenia.

"Do you take the dog with you when you *do* go out?" asked Inez.

"Of course I do," answered Maxie. "Winks would howl the house down if he was left alone."

"Any promising looking types ever come up and pet him?" demanded Ruth, hoping that perhaps Winkie Boy was doing her friend some good in spite of herself.

"Whenever they do," answered Maxine, "he bites them. Don't you, Winkie Boy?" she asked fondly.

Another grim exchange of looks traversed the space between Ruthie and Inez.

"It was the fatalist error I ever perpetrated," commented Ruth, "when I got that dog for you."

Seeming to take a perverse joy in their attitude, Maxie grinned.

"I've got a chance to audition for Global Films next week," she now announced, "and I'm scared to death."

The delayed good news cheered her friends exceedingly.

"Why should you be frightened?" Inez spoke up with confidence. "With that voice of yours, and that red hair, and those green eyes, you can't fail!"

"I'm not thinking of that," Maxine answered. "I'm worried about what to do with Winkie. It's going to take all afternoon and I can't leave him alone."

"Look here," said Ruth irately, "you're not going to let your life be ruined by that blasted dog."

But her gaze resting on Winkie Boy, Maxine didn't even hear.

"Look at him now!" she exclaimed in tones of fond delight.

They looked. Winkie Boy was tearing the corner out of Inez' pocketbook in frenzied ecstasy over its underlying glue. Inez leapt to rescue her pocketbook but had to win a ferocious attack on her big toe before it was once again safe in her possession.

Delighted at his prowess Maxie reached for her child and cuddled him, while Winkie Boy, laughing all over his face, playfully executed a series of darts at her nose pretending to bite it.

"From where I sit," Inez spoke up suspiciously, "Max is going to cancel her audition at Global to play nurse maid to that flea ball."

"Oh, no she isn't!" stated Ruth firmly. "Because I'm going to take care of him while she auditions."

"If he could get used to you beforehand," agreed Maxie, "it *might* work out."

Ruthie looked at Winkie Boy as, panting with pleasure, he was gazing ecstatically into her friend's face. He *was* a pretty thing. He looked just like a little red fox, and he *did* have personality, no doubt of that. She went over to him.

"Hello pal," she said, "will you let Auntie Ruth come and spend the day with you?"

With the dart of an adder, Winkie Boy struck out and bit her nose. Ruthie slapped him.

"You get out of here," Maxine cried out, irately.

"Well, how do you like that?" gasped Ruth. "I gave you the darned dog, didn't I?"

"You hit him!" declared Maxie.

"He bit me."

"He's no fool. He knows you hate him," said Maxine. "Now you get out!"

This was indeed a situation. The three girls had been inseparable chums from their first days in Hollywood as inmates of the Studio Club.

Ruthie turned to Inez.

"Come on," she said, "let's blow this place before we get hydrophobia."

But as they were starting out the door, Ruth's heart softened and she turned back.

"That offer to take care of him while you test still goes," she said.

"I wouldn't trust you now," Maxine spoke up, unforgivingly. "I'm going to take him with me."

Exasperation overtook her friends.

"They don't allow anyone to bring dogs on that lot," spoke up Inez.

"I'll hide him under my coat," declared Maxine. "They won't even see him."

The two girls exchanged another eloquent glance and then gave up. Ruthie slammed the door as she and Inez left.

.   .   .

When Maxine smuggled Winkie Boy through the outer sanctum at Global, she did it almost as a matter of defiance, and there was a chip on her shoulder as she placed Winkie on the floor in Mr. Slavik's private sanctum.

Mr. Slavik, who had risen to producerdom the easy way, by means of that little word, "Yes," which is so dear to Hollywood, was not yet easy enough on his throne to admit of so human a touch as a love for dogs, even if he didn't love them, so after one quick glance at Winkie Boy, he disregarded him.

While he talked to Maxine disjointedly, their conversation interrupted by endless telephone calls, Winkie Boy proceeded to investigate the office. With an expert air, he carefully measured the length, width and depth of all the furniture, paced off the distances between various pieces of it and finally disappeared in the space under Mr. Slavik's desk which was relegated to Mr. Slavik's imperial legs. He had been there a few moments when, to Maxie's perturbation, a trickle of wetness began to ooze from under the desk. Remembering the dire prophecies of Ruth and Inez, Maxie bit her lip and tried to keep the contretemps from shaking her.

Mr. Slavik finally went for his royal accompanist and ordered him to take Maxine to a music room where he would join them as soon as he was able. Maxine achieved a reunion with Winkie Boy without disclosure of his under-desk activities, and followed the accompanist.

In the music room, she ran through a couple of songs and the accompanist picked out a Debussy.

"The good composers impress his nibs," he told Maxine, "then he shoves you into a musical and you come out singing, 'No Love, No Nothin'.' But that's life!" he sighed.

Maxine admitted that it was, at which Winkie Boy, as if in agreement, raised his chin and started in to howl.

"What are you going to do with the pooch?" asked the accompanist. "Does music make him nervous?"

"It does a little," admitted Maxine, "but if I put him somewhere else he'll only howl all the louder."

"We could put him next door," suggested the accompanist, "and it wouldn't matter. This room is sound proof."

He helpfully went to pick up Winkie Boy, at which Winkie Boy crouched, growled and bit him. Apologizing, Maxine went to pick him up, but Winkie Boy was no fool. He knew ejection was in the offing. So, in order to remain by her side, even though it hurt him more than it hurt his beloved mistress, Winkie Boy bit her. Speaking soothing words of comfort, Maxine finally gathered Winkie Boy into her arms and transported him to the next room where he was shut up for the duration of the audition.

Maxine proved to be a qualified success. Mr. Slavik was pleased with her hair, teeth, eyes and ankles, and approved her personality, but her voice, he said, had no chiaroscuro. So his proposition was to use the former items, and dub in a voice that had. Maxine was indignant.

"Mr. Slavik," she said, "chiaroscuro pertains to painting and not to music. You're all mixed up and I don't think you know a voice when you hear one."

Mr. Slavik looked frantic. Dictatorship he could handle superbly, but not an argument. He hardly knew what to say.

"If that's the way you feel about it," he finally remarked stiffly, "it's okay with Global."

As he opened the sound proof door to start away, there rose from the next office the banshee cry of Winkie Boy.

Mr. Slavik stopped alertly.

"What's that?" he asked.

Knowing she was through with Global come what may, Maxie bridled.

"It's my dog," she said as she went to retrieve Winkie Boy, "and that gives you a rough idea what he thinks about Global."

Mr. Slavik started away, but as Maxine emerged from the adjoining office with Winkie Boy pressed close to her breast, he turned back.

"Wait a minute," he said.

Maxine stopped, half expecting to be presented with an ultimatum regarding Mr. Slavik's office carpet. But it was something of greater moment.

"We've been looking for a sound track for that off-scene crazy woman in 'Jane Eyre' for the last three weeks," said Mr. Slavik. "If you want your dog to make a test for it, have him here at eleven o'clock in the morning."

Maxine was about to refuse with indignation when she suddenly thought what effect it would produce on Ruth and Inez should Winkie Boy end up with a contract at Global.

"The job pays twenty-five dollars a day," tempted Mr. Slavik.

"All right," said Maxine, "we'll be here."

Feeling vastly more secure now that he had achieved a better exit, Mr. Slavik went on his way.

On the day Winkie Boy cashed his pay check for the off-scene howl of Mrs. Rochester, Maxie called her chums up in a spirit of triumph which was tempered with forgiveness and the three girls met in Schwab's Drug Store for a big thick steak on Winkie Boy. Two days later Winkie Boy won mention in the column of Louella Parsons, along with a lot of humans. He took it in his stride however, considering himself no different from the others.

Suggestion for Keaton Story

Buster is an enormously rich young man, whose money came from very lowly sources. He is terribly in love with the daughter of a very poor but aristocratic family—Mary Lord. Mary does not love Buster, but her family is so insistent that she marry him that she finally agrees.

Buster has no illusions as to why she has married him, but he is so in love with her that he takes a chance on winning her love in time by kindness.

Buster and Mary start on an automobile honeymoon, accompanied by Buster's valet, Jimmy Durante. While motoring along a beautiful mountain road Buster stops at a little railroad station and picks up a newspaper, the first they have seen for several days. He tosses it into the car and drives on; but presently, as he is driving, something on the front page catches his eye. He looks further and sees an article to the effect that he has lost every dime of his colossal fortune.

Everything goes blank before him, and the next thing Buster knows he finds himself, his bride, and Jimmy, in the bottom of a ravine with their automobile on top of them.

They are picked up in pieces, taken to the hospital and stuck together again. Buster's only concern is for his bride, whose eyes have been affected by the smash.

He interviews the eye specialist, who tells him that he believes Mary's sight can be saved, but she will have to have her eyes bandaged for several months. He also tells Buster that he must be very careful that she suffers no shocks of any kind.

Buster is at his wit's end. To tell Mary about the loss of his fortune may be a shock that will kill her.

Presently Jimmy, the valet, gets an idea. So long as Mary is not able to see, why not take her to Buster's enormous family estate (which has not yet been foreclosed on), and pretend that everything is as it should be, so that Mary knows nothing about her husband's loss of fortune.

Mary is escorted to Buster's home, where Buster and Jimmy establish her comfortably, and then set out to be an entire staff of servants to keep the place in running order. Buster has to pretend to be Mary's maid, the cook, the butler, the chauffeurs, the grooms, and even the animals on the estate—all of which have been sold.

In order to get money for expenses, Buster and Jimmy have to sell off the furniture—so that they have to move the few articles left from one room to another in order to keep Mary from realizing that she is living in a practically unfurnished house. Things get so tough that Buster finally sells his bed, saying philosophically, "It's okay. Mary will never know it's gone."

Mary longs for company, so he and Jimmy give big parties at which they, being the only two people present, impersonate dozens of guests, entertainers, etc. It is easy for Jimmy to provide ha cha in the way of musical numbers, but when Mary asks for Giovanni Martinelli to be sent for to sing her a little Grand opera, Jimmy has to strain himself no end to produce the required effect.

They give large dinners at which a table is set for twenty people— Buster and Jimmy cook and serve the dinner and scramble about from one chair to the other at the table, impersonating guests.

The time is rapidly approaching when the doctor is to remove the bandage from Mary's eyes. Buster realizes that once she is cured his bluff will be called, so he prepares to walk out and leave her in peace. Since she has married him only for his money and his money no longer exists, he has no right to be her husband.

However, the day before the doctor is to remove the bandages, Mary gets so anxious about whether or not she is going to be able to see, that she sneaks the bandages off herself. She finds out that she is cured. However, she says nothing to Buster about it, and the result is that she goes through the whole day of seeing poor Buster's frantic efforts to keep up the luxuries with which she has been surrounded, and learns what has been going on. She also sees that Buster is preparing to leave her the next day.

When the doctor arrives the next day, officially removes the bandages and pronounces Mary cured, Buster makes a high dive off the front veranda into a waiting car—an old, broken down Ford, which is all he possesses in the world, and starts away, accompanied by Jimmy.

Mary grabs the doctor by the hand, pulls him out of the house and into his car, and gives chase.

Mary catches up with Buster, tells him that she doesn't care how little money he has—she loves him.

Evelina

A Brief Synopsis of a Musical Comedy
Which Could Be Developed and Tailored
by Anita Loos for Jeanette MacDonald

The first scene opens on a bedroom . . . a very luxurious bedroom . . . but obviously a man's bedroom, the owner of which lies in bed, asleep and snoring. It is quite evident that he has come home very tight for he is sleeping in his dress shirt, and the remainder of his evening clothes have been thrown about on chairs and tables, one of which has been overturned.

(The man is Freddy Hislop, aged thirty-two. He is rich, of a prominent family, very charming, but a little bit on the stuffy side.)

Into this scene of luxurious disarray bustles Evelina, followed by Freddy's valet and her own maid. Although it is only nine o'clock in the morning, Evelina is fully dressed in a charming but completely unseductive street gown which needs only a hat and wrap for her to step out onto the Avenue. Evelina is against negligees. Evelina is energetic. To set her household going in top form, Evelina rises at seven o'clock every morning and dresses herself for the day.

(It is one of Evelina's amusing characteristics that, although she has an excellent personal maid, she spends most of her time not only waiting upon herself but even waiting upon her maid. For Evelina was not born to luxury and is much too energetic ever to have achieved relaxation.)

Evelina is deeply distressed that Freddy has to get up at this (for him) early hour, but his office has called several times to say that he is due for a conference with an important Big Shot and there is nothing else to do.

Now comes the ceremony of waking Freddy up and doing it as painlessly as possible. To the great disgust of Freddy's valet and her maid, Evelina insists on waking Freddy by means of the music from a portable radio which she gently carries closer and closer to Freddy's ear, singing as she does so, until slowly and painfully Freddy wakes, complaining a little petulantly about the particular musical number with which Evelina has brought about his consciousness.

Now follows a scene of the most charming domesticity . . . domesticity which Freddy, in his male selfishness, smugness, and complacency is utterly incapable of appreciating. Evelina steadies him to the bathroom where he proceeds to take his shower (off stage).

While Freddy is showering, Evelina proceeds to direct the tidying of the bedroom. With the assistance of Freddy's valet and her maid the disarrangement is rapidly done away with. Fresh flowers are brought in and the draperies are parted to let in the brilliant April sunlight.

Now Evelina selects Freddy's clothes for the day . . . pays particular attention to his tie. He is a little bit yellow from dissipation, so his tie must be blue, a color designated to make him appear at his best.

It is quite obvious that Freddy is going to be late to the office, so Evelina gets on the phone and squares him with the important Big Shot who is already waiting for him.

Freddy comes out from his shower grumbling, "Why is Evelina so chipper at this hour of the morning? Why is she so completely dressed?"

Evelina explains that she has a luncheon engagement at the colony.

"But why get ready for it so early?" persists Freddy.

Evelina explains that she has errands to do. Evelina does all the marketing herself. Freddy must have the best of everything. Evelina believes in his getting his vitamins through food and not through pellets.

Freddy's perfectly appointed breakfast tray appears, graced with a potent pick-me-up, and while Freddy is regaining a state of normalcy, the telephone rings. Evelina answers the phone. On the other end of the wire is a young woman who, from Evelina's reactions, we realize to be a rather rowdy Park Avenue debutante named Sissy Knowlton.

With a sinking heart Evelina calls Freddy to the phone where Freddy proceeds to date Sissy up for dinner, the theater, and some nightclubbing. Freddy now hangs up the receiver and turns to the crestfallen and dazed Evelina.

"We've got to have a serious talk, Evelina," says Freddy. "I'm nearly thirty-three, you know," he adds. "It's time that I got married."

And now, in a scene which is both tender and cruel, Freddy lets Evelina know that he is leaving her. They have been together for five years . . . five years which have been full of happiness and tender memories . . . but Freddy is fed up.

And as the scene progresses, the audience indirectly and subtly learns that what Freddy is fed up with is *domesticity*. The life he leads with Evelina is much better ordered and more domestic than the lives which most men live with their legally married spouses. But Freddy is bored with order, attention, and a devotion which can only be called "wifely." Freddy of course doesn't know it. And poor, conscientious, earnest, and loving little Evelina knows it even less. And so, wishing to break the tie which binds him to Evelina, Freddy has simply picked on the old stock excuse . . . the excuse used by all men who want to break with their mistresses . . . the excuse of a desire for marriage. He doesn't see in the least that Evelina is as much a wife to him as any legal wife could ever be.

(Throughout this scene the audience must see very clearly that Evelina's heart is breaking. But Evelina has courage. Evelina's chin is up and she takes the blow without flinching.)

In his bigotry, Freddy now proceeds to be very generous. He wants to set Evelina up for life and to see that Evelina gets everything her little heart desires but as he is speaking to her, we can clearly see that Evelina's little heart desires only [one] thing in the whole wide world . . . and that is Freddy.

Freddy proceeds to be terribly, terribly sorry that things have ended as they have. But after all there is nothing in the world like marriage.

"As a matter of fact," Freddy states fatuously, "you *might* make a very good little wife for some man. I think that is what you ought to try for too, Evelina."

Conquering her tears, Evelina replies that she has been so long out of the world since she has been with Freddy that she has no social connections, no activities, no friends. She doesn't even know anybody who might invite her to tea, much less ask her to marry him.

This suddenly gives Freddy his most noble impulse of all.

"Evelina," says he, "I am going to see that you are happily married *before I marry myself*."

He runs through a list of the men who might be marital possibilities for a good girl like Evelina and forthwith arranges for her to meet them.

We now go into a *series of scenes* in which, against backgrounds of great glamour and luxury, Evelina once more enters the world in which she lived when, as a coquette, she first made her connection with Freddy. And gradually Evelina once more becomes the coquette.

Evelina buries her rigid principles, because one must never show one's rigid principles to any man with whom one wishes to succeed. To be a true success with men, one must seem to be quite lazy and helpless and casual. Therefore, Evelina proceeds to give a convincing picture of laziness, of casualness and helplessness.

Evelina lets herself go. Evelina gets tight. Evelina gets slightly disheveled. And as Evelina becomes once more the true coquette and lands herself a proposal from a man much richer, more powerful, and more important than Freddy, Freddy falls madly in love with her and, in a scene of passionate intensity, carries her off to be married.

In the last scene we are again in Freddy's bedroom. Everything is in disarray and so is Evelina. Freddy is sound asleep, snoring, and *so is Evelina.* Freddy's valet has a hard time waking Freddy up, but even *Freddy himself* can hardly wake up Evelina.

Everything in the whole house is at sixes and sevens. The coffee is cold. The valet has allowed Freddy to run out of his pickup medicine. The cook has departed for parts unknown. Freddy's household is a mess but my God, how Freddy loves Evelina!

The moral of this little operetta is that every good wife should also be a good coquette.

NOTES ON THE DEVELOPMENT OF THE ABOVE MATERIAL

The scenes in which Evelina charms, delights, and entrances the men to whom Freddy introduces her, should show every facet of our star's capabilities. With one man she should be dumb because the man is a type who adores dumbness in women. With another man she should be witty because he is the type who desires wittiness in his women. With yet another one she must be mysterious because this is a man who likes mystery in his women.

Whether these should be separate scenes or whether the whole gamut of MacDonald's charm could be run in one large scene is a question to be decided in a further working out of the material.

I feel that all of these episodes should be completely honest and should be attained without any tricks of makeup or other stage devices. In other words, the progress of the girl toward her goal must be done in terms of honest characterization. It is only in this manner that we can get true satire and *believability,* without which no musical, to my way of thinking, is worth a dime.

The scenes of tender reminiscence with Freddy should have plenty of heart in them . . . heart which can be expressed both in dialogue and in music.

Naturally I have had little time to give this any thought, and the outline may sound rather meager. I believe it is enough however to illustrate the basic idea of the plot, and I shall be most interested to hear your reaction, also to hear Cole's reaction and if you are both interested, to get together with Cole out here whenever he is able to devote some time to the matter. I have frequently worked with MacDonald and feel that I know her points pretty well and that all her capabilities could be put to use during the development of the material.

Women in Uniform

Draft Treatment for Film

AUGUST 1942

[Anita's note:] This is the first draft of a story which, naturally, will be changed in various details as it is improved and developed into a screenplay.

We open on shots at various railroad stations throughout the United States and show recruits of the Women's Auxiliary Army Corps (WAACS) saying good-bye; kissing mothers, sweethearts, children, just as soldiers have been used to doing.

There are all sorts of women from the ages of 21 to 49. 78% of them are college women so they are of the high type. Many of them are saying good-bye to husbands for the majority are married—some to men in uniform.

After we establish a great variety of good-byes being said at stations throughout the country we show a scene of great excitement at the leave taking of our heroine, Paula Essery.

(Paula is the beautiful, pampered and spirited wife of an important industrialist in a small city in Ohio. Her husband is a self-made man who has developed a great industry out of his own inventions. Like many wives of prominent men, Paula's chief interest in life is to try and prove to the world that she is at least as great as her husband, if not actually greater. She has never been content with being merely Mrs. Essery, the mother of a charming little boy and the social leader of her own particular clique. It has always embittered her to stand in the shadow of her husband's importance—to be prominent merely because she happened to marry J. P. Essery.)

In her strivings to conjure up some sort of limelight for herself, Paula has neglected her husband, her son and her home and run after a dozen different "careers," the latest of which has been the writing of a book.

Paula's husband, who adores and idolizes her, has treated her book as he has treated all her attempts at 'self expression'. He laughs about it as being merely another passing hobby. But by this time Paula's egotism, petulance and desire for acclaim has reached such a climax that her book has come to be a real issue between them. And when the manuscript begins to be returned from publisher after publisher, it seems more and more apparent that her husband's criticism of her effort has been correct. The strain on Paula's egotism mounts.

By this time the war has started and J. P.'s prominence as leader of an essential war industry has been greatly stepped up: he is beginning to be a prominent figure not only in Ohio but in the nation's capital as well, a fact which further thwarts Paula and makes her feel more unimportant.

Paula has done a tremendous amount of talking about this novel and the fact it is being rejected over and over is another horn in her super sensitive egotism. At first she said that revisions have to be made. After awhile, the war itself becomes her alibi. It is so easy to say that the publication of a novel seems like "such a silly thing" in the light of world conflict. And then into the war picture there emerges the WAACs. To join the WAACs will not only be the perfect alibi for her failure to complete the book for publication, but it will give her the opportunity to get back at J. P.; literally to walk out on him for what she chooses to believe is his complete lack of appreciation of her innate greatness.

Naturally J. P. can do or say nothing against Paula's 'joining up.' There is apparently no reason why she should not. He, himself, must spend a great deal of time in Washington. Their child of eight has to be away at school . . . he has always been away at a special school for children of defective health for little David Essery has an eye condition which requires very special attention.

And so we find J. P. at the railway station, covering a great anguish over the departure of his adored and beautiful wife. As this scene is our first introduction to Paula, we are going to believe just what the scene suggests on its surface—that Paula is a gallant woman giving up an 'adored' husband and child and the luxury of a lovely home out of pure love of country.

What we do not know at this time is that Paula's induction into the service of her country is only just one more of her whims, one more of her attempts to show off. And this time it looks at last as if she has succeeded brilliantly.

Paula's departure for service is news of the first order and she is surrounded by cameramen and interviewers. Innate actress that she is, Paula's attitude is one of great sincerity. She gives a stirring interview to the newsreel cameraman in which she states that her reason for going into the WAACs is that she couldn't bring herself to face a life of leisure at a time when women have been given the greatest opportunity in the nation's history—the opportunity to serve in uniform.

Among the mob of people seeing Paula off is her maid, Gussie. Their good-bye to each other is touching and Paula explains to one of the newspaperwomen that Gussie was her governess when she was a child and has been with her for over twenty years.

During Paula's touching farewell to her husband we note that Gussie slips a little envelope into her mistress' pocketbook, handing it back to Paula just as she makes a hurried and excited dash onto the train to leave in a blaze of glory.

And now we are resolving to the Railroad Station in Des Moines, Iowa:

The train from Chicago is pulling in—and out of it troop numberless WAACs, for there are 800 of them due at Fort Des Moines this morning.

Paula has gotten herself up with special care for this entrance into her new life, wearing an extremely simple suit and carrying her own luggage. News cameramen are stationed at the depot and the girls go through another session of having their pictures taken. Paula's attitude at this time is charming. She forces the other girls to stand ahead of her in the news shots and completely charms everyone by her modesty, simplicity and the earnestness of her attitude. (We are still not 'on' to Paula.)

Waiting at the station are some Army busses which are anything but luxurious, the seats being wooden benches. There is great jostling, excitement and joking as the girls get into these busses and start on their way to Fort Des Moines.

(The drivers of these busses are the first of the regular Army men who enter our picture and their facial expressions as they welcome these girls into Army life is worthy of note. Quizzical is probably the word that best describes it.)

And now we dissolve into Fort Des Moines itself. It is one of the most lovely spots imaginable. The buildings are of red brick, with white porticos and columns, and they face a tremendous parade ground which is all in lawn. The walks are shaded by enormous oak trees and elms and the entire place is redolent of tradition—the finest American tradition of architecture and the spiritual simplicity which our native Colonial architecture symbolizes.

This is the opening day of the WAACs training and 800 officer candidates are entering camp. Some have been there for several hours and are already in their brown and white striped seersucker play suits which are exactly the type which women would be wearing in civilian life at a resort. The majority, however, are in their own civilian clothes.

The press has been allowed in for the day and the camp is swarming with cameramen and newspaper people.

Here again we note the attitude of the regular Army men stationed at Fort Des Moines. It is apparent from their expressions that orders have been given to treat the whole situation as if it were mere routine. But from the expression on the men's faces we can easily gather their attitudes. Some of them think the situation funny, others are annoyed, others merely curious.

As Paula's bus heads into the Fort the girls react with great enthusiasm over the look of their training quarters. None of them has ever heard much about the Fort and they are not expecting to find a place so outstandingly attractive as this.

Among the girls in Paula's bus is a very quiet young woman of foreign aspect who speaks with a pronounced accent. She is the one who explains to the other girls that the Fort was built in 1848, after which she gives them a brief history of it. Paula is surprised at their foreign girl's knowledge about the place.

"How do you happen to know about Fort Des Moines?" she asks the girl.

"It has been a pleasure for me to read about our country," answers the girl with her pronounced accent. "I am a naturalized American, but my family is still in Poland."

News that Mrs. J. P. Essery is arriving in the Army bus has caused quite a little interest among the other recruits and a number of them gather around as she alights in front of the Registration Office.

We here establish one tough Army man, Sergeant Sullivan, who has been with the forces since before the last world war. His one great desire at the present moment is to be in the thick of things in Libya, and here he finds himself in Fort Des Moines having to nurse a lot of females into jobs for which he considers them eminently unfitted.

And now we move into the registration office and see the first episode in the induction, via the making out of questionnaires by personnel experts in the Army. For her questionnaire Paula draws the tough old Sergeant Sullivan, the guy who wishes he were in Libya. The man is a master of psychology and as he asks Paula the pertinent questions of the exhaustive questionnaire we get our first small hint from his reactions that perhaps Paula is not just exactly the selfless and high minded creature she has seemed to be in our first thrilling introductions to her.

At the end of the scene, Sergeant Sullivan looks at her quizzically and says, "Well, Mrs. Essery, you're in the Army now."

Paula nods sweetly, but we can see that she resents this man's attitude and this scene is the beginning of a feud between them which ought to parallel very amusingly the well known feud which always exists between the tough top sergeant and the new recruit.

I think it is important to work into this sequence several of the girls as they answer their questionnaires. One of them with great simplicity states that she was married but that her husband is dead; that he died on December 7th in Pearl Harbor. Their one child was killed in an accident two weeks later.

"You've had it pretty rough, Mrs. Fellows," remarks the officer in charge of her questionnaire.

Mrs. Fellows smiles. "I've still got the greatest country in the world," she answers.

"That's right," answers the officer.

We now go to the large fitting room in which the WAACs are outfitted. Over the door someone has placed a sign which reads, "Through these portals pass the best dressed women's army in the world."

The storeroom is manned by clerks from the big department store in Des Moines who are experts at fitting and selecting the sizes of articles of wear. There is much joking among the WAACs about their outfits. Their dainty pink seersucker pajamas, their pink satin bras, their short khaki colored rayon panties and the hats. The hats are a miracle. They have been designed so as to be becoming to practically every shaped face. The uniform too is the last word in chic. The skirt is a masterpiece designed by one of the greatest women designers in New York and its slenderizing effect delights everyone. The shoes are so smart that they are likely to have an effect on women's styles. They are anything but 'ground grippers', the heels being rather higher than the ordinary type of walking shoe. Garments are put into a large blue canvas bag and by the time Paula has secured her outfit it is the noonday lunch hour.

Lunch is served cafeteria style in an enormous building. The scene in the cafeteria is of great interest and amusement. The army cooks are men, but one motherly looking WAAC of about 42 explains that this is all going to be changed when the WAACs get going; that she closed down her restaurant in order to join the Army and she is going to take charge of the stove department just as soon as Uncle Sam gives her the word.

Lunch is hearty and wholesome. Paula has brought along a small package of Swedish health bread. Paula has never eaten white bread on account of her figure, but Paula has never been as hungry in her entire life and before she finishes her meal, she eats her health bread, plus a large amount of the so-called fattening white bread the Army serves.

Some of the forty colored girls who are in training make their entrance into the cafeteria. These are girls who have already gotten into their uniforms and I am here to tell you that you have never seen any uniform worn up to its hilt until you've seen a snappy colored girl in the WAAC outfit.

On their way back to the barracks after lunch, the girls learn that they are to be addressed by Mrs. Hobby. They troop up towards the steps of the Press Building and we could here show some of the newsreel shots taken of Mrs. Hobby as she addressed the girls on opening day.

(N.B. If we do not use Mrs. Hobby's speech, we can have a character similar to Colonel Faith, the officer in charge of the Fort, who makes an induction speech in which he states that these 800 women are at the birth of a great historical movement. That from the time of Molly Pitcher to Amelia Earhart, gallant women have served their country without the recognition of the uniform. Now the uniform has been granted to them and that it is a reward which the women of America greatly deserve. They are starting that day, July 20, 1942, on a tradition which will remain forever in the annals of the country whose cause they serve. That on this day they are given a clean page and that what they do in the weeks to come will be written on that page and remain in American history for all time to come.)

During this address we cut around to show close-ups of various listeners. They are all girls on whose faces we read the greatest respect and attention, a number of them are so inspired that we see tears in their eyes.

And now, for the first time, we read on these faces the emotion which has motivated all these women to give up jobs, homes, the easy opportunities to make money which always exist in war time, and go into the humble service offered by the WAACs. That emotion is gallantry; these are gallant women.

At the end of this episode, which should be greatly stirring, Paula and the group of girls who are with her are ordered out to march on the parade ground. In this, Paula's first drill, she looks up at a particularly large and beautiful American flag flying over the highest building on the Fort grounds. Her gaze remains on it dazedly and in spite of a nature which we have begun to realize is not completely worthy, Paula is beginning to be touched by the vital experiences through which she is going.

Now we are dissolving to a scene where Taps are being sounded and the big flag is being taken down. Inside the barracks, Paula is seated on her cot. She is dead tired, physically tired for the first time in a long while. The other girls are getting ready for bed. It is at this moment that Paula organizes the little group of five or six girls who are to be her satellites during the time to come.

During apres-bedtime discussion, some of the girls state their reasons for joining the WAACs; one of them has a husband who is a prisoner of the Japanese. She has given up a high salaried position as an executive in a department store so as to feel that in the closest way possible she is helping her husband.

Another girl, the only daughter of a military family, states that in every American war since the Revolution her family has had a member serving in the fighting forces. The establishment of the WAACs has given her the opportunity to carry on unbroken the tradition of her family.

Another girl has signed up because her mother is gradually being starved to death in France.

Another girl says it is her belief that youth must have a vital place in the world after the war is over. "I don't think we could take that place," she states, "unless we have done our part in the conflict."

One motherly looking woman of 46 says that her son is in the Marines and she wants him to be proud of her.

Another girl states that she can't bear sitting on the sidelines in this great conflict. "I happen to be the type," she states, "that likes a front seat."

One of the girls who is to play a main part in our story is Molly Self-ridge. Her reason for joining up is that her husband is out on a Pursuit boat in the Atlantic and she isn't going to sit about loafing while he's dodging German submarines.

Now one of the girls speaks up to say that Paula has probably given up more to enter the WAACs than any other girl in the outfit. Paula, reveling in the opportunity to show off, gives a very convincing performance of a woman whose heart is torn between having to leave her husband and her adorable child, to say nothing of the book she has been writing which had only a few weeks' revisions to be done on it before publication.

Preparing to get into her pink pajamas, Paula reaches a particularly touching point in her narration when she happens to open her pocket-book and finds the note which Gussie gave her at the railroad station. The finding of the note gives Paula a further opportunity to throw her weight around.

With tears in her eyes, she remarks that her darling maid who has been with her from childhood has slipped one last little word of good-bye into her purse. Thus giving a great performance of someone deeply touched by the action of a well beloved menial, Paula opens the note and looking over her shoulder, we read in Gussie's handwriting:

"This is the first chance I've had in 20 years to say what I feel, Madame. With you in the Army, heaven help Uncle Sam."

Outraged, Paula quickly destroys the note and now she tries to go to sleep, but a mixture of emotions is now surging through her mind and heart; fury at Gussie, perhaps a guilty conscience and a certain sense of shame in the presence of these gallant, earnest women who believe in her. Then, too, the bed is hard and she is beginning to miss the comforts to which she is used; comforts she never really appreciated until this very moment.

We now follow with scenes of the training routine during which we develop the stories of our other main characters and their relationship to Paula and to each other.

We see Paula learn to make a bed, we note that she hates doing it and subtly works on one of her satellites to do it for her. We are present at a lecture on Army discipline given by the tough sergeant who wants to be in Libya. The Sergeant lets Paula know that he is 'on to her' just as he did the day when she filled out her questionnaire. Inwardly she hates this man. Outwardly she is so superior to him and so sweet that she would try the temper of an angel, but this Sergeant is an angel and manages to restrain himself.

One of our scenes takes place in the Post Exchange where from 1848 the men at Fort Des Moines have bought tobacco, pipes, socks and other male necessities. Now one of the counters is being stocked with powder compacts, lipsticks, and rayon stockings. The expressions on the faces of the old line Army privates over these innovations are well worth featuring.

Another episode shows a grizzled old Cavalry Captain as he watches the removal of his beloved horses from their comfortable stalls in the impressive old barn, which is now to be converted into a WAACs' classroom.

We go into the colored girls' barracks and hear one of their number who was a café entertainer singing for her comrades as they do their chores.

By Friday, the end of the first week of training, Paula has come to realize that the limelight, for her, is over. Other women are signing up who are as important and as glamorous as she is. With something like despair, she notes herself becoming merely one [of] a group; moreover a group in which she is not very likely to distinguish herself.

As she is facing the lowest moment of realizing the dread future [into] which she has plunged, there arrives a telegram from a certain Patrick Stokes, a member of one of the last publishing firms to which Paula sent her book. Stokes wires that he would like to know when he can fly out to Des Moines from New York and see her.

Paula is beside herself with curiosity. What can this man want? Has he, perhaps, reversed his decision on her book? She wires him that she will be 'on leave' Saturday afternoon and will meet him at the hotel in Des Moines. Then she proceeds to do a little self-advertising among her fellow WAACs concerning her forthcoming conference in Des Moines with 'her publisher.'

Saturday afternoon comes and Paula is released. She hurries to Des Moines to keep her appointment. As she makes her way through the lobby of the hotel we see it seething with military life. Numbers of the WAACs have come in to spend their first leave and all of them are in uniform. We meet many of the same girls whom we saw arrive on that first day and we see how two weeks of training has changed them, invariably for the better. One of the girls, who was slightly overweight, is already a trim figure in her uniform. All the girls have a more serious air, an air of more authority.

As Paula is entering the elevator to go up to the suite of rooms she has engaged for herself, she runs into Molly who remarks that "somehow 'civvies' seem a little dull in comparison to their uniforms," a statement to which we realize Paula doesn't agree.

Paula enters her room where the best hairdresser and manicurist in Des Moines are waiting to help her become once more her own glamorous self.

(I do not know whether the WAACs are allowed to wear civilian dress 'on leave,' but whether they are or not, Paula has ordered an exciting new dress from New York with which to impress 'her publisher.')

She is a vision of loveliness by the time Patrick Stokes phones and states that he will be waiting for her in the Gotham Club which is located in the hotel. Paula enters the Club to find it a really glamorous spot, very like a luxurious New York nightclub, with seductive lighting and an excellent orchestra. The aspect of the place, after her seemingly endless incarceration in barracks, bucks her spirits enormously.

Pat Stokes is waiting for her at a secluded table. He is a very attractive man of forty five who fell under Paula's spell at the time she brought her novel to New York to submit it to his firm.

From the moment of his greeting to Paula, we are able to gather that he has developed a big crush on her in their previous encounters. Now he tells her that he is withdrawing from his firm, plans to go into business on his own and is willing to bring out her book as one of his first ventures.

During their scene it develops that his motive for publishing Paula's book is partly based on his fascination by her as a woman, and partly on the publicity a book from the wife of a prominent man may give his new venture.

On her part, Paula finds 'understanding' at last of her great talent and the satisfaction of being treated accordingly; she always knew her book was great. This man Stokes has had the vision to see it; she will be a famous author; she will show her husband how criminally lacking in appreciation he has always been.

But why, oh why, hasn't this happened before? Before she petulantly signed up with this annoying gang of ardent women patriots for the entire duration of the war and six months afterwards?

However, a couple of bracing cocktails makes her feel that life is pretty rosy. Her flirtation with Stokes is a different type than any in which she has ever indulged . . . a literary flirtation . . . a highbrow flirtation . . . one which has opened up a whole exciting new world for her intense egotism.

But just at the high point of this soul-satisfying conversation, Paula is paged and told that her husband is waiting for her in the lobby. Paula hears this news with a mixture of emotions, the first being indignation that J. P. should crash in and interrupt her at a time like this. But following immediately is another emotion—a sense of joy over the scene of justification into which she can now plunge . . . the chance to prove to her husband that he has been wrong about her literary aspirations all the time . . . the chance to show him that he has always underrated her . . . has never given her the respect which is her due.

Bristling with indignation at J. P., Paula is rising to meet him when she looks up and sees him entering the Club. He is smiling happily and there is an air of mysterious excitement about him, which Paula, in her preoccupation with herself, does not notice. She greets him, kisses him briefly and introduces him to Stokes. Then with a tinge of smugness, she proceeds to tell J. P. her great news. Just as she imagined, J. P. hears it without being greatly impressed. His attitude infuriates Paula, and presently causes Stokes to bring his interview to a close, stating that he must catch his plane back to New York. Then he leaves.

Now Paula turns petulantly on her husband and tells him that they had better go up to her suite and have a talk. By this time, J. P. has come to a full realization of his wife's ungracious mood.

"That's just what I came for," he answers quietly.

They enter Paula's suite and she at once launches into a petulant tirade over her husband's disregard for her success. He has never understood her—he has always belittled her—she feels that the time has come for her to assert her individuality—to be 'true to herself.'

She is an independent woman now—a free woman—a woman who has proved herself. She doesn't need J. P. Not even financially. She already has a large check of her own earning in her pocket. She feels that it will be much better for them both if they separate and find their full self-expression in freedom.

Stunned, J. P. listens to his wife's outburst, and in retaliation lets her have some pretty bitter truths about her shallowness, her egotism and exhibitionism . . . truths which are all the more infuriating because they are true. Then, in continuation, he states the reason for his trip to Des Moines. He has had an interview with a New York specialist who has recently worked out the technique of a new operation through which there is a great chance of a cure for little David Essery.

Paula's heart leaps with joy at this news. She asks a dozen questions all at once, as to when the operation could be performed . . . where it could be performed . . . how soon.

"As soon as you can get a few days leave to be with him," answers J. P. "If you're there to hold his hand, the little fellow won't mind anything."

Then he tells Paula a brief good-bye and leaves her alone . . . alone in the joy over the chance of her boy's recovery . . . alone in the satisfaction of her career and of the exciting new friendship with Stokes . . . alone in the bitterness of her husband's lack of understanding.

And now a wave of self pity and anguish engulfs Paula. Why didn't she know about her book before she joined this silly women's army? She goes to bed . . . tries to sleep but can't. Maybe the bed is too soft . . . maybe she misses the other girls. Then, too, maybe she is thinking just a little bit of the idyllic love of the early days of her romance with J. P., of her son and the neglect with which she has always treated him.

Presently, there is a tap on her door. Paula opens it to find Molly standing outside. On Molly's face is a confusion of the most vital emotions. She has something to tell Paula at once. The two girls sit on Paula's bed and Molly announces she has just learned she is going to become a mother.

They have an intimate talk about motherhood and Paula finds herself telling Molly things about the birth and early infancy of her own little boy. As she talks to this eager young woman who is so in love with her sailor husband, so proud of the work he is doing out on the Atlantic, something of sympathy and understanding starts to stir in her . . . something she doesn't quite like . . . it makes her uncomfortable . . . makes her feel somehow rather second rate and ashamed.

After the scene is over and Molly has gone off to sleep, Paula's resentment at the fate which imprisons her in the WAACs becomes increasingly bitter, even though in her heart she knows how petty and unworthy she is being.

On Sunday evening, as Taps are being sounded at Fort Des Moines, Paula makes her disgruntled way back to her barracks.

Now she sets about trying to get out of the Army. She pulls every wire she can think of, but it is no go. She is in for the duration and six months thereafter. But then comes an inspiration . . . the thought of using her child as reason for her release . . . not for the several days suggested by her husband, but a permanent leave because of the forthcoming operation and convalescence of her child. An emergency leave is granted with release to follow.

Paula's departure from Fort Des Moines is dramatized by sudden word from the Navy that Molly's husband has been killed in action on his Pursuit ship. The scene of good-byes between the two girls and their fellow officer candidates is one of great poignancy. Molly is forced to leave the WAACs because of approaching motherhood, while Paula, exhibitionist that she is, is able to give a performance which is almost as convincing as the actual grief and anguish of the poor little Navy widow.

Paula goes to New York to see the famous specialist who is to operate on her boy, but while in the city she has another encounter with Pat Stokes and enjoys a first small taste of the life she is to have as a woman of importance. Stokes makes a dozen dates for Paula . . . to address clubs . . . to meet other writers . . . to have parties given in her honor. She has never been so thrillingly happy and important in her whole life and Stokes himself is overcome with joy on learning that Paula will soon be free of her involvement in the WAACs.

After several days, Paula has made the arrangements for her boy's operation and she departs for his school. Her leave-taking with Stokes is practically a love scene, with more romance to follow as soon as she can conveniently return.

Paula's arrival at her son's school makes a sensation. Word has run through the institution that little David Essery's mother is a real, genuine soldier. Since Paula's induction into the WAACs she has never realized what the uniform meant. But now she realizes it in the dramatic situation. She begins to hold her head high . . . square her shoulders . . . to be proud.

She has a scene in private with her son. Paula and her son have never been very close. The boy has always adored her as the most beautiful creature he has ever known, but the obvious fact that he has been in her way has made him shy and reserved. Now his shyness has all been removed . . . now he sees his mother, not as a beautiful butterfly, but as a glorious patriotic symbol . . . someone of whom he can be proud for the greatest reason in the world.

Paula has to speak up now and tell him that she is going to put aside her uniform in order to stay with him always. The boy's first reaction to this is delight, but he presently grows thoughtful.

"You know, Mommy," he tells Paula, "I doubt that I'll ever be able to wear a uniform and Daddy can't because he's too busy in Washington. And the thing that makes me happiest in the world is that you are wearing one for Daddy and me."

Little David Essery is to be operated on the day following the closing of school, but at closing day Paula is asked to tell the boys something of the Women's Army. These pathetic little creatures . . . boys who are not well enough to indulge in patriotic games which are so dear to every child's heart in wartime . . . and as Paula stands on the platform facing the eager admiration of these children, there begins to stir within her something of the spirit she has subconsciously developed during her enforced enlistment in the WAACs.

Paula begins to tell the children of the origin of the WAACs . . . of the brave women in the First World War who served in Flanders in the uniform of the French army because the United States, the land of their birth, at that time had no uniform for them. She tells how Edith Norse Rogers, who was one of these women, made it her life work to rectify this situation and to see that Uncle Sam would give his gallant daughters the same chance that his gallant sons had always had. She tells of the terrific fight Mrs. Rogers made in Congress, and of the great work of Senator Thomas of Idaho, who carried the bill through to its successful conclusion.

Paula's words, as she speaks, become increasingly inspired, for without knowing it herself, and even against her own will, she has become imbued with a terrific respect for the organization against which she has been fighting outwardly. Her speech is brought to a close amidst touching applause.

The next day, Paula is sitting at her son's bedside in the infirmary after the operation, which has every indication of being successful. Paula is feeling very benign this morning. She has made arrangements for Molly to stay with her boy . . . to look after him while Molly is having her own child. It will give Molly something to live for and naturally will leave Paula free to spend plenty of time in New York. At last Paula has everything within her grasp . . . everything she has always wanted . . . a chance to show off brilliantly in a brilliant circle . . . a chance to carry forward that soul-satisfying literary flirtation with the intellectual and understanding Patrick Stokes.

But Paula has to go back to Fort Des Moines for her release. She arrives there during the ceremonies of the completion of training of her fellow candidates. She stands on the verandah watching them . . . watching them march . . . watching them stop in formation under the big flag at the head of the parade grounds . . . watching them salute that flag. And now there are stirring within her a great multitude of new emotions, as everything that is good in Paula is rising to the surface.

She goes to the tough Army Sergeant who has been handling the matter of her release. Sergeant Sullivan looks at her and in his face she reads his contempt as he announces that he has 'overlooked' attending to her release and that she is still with the Army. Naturally, Sergeant Sullivan has done it purposely to get back at this silly creature, so he is almost knocked over when Paula breaks into tears of joy and thanks him from the bottom of her heart. For Paula's regeneration, which has been subtly working within her from the first moment of her induction in the service, has finally worked its way through to the surface. With the deepest feelings of relief, she rushes to rejoin her company— to lose her identity—to do a humble service—to be one, merely one, of the women in uniform.

As a comedy finish, we see one of the toughest old Army men being released to go into combat service through having a buxom WAAC of 42 take up his duties at Fort Des Moines. The picture closes on the lately disgruntled soldier giving the motherly looking WAAC a great big kiss.

THE END

Aunt Anita's Romances
and Friendships

Mary Anita Loos

Friends were always very important to my Aunt Anita, and she had more of them, of every different stripe, than anyone I have ever known. First on the list, and most difficult to explain, has to be her husband, John Emerson.

Anita met Mr. E., as she always called him, shortly after he had arrived in California to direct films. Seeking material for Douglas Fairbanks, Emerson found a witty collection of story ideas by someone named A. Loos. He took it to Griffith for his approval, but D. W. warned him, "The laughs are all in the lines. There's no way to get them on the screen." Emerson suggested that he would like to take the chance on one called *His Picture in the Papers*. Griffith just let him go, thinking he would edit it down later and actually even withheld it from release, but when one New York theater failed to receive the picture it was supposed to run, *His Picture in the Papers* was sent over as is, and the audience loved it. It was a smash.

John Emerson reacted to Anita's youth and tiny stature with surprise. He was amused with her piquant personality, but most of all he was impressed by her brilliant writing. It was obvious from the beginning that

Anita was intrigued with a man who was not only tall and handsome (as James Montgomery Flagg's portrait proves) but also more sophisticated than her young-fry pals around the studio.

Emerson, in a sense, was a more elegant version of the father she adored, a dandy full of big plans. He told Anita he had been briefly married once before and wasn't planning on marrying again, but he wasn't about to lose this woman who had proven her worth as a meal ticket. Emerson and Anita were married in June 1919.

Anita was his pigeon. He took advantage of her great drive and creativity, showed her a few tricks in presentation, corrected a few commas, and, in a psychological way, took over where her father had left off. From the midteens until the mid-1940s Emerson put his name on almost everything she wrote, often in front of hers and in capital letters. He also arranged the deals that included his service as director or producer to go with her writing, paying himself more than she was paid.

He attempted to halt the publication of *Gentlemen Prefer Blondes*— was it because he didn't understand her original wit and satire, or was it because he was jealous? When it was a success, he drafted a dedication for the book that credited himself with everything Anita knew. That dedication was stopped by Anita's outraged friends and became, simply, "To John Emerson."

He spent her money lavishly (including the bonanza of *Gentlemen Prefer Blondes*) on himself and other women and lost Aunt Anita's entire fortune and their New York home. He put all their property in his name only and attempted to throttle her, claiming she was "too good to live." Fortunately, Anita's faithful driver interfered and called my father, who immediately took Emerson away to the Las Encinas Sanitarium in Pasadena, where he was diagnosed as manic-depressive.

Emerson resided in elegant comfort at the sanitarium for almost twenty years. (It was the drying out and mental support center among wealthy patrons in the entertainment industry.) A woman driver/ companion cared for him, and pretty nurses fled from his approaches. He was taken to fine restaurants and theaters in the Los Angeles area and, unfortunately for all of us, to many visitations at Anita's Sunday luncheons, where he would advise everyone on how to run their lives.

Anita never would divorce him. She said she could always make a living and "Poor Mr. E. is unable. . . . [H]e's ill." She treated him with constant affection and went on with her lonely life.

I don't think many of her friends ever confronted her about Emerson. I know I did only once. It was on a Sunday morning before one of her traditional luncheons with her favorite friends. Everything was in order. Hallie and George Jenkins were working together, preparing the seafood salads, mélange of homegrown vegetables, and enchiladas. As Anita and I left to walk down to the Santa Monica pier, I noticed Emerson's scotch scarf being hung over a chair. The thought of that man's appearance along with Aldous Huxley, Dr. Edward Hubble, and visiting celebrities from New York and Europe troubled me; and as we walked along the sand, I could not hold back my distress.

"Anita," I asked, "why do you have to invite Emerson? You know he butts in on Huxley and Dr. Hubble and, of course, you. Why don't you give him up on Sundays?"

After taking two steps to every one of mine, she stopped short and looked up at me, I realized, with anger, something I had never seen before on her.

"Don't you know?"

I could only stare at her.

"I am to blame," she said.

"How?"

I only heard the sound of the waves, and I felt like I was in the midst of a bad dream.

Gently she started walking again.

"It goes back to the day I met him. Mr. Griffith, yes that's what all of us from Lillian Gish to his cameraman, Billy Bitzer, called him, decided to give a little class to his studio by hiring a director from the theater. He was John Emerson, and Mr. Griffith himself brought him to my tacky

Anita's mother, Minnie Smith Loos. Mary Anita Loos private collection.

Anita and her sister, Gladys *(standing),* in the San Francisco stock company production of *Quo Vadis,* San Francisco, 1897. Mary Anita Loos private collection.

Anita Loos, six years old. Mary Anita Loos private collection.

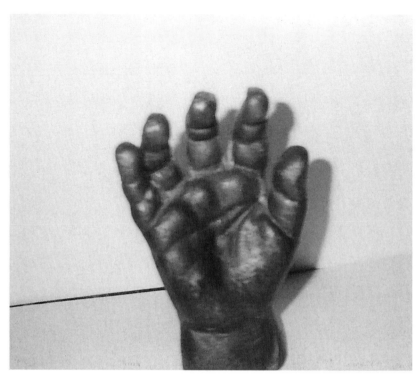

Cast of Anita's hand when she was four made by her father in his print shop in Etna, California. Mary Anita Loos private collection.

Anita in an outfit she designed herself, San Diego, 1913. Mary Anita Loos
private collection.

Anita hamming it up for the photographer at the Del Coronado in San Diego, circa 1914. Mary Anita Loos private collection.

Anita on the beach at the Del Coronado with her first husband, Frank Pallma, 1915.
Mary Anita Loos private collection.

Hollywood at last! Anita at her outdoor desk, 1916. Museum of Modern Art/Film Stills Archive.

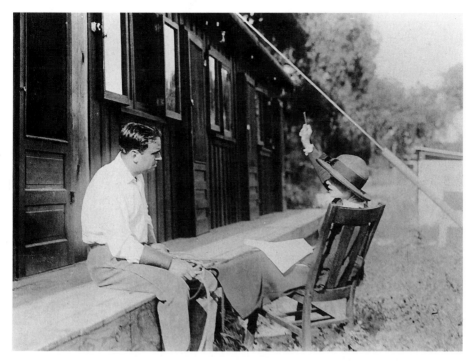

Douglas Fairbanks and Anita Loos, 1917. Museum of Modern Art/Film Stills Archive.

Above and opposite: John Emerson and Anita Loos. These photos, taken in 1918, a year before they married, are typical of the publicity shots Emerson arranged for himself and Anita. The one of her reading the newspaper while he works away is particularly ironic since it was Anita who did all the writing. Museum of Modern Art/Film Stills Archive.

Lined up for inspection. Candidates for the role of Lorelei in the Paramount film *Gentlemen Prefer Blondes,* 1927. *Left:* Anita Loos, Malcolm St. Clair (director), and John Emerson. Publicity photo.

Anita at MGM, 1930s. Mary Anita Loos private collection.

Anita *(right)*, with Frances Marion and Victor Fleming, dressed for Marion Davies's costume party, early 1930s. Frances Marion Collection. University of Southern California Cinema-Television Library.

Anita and her writing partner at MGM, Robert "Hoppy" Hopkins, mid-1930s.
Mary Anita Loos private collection.

Mary Anita and Anita, mid-1930s. Courtesy of the Academy of Motion Picture Arts and Sciences.

Anita and her brother, Dr. H. Clifford Loos (Mary Anita Loos's father), 1940. Mary Anita Loos private collection.

Aldous Huxley, Anita, Peter Duchin, and his nurse, Rita Chisholm, 1939. Mary Anita Loos private collection.

Anita Loos, Mary Anita Loos, and Eddy Duchin, Los Angeles, 1938. Mary Anita Loos private collection.

Sunday gathering at Anita's, Santa Monica, 1950. *Front row, left to right:* John Emerson, Anita Loos, and Cecil Beaton. *Back row, left to right:* Aldous Huxley, Ruth Gordon, Ruben Mamoulian, Azadia Mamoulian, Maria Huxley, Dr. H. Clifford Loos, Mary Anita Loos, and Richard Sale. Mary Anita Loos private collection.

Mary Anita, Anita, and Richard Sale in Paris shooting Anita's *Gentlemen Marry Brunettes,* 1955. Mary Anita Loos private collection.

Anita at Mary Anita's home in Newport Beach, 1964. Mary Anita Loos private collection.

Anita in Newport Beach with her great-nephew, Edward Sale, 1964. Mary Anita Loos private collection.

Anita's eighty-fifth birthday, 1973. *Left to right:* Mary Anita Loos, Anita Loos, and Helen Hayes.
Mary Anita Loos private collection.

little story editor's office and explained that Mr. Emerson was a Broadway actor and director who was considering joining the group.

"'He looked through the files and laughed at my purchases of your stories,'" Mr. Griffith said. "'And laughed again when I told him that they were too witty for words, but he enjoyed reading them.'

"John looked at me with surprise," Anita went on. "Again, my damned tiny figure was against me. . . ."

She paused a moment. She walked on, and so did I.

"He took my hand and held it. And you know what happened? This handsome man took me under his wing. John asked me, a nobody, to work with him. And we worked successfully. I can tell you, a director can misuse your story and spoil it. John never let me down with what I wrote."

I was thinking about all the scripts she wrote where he had added his name after a few small corrections, but she gestured toward the last southern house in the great enclave where most of the moguls and stars from William Randolph Hearst to Irving Thalberg resided in those glamorous days of the Gold Coast.

"Look at that," she gestured expansively. "The galaxy of stars we knew, the trips abroad, the world. Here I was, courtesy of John Emerson, who chose me as his partner when I was nothing. He was so handsome and I, little Anita Loos from San Diego, a girl who never had a date in school, bucketing around cheap theaters playing Little Lord Fauntleroy because I was so small, and we were married in the elegant home of Norma Talmadge.

"As a team, we photographed like a dream. I wrote well . . . [and] he directed well. . . . Yes, I learned he was paying attention to other women. He did what many other men did. Our successful work brought us together, and I found my intellectual group and he found his social group.

"It wasn't the depression that ruined us. Everyone knew about that. We made so much money at one time that it didn't make much difference."

She stopped suddenly and turned away from me.

"Lots of things could have broken us up. But—but—it was *Gentlemen Prefer Blondes* that did it."

I was aghast.

"I was suddenly internationally famous," she continued in a smaller voice. "Poor middle-aged John could not bear the fact that everyone wanted to know me, be with me, quote me. He felt he must seek self-satisfaction, and he became desperately mental."

She looked out to the hissing sound of the sea on sand.

"So now you know," she finished. "Let's go back."

Anita did have a few other romances in her life. One of the odd characters who hovered in and out for many years was Ray Goetz. "Plump and fortyish," as Anita described Ray, he was not an ideal, but he did adore her. After a short, successful spell in Tin Pan Alley, Ray had traveled about Europe with Puccini. Ray had made a brief flashy marriage with a French chanteuse, Irene Bordoni (his sister Dorothy had married Irving Berlin in 1912, but she died five months later). Through connections with his brother-in-law, Berlin, and his friend Cole Porter, Ray had some success as a producer of their early musicals. For Ray it was like finding two bottles on the sand with genies inside them; however, that ended when he was caught pocketing some of the royalties. Ray did manage a few legitimate ASCAP royalties from songs he cowrote, including the popular tune "Bells Are Ringing for Me and My Gal," but most of his income came from his family. Ray first came into Anita's orbit in Palm Beach as he was also a friend of the Mizners, and when Ray later lived in a guesthouse up the canyon in Santa Monica, he fervently courted Anita.

Anita occasionally considered the possibility of marriage, in part because she was at times genuinely lonely and because it would be nice to have a dependable escort; also, it was awkward for her to go on her own with other couples.

Still, I remember her calling me one night in the mid-1930s to say,

"Guess what? Ray just proposed to me. We were at that little Sign of the Cock restaurant on the Strip. Anyway, it was a good meal."

The best thing about Ray was that he was available, but Anita never could take him seriously for any length of time. Even though she had sympathy for a list of has-beens, Ray was finally abandoned because he had not even been an important *been*.

For years Anita would go back and forth in her own mind over what to do next on the romantic front. She was in New York in the late 1940s when she wrote me:

> Sometimes I get a neurosis about facing the future alone to the extent that I slightly entertain the thought of marriage. But when I realize the most reliable beau I have had through the years is Ray Goetz, who is certainly no Rock of Gibraltar, I think that perhaps the frying pan is better than the fire. Ruth Dubonnet met my Harvard professor while we were visiting at Jack Hanson's place at Gloucester a couple of weeks ago and she feels I could concentrate on him, However, as much as I love Boston, I'm afraid that isn't such a bright idea.

I never met the professor, but I do remember another beau, a newspaperman she had met in New York. Anita invited him to visit her in California, and he was delighted to leave the jocks at Toot Shor's saloon for the beach three thousand miles away.

Everyone was curious to meet him, of course, and he picked up the nickname "Sugah" because that is what he called Anita. Certainly more endearing than Emerson calling her "Bug," but when Emerson appeared at one of Anita's lunches and met "Sugah," he wasted no time in taking me aside to let me know what he thought.

"The guy is a bum," Emerson told me. "No good. It would be just like Anita to let him make a fine catch with her," waving his finger at me as if I were a naughty child.

"You should know," I thought to myself; he'd been living off her talent and income for decades. Unfortunately, he turned out to be right about Sugah, and he never let me forget it.

Sugah escorted Anita to a high-profile Hollywood dinner, well attended by studio executives. After a drink or four Sugah had the audacity and stupidity to get into a loud argument with Frances Goldwyn, the current totem of good wives.

If that wasn't enough, the car that Anita had bought Sugah, so he could drive around town while she worked all day at the studio, was stolen outside a pub in Venice. He took a cab back to Santa Monica, and Anita's cook paid the fare. The car finally turned up in Santa Barbara, pocked with bullet holes.

When it was returned, Anita gave it to me. My first car.

Sugah was escorted to the airport by Anita's devoted chauffeur, George, who waited patiently for the plane to take off so he was sure Sugah was indeed heading back to New York. I went over to check on Anita and found her on her bed, curled into a fetal position. It wasn't that she was in love with him; she was just upset that his antics were being broadcast by phone throughout Hollywood and New York.

A few years later we heard Sugah had married a well-off divorcee, a petite brunette who would take good care of him. "Well," Anita said, smiling wryly, "Sugah got what he wanted. Let's drop the subject."

One other romance bears more than a mention. When Anita and Emerson were taking their annual pilgrimages to Europe in the 1920s, Anita met and intrigued Viscount D'Abernon. The tall, elegant man about town introduced her to the cultural and social elite of London. Since Emerson was busy on his own, chasing women and ordering a tailor-made wardrobe, he couldn't have cared less. Anita was free to enjoy the attentions of the viscount, who she learned was the illegitimate son of King Edward VII by a Spanish dancer. Anita and the viscount were soon a familiar pair at social events, as well as at art galleries and exhibits.

Near the end of the first season they spent together, they returned to her hotel suite for tea, and as he put his cup down on the saucer, the viscount very politely asked her if she would care to step into the next room with him. The only other room was the bedroom, and Anita was so startled by the question coming out of the blue that she responded with a simple, "No, thank you." He picked up his teacup again as if nothing had changed and the possibility was never mentioned again. They did keep up their friendship and their shared love of art, and among the treasures he sent her were two prints by their favored artists, Brueghel and Cranach.

Twenty years must have passed because Emerson was safely tucked away in the sanitarium in Pasadena, and Anita was living in New York when she told me D'Abernon had written her that it was time to finally break out of the prison of propriety that had limited their friendship. He proposed that they travel Europe together, searching for Cranach's lost masterpiece *Hares Catching and Roasting a Sportsman,* which had been the intrigue of art circles since it vanished in the sixteenth century.

"Why not?" thought Anita, and I was pleased she was planning for this adventure that might truly bring her happiness. But it was only a few weeks later that Anita picked up the *New York Times* and saw the viscount's obituary. So much for the ideal romance with the man who had been such a valentine in her life.

Anita's fascination with con men was not limited to Emerson and Sugah. With the attraction set at an early age by her father, men like Wilson Mizner drew her like a magnet. In fact it was one of Mizner's former errand boys, Robert Hopkins, who made life at MGM in the 1930s so fun for Anita. Hoppy, as everyone called Hopkins, was one of the fascinating characters, with their intriguing mix of sin and fun, produced by San Francisco's Barbary Coast before it was destroyed in the 1906 earthquake.

Somewhere Hoppy heard about the treasure earned by the gag writers of Hollywood, and he began his movie career in the mid-1920s as a member of Mack Sennett's "think tank," specializing in zippy one-liners that became subtitles. With the new world of sound films Hoppy progressed to MGM, where he was often credited with "additional dialogue," although he never actually got into the intricacies of script writing.

As a matter of fact, Hoppy never actually wrote *anything* down. He wouldn't even answer a telephone. If Anita happened to be there, she would pick up the receiver and then put it down on the table so Hoppy could keep pacing as he shouted out a conversation.

Although Hoppy's wit and ability to throw off a clever line at a moment's notice had kept him employed, he was in a tenuous situation when he and Anita got together. She interpreted his ideas, and of course did all the writing, and the height of their unique collaboration was the creation of the film *San Francisco*. Anita and Hoppy shared a love of San Francisco and their mutual idol, Wilson Mizner, who had died in 1933. It was an emotional experience for Anita and Hoppy to create the role of the gambler with the heart of gold, Blackie Norton, modeled on Mizner and brought to life on the screen by Clark Gable. However, Anita was so concerned about Hoppy keeping his job at MGM that she insisted he receive sole story credit, so he alone received the Academy Award nomination for best original screenwriting in 1936.

If you look at the film's credits today, you'll also notice John Emerson listed as the producer—Anita had arranged with Thalberg to cut her own salary and give the other half to "producer" Emerson—it was the only way he could get a job.

Hoppy came by Anita's house to go over what she had written and was often invited to her gatherings. He was an amusing conversationalist and a ringer for Leopold Stokowski—thin and white-haired, with hand gestures similar to those of the flamboyant symphony conductor, who was in Hollywood in 1936 to appear in the film *One Hundred Men and a Girl*.

There was a brief period when Anita thought she had finally found an intellectual equal who had possibilities as a lover. Stokowski was headlined in big letters in Anita's appointment book every day for a week. When he asked if he could bring his friend Greta Garbo one day for a visit, Anita phoned and instructed me to saunter down the beach at a certain time with my Yorkshire terrier. Everything went as planned, with Anita feigning surprise as she announced, "Oh, here comes my niece," and I joined the threesome, thrilled to meet Stokowski and, most of all, the elusive Garbo. I even managed to have a pleasant visit with Garbo while Stokowski chatted on with Anita. Garbo asked what I wanted to be, and I said, "Either a writer or an archaeologist—I am too tall to be an actress." Garbo picked up a book and backed up against me, measuring the tops of our heads. "No," she announced. "You are exactly my height and I have no problem." Overwhelmed, all I could say was, "But you are Garbo!"

Anita was all eyes for Stokowski until he told her the reason for their visit; he wanted Anita to take Garbo to Bullock's Wilshire and help her choose some decent clothes because they were about to leave together on a trip.

That ended the large letters in her appointment books, but it was during the time of the Stokowski-Garbo affair that Anita's longtime friend Paulette Goddard happened to drop by and, finding Hoppy alone in the living room, mistook him for the great Stokowski.

Paulette turned on the full charm. At first, Hoppy was surprised and intrigued, but when Paulette began chatting about music, it fortunately left Hoppy speechless, or the mistaken identity would have been quickly revealed. It wasn't long, however, before Anita came downstairs and introduced her cowriter, breaking the bubble of Paulette's dream of winning a man away from Garbo, which would have been an incredible feat.

Paulette Goddard was a friend of Anita's throughout their lives. Paulette was a beautiful and accomplished actress who was also well read, erudite, and intelligent. Of course, she also had a great sense of humor. She had several husbands, including Charlie Chaplin and Erich Maria Remarque (the latter was the brilliant author of *All Quiet on the Western Front*), but when I got to know her well, she was married to the stage and screen actor Burgess Meredith. They lived on the beach near Anita, and often in the late summer afternoons Paulette and I would swim out beyond the breakers and paddle until the first star came out, talking about life, careers, people, and dreams. She even made me, as a young girl, feel special, and I realize now that her magic was to do this with whomever she was with.

One of the results of Paulette's magic was a large collection of "headlight" jewels she so casually wore. One night she and Burgess were returning from a trip, and they stopped at a diner on their way home. Paulette carried a bag with her jewels in with her, but when she got back into the car, she realized they were gone. "Oh, well," was her attitude, but the next day the phone rang and a voice told her the jewels had been found. Some boys playing near a tunnel had found the bag, obviously dropped by thieves being pursued. The boys' honest parents had found her name and number in the bag, and Paulette had her jewels back.

Emeralds and rubies were her usual fare, so I remember how surprised Anita and I were one day during the war when Paulette arrived for tea wearing a gold thistle brooch set with a semiprecious topaz. "Where did you get this?" Anita asked. Paulette told us of meeting a Scottish lord (if Mary Queen of Scots had won, he might have been king) who was visiting Hollywood and well, Paulette explained with a smile and a sigh, "It was the best he had."

Another time I remember Anita and Paulette laughing together was when Hollywood was in the midst of helping the war effort. Even those with estates and limousines worked like fiends in their "victory gardens." Anita and Paulette started crocheting like mad, but I could not figure out what they were making that was giving them such delight. On close examination their concoctions looked like multicolored crocheted sausages.

When I asked, "For heaven's sake, what are they?" they both started to giggle.

"It's very cold where the boys are and we thought it would be a real treat to send them these," Anita answered.

"These what?"

"They are peter heaters." And with that, both of these sophisticated women burst out chuckling. They seemed convinced they had hit upon a great idea, but I couldn't help thinking that as fascinating as their new inventions were, the boys would have rather had a signed picture of Paulette.

As the woman who wrote *Gentlemen Prefer Blondes,* Anita was obviously a student of femmes fatales, and Paulette was a living example. She attracted men as diverse as George Gershwin, Aldous Huxley, and Howard Hughes. Huxley made her his ideal in his novel *After Many a Summer Dies the Swan,* and Gershwin was rumored to have written "They Can't Take That Away from Me" for Paulette. She would play golf with Howard Hughes and bet him five thousand dollars a hole. If she won, he paid. If she lost, she laughed.

There were many other lesser-known conquests as well. For example, I remember lunching with Anita and a very elegant gentleman at The Colony Club in New York. He spent a great deal of time over a demitasse to consider how he could find a certain velvet ribbon to exactly match some rare, white violets he had been growing in a hothouse specifically to give to Paulette when she arrived in New York.

Later, in the taxi, Anita turned to me and said, "You know, there is no one like Paulette. She's a natural beauty, she's a real athlete in great condition, she doesn't need fancy clothes, and she's not only intelligent, but she's fun."

Anita, who always liked the cerebral approach, paused and then added, "You know, words aside, really, I wonder what she *does!*"

We both laughed heartily. There was a time when I thought perhaps we would find out because Anita was at work with Paulette on a book. They took even longer walks than usual as they went over Paulette's life and the material that Anita would write. Then one day Paulette turned to her and said, "Of course, I don't want to mention my marriage to Charlie Chaplin."

Well, Anita tried to explain that they couldn't have a book about her life without that, but Paulette would not budge, and that closed the pages of an interesting, unwritten book.

They stayed friends and continued to make each other laugh during lonely times, and among Anita's papers was the following page that gives Anita's explanation of Paulette's magic:

Women have for so long been in pursuit of men that, on catching one, a woman sometimes has a basic feeling of guilt—as if she were a thief. This utterly destroys all romantic feeling between them. No longer is the woman the giver of emotional experiences—of glamour—of fantasies—of quirks and jokes; she is the "taker," the "remover" of romance, of money, of fantasies, of emotions and jokes—the man goes home to a life of depletions and not of fulfillments.

In the viewpoint of Paulette Goddard, a woman bestows innumerable blessings on a man by her interest. Even her gold digging provides for him the grandiose feeling of generosity—it makes him, for the moment of giving, a god. Because to Paulette there is no sense of guilt of the thief—she really and truly loves men—is sorry for them—and compassionate. She knows herself capable of supplying them with their utmost needs—not only physically, but emotionally, spiritually and romantically. She puts a man, as it were, "on the man."

Instead of degrading him by feelings of a thief, she uplifts him, making him the great giver of all good things. She does not do this with humility—she is a goddess accepting the homage of a god.

She respects very deeply her powers as a woman. In fact, she respects the powers of all women—and by so doing, raises their status into true dignity (which, alas, it does not always deserve).

There is in her no touch of bitchery—she respects women as deeply as she loves men. By doing so, she makes them better than they actually are. . . . [T]hus is she the great benefactor.

Another equally important friendship to Anita was the one she shared with Helen Hayes. Anita and Helen first met at the Algonquin Hotel in the 1920s because the sweet innocent actress had enchanted the accomplished playwright Charles MacArthur. Anita had no love lost for what she considered the show-off wits at the hotel's famous round table, but Charlie was an exception. The handsome Charlie had proven his talent writing *The Front Page* with Ben Hecht, and most everyone was surprised when Charlie decamped from his eccentric relationship with the great wit Dorothy Parker and found Helen to be the love of his life.

Helen sought out Anita to help her dress with the style required in her life with Charlie, and Anita found her a delight. A great sense of humor helped, of course, but the actress also took her work seriously while treating herself lightly. Charlie claimed to be enchanted with her grace and beauty, but Helen told Anita she thought the heart of his adoration came from her eager, honest, and constant attention.

Helen and Anita had known each other more than fifteen years when, in 1940, Anita was tired of Hollywood and Helen was tired of being engulfed in period plays. As stimulating and successful as her roles as Queen Victoria were, she longed to create a character onstage that was much like herself, where she could kick up her heels and dance.

"Write me a play that is full of fun and gayety," Helen pleaded with Anita. "I will be free of my crinolines and you will be free of Hollywood."

Such idle comments do not usually lead to anything, but Anita picked up her trusty pen and wrote the play *Happy Birthday* for Helen. Helen got to wear short skirts and dance on a table, and Anita moved to New York and into a successful second career as a respected playwright.

Anita shared Helen's heartbreaks as well. Helen and Charlie's beloved daughter, Mary, died of polio while she was still in her teens. They adopted a son, James, who later became a successful actor (costarring in the long-running TV series *Hawaii Five-O,* among other roles in film and television) and the joy of their lives. I remember being with Helen in London in the 1950s, and she always carried pictures of her Charlie and her children in silver frames. She had the loveliest smile on her face when she said, "Here they are, the most beautiful people in the whole world."

Helen had a love-hate relationship with Queen Victoria. She had found great success on the stage playing the monarch, but one of the results was, she said, "My house in Nyack is crammed with Victorian junk. Don't let me buy any more." Yet on the return trip from Brighton we had a hard time getting another passenger in the car—a life-size statue of Queen Victoria that Helen just hadn't been able to resist.

Later still, in 1970, after Charlie had passed away and Anita and Helen were both living in New York, the two of them decided it would be fun to revisit their favorite New York haunts and discover new ones by doing a book together.

The result was *Twice Over Lightly: New York Then and Now.* It is hard to say if they had more fun writing it or promoting it, and I was able to travel with them because one of my own books, *The Beggars Are Coming,* was published at the same time. Mine was a Bantam Super Release, the first massively promoted, straight-to-paperback book, and it sold more than a million copies. Part of the promotion was a book tour, and both our books were handled by the wonderful publicist Jay Allen, who escorted us in and out of television and radio stations and to social events. Since Jay was six foot seven and Helen and Anita both hovered at five feet, he had a difficult time opening the door or lifting a drink without hitting them in the face with his elbow. We had a wonderful time together, but I think the best part for me was knowing Anita was so relieved by my success—I wasn't going to disgrace her or worry her by just writing for the movies. And watching those two wonderful women enjoying their later years was truly an inspiration.

Yet another character in Anita's kaleidoscope of favorite personalities was the party giver extraordinaire and con woman Elsa Maxwell. Others found it perplexing that such a Mack truck of a woman could rise to fame and some fortune by throwing parties for the rich, who certainly should be able to take care of themselves; but it made perfect sense to Anita, who explained it as follows in her personal papers:

> So many rich people, through never having to have exercised their resources, have no vitality. They can only feel alive by synthetically

taking on vitality with those who have an over abundance of it . . . through making a connection with the vital stream of someone else. Whatever Elsa is, these people quicken to life and connect with the surge of her own over-vitality. They live for the duration of that connection.

Not surprisingly, two of the people who depended most on Elsa for fun were the duke and duchess of Windsor. They counted on her to surround them with interesting people from all walks of life, down to the details of the invitation list, party favors, and themes that were the rage. Elsa often organized her parties under the guise of supporting charities such as the Free French, and only occasionally would questions be asked. However, it was noticed that the funds going to the French were minimal because most of the proceeds went to picking up Elsa's tab for her suite at the Plaza for the duration of her stay in New York, along with all the drinking and dining.

Elsa's close, longtime friend was Dorothy Fellows Gordon, a handsome, easygoing woman who had left such gentleman suitors as the current duke of Alba to follow Elsa's rocket action. With some inherited wealth of her own, Dickie, as everyone called her, bought a house in the south of France outside of Cannes, which became Elsa's base of operation when she wasn't traveling through the States or Europe.

Keeping on the move was a key to Elsa's success, and when she and Dickie arrived in Los Angeles, they often stayed with friends. Jean Howard told the story of Elsa camping at the home of Jack and Ann Warner when Ann, who always slept until noon, was awakened one morning by a call from the butler.

"Does Mrs. Warner plan on joining the lunch?"

"Lunch, what lunch? You know I never eat lunch."

"Well, Miss Maxwell wanted me to ask if you were joining your guests. She says she has invited almost fifty." All on the Warner's tab, of course.

So, even within Hollywood, Elsa had to keep moving, and therefore I was taken aback only a little when Anita informed me one day that

Dickie and Elsa were staying in her guest quarters. Elsa was writing a gossip column of sorts at the time, so she was always on the lookout for tidbits about the stars; but it seemed to me that she was her own favorite subject. She was the only woman I ever knew who literally carried her memoirs in her purse. She would guide conversation into something she had done, à la Oscar Wilde, and then pull out a clipping of some past success and read it aloud.

Anita was amused, but she didn't see her guests often. Elsa and Dickie slept in late, and Anita was up with the dawn to write. While she was at the studio, Elsa entertained guests at the house and, as Anita found out later, called all over the world using her hostess's phone. Dickie and Elsa left after a few weeks, off to New York on the Super Chief to free more French before the phone bill arrived.

So it was all the more astonishing when I answered the door the day after their departure to find an elegant delivery truck with an enormous package. To Anita's amazement Elsa, never known for reciprocating, had given her a splendid gift: a complete collection of Louis Vuitton luggage.

Anita used and enjoyed the luggage, and then, about a year later, we were sitting around her pool on a Sunday morning reading the newspapers. Anita suddenly let out a loud chortle. She handed me the page and pointed to the article revealing that a well-known luggage shop on Beverly Drive was suing Elsa Maxwell for a large unpaid bill for a set of Louis Vuitton.

Anita was still laughing. "Well, the luggage is secondhand now. And I know I am unique—I actually got something from Elsa. It was great fun and God love her, she is still out of jail."

And I still have and use one of the overnight cases.

While we are on the subject of outlandish women, there is one other set of Anita's friends I cannot resist including here, the Gabors.

Anita adored bigger-than-life characters who had created themselves, and that certainly describes the Gabors. Another reason they intrigued her was, as Anita said, "The Gabor family is composed of women who idealize sex and find it, in each and every one of its manifestations, utterly delightful."

In spite of the Gabors' outward attention to the supercilious, Anita found them genuine at the core. Always cerebral, Anita used her writing as a way to investigate and think about the Gabors' approach to love and men, so different from her own, and even went so far as to write the following opening to a play about them:

> *Act 1, scene 1: The party is over. The four are saying a quiet good night to the last guests to leave.*

JOLIE: We're one man women—but the tragedy is there's never a man who measures up to us. What kind of men do we attract? Pimps who think we have money that we haven't got . . . publicity seekers who want to ride into the El Morocco on our notoriety and get their names in the columns . . . weaklings who are so half-witted they really fall for us . . . But a MAN—a real man—Never!

But darlings, we are WOMEN. We're a hell of a fine type of women—there's more woman in one of us than there is in a whole roomful of American girls! I'm a whale of a woman . . . all my life I've been a whale of a woman . . . but have I ever even met a whale of a man? No!

When Einstein was looking for a wife, did he ever give me a tumble? Or General Mark Clark? Or Eisenhower? Or Winston Churchill?

All my life I've been temperamental, but do you know why? It is to plague the silly men I've gone with . . . to make them turn into men—the kind of men who would punch me in the nose. But what happened? They all became Mr. Jolie Gabor and it reminded them how ineffectual they were and they ran off with some nondescript female who made them look important.

JOLIE: (to Zsa Zsa) Are you happy?

ZSA ZSA: Happy? I'm the most miserable person in the whole world. I'm in love with a man I can never get—he doesn't even like women.

JOLIE: (to Magda) And you?

MAGDA: All I want in life is a home someplace in the country with children and dogs. I don't want to be glamorous! But when I'm not glamorous, I'm nothing! So I dress up like little Bo Peep and go to the party.

JOLIE: (to Eva) Are you happy?

EVA: Yes, Mamma, I am happy. When I get a part in a play or in a t.v. show and I am working in front of audiences and lights and wearing glamorous clothes—then I am happy.

JOLIE: If you don't want men, you are lucky. But take me. . . . I've been living a long time and I've had a lot of things. But there's just one thing I've found that brings completely delirious happiness. To sit at a table in a quiet place with a man who, for a moment, gives the illusion that he's in love with you—and, for a moment, he is. And you drink Tokay! And you listen to Hungarian music! And you eat delicious Hungarian food and you talk about love. How can anyone talk about love when you're eating a sandwich and a coke in a corner drug store? But moments like that, they are worth all the baseball games—all the t.v. shows—all the 4th of July celebrations . . . everything. And, if the man was only big enough to laugh at our nonsense . . . to think it was a big joke to be called Mr. Jolie Gabor . . . then it might go on forever and ever and we could find the one thing that makes life worth living . . . a perfect marriage.

Every time a man leaves one of us, it is like a funeral. And in my life, I have had fifty funerals! It's too much!

Jolie, the mother of the Gabor brood, had raised her daughters to be courtesans, and she herself was a definite role model in the way she enchanted men. To Jolie the zenith of romance was to sit in a restaurant listening to Hungarian music, eating great food, drinking fine wine, and listening to the compliments of her escort. The father of the girls had been left long ago and was rarely seen, but when I met him, I found he bore a remarkable resemblance to Conrad Hilton, one of Zsa Zsa's many husbands.

The Gabors arrived on American shores one by one, and the first to reach the United States was Zsa Zsa. She was running from an alliance with a Budapest big shot and, once here, managed to have such a remarkable success that it was obvious her sister Eva would follow. Among the men who found her delightful was Ernst Lubitsch, who gave her a break in films, and he basked in the joyfulness and ambition that always went with the girls. Eva, unlike her sister, was happier being on the stage or on a set than just being in the arms of an ardent lover.

Eva became hugely popular while starring as the wife on *Green Acres*, playing a character very much like her real self. Her costar, Eddie Albert, cherished her but on more than one occasion found her Hungarian sense of reality frustrating if bemusing. As an example, Eddie told me of the time they were ready to go before the *Green Acres* cameras when he caught his first glimpse of Eva's costume, a gorgeous negligee rimmed with thousands of marabou feathers. Eddie, ever the environmentalist, winced and told her, "Oh, I wish you wouldn't wear that."

"Don't you like it, dahling?" purred Eva.

"You are beautiful, but I am thinking of all the birds who died to create that gown. If you wear that on television, millions of women will want one just like it and millions of birds will die," Eddie pleaded rationally.

"Oh, darling," replied Eva. "These feathers don't come from birds—they come from pillows."

Yet under those ditsy exteriors lurked true pragmatists. After Zsa Zsa and Eva were firmly entrenched in America, they sent for their sister Magda.

Word leaked out yet another glamorous Gabor was about to dock, so photographers lined the gangplank, but Zsa Zsa and Eva were not about to let the world see Magda before they had a chance to do what they knew they had to do. They arranged to take the pilot boat to meet the liner as it entered the harbor and boarded before it docked. They found Magda, who had yet to develop her sense of timing, readying herself to be photographed.

Instead, her sisters hid Magda until all the other passengers and the disappointed photographers had dispersed, bundled her up, whisked her through the now almost empty customs, and into a waiting ambulance. From there it was straight to the hospital, where a plastic surgeon was in attendance to perform a nose job.

Three weeks later Magda was officially presented to the press as the third gorgeous Gabor sister.

New York at Last, 1944–1981

The fact that Anita had been released by MGM was slow to sink in. A part of her was excited to be free, but she also chafed under the uncertainty. Income came from a variety of freelance assignments, including work on a Dorothy McGuire story for Joe Schenck and a treatment for Darryl Zanuck. She also met with director Michael Curtiz about a rewrite on *Mildred Pierce*.

Her beloved father, R. Beers Loos, died in 1944, and although Anita continued to write almost every morning, she was depressed and wrote vaguely of feeling suicidal. She convinced herself that her salvation was in New York, and it was Helen Hayes, known primarily on Broadway for her portrayals of Queen Victoria and other period characters, who came to Anita's rescue. One day over lunch the two old friends were discussing their dilemmas, and Helen said they could both solve their problems if Anita wrote her a play where she could kick up her heels in modern-day clothes.

Originally titled *Addie Beamis*, after the main character, the renamed *Happy Birthday* went into rehearsals in New York in September of 1946. Rewrites and agonizing previews followed, but Anita was in her element. When the *New York Times* raved about the play and a "new" Helen Hayes, the line for tickets laced around the block. *Happy Birthday* ran for more than a year, and Anita was finally in New York to stay.

Now an established Broadway success, Anita began working on several plays, including one for ZaSu Pitts called *Mother Was a Lady*. Her coplaywright was Frances Marion, who had also given up on Hollywood and found a renewed love of life in New York. Both women were disciplined early risers, and Marion joked that Anita had been writing for several hours when "I drag in at six in the morning."[1] George Abbott

was set to produce *Mother Was a Lady,* but the play was pulled during
the tryouts in New Haven because of disagreements over the third act.
For once Anita wasn't crushed because she had already been approached
about turning *Gentlemen Prefer Blondes* into a Broadway musical. Anita
and composer Jule Styne saw Carol Channing in *Lend an Ear* on Broadway, and Anita said, "There's my Lorelei." She had to fight with the producers to cast Carol in the lead, explaining, "You can cast Lorelei two
ways, with the cutest, littlest, prettiest girl in town or with a comedienne's
comedy comment on the cutest, littlest, prettiest girl in town. I wrote
her as a comedy, and Broadway is attuned to satire."[2]

Carol was thrilled to land the part and tells the story of how Lorelei
had first impacted her life when she was a six-year-old girl in Seattle.
"The popularity of [the book] *Gentlemen Prefer Blondes* had so swept the
country that I just had to cut my own hair into a "boy's bob" just like
her heroine's. Little did I dream that twenty-four years later, Anita herself would take me by the hand to a leading New York salon to have it
bobbed again so that I could play her Lorelei on Broadway."[3]

One critic called Carol as Lorelei a "triumph of miscasting," but as
Carol's father pointed out to her, *triumph* was the key word. Featuring
Jule Styne's now classic songs such as "Diamonds Are a Girl's Best
Friend," *Gentlemen Prefer Blondes* opened in December of 1949 and ran
on Broadway for almost two years. The play also brought Anita a new
round of media attention, and she basked in being heralded as the tri-
umphant survivor that she indeed was.

Anita went to France in 1950 and collaborated with the grand dame
of French literature, Colette, on the play *Gigi.* One can only imagine the
conversations between these two women whose beginnings were so similar, who were both prolific from an early age, and who both had sup-
ported older men who claimed credit for their work.

George Cukor, a stage director before he had hit it big in Hollywood,
was set to direct *Gigi* on Broadway, but in the end he could not get out
of his film commitments. Anita was disappointed that "dear George"
would not be joining her in New York, but she and Colette were both

excited about their new discovery, Audrey Hepburn, to play the title role.[4] The rehearsals were bumpy, as always, but the play was a hit on opening night. Anita sold her play outright to Hollywood, and her old friend (and Marion Davies's nephew) Charlie Lederer adapted *Gigi* for the screen.

In 1951 Anita's novella *A Mouse Is Born* was published, and she adapted another Colette story, *Cheri,* into a play. Anita was in New York when Emerson, the hypochondriac who had claimed to be on the verge of death since the early teens, died at Las Encinas at the age of eighty-four in March of 1956. Except for one thousand dollars that he left to his nurse companion, Mrs. Butterworth, the estate went to Anita.

She continued to blame herself for the failure of her marriage for the rest of her life. When she was feeling particularly doleful, she would moan, "If only we'd remained sympathetic co-workers without the complications of marriage," and believed that her success had turned "a strong willed character I adored into a sick man."[5] We can only hope in her heart she knew better.

I have left it to Mary Anita and her firsthand accounts to give the reader details of Anita's friendships and romances, but the historian in me would like to set the record straight on one of the rumors that I ran across in researching the women behind the cameras in early Hollywood. Several people questioned Anita's sexual preference; after all, they conjectured, Anita was a friend of Greta Garbo's and of Garbo's lover, Mercedes de Acosta, as well as being a friend and neighbor of another of Garbo's close friends, the screenwriter Salka Viertel. Elsa Maxwell and her partner, Dickie Gordon, were friends and occasional houseguests, and Anita seemed very comfortable in the company of gays. From these coincidences some jumped to conclusions, even though there were no love letters or interviews with anyone claiming to have participated in or witnessed such relationships.

This did not stop some biographers of other figures from making assumptions about Anita's inclinations. For example, a Paulette Goddard biographer quoted Paulette as being irked because instead of coming to visit her, Anita stayed home to be with Gladys and a "Miss M." From that the biographer inferred Anita's involvement in an all-female ménage à trois. However, if the writer had done her homework, she would have learned that Gladys was Anita's housekeeper and that "Miss M" was the pet name for the housekeeper's adopted daughter.

Jumping to conclusions like that is particularly frustrating because they tend to be propagated once in print, yet I tried to keep an open mind to all possibilities. The first time I read through Anita's appointment books, I watched for notations that might signal an intriguing rendezvous, but there were none. I did, however, notice several weary, tear-stained references to being miserable over men, particularly Emerson, revealing that although she would publicly make light of his escapades, she had been genuinely crushed by them. Still, when I felt I had come to know Mary Anita well enough, I asked her if she thought there was a possibility that Anita had relationships with women.

"Oh no, no, no, no," Mary Anita insisted, shaking her head. Yet something was still bothering Mary Anita, and she surprised me with her clarification: "Not that Anita might not have been a lot happier if she had been. I can just see that tiny figure, almost fetal in an overstuffed chair, crying over some man. She so longed to be loved."[6]

Of course Anita was loved but, too often, not in the way she desired. Many intelligent men adored her as an equal and valued her as an intellectual playmate, but not as the lover she also wanted to be. So many pages of her musings and character ideas deal with the mysteries of relationships between men and women, and she never stopped trying to figure it out.

Anita was constantly at work on something, and her files contain innumerable partially completed plays and stories. In addition to *Old Buddha,* the play she had written for Ethel Barrymore about the last empress of China, there are half a dozen other complete plays that were never produced or only got to the preview stage.

The renowned Hollywood gossip columnist Louella Parsons is the subject of *The Gay Illiterate.* Using the same title of Louella's autobiography, Anita's dramatic comedy celebrates the "mystery" surrounding the notoriously ditsy yet smart-as-a-fox legend. Unorthodox, path-blazing, determined, self-absorbed, and disciplined, the character of Louella is showcased as a single mother and a film writer in Chicago in the teens before her rise to popularity and power.

Anita adapted Ludwig Bemelmans's book *To the One I Love the Best: Episodes from the Life of Lady Mendl* into a play she called *Every Girl Needs a Parlor*. Both the book and play focus on the later years of Elsie Mendl, bypassing the earlier time when, as Elsie de Wolfe, she shared homes and lifestyles with the international literary agent Elisabeth Marbury and became famous as one of America's first interior decorators, introducing chintz into thousands of living rooms. The delightfully eccentric Elsie surprised all her friends by marrying Sir Charles Mendl late in life, and the play is a comedic homage to the ramifications of their relationship and Elsie's unique personality. Anita's copy of the play lists Charlie MacArthur as the coplaywright, but never in her appointment books does she note enough time with MacArthur to reflect the time it would have taken for them to have actually written it together. More likely, he suggested the idea or passed the book on to her.

The Amazing Adele, a play about Fred Astaire's dancing sister and early partner, opened in Philadelphia in 1955 but never made it to Broadway. Anita also adapted *The King's Mare,* about King Henry VIII and his relationship with his wife, Anne of Cleves. Anita thought that the combination of the tall, German Anne and the short, rotund Henry, the queen's attempts to learn English and to improve her new country's cuisine, and the methods she employed to ensure she would live a full life, in contrast to Henry's other wives, provided many comedic possibilities. *The King's Mare* played briefly in London in 1968, and in spite of Anita's attempts to turn it into a musical called *Something about Anne* and to have it star her Broadway Lorelei, Carol Channing, the play never opened in the United States.

However, *The King's Mare* did allow Anita to have a grand trip to London and Paris with Carol Channing. "Anita spoke French fairly easily, and everything was new to me," remembers Channing, who had never been to France before.

> I saw my first bidet in our Paris hotel room, and of course I asked Anita what it was. "Well, dear," she explained, "first you have to understand that the French are the dirtiest people in the world. But there is one little place they believe in keeping clean. . . ."
>
> Anita was just so much fun to be with. She knew everyone, everywhere, and she kept that little body in shape through long walks and an hour a day at the ballet barre. Of course we went to the couturier salons. Sometimes we even wore matching Middy blouses. And there I was, six feet tall in heels, and there was tiny Anita. . . . I never actually saw us together and I never asked.[7]

In 1961 Anita satirized Hollywood in another novella, *No Mother to Guide Her. A Girl like I,* Anita's autobiography of her early years through the publication of *Gentlemen Prefer Blondes,* was published in 1966. Its light, gossipy tone covering the silent-film years sold very well, particularly in big cities. And again she garnered incredible publicity, both for her book and herself.

Anita enjoyed the company of old friends like Helen Hayes, and after Helen's husband, Charles MacArthur, died, Helen and Anita spent a year traveling around New York City together. They revisited old haunts and made new discoveries; the result was the delightful book *Twice Over Lightly.*

Another Hollywood veteran who kept up a busy pace in New York was Lillian Gish, and she and Anita often went to films together. They particularly enjoyed the retrospective screenings at the Museum of Modern Art, and Mary Lea Bandy, current director of the MOMA film department, says, "They were such fixtures going in and out that everyone just took them for granted. Can you imagine?"[8]

Jim Frasher, Lillian Gish's manager for the last thirty years of her life, looks back fondly on how Anita and Lillian enjoyed each other's company. "I remember one day we had a long drive and Anita regaled us with raucous tales of who was doing what to whom. As soon as we de-

livered Anita to her apartment, Lillian turned to me and said, in no un-
certain terms, 'Now you must never repeat those stories to anyone.' I was
crushed of course so I asked her, 'Are [the] stories not true?' 'Oh the stories are accurate enough,' Lillian replied. 'It's the people she gets wrong.'"
Jim still harbors the suspicion that the stories were deadly accurate on
all counts, but what Lillian said still goes. "And whether or not they were
true," he adds, "Anita was a wonderful story teller."[9]

Another "old" friend she saw often was Peter Duchin. His famous
bandleader father had died when Peter was in his early teens, and the
Harrimans had become his surrogate parents. Peter had grown into a
healthy, tall, classically good-looking young man, and Anita saw him
often at parties at the Harrimans' Sands Point, Long Island, home. He
also visited Anita at her apartment across the street from Carnegie Hall.
Anita, her housekeeper, Gladys, and Peter would trek to Harlem for
dancing, and when Peter began his career as a professional pianist and
orchestra leader at the Maisonette at the St. Regis in New York, Anita
was among his boosters. Rudy, the maître d' at the Maisonette, adored
Anita, and he referred to Anita and her friends like Marie Harriman
(whom Peter called "Ma"), Madeline Sherwood (widow of the writer
Robert Sherwood), and Virginia Chambers as "the girls," even though
they were all pushing seventy by this time.

"I remember one wonderful evening when 'the girls' came in and
were having a particularly good time," remembers Duchin. "Ma, Ginny,
Madeline, and Neetsie were sitting at a table, tearing down just about
everybody in the world and having a marvelous time. How they could
laugh. I came over and sat with them between sets and then again when
the show ended at two, but they were in no mood to go home. They
wanted something to eat, but when they were told the kitchen was closed,
Madeline said, 'Well, that shouldn't stop us.'"

With Rudy's cooperation the group ended up raiding the kitchen at
the St. Regis, and "at three in the morning, Ma, Neetsie, Ginny, Madeline, Rudy, and I sat down to a fabulous breakfast of buckwheat pan-
cakes and Dom Perignon."[10]

Anita was still taking years off her age when she claimed to be celebrating her eightieth birthday in 1973. It was really her eighty-fifth, but
she could have passed for seventy-five with her short hair and chic
clothes. In fact she wore a sable coat and carried a Gucci bag during an
interview the following year focusing on the publication of the second
volume of her autobiography, *Kiss Hollywood Good-bye*. Rarely shy with
opinions, Anita used the occasion to blast recent Broadway productions.
("Last night I went to Neil Simon's play. My God it was awful—crass,
unforgivable.") But just in case anyone might think she was out of sync
with the times, she praised the latest films, singling out Fellini and Lena
Wertmuller as "brilliant."[11]

Anita wrote two more books over the next few years, *The Talmadge
Girls,* celebrating Norma, Natalie, Constance, and their incredible mother,
Peg; and *A Cast of Thousands,* a delightful autobiographic large-sized pic-
ture book laced with vignettes about her friends and colleagues.

Cleaning out her files in 1980, Anita decided to auction many of the
letters she had kept over the years from other writers, including William
Faulkner, F. Scott Fitzgerald, Alice B. Toklas, Aldous Huxley, and H. G.
Wells. Many of these were letters between friends, but some, like those
from William Faulkner and H. L. Mencken, were in praise of *Gentlemen Prefer Blondes*.[12]

Anita's popularity and celebrity were still such that when she died of
heart failure on August 17, 1981, her obituary occupied a full page in the
New York Times and in many papers throughout the country. She had
been fibbing for so long and so often about her age, many newspapers
didn't know what to do, and she was dubbed every age from seventy-
nine to ninety-one. In reality she was ninety-three.

Having left instructions that she wanted no one to cry, friends and
Mary Anita arranged a memorial service where tales were told and the
laughs kept coming through the tears. Another tribute to Anita's popularity: the memorial service received full coverage in *Variety*. The
speeches from that memorial service constitute the final chapter of this
book. Space does not allow us to include one of Anita's full-length plays,

but what follows here are several of the short stories and one-act plays Anita turned out in her "spare time" in New York.

It Pays to Advertise is a satiric spoof of the upper classes. Although Anita was pleased to consider herself a New Yorker, and joined in putting down Hollywood, she poked gentle fun at her new home as well. She found New Yorkers in some ways as celebrity conscious as her friends on the West Coast. And she was always bemused over the upper class's need for someone like her friend Elsa Maxwell to instruct them on how to entertain themselves.

One More Heroine is a character study of a lonely woman and an injured veteran who live for each other but never actually meet. Anita enjoyed writing the occasional story that would not be subjected to a producer's whims, actor's revisions, or director's changes. In *One More Heroine,* and in the story that follows it here, *Mr. Sherard,* Anita was able to paint descriptions without concern for set decorators and to create situations that didn't require camera pans or fadeouts.

In *Mr. Sherard* Anita contrasts the outlooks and expectations of young people and those near the end of their lives. She poignantly investigates the impact of assumptions and the lack of communication on couples. In *Mr. Sherard* advice is easy to give and difficult to actually apply to one's own life.

Both *Mr. Sherard* and *One More Heroine* are heartfelt stories without the happy ending required by the movies. Although both have their own twists, they are very unlike the cute little twist-of-fate stories Anita wrote from her home in San Diego fifty years before. These stories are written by a woman who has seen the world, been disillusioned in love, appreciates the importance of friends, and is no longer looking for simple answers to complex questions.

Cari Beauchamp

It Pays to Advertise

A one act play by Anita Loos

*The setting is the red and gold salon of the old REVELL home
in the once ultra-aristocratic Murray Hill district of NEW
YORK.*

*The atmosphere breathes long-standing tradition, and
an elegance that has stood a little too long. The room is filled
with family portraits autographed, photographs on royalty,
furniture that was once elegant and old fashioned objets d'art.
But everything is desperately run down.*

*Seated R, is Mrs. REVELL, aged 52. She belongs to the
elegant nineties, and is of a fine old family, but she is not very
bright and is in a constant daze over the terrible things that go
on in modern life. An utterly helpless, fussy old girl, completely
at loose ends about everything. She is nervously and desperately
biting her fingernails and looking helplessly about.*

*Enter JULIAN REVELL, her husband, who hasn't been
sober since 1890. He is not in a staggering state, but only a
bit unconscious and likely to doze off the moment he is seated.
It is also rather difficult for him to finish a sentence, as he can
never remember what he started out to say. The only subject
that really touches his heart is the subject of liquor.*

JULIAN: (brightly) Well, my dear? They said that you wanted to see me.

MRS. REVELL: (almost on the verge of tears) I wish you wouldn't be so cheerful, Julian. Our daughter didn't get in again this morning until ten o'clock.

JULIAN: (starting out to be serious and fatherly) What? Ten o'clock this morning? Well-Well-Well. (by this time he has forgotten his outraged father's mood, and wanders off into speculation) She must know some good places!

MRS. REVELL: (more hurt than angry) Julian, do try to concentrate! I fear that the worst has happened to our child.

JULIAN: Dear me—You don't tell me!

MRS. REVELL: I've tried to overlook Judy staying out all night, and going to terrible parties, because all of the other girls do it.

JULIAN: Very rowdy of them. Should be stopped!

MRS. REVELL: But this morning I found out that she is accepting money from a strange man!

JULIAN: You don't mean to say!

MRS. REVELL: Our daughter—a REVELL whose great-grandmother carried water to the Continental troupes on Morristown Heights.

JULIAN: (breaking in) Should have carried brandy my dear. Nothing better for fighting men than a good stiff hooker of brandy.

MRS. REVELL: (almost in despair) Julian! Will you try to concentrate! We've got to have a family conference on the subject of Judy. I've sent for Cousin Connie.

JULIAN: Ah yes. Cousin Connie—married some titled fellow—crowned heads of Europe, I believe—

MRS. REVELL: She hasn't been home for fifteen years—what will she think of America?

JULIAN: Gone to the dogs—Ashamed to have her see it!

MRS. REVELL: What will she think of Judy, a debutante who—who—who stays out all night—who accepts money from strange men!

JULIAN: It's a terrible thing—ought to be stopped—girls taking money from men—has cost me a devil of a lot in my day.

MRS. REVELL: What did you say?

JULIAN: (realizing he has said too much) I said it's a terrible thing, ought to be stopped. Just give her a good talking to—wait till I see her—(Judy enters—a very pretty flapper of 19—very angry—holding out a small evening bag)

JUDY: Mother—somebody's been going through my evening bag—and stolen a check for two thousand dollars.

MRS. REVELL: I don't deny it, Judy. Your actions do not warrant that your parents trust you any longer. We never know where you are or what you are doing. I began to fear the worst. I went through your things and I find you accepting money from strange men.

JUDY: Yes—and the Revells have been broke for years—I'm the only one I know that's been able to go out and sell myself.

MRS. REVELL: Judy!!

JUDY: Besides if you'll be patient you'll find out about it—because it's going to be spread over all the newspapers soon enough.

MRS. REVELL: Judy!

(Enter Cousin Connie, an American—a very smart woman of the world married to a titled European—She is in America for the first time in 15 years.)

COUSIN CONNIE: (entering, full of spirit—she has overheard Judy's last words) What's going to be spread all over the newspapers? Some delicious scandal I hope.

MRS. REVELL: (rushing up to greet her) Connie. Welcome home. (looking her over) Why you haven't changed a bit!

CONNIE: Why should I? Japanese massage darling, paraffin baths, and a marvelous new system of slapping the face into shape; (noting Julian who is asleep) Don't tell me that's Julian!

MRS. REVELL: (running to Julian and shaking him) Julian! Julian! Wake up. It's Connie—back home after fifteen years!

JULIAN: (waking up) Connie? Connie back home? Didn't know she'd left.

CONNIE: Julian darling! (rushing over and kissing him; then signifying that his breath is pretty strong with liquor) Whew! (to Mrs. Revell) why the blessed lamb hasn't heard of prohibition!

MRS. REVELL: I've tried to tell him; but he won't listen.

CONNIE: (looking about and spotting Judy, who stands sullenly upstage)—And so this is Judy?

MRS. REVELL: Judy, go greet your aunt.

JUDY: (still sullen, goes up and gives Connie a cool kiss) Welcome home, Aunt Connie.

CONNIE: Thank you my dear. (She stands back a step in order to look Judy over—then to Mrs. Revell) She's not bad—not bad at all! (to Judy) Turn around child; (Judy sullenly turns around) Now let's see your knees. (Judy ungraciously raises her skirt about two inches—Connie turns to Mrs. Revell) Never want to judge a girl from the knees down—bathing suits are too important—H'mm. Not half bad. Ought to be able to do something with her! (to Judy) Are you what is known as a good girl?

MRS. REVELL: (bursting into tears) That's just what we want you to help us find out!

CONNIE: Dear me! Dear me! Why what's all this?

MRS. REVELL: We've every reason to believe the worst.

CONNIE: Judy, I hate to be a prig—but if you've lost your good name it's a great mistake. Wouldn't matter in the least if you had any talent—but you debutantes who have nothing but a good name certainly ought to hang on to it. (Judy turns stubbornly away.)

MRS. REVELL: Oh Connie—The things that have happened in America since you were a debutante!

CONNIE: Yes I must say I notice a change. When I was a young thing the drinking was all done by men at stag parties, or in their own clubs. None of us girls ever saw any of the fun. Now I find everybody getting tight together— right in your own salons—and no end of amusement—but very bad for matrimony!

MRS. REVELL: It's fatal!

JUDY: I don't know why I have to get married—I have much more fun being free.

MRS. REVELL: Listen to her!

CONNIE: It's amazing! Fifteen years ago if a man was caught kissing a girl without proposing, her family forced him

to marry at the point of a gun. Today even the classic
excuse for a military wedding doesn't hold good.

JUDY: Well, I think things are much better as they are now.

CONNIE: I agree with you in a way—more amusements—better
scandals, lower and funnier conversation—but how
is a poor girl with no ability going to hook herself a
husband?

MRS. REVELL: That's what I tell her—it's terrible. She didn't get
in this morning until ten o'clock.

CONNIE: Ten o'clock? Oh that's ridiculous, child. Don't you
know there's no fun to be had after six?

JUDY: I wasn't out for fun—I was out for money.

CONNIE: Ah well . . . that's different. And, how much can you
make on a night of work?

MRS. REVELL: This morning I went through her things and found
a check for two thousand dollars.

CONNIE: Two thousand? Well, it's been done for less. Who was
the—uh purchaser?

MRS. REVELL: (fishing in her dress and pulling out a check) It's signed
with the name of a strange man.

CONNIE: Let's see it. (she takes the check and reads) "Pay to
the order of Judy Revell, two thousand dollars," signed
Herman Glickman. Herman Glickman! There's romance for you! (Judy turns sullenly away) Judy, who
is Herman Glickman? Is he handing out two thousand
dollars for nothing?

JULIAN: (coming to life) What's that? Two thousand dollars for
nothing?

CONNIE: Shut up Julian. This is going to be interesting. After all
that these flappers give away gratis, I'm dying to hear
what they'll do for two thousand dollars.

JUDY: (defiantly) I don't consider that it's anybody's business but my own.

MRS. REVELL: (going to Julian) Oh Julian, can't you do something? Try to realize that your daughter's good name is gone beyond recall.

JULIAN: (rousing himself) Just so! Just so! (to Judy) I think that you, my daughter, should so far forget her good name as to—as to—as to . . .

JUDY: Yes, father—go on.

JULIAN: Exactly—best apples in the world—right on the old Revell place in Reinebech—best hard cider in the world! (he relapses into complete contentment)

CONNIE: (to Judy) Where did you pick up this—this Herman Glickman?

JUDY: I met him at a cabaret up in Harlem with the Duchess of Dexter.

CONNIE: What? With Dolly Dexter?

JUDY: Yes, she has been chasing after him for weeks.

MRS. REVELL: You see what goes on in America!

CONNIE: Well, Herman Glickman must have charm because I have never known Dolly Dexter to waste her time.

JUDY: He's not supposed to be charming, but he does pay— the Duchess got five thousand out of him.

CONNIE: Might I be permitted to ask what Dolly Dexter delivered for five thousand dollars?

JUDY: Well, she didn't have to do as much as I did, but then she has a title. And Herman is crazy for titles so he considered that she was quite a feather in his cap.

CONNIE: I'll be bound! Are we to understand that you took Herman away from the Duchess?

JUDY: She didn't mind. She was through with him.

MRS. REVELL: You see!

CONNIE: Now look here Judy—after all, you owe something to your family and you've worked my curiosity up to a pitch where I can't control it much longer. What did you and Herman Glickman do at ten o'clock in the morning?

JUDY: I'm not going to tell because you'll all make a furious fuss and really—it isn't anything.

CONNIE: On Park Avenue, evidently not!

JUDY: He simply made me a proposition and I agreed.

CONNIE: For two thousand dollars!

JUDY: And we spent the night out in order for him to get into his office this morning, for the money, then we had breakfast at the Astor and came home.

CONNIE: (to Mrs. Revell) Well, Emma, do you want to hear more?

MRS. REVELL: Is—is—this Glickman married?

JUDY: How should I know? I don't know anything about him really—except that he's the best advertising agent in New York. And his proposition was all right.

CONNIE: I think I'm beginning to tumble, so Judy, you might as well tell the whole story—go on—there's a good girl.

JUDY: Oh, all right! I signed a paper allowing him to use my name and photograph and pedigree in some very high class advertisements that go into the best magazines saying that I have been cured of seborrhea.

MRS. REVELL: (gasping—but hardly understanding) What's seborrhea?

JUDY: Well, it's something to do with the breath.

CONNIE: (to Mrs. Revell) But you'll never know whether you

	have it or not, Emma, because I've read those advertisements and they say that your best friend won't tell you.
MRS. REVELL:	I think I'm going to faint.
JULIAN:	Quick—some whisky. (He pulls a flask out of his pocket, uncorks it and takes a drink.)
MRS. REVELL:	When I think that a Revell—a direct descendant of Georginaud Revell of Morrison Heights—could—Oh—it's so terrible!
JUDY:	I knew just what would happen if I told you and I'm not going to stay here to be insulted by petty minds.
CONNIE:	And why should you when every first class magazine in America will soon be on the job?
JUDY:	(to Connie) I must say, Aunt Connie, I did think that you would understand!
CONNIE:	(thinking a moment) As a matter of fact, Emma, perhaps we are taking this thing too seriously.
MRS. REVELL:	Connie! How could it be worse?
CONNIE:	Easily! The advertisement says that she's been cured of seborrhea. Suppose it said she still had it!
JUDY:	Oh mother—it isn't as if I were the only one who ever did it. (picking up a magazine) Why this magazine is full of people we know.
CONNIE:	(thinking very deeply) Let me see it. (She takes the magazine and starts to look through it.)
JUDY:	The Queen of Numania gets as much as twenty-five thousand for an advertisement.
MRS. REVELL:	The Queen of Numania!
JUDY:	Certainly—because she is royalty. And the Duchess of Dexter is worth real money too—but with our ancestry, they only pay two thousand.
MRS. REVELL:	Our ancestry? Why we're the best name in America!

JUDY: Yes, but what does an American name count for anyway. We only date back a hundred years or so. If we had a really old name, we would be worth more money to this cure for seborrhea.

MRS. REVELL: Judy! Does your ancestry mean no more to you than that?

JUDY: Well, mother, what else can ancestry do for you these days?

CONNIE: (looking up from her magazine) She's right. Why this is marvelous! The best names in America sold out to silverware, stationery, dressing tables, curtains, cold cream, yeast, radios and radiators. (turning to Judy) What's the address of Herman Glickman?

MRS. REVELL: CONNIE! You're not thinking . . .

CONNIE: Why not? If Judy's name is worth two thousand, that moneyed title of mine ought easily to bring five.

MRS. REVELL: Connie!

CONNIE: As for you Emma . . . How about a kind word from you about—let's see—(flips through magazine)— bathroom fixtures?

MRS. REVELL: (going over to Julian who again is asleep) Julian, Julian, wake up! Connie is insulting me—She is suggesting that I sell my good name!

JULIAN: (opening one eye and looking her over, then shaking his head) You'll never find a taker!

CONNIE: Julian! Come to life will you—Here's a chance to clean up.

JULIAN: What? Where?

CONNIE: (handing him the magazine) Here! Look at that! (quoting from the magazine) "Well-known man about town regulated by yeast!"

JUDY: Oh yes, that yeast company pays three thousand.

JULIAN: Three thousand? For what?

JUDY: For anyone who's been cured by yeast.

JULIAN: All right, where do I collect?

MRS. REVELL: Julian!

CONNIE: (handing her the magazine) Emma, just look what Julian will get, a beautiful full page advertisement all in color.

MRS. REVELL: (looking like a ghost) Why—why—that picture shows the man's insides.

CONNIE: You should be proud. It will be the first time in history that anyone ever suggested that Julian had anything in him.

MRS. REVELL: I'll die of shame!

CONNIE: Shame? Nothing! It's just nerves . . . (flips through the magazine again) All you need is—let me see—ah, yes, here it is—Sanatogen—Look at what it did for Mollie Vanderlip (Mrs. Revell turns away, hurt) Removed her double chin and left the dimple. Marvelous!

JUDY: Well, I'm sorry, Aunt Connie, but I can't stay on . . . I've got to go and get dressed.

MRS. REVELL: You're not taking one step out of this house again unchaperoned.

JUDY: Mother, don't be stupid. I'm going to the Joshua Alderson lunch for the Bishop.

MRS. REVELL: Now I know you're lying to me—wild horses wouldn't drag you to a lunch for the Bishop.

JUDY: Maybe not—But I had to promise Herman Glickman that if he advertised me as socially prominent I'd change my way of living! Now I have to accept every dull exclusive invitation that comes my way.

CONNIE: Why, Emma—listen to the child. This is wonderful. Neither you nor Julian have been able to do anything with her. Judy's breeding, education and family name—none have been enough to keep her from going rowdy. Now along comes Herman Glickman and for two thousand dollars and a little publicity, she is willing to step up to her position in society. I think you owe him a big vote of thanks.

MRS. REVELL: Oh, I don't know what to think!

CONNIE: (to Judy) Run along now child, don't be late for the dear Bishop—and bless you. (she kisses Judy—Judy exits)

MRS. REVELL: Oh dear—do you really think she'll lunch with the Bishop?

CONNIE: Certainly—I think your troubles with Judy are practically over. And now, Emma, don't you be a fool all your life. (opening magazine) Here's some magnificent coconut oil—excellent for the hair. All it needs is a life sized reproduction of that false front of yours to bring it to the attention of every sales girl that rides the subway. Come on now!

MRS. REVELL: Never. I've never used anything on my hair in my life.

CONNIE: Then it's time you did. Don't spoil this beautiful morning by holding out on us.

MRS. REVELL: (walking) But never has our family done anything like this before.

CONNIE: Yes, well, our family hasn't done a darn thing worth anyone's notice since great-great grandmother carried water to the Continentals on Morrison Heights. And here is an opportunity for you to carry oil to those who are fighting just as hard to keep their hair.

MRS. REVELL: But Connie . . .

CONNIE: Emma, it's your duty!

MRS. REVELL: Well, if you put it that way, I might buy some and if it did do my hair some good, I suppose I ought to let the American people know about it.

CONNIE: That's the girl. It might not do it a darn bit of good, but nothing in life could make it look worse—and think of the money.

MRS. REVELL: Yes, but still, it does seem horrible. What is society coming to? Where is breeding? Where is pride? Where is privilege?

CONNIE: Don't be silly. Where is Herman Glickman?

(She grabs Julian and Mrs. Revell and they all start for the door.)

CURTAIN

One More Heroine

It has always been my boast that I have kept a respectable house. It's hard enough to do as any landlady in Philadelphia can tell you, but my lodgers have always been just the same to me as members of my own family. I've always watched their comings and goings and seen to it that they kept out of mischief just the same as though they were my own children. I seldom have anyone for very long, which, of course, is because it is a transient neighborhood. That's the reason why I have to be so careful. But when the one lodger I could have banked on, a woman I have known intimately for fifteen years, who was everything that a good Christian ought to be, suddenly becomes a hussy over night, spends her savings on immodest, colored undergarments, and dies under the most awful circumstances, causing my house to be investigated, I simply give up. I'm through with trying to understand human nature.

Ella Craigen first came to me fifteen years ago—and she wasn't an entire stranger then. She was an old friend of Cousin Abbie's who sent her to me because she was a stranger in Philadelphia and wanted a quiet, respectable place to live. I saw at once that she was a good girl. Her eyes weren't exactly crossed but they had a sort of cast in them. She was very thin and pale. She had a sharp nose, very light blue eyes and thin lips and was not given much to talk. She had a position teaching—which she held with honor up to the end. That shows what the Board of Education thought about her!

As I say—she was everything that a good girl ought to be, all those years until the end. There was only one thing about her that might have given me a clue. She did have beautiful hair. It was long and golden and very thick—although I will say that she never made a boast of it and always wore it straight back in a very modest, unbecoming bun. I suppose if I had been a professor of psychology that hair might have given me a clue.

When I think of her as she was all those years! I thought—in fact we all thought—that she was the most modest creature in the world. The men all used to notice it. I never knew she spoke to a man for over a minute in all her life. She always pretended to have the greatest contempt for them and although she was so modest and all, I think she could have held her own against any of them. She had that sort of constant, righteous indignation that God gives good women for their defense in this world.

Not only was she self-respecting and quiet but she had a very bad case of heart trouble that made her all the more retiring. She had to be very careful to keep from excitement of any kind and always took two minutes to climb the stairs. She used to do it with her watch in her hand.

After she had been with me about two years, we became quite friendly. She took the Nautulus [*sic*] and I took the *Ladies' Home Journal* and she used to come downstairs two or three times a week and read aloud while I did my mending. She was great on improving the mind, and never did anything without making sure it would benefit her.

She used to read the *Ladies' Home Journal* from cover to cover to me, but always skipped the radical parts about sex and hygiene and such things. I'm just telling this to show how she fooled me for fifteen years.

She never had a male caller, and very few women ones. There were other teachers who used to call once in a while when she was sick. About the only mail she got was a few motto post cards at holiday times. She had these mottos hung all over her room. She was very advanced on New Thought lines.

The first time I ever knew her to take any interest in men, whatso-
ever, was after the war started and then, of course, we were all trying to
help the soldier boys, so I didn't think anything of it. She used to sit in
her room night after night till sometimes one and two o'clock making
New Thought scrapbooks for the wounded boys. She would get all
worked up making them—she was terribly patriotic. I used to go up
and try to make her go to bed. Her cheeks used to blaze and her eyes
sparkle and I know it was bad for her heart. But she wouldn't listen to
me. She used to say, "What is this in comparison with what those brave
boys are doing over there?"

She really became half daft about the war. She had a map in her room
and followed up every day with colored pins.

When the wounded boys started coming back she got worse. She used
to turn out New Thought scrapbooks at the rate of two a week. It took
a good deal of her money, too.

When the restrictions began she did more than her duty. She wouldn't
touch sugar or meat and she got along with scarcely any heat or light.
But in spite of everything, her health seemed to be improving—she had
color all the time—and life. She was all stirred up.

Then an incident happened—it was about the light restrictions. It always took her about twenty minutes to comb her hair in the morning as
she was very neat about keeping it clean and healthy. When the light re-
striction went on she wouldn't turn on the electricity in the morning and
her room being so little and dark with only one window, she had to stand
right in the window to get enough light to see at all.

Right across the street is a big hotel—the Touraine. One morning as
she was combing her hair at the window she looked across and saw the
boldest, foreign looking man, sitting in the window—*in his night shirt,*
glaring right at her. She was terribly mad (or so at least she told me) and
she motioned him to get away but he only grinned and went right on.
She tried to draw the swiss curtain but then she couldn't see to put on
her hair tonic—so she had to go and put on her waist and collar and
comb her hair that way with him leering over at her all the time. She

came downstairs and told me that it was disgraceful that this grinning foreign monkey could spend his time like this when our boys were fighting and dying over there. She never had much use for foreigners—and I think this was the first time she had ever been insulted by a man. She *seemed* terribly upset—and I believed her.

She worked longer than ever on her New Thought books that night.

The next morning when she came downstairs she was almost pretty, she was so lit up and excited. In the first place this foreign monkey had been at the window and behaved exactly like he did the morning before. That made her mad. But what made her excited was that they had phoned from the hospital that she could come down and help entertain the wounded boys. She had made application months before. She had three of her New Thought scrapbooks under her arm and was going down straight from school to read to the boys out of them.

I told her to be careful of her heart—but she said the doctor told her that it was lots better. She had never felt so well in her life. And she sailed off.

I could hardly wait for her to come in at dinner time. I heard several go upstairs—but no one went slow enough to be her. It got to be eight o'clock. Finally I heard young Mr. Rance come in. He went to the hospital often to see one of his friends, so I went out into the hall and asked him if he'd been there. He had, so I asked him did he see Miss Craigen. He said yes, and told me what happened.

It seems the boys weren't advanced enough to appreciate her New Thought books and there were some variety girl singers down there—all painted up and singing ragtime songs—so they didn't pay any attention to her at all.

I rushed upstairs and listened at her door. Sure enough—she was in there—crying. She felt she couldn't face me and had *run* upstairs so I wouldn't know she had come in. I didn't know what to say, so I just tiptoed back again.

The next morning when she came down, she didn't say a word about what happened. But she didn't look like she had for the last few months.

She was pale and tired looking. But she was terribly indignant. The foreigner was still at the window in the Touraine. I think she was a little bit glad to have this to talk about as it covered up the other and how the boys didn't appreciate the New Thought. She went on quite a tirade about men, about how common their tastes were, and this one in particular, and said she'd show him his place if it was the last thing she did.

That night, without a word, she came downstairs with her magazine and we had our evening just as though the war had never broken in. There was no talk of scrapbooks, and I noticed she tried to skip everything in the magazine about soldiers. That was our last night! When she went to go upstairs she told me that she was not going to endure the foreigner another day. She had done the best she knew how to help men and they didn't seem to appreciate it and she wasn't going to let one of them make her life miserable.

She went out earlier than usual the next morning, and I watched out of the front window to see what she did. Sure enough—she went into the Touraine. She stayed there about fifteen minutes and when she came out her face was set and white. She went around the corner and I lost sight of her.

She came in at the usual time that night—went upstairs as usual, taking two minutes. I could hardly wait to get up to her room and find out what she had done to that foreigner—but when I got there she didn't seem to want to talk. She was putting something away in the bureau drawer (I found out later what it was, the sly thing). She said she wanted to be quiet and go to bed so I left her.

Then came the morning! What a morning. Never again will I believe in *anybody.*

She did not come down at her usual time. It got later and later and I began to be worried. Finally I went upstairs and knocked. There was no answer. I knocked again. No answer. I opened the door with my pass key and walked in. There she sat—at the window. Her hair was down— it did look beautiful. But she was clothed in the most brazen pink colored undergarment. From the waist up she might as well have had nothing on at all. Her face was smeared with rouge! I stood rooted to the spot. Finally I got my breath and said "Ella Craigen!" She didn't answer. I went over to her. I shook her. Her shoulder felt like ice. She was dead. Her heart at last! But on the threshold of death she *had gotten herself up regardless in order to attract that foreigner across the street.* And she had pretended all the time to hate him—she had gone over to the hotel on the pretense of complaining about him—and probably all the time it was only to see him closer. I was simply stunned but I did have sense enough to cover up her naked body and put her on the bed before I called for help.

We sent across to the Touraine for Dr. Gregory. Before he got here I had rubbed the paint off her face and had her in a decent flannel nightgown.

He was quite interested in the case—it seemed as if he had seen her before—although I didn't think she ever went to him. I told him she died decently in bed—that was a white lie, Heaven knows! He said that it was her heart—that she showed evidences of an emotional struggle of some sort. He could tell that because her nails had dug into the flesh of her palms and her face was all contorted. I knew this was because her better nature had come to and the spirit had probably done its best to fight the flesh before she passed on.

We finally got her buried quietly. But that woman certainly spoiled my belief in human nature. I am through with taking chances.

. . .

Dr. Gregory dropped into his club that evening after a trying day. He had had two deaths—one of them a heart case, a little old maid school teacher with whom he had had a peculiar experience the day before. The other was Lieutenant Bellini, the famous Italian Ace who had been confined in his rooms at the Hotel Touraine for several months—a victim of shell shock.

The Italian was an adorable boy—sweet, warm of nature and child-like. The doctor had learned to love him, as had everyone with whom the lonely, whimsical foreigner had come in contact.

The doctor felt talkative and made his way toward a friend.

"I see that Bellini died," the friend said as he looked up from his newspaper. The doctor settled himself in the easy chair, lit a cigar and began his story.

"Today," he said, "I saw death take two of the most contrasting natures—with a strange bond between them." The friend was interested and put down his paper.

"Young Bellini had been in a bad way, nervously, for months!" said Dr. Gregory, "when, one morning I found him almost normal and quiet. Then he told me what brought it about. It seems that there was a woman in a cheap lodging house across the street who had appeared at her window and combed her beautiful yellow hair. Bellini had been terribly homesick, and the sight of that hair brought to his mind a little sweetheart he had had once in Venice. It cheered him so that he spent one whole happy morning—and even in the afternoon when his attacks came back, he kept amused, wondering if the girl would be there the next day. Sure enough she was—and every day after—and Bellini watched her and found calm and contentment. Of course, I knew he couldn't pull through—but I was grateful for those few cheerful moments he had.

"Yesterday I was in the parlor of his suite talking with the nurse when someone knocked. It was the owner of the hair come over to complain and say that if the boy's interest in her didn't stop she would report it to the hotel.

"She was a poor, little, faded out school teacher—with this incongruous mop of what one might almost call voluptuous, golden hair. Puritan—of course, to the finger tips, and full of righteous indignation. I explained things to her and told her that if she was able to give this poor soldier a little camouflaged thrill, she ought to be happy to do it and mark it down as war work. I described the little Venetian sweetheart sitting in the window in her rose chemise (as Bellini had described her to me), smiling down on him as he lay in bed in the late mornings. I asked her why she couldn't go on combing her beautiful hair and bringing back those happy days to the poor boy. Of course, that shocked her—poor soul!" The doctor smiled, reminiscently. "I didn't mind shocking her a little bit—perhaps a good shock administered in early life might have made a human being of her. She was far from unattractive, in a way. However, she was a true product of Puritan training and outraged to the very soul. She began to cry and said that men were beasts and that they didn't want good women to lift them to higher things.

"It was useless to argue with her and I was in a hurry so I patted her on the shoulder, told her to think things over and see if she could find it in her heart not to blame the poor homesick boy who had given his life to his country. She made some curt reply about men in general, Bellini in particular, added a little slam at me, en passant, and left with a set, hard expression on her face.

"This morning, early, I was called over to the lodging house and found that the poor soul had passed away. Her heart had been in bad shape for years and she had evidently suffered some shock that brought on the final attack.

"I no sooner got back to the hotel than I was called up to Bellini's room. He had had a bad night but had quieted toward morning. The nurse left him, and, hearing no sound from his room, had not entered it until seven-thirty. When she did go in, she found him seated at his window, dead, his eyes staring out across the street, with a serene and beautiful smile on his face. But the most we could have asked for him was granted. He had a peaceful death."

THE END

Mr. Sherard

Mister Sherard was dying. There was no doubt of that. He lay awake and feebly restless in his small room at the hospital. A young nurse was seated near by in a flood of light that poured down from under a newspaper that was pinned as a shade on the electric lamp, making a sharp shadow and leaving the remainder of the room in twilight. She was fidgeting, too. It had long been her patient's habit to sleep through this hour, and she had hoped to escape for a few moments, steal out, and in the dark shadow of the cozy church that shared a city block with the hospital, meet her young man whose cautious whistle now faintly reached her ears. Nervously she fingered a small box in her pocket. In it was an opal and diamond stickpin which she had brought as a surprise for his birthday. She kept looking over in exasperation toward Mister Sherard and noted each time that he was still awake.

His entrance into the hospital a few days before had caused something of a flurry. The fact of his illness had prompted newspapers to dig up the half-forgotten story of his romance and elopement with the wife of an English captain who had been a stage favorite and great beauty of her day. The beauty had followed him off to China, in the most romantic manner, sacrificing reputation, country, husband, friends and a still possible career, but about the time the English captain freed her by divorce, a fresh scandal broke out in which she publicly accused her handsome lover, banteringly nicknamed in the journals of that day "Dashy-Eyed" Horace Sherard, of a liaison with one of her friends, an Austrian countess. It was finally denied, however, even by the beauty herself, who set the charge down to an attack of temperament. The Countess left China and went back to Austria. The two were married and settled in Peking, where Sherard managed to fill his time artistically enough because of a fine appreciation of horses, wine and cards. Still beautiful, Mrs. Sherard died some few years later of delirium tremens and nothing more was publicly known of Mister Sherard, because after that he had buried himself in Vienna.

Years passed, and at the age of fifty-two he had come back to New York to attend to matters involving an estate, had been stricken with heart trouble, and now he was dying. And so this hero of a romantic love affair was welcomed into the hospital with a flutter of curiosity on the part of the nurses. But he did not prove an interesting patient. He had none of the garrulity of the invalid, and in fact spent a great deal of time sleeping.

Tonight, however, he would not sleep. He lay there, in his fine frilled linen nightshirt, looking like a clean-shaven, white Mephisto. The nurse was growing frantic. She heard again the faint whistle of her young man and wondered how much longer he would wait. She finally took the little jewel box from her pocket and stole a look at the stick pin. Light struck the opal and glanced off straight into the eyes of Mister Sherard.

"An opal?" he inquired.

The nurse jumped at the sound of his voice. She looked up and noticed that he was feebly holding out his waxy hand. She took the pin from its box and brought it to him.

"It's only an opal," she said, as though an opal had to be apologized for, "but it's surrounded with diamonds."

He took it and looked at it curiously while she adjusted the shade on the lamp so that he could see it better. Finally he handed it back.

"It's for—?" he stopped and looked up.

The nurse was pleased and self-conscious.

"For my—beau," she answered.

For a moment Sherard thought—and then with an altogether un-called for emotion he gasped.

"Don't give it to him!"

The nurse was surprised. This was unlike her quiet patient. Then a flicker of understanding crossed her face.

"Oh, I see. You're superstitious. But it's all right. It's his birthstone."

Sherard, still peculiarly impatient, said:

"I wasn't thinking of that." Then, "Don't give it to him," he whined.

The nurse didn't know whether to be interested or not. Probably he was merely out of his mind. However, she ventured a query. In answer to which he said with feeble vehemence:

"It cost too much!"

The nurse decided to humor him. Not, however, to the extent of giv-ing up an argument. She smiled.

"I enjoyed saving for it," she said.

"Of course you did," he answered impatiently. "That's your woman's nature. You enjoy making sacrifices."

"That's right—all right," she broke in glibly.

"Then you've had your fun out of it! Be satisfied! Throw it away!"

Thoroughly convinced now that he was out of his head and, hoping to send him off to sleep, she started smoothing out his bed covering.

"Please listen to me," he went on. "You're going to spoil your life!"

"Sh!" she whispered, trying to soothe him with her best professional softness. "Go to sleep."

At this juncture there was a soft tap at the door and as if by magic, another nurse stood in the room, so expertly had she managed her en-trance. She looked at Sherard's nurse significantly.

"I'm just going out," she said. "Can I do anything for you?"

Sherard's nurse joined her by the door and whispered: "Tell Jimmy I'll be out as soon as I can get the old man to sleep."

The other nurse nodded. Skilled at whispering, the first one quickly recounted her troubles with her patient.

"Does he ever tell anything?" asked the other.

Sherard's nurse shook her head wearily: "He's just raving tonight, but he'll tire out soon."

The other nodded, whispered assuringly: "I'll tell him to wait." And glided out. With a deep sigh the nurse looked after her escaping co-worker, then turned back to the bed resigned to be patient for half an hour at least. But Sherard was more wide awake and more querulous.

"Who is your young man?" he asked.

Glad of a sane subject of conversation, she answered: "He's on a news-paper now—but he's already had things in the magazines."

"And he's having a birthday?"

"Yes."

"Throw that thing away and give him a handkerchief."

Mr. Sherard's attitude had assumed the importance of one not to be denied. Raving he might be, but there was nothing of vagueness about it. Something complete was in his mind, ready to be born, and even the thoughtless nurse realized that she had best help him to get it out.

"I wish you'd explain just what you mean, Mr. Sherard," she said.

"Get over into the light, child." He gestured toward the shaded electric table lamp. "I've scarcely taken a good look at you."

She stopped and adjusted the newspaper so that the light shone on her face. Vanity touched, her interest was awakened. It seemed, too, that Sherard had ceased being merely a patient and was a man again—the figure of romance who had stirred her curiosity at the beginning. Something fired him. He leaned quite steadily on his elbow and gazed at her intently with glistening eyes.

"Tawny hair, pretty teeth, blue eyes," he repeated.

The blue eyes bashfully looked down and for a moment she was altogether charming.

"You have better features than the most lovable woman I ever knew."

Straight away the nurse thought of the great English beauty and gasped. This was extravagant! But Sherard smiled and shook his head.

"Not that one. You've been believing the newspapers," he chided.

At that note of intimate irony the nurse seemed suddenly to come into the presence of the full charm of this man whose whole gay, irresponsible, half-tipsy way through life had been flowered by the loves of men and women. She became aware of exquisite friendship and there commenced her small moment of it—that love which passed all understanding of her sort, to whom love seems to have some eternal connection with family ties, God, Mother, sweetheart and kisses. He gallantly motioned her to be seated and, like the conductor of an orchestra, directed her movements until she made her loveliest picture.

"Now," he said, "the opal—at your throat."

She fumbled in her pocket, produced the pin and did as he told her.

"That's better," he said. "The devil devised uniforms."

He looked at her a moment in silent contemplation, and then went on.

"Did you ever notice that there's always a glint of gold about a nun? Gold tooth or eyeglass frame, or sometimes both."

Her mind seemed to be getting keen. She nodded and thought she had noticed. Mister Sherard shuddered.

"How hideous that any woman should have to wear her spangles dishonestly."

The nurse looked at him in awe, but in understanding. She was a Catholic. Here indeed was a thought for tomorrow.

Sherard now leaned back and gazed at her through half closed eyes.

"Keep your pretty pin, my dear, and wear it yourself. It makes your throat appear still whiter—and to make your throat whiter for your lover is so much more charming and considerate than to pin so many kronens worth of—(he paused) pardon me—my mind is halfway in Vienna—so many dollars worth of precious stones into his necktie."

"You mean, it will make him feel cheap?"

"Something like that."

"Even though I loved saving for it—even though it gave me pleasure—"

"You women—with your perverted love of making sacrifices! You don't care whom you humiliate by them—even the ones you love most. Do you want him to marry you?"

The blue eyes glistened in tears.

"I want him to love me always—even if he doesn't."

"Oh," he said, "so that's the way it is!"

She became conscious of the bright light beating down on her from under the newspaper shade. First her face went a deep pink, and then she slid from her chair in one quick movement to the floor beside his bed, her head within stroking distance of his hand.

"I thought if I did everything for him—" she sobbed.

"You could put him completely in your debt, eh? My dear, my dear— since when have we humans learned to love our creditors?"

"Life is awfully hard on women."

"I know—we love you for your faults—and you have so few of them."

She sobbed for a long moment. All that Mr. Sherard said was reaching her frail consciousness, so unused to the experience of being touched by thought. She suddenly felt her vaunted love for Jimmy to be weak and slovenly—not a strong and proud thing that he would cling to—but a ragged weed he might uproot at any moment, and feel relieved for.

Finally, when she was able to speak through her sobs, she said, "I will be harder on him. I won't give him the pin. I'm glad I've kept him waiting tonight."

"He's waiting for you?"

"Yes—outside."

"That's good. Now listen to me, my child—there—there—stop crying and listen to me."

She tried to check her sobs, succeeding a little.

"You'll soon be through with me—oh yes—and after you are—I want you to take your lover by the hand and step out into life with him exactly as though you were two children going into the back yard to play—not into the front yard where you are too likely to be on your dignity and conscious of passers-by, but into the back yard where you can wear your old clothes—throw off your hat—and, by all means, play a bit in the mud. Do you understand?"

"I think so."

"Be healthily selfish—like a child."

"Yes."

"And when you are tired of the mud—get out your best paraphernalia—and play at being queen."

"Yes."

"Oh—it's not so easy as that—it's always hard for a woman to be queen—but you must practice and learn. Be the one to supply his glamour. We men have to have it! Be his queen—and his playmate—but nothing less than that—and by all means nothing more. It is so easy for a woman to be a saint or a slave! It does her little credit—is that his whistling I seem to hear?"

"Yes."

"Run along to him—I'll be all right. I'm tired."

He had become the invalid once more—his voice sounded broken and weary. She rose, smoothed his pillow in silence and gave him a drink of water. She wanted so much to help him as he had helped her. She felt that he had given her a subtle strength that was to last all her life—the wisdom of the serpent perhaps—that would make her mistress of life, love and Fate. She saw herself meeting Jimmy, clear-eyed, with a smile. No sticky sentiment would come into their comradeship from now on— together they would laugh at and enjoy everything—even sin. And then, as a revelation—it came upon her that there was no such thing as sin— nothing to fear in all the world.

"Can I do anything for you, Mister Sherard?"

The sound of her own voice surprised her. It ought to have been husky, after her little cry—but it was strong and clear.

Sherard motioned toward his bed table.

"Yes," he said. "I have written a cable—it's here—under the glass of water—take it to the desk and see that they send it tonight."

The nurse took his cable message—as she had every night since his advent at the hospital. She hesitated—

"The lady in Vienna—was like—like that?" she ventured.

"She is like that. She has been for twenty years."

"Will you tell me more about her—I'd like to be—like that."

Sherard smiled, in tender reminiscence. He took a deep breath—this was causing him effort.

"She is strong, and sweet and penetrating—like the peppermint candy I used to buy when I was a little boy. She loves herself better than anyone in the world, and that's what makes it so great a compliment that she loves me next. She doesn't like children. She's such a child that she would be jealous of them. She lives informally as an Arab. I could never get her to wear a hat. The greatest thrills I've had in life have come at the sound of her footsteps toward a door—and if I were to hear them now in the corridor," he smiled feebly, "I shouldn't be dying this week."

The nurse put her hand on his in a gesture spontaneous with sympathy. It was no time for nonsense—so she did not deny him his prophecy.

"Good-night, and run along," he said. "I'm tired. I shall be asleep when you come back."

"Good-night."

"Remember what I've told you," he smiled whimsically. "I have the right to be a prophet tonight. Keep your pretty pin. It's a symbol of your happiness. If you give it to him—you'll lose him."

"I'll remember." Another hand squeeze—in a moment she was out the door and two more humans had parted for that space measured in Mr. Einstein's fourth dimension as forever.

Up and down under the trees of the old churchyard strode Jimmy Farrell. He had started the evening by wondering why he waited at all for this girl who had begun to lose charm for him—but the longer he waited, the less he wondered and now that she had been unbelievably long in keeping their rendezvous, he was actually getting keen for her. When at last he saw her hurrying through the shadows toward him, their affair seemed like an adventure once again.

He took her in his arms. As she raised her face to be kissed he saw through the thin shadow traces of tears in her eyes that set his interest wavering again. "What have I done now?" he thought, but "What's wrong, old girl?" he asked.

"It's my patient," she said. "He's worse tonight."

He patted her shoulder. How sweet she seemed! It was the first time he had ever seen her in tears, as a disinterested spectator. He took out a clumsy handkerchief and started to dry them. A great cord of tenderness seemed to bind them, but almost with terror the nurse felt rising within her an aching insistence to do something for her lover, a great service of some sort—to give him something—the best she could afford—the opal pin—NO!

She took a deep breath and tried to hold herself.

"What did you do today, dear?" she asked.

He pulled her deeper into the shadow of a tree and they sat with their backs against its trunk. If he had only started to make love to her—then at least she could have returned that to him and so have eased that beating, terrible tenderness that was crying for an outlet. But he didn't. He leaned back against the tree, tiredly, and launched into a tale of his day's doings, just as though she had any interest in them, of themselves. It was so pathetically mannish! She fondled his hand and felt that she must cry. She knew that she was slipping—slipping—the opal burned her throat.

It seemed that some low moraled host had served Jimmy with etherized beer the night before and his head had ached all day. His headache leaped to her heart and lodged there—an insistent pain. But, thank God, at last she could serve him. She started to jump up and go for aspirin—but he pulled her back.

"Don't fuss," he said. "This quiet is great—I feel better."

That was a subtle compliment, but some way, it floored her. All she could do for him was to rub his tired head—and that wasn't enough. Her feminine soul could not hold itself much longer. The opal burned more deeply. She heard little of Jimmy's adventure in a Harlem murder— for her own reasoning had come to her rescue and had started to comfort and relieve her. "What if a cold-blooded creature in Vienna had kept a man amused for twenty years—was that at all typical—he needed a real woman—why had she listened to Sherard. His charm was like the charm of a devil—he was a hypnotist."

Jimmy's day had ended by a fight with a drunken barber, who had to be written up for his exploits in terrorizing a neighborhood. He was simply tired out! All he wanted in the world was a blank space of quiet in a woman's arms—*and no fuss*. Like the mother of the world, she gathered him in and put his head upon her breast. The tenderness within her throbbed and grew—and grew and grew until it had to burst.

"Jimmy—" she whispered.

"Yes?"

"Do you see something shining on my dress?"

"What is it?"

"It's a stick pin—for your birthday!"

.   .   .

Mr. Sherard must have been wrong for the time came when the nurse— now Mrs. James Farrell—could happily combine business with pleasure in nursing her husband, the young writer, through a broken leg. She lived in a delirium of happiness—so much service required and she so grateful to give it. She kept their small apartment as clean as a diet kitchen. She was a whirlwind at any work which required her presence away from their bedroom where he lay. He, too, was very cheerful and sweet through it all, in spite of the pain and many weeks of inactivity.

The nurse was almost too busy to think—but sometimes at night— when Jimmy lay in fitful slumber, and she could not sleep for fear he might waken—she remembered that vivid evening's talk with Mr. Sherard. It amazed her to think of how very true his words had sounded at the time—and as she recalled them, somehow, they still sounded true—even now when they were proven to be so wrong. Jimmy loved her. She was the first one he sent for after his accident. He had taken their marriage for granted then—as she had. She reveled in slaving for him—giving, giving, giving—he had *married* her—what more proof could any woman require. But, in the reel of her memory, blurred and undistinguished as it was, there was one well developed picture—that scene with Mr. Sherard in the hospital room. She could not blot it out. Often and often she had tried to conjure up the picture of that heartless, cold-blooded creature he had loved so much—though surely not as much as her Jimmy loved her. How happy she was—how tired and how satisfied after every day of loving service.

Jimmy had a few friends who came to see him. One of them, a special crony, a sporting writer known as "Musty" Miller, carried about with him so great an atmosphere of the blind pig, the reading stable and those spots sacred to men that the nurse felt out of place in his presence and delicately withdrew whenever he paid a visit, leaving the two alone. These were bright spots in the sick days of James Farrell.

Jimmy was well liked among the newspaper crowd, and genuinely missed at the Dutchman's, one of the best places on Fortieth Street to get good beer since prohibition went into effect.

Some of the boys were sitting about there drinking and talking one night when Ben Hibbens, who had been away on a long murder case in Florida, returned to the rendezvous. After greetings were over and more drink had been ordered, one of the first things he said was, "I heard that Jimmy Farrell married that nurse he used to hang out with."

The boys stated that the report was true.

"How come?" asked Ben. "When I left town she was rather heavy on his hands."

"I guess he liked her better than he let on," said one of the others. "She's not such a bad egg and she's done a lot for him. He was out of a job with a broken leg when they were married—they're living on her little bank roll now."

"And Great Scott! How she's improved," spoke another. "I went up to see him one day and I hardly knew her when she let me in. Used to be rather undecided as to looks—but you should see her now. She's blossomed out like a red rose. I vote he's a lucky guy."

"Anyone's a lucky guy that has a sweet little woman ministering to him when he's out of luck," spoke one who had spent most of the afternoon—and thus far, the evening—at the Dutchman's. "I tell you boys, it's the only thing in life when you're out of luck—a little wife who loves you and a little home, and a sweet little—"

At about this point matters were broken into by the arrival of "Musty" Miller who also had to greet the newcomer and order more beer. Such like talk being gotten over—conversation started again.

"We were speaking of Jimmy Farrell getting married," said Ben.

"Just came from there," said Musty. "He's getting along fine. His wife's a swell nurse. That reminds me, I've got to watch the clock—got to get over to the Music Box before that little Mexican gets away."

"What little Mexican?"

"Tenita Vallejo—the dancer—you've seen her act. She's got Jimmy into a jam."

"How?"

"Well—he gave her a pin his wife gave him before they were married—and when his wife asked what happened to it, instead of using sense and saying he lost it, he tells her it's in hock. So then she gives him the money to have me get it out."

"What are you going to do about it?"

"Now I've got to borrow the pin from Tenita and hunt up another one just like it."

"Why don't you buy the pin back from her?"

"Well, that's where Jimmy is an underdeveloped moron again. She told me she'd sell it back to him—but the poor imbecile wants her to keep it on account of sentiment—and so I've got to go chase up another one. And that isn't all. He's made me promise to have my wife take his wife out to lunch Friday so Tenita can come up to see him. So I've got to go over and catch her after the show and ask her if she'll do me the

favor to go see a poor sap with a broken leg and a lame brain and a penchant for trouble."

"Isn't it the truth?" spoke up one of those Fortieth Street philosophers,
"that the harder they're boiled—the harder they strike?"

.   .   .

In a garden of Vienna (that city so swimming in a sea of sensuous music that in spots, the music has crystallized like meerschaum and taken
lovely solid forms), there is a monument to Johann Strauss. The composer, all gold, stands playing his violin in evening dress (very chic, tight-
fitting evening dress) which does not deprive posterity of the knowledge
that he was a fine figure of a man. He is playing that last movement of
The Blue Danube Waltz. Floating about him in the purest white music—beg pardon—marble are the faces of delirious lovers who have been
set quite mad by the strains from that golden violin.

Up and down the gravel walk before this shrine, there paced an Austrian countess. She was about forty-eight, although her golden hair was
nearer thirty. But her heart had reached a hundred since the death in New
York of Horace Sherard. She was waiting for her lawyer—her advocate—
to whom she had given this rendezvous because it was pleasanter than
his office (she could never endure offices), and because she knew the park
to be on the way to his favorite coffee house at which he daily met the
hour of three.

Presently she saw him coming down a flowered alley, a little late, but
not allowing that to stop him from looking over three pretty girls who
passed at different points.

"Countess—my dear friend—a thousand pardons," he spoke as he
came up—and muttering many more sweet nothings, he kissed her
hand.

"Don't mention it, dear, dear Doctor," said she. "Have you a butt?"
(This being the only way to say in English the charming Viennese of
"Have you a cigarette".)

He gave her a cigarette and lighted it. Then they walked to a bench and seated themselves.

"The papers arrived today," he said. "It's all quite simple. He has left you everything."

"So?" she asked listlessly.

"My dear child," he said, "might I be permitted to say that 'everything' in American dollars means a lot."

"What can it mean to me—now?"

"Ah—that's just what I have been thinking. I have made such plans for you! Your son—standing just at the threshold of life. There is no reason why you cannot reveal yourself to him now—think what the money may mean to him."

"Money!" she said bitterly. She opened her little silk handbag and took out a letter.

"Read that!" she passed it to him. It was from the nurse who had raised the boy and then become his housekeeper. He had been a brilliant student of philosophy at the college which had been endowed by a fabulously rich American of Austrian birth. The American, an idolater of learning, like so many of his type, had brought his family that year and the daughter of the house had fallen in love with the brilliant student. They were engaged and already the culture-crazed American family was enthusiastically closing in on him—to separate him forever from Austria—and from need of other love—or other money.

The kindly Herr Doctor read the letter and knew not what to say. He pressed the Countess' hand—and then removed and wiped his spectacles.

"So," said the Countess, "everything goes from me—like that." She blew a puff of smoke into an overhanging lilac branch. "I've had too much happiness—now I must pay up."

The Herr Doctor shook his head. "How can you say that, my dear child. You whose whole life has been a sacrifice?"

"Such a funny, crazy life I've had—Herr Doctor—two lives you might say—living with Mr. Sherard—and trying to see my boy—on the sly. It wasn't often easy. Horace hadn't so much money then. I had to skimp and save to keep my boy in just the simplest style, and often I had to be far away from him. Travel is so expensive—we couldn't both take all our journeys. But I was so happy at having him anywhere."

"Do you know the thing I've loved most in the world is a new hat—but I pretended I didn't like hats—so I seldom wore one—and almost never bought one—in order to save the money." She laughed aloud. "You've no idea how many hats it takes to keep a boy."

"I know," said the Herr Doctor, "I keep a wife in hats—and two boys. And you never let him know he had a son!"

"How could I? When I left him in Shanghai, I didn't know myself. He was to have followed me—and then I heard he had married the English woman. Someway the English get what they want! Of course, it would have embarrassed him then—to know we had a child. After she died—he came to Vienna. She had made him wary! How he hated ties—of any kind! He always pretended that he came to Vienna on business—and that when he found me here it was quite by chance. It made him so happy to take our affair very lightly! I knew then that he would live the remainder of his life, by chance. A plan for tomorrow bored him. By that time I had grown so used to hiding the boy that it was a second nature with me.

"For years I watched for a cue that might encourage me to let him know—but it never came. Then too—to tell him would have made such a ridiculous scene. I never could have played it through. I might have let him find me sewing on little garments—but when he took them out of my hand they would have dragged on the floor! My darling was so big—even for his age!

"Do you remember the time we were at Sommering? It was the first time Horace had seen winter sports and he went quite mad—we were at them day and night—tumbling about in the snow—and our boy was with double pneumonia. I thought one day I should have to tell him—but I didn't—thank God!"

"You should have married him, Countess."

"How could I—after his life with that dreadful English creature. They made fun of him for marrying her—poor boy—as if he wanted to. That turned him against marriage for all time—he mentioned it to me—once—but I wouldn't trick him into it."

"You would not be quite so friendless today if you had."

"Yes, but it gave me a bit of glamour—being his—not his wife—and he loved glamour."

The Herr Doctor took her hand and kissed it.

"The one woman I know who has had a happy, lasting love life—and—my God—how full it is of tears."

"He never saw them, Herr Doctor."

The Herr Doctor pressed her hand in quiet sympathy.

"My God," she said. "I'm pitying myself!" She smiled through the tears she was trying to hold back.

"Tell me, dear friend," he asked, "has it been worth it—the giving up of child—family—friends—the many, many years of sacrifice?"

"Shall I tell you the truth, Doctor? The sacrifices were easy—they do come easy to women. We're soft things. They were all easy but one."

"And that was—?"

"To seem not to be sacrificing. To give—and seem to take. To be hard and brilliant when one was melting to be soft. But it was very much worth while—for twenty years I lived—and I was very happy."

The Doctor looked at his watch. It was near the coffee hour. He tried to think of a cheerful speech to end their interview. But she understood that it was difficult and took it out of his mouth.

"Don't worry about my future, my dear friend. Some day I shall take a trip to America and perhaps meet my son again—socially."

She stood, giving him leave to go. He kissed her hand—with her other she brushed away her last tear.

"May I have the honor to escort you somewhere?" he asked.

"No thanks," she answered.

The Herr Doctor bowed deeply, kissed her hand again, and turned to trot to his beloved coffee. The little countess standing in the pathway seemed to waver. She looked up at the golden figure of Mr. Strauss—but he was no longer playing the last movement of The Blue Danube. He was playing a Bach fugue—and the faces about him seemed to be weeping. Two little children ran down the flowered alley and jostled her. She put her hand on the head of one of them, partly in tenderness and partly for support, but it wriggled away, and soon she heard their childish laughter dying down another alley. She was frantically alone. She steadied herself against a bench, then turned and ran quickly down the alley after the good Doctor who had almost reached the street.

"Herr Doctor—Herr Doctor!" she called. He stopped and waited till she caught up with him. "I'll walk a way with you toward the Kartner-strasse," she said, quite out of breath. "And if we pass a hat shop, I may go in and buy myself a new hat."

Travels with Aunt Anita

Mary Anita Loos

As adults together, Anita and I shared many wonderful times. Anita was so tiny that it was difficult for her to pull open heavy doors or even use kitchen equipment, so when we both lived in Los Angeles, I became her driver, shopper, and handyperson when the help was off, and that was great fun. When I stayed over, I was careful never to interfere with her working life. No matter where she was, that light by the bed would snap on before dawn, and she would pursue the long-tread path of her imagination and talent. Those early morning sessions were her sanctum sanctorum, and her throne was a chaise lounge in her bedroom; she perched a large, yellow pad on her lap and penned hundreds of pages. I was careful not to disturb her, and her own desire to please and to avoid confrontation extended even to her Pomeranian. In his cashmere sweater that she had knitted for him, that dog would bark when the light was on, so often Anita would get under the sheets with a light to write. Later in the morning she would talk on the phone to intimates, groom herself for the day, and turn the pages over to a secretary to type. Then she was off to a studio conference, lunch meetings, or to her bungalow office, after which she would return to the now-typed pages, edit them, and start writing again.

As great as those times in town were, it was during our travels to-gether that I learned the most from my Aunt Anita. I remember one particular trip the two of us took together after her husband, John Emerson, had finally been put safely away in a sanitarium in Pasadena. Anita and I were both working at MGM at the time; she was finishing up the script for *Susan and God,* and I was in the publicity department. We decided to drive north and revisit the places of her youth. Our first stop was Monterey, and as we checked into the Del Monte Hotel, I was struck by how impossible it would be for Anita to travel alone because of her difficulty with handling a car door or luggage. In spite of the hotel's luxuries we soon headed out again to drive along the famous Seventeen Mile Drive, where my mother's aunt and uncle had once owned a beautiful estate, and then dined at Pop Enst's restaurant at Monterey's Fisherman's Wharf, where Anita remembered her father taking her and splurging on abalone steaks costing $.50 (they were up to $1.75).

The springtime air was lovely as we returned to the hotel, and I was looking forward to a quiet time together when Anita said, "We are hav-ing such a good time that I think we ought to have poor Mr. E. come up and join us. It would do him good."

After all she had suffered living with him and all she had gone through to get him into the sanitarium, she could not stop trying to help him. I knew there was nothing I could say that would make her change her mind so I swallowed my despair and said, "Well, if you really want to . . ."

Emerson had been put on the train by his nurse/companion, Mrs. But-terworth, and he arrived the next day, along with his bottle bags, med-icine kits, lap robe, overcoats, and a manuscript carrier, no doubt in hopes that Anita would write something he could put his name on again. Din-ner was a disaster as he sent back half the food and spent half an hour sipping his decaffeinated demitasse and complaining about the draft. Fi-nally he agreed it was time for bed, but that was hardly the end of the evening. Anita was called to find his proper pills and after everything was set up just as he insisted on his bedside table, he announced, "I just have to sit in a tub of hot water to stay alive."

Anita and I got him into the bathtub, and then she said, "You go along. I'll stay with him and he'll have to move eventually." But half an hour later he decided he couldn't move at all, and I was called back to use all my strength to get him out of the tub. Anita put him into his flannel pajamas, then called the night porter for a hot-water bottle, and when Emerson finally settled in for the night, he smiled up at Anita and said, "Just like old times, Buggie."

As Anita and I finally got into our beds, I asked incredulously, "Did he always do this?"

Anita nodded and I couldn't resist asking, "How did you ever do it?"

She shrugged, "I guess I was younger then."

The next morning, after his breakfast in bed, Emerson retreated to the bar, where he sipped warm milk while taking his pills, and Anita and I investigated the train schedule.

The half-hour drive to the Salinas station seemed endless, but with the help of several porters, tipped lavishly by Anita, Emerson was finally put onboard with all his luggage. We waved a happy good-bye, but as the train pulled out I realized I never had seen anything move so slowly in all my life.

"I think we have had enough of Monterey," Anita said as we drove back to the hotel. "Let's go on in the morning."

We didn't speak of Emerson again until that night as we went to bed, and she said something to me I had never heard her admit before.

"I guess I was just born to be a patsy."

Our spirits rose the next day as we entered the beautiful city of San Francisco. "This was my escape hatch," Anita said, as if she and her memory were twins. "I guess I was about six years old when we moved here from Sisson. We had rich times and poor times, and I know it was tough on Mom, but I always had a great time because of Pop.

"Pop brought home Jack London before he was famous," Anita continued as we drove up the hills. "Like so many other women of every age, I had a crush on Jack. He used to recite poetry to me after Pop slipped him a drink or two behind Mom's watchful eye. Then there was the trunk Pop kept in the living room for a friend who was out of town. It turned out to be the gear of the great escapist Harry Houdini!"

As we approached Telegraph Hill, Anita gestured toward the place where our ancestors had been announced by the semaphore as their clipper ship approached the narrows of the Golden Gate.

"You can never know what Pop put us through, but what fun he was for me. He even tried to make me into a Spanish dancer. He billed me as Nita Loos, but I am happy to say as a Spanish or as a dancer, the public wasn't interested. My sister Gladys was two years younger than me and a pretty blonde. We were great pals and we were both in Pop's stock companies to bring in the rent. He put us in *Quo Vadis,* and I played Lord Fauntleroy well into my teens because I was so small."

"You know," she smiled, "I never told you this, but I was once worried about your father. Before he decided to become a doctor, he went off on a vaudeville tour one summer under the name of Harry Clifford. He was handsome and had a singing voice the ladies adored. Pop even made a life-sized poster of him he dragged around for years. Think of it, your father might have been a ham!"

She shook her head, for in her idiom the word *ham* meant actor, and, with few exceptions, she thought they were a lightweight group.

This was all news to me, as, indeed, my ambitious father, who married my socialite mother, would never have brought it up. As we turned onto Turk Street, Anita said, "It's all changed since the earthquake. As a kid, I would walk here early in the morning with Pop, who told me the hookers were the only other people up at that hour, either getting hot coffee or a growler of beer to take home to the pimp who was still in bed. Your dad went through the quake when he was an intern at the German hospital and he told me tales of rescuing the living and leaving the dead to the fire. He heard that with the Barbary Coast wiped out, the ladies of the night had to find some other place to meet gentlemen, so they started congregating on the steps of the Mint."

She was laughing at this and other memories and smiled again as she directed me to turn onto Union Street. "Now I'll show you the glamour we had for a short while.

"Here it is," said Anita as we pulled in front of a handsome, two-story house with bay windows. "Grandpa Smith left Mom an opportunity for her dream of a lovely home, good schools, and a chance to live a normal life. Thank goodness he also set aside a fund for your father to go to Stanford Medical School, because it didn't take Pop long to go through Mom's inheritance. It must have been so hard for Mom. I remember Clifford taking care of Gladys and me while she put out Pop's newspapers because he was off on one of his flings."

My father had told me some of these stories of course. He said he was ashamed of himself as he remembered one Christmas as a little boy when the table was set with bread, stuffing, homemade cranberry sauce, and a thick gravy but no turkey. And under the pathetic little forest cut tree were such pitiful grocery store toys that, in memory, he had said, "Is that all?" And Grandma had held her handkerchief over her eyes.

And yet that handkerchief often held tears of laughter as she listened to her husband's witticisms. When my husband, Carl, saw R. Beers carefully pushing Minnie in her wheelchair, he said he had never seen a couple so devoted to each other. Perhaps Anita hoped one day it would be like that with her and Emerson.

Anita and I drove in silence to the comfortable St. Francis Hotel and meandered through Gumps and then up the hill to colorful Chinatown. This was the one place where Anita could buy little slippers that fit her size-one feet, and she found a simple little Mao jacket with frogs instead of buttons. It was made for a child, but it fit her perfectly.

The next day we drove across the Golden Gate Bridge, and Anita looked back wistfully. She said nothing, but I could tell from her face that not all of the many memories that had stirred her were happy ones. Gone was the romantic city she had resurrected in *San Francisco,* her box office success of several years before.

Our destination was Mount Shasta, several hundred miles north, where it stood as a sentinel, rising in its high glacial splendor from the lower plain. Grandpa had told me how the Indians revered its mystery and never went above the snowline, and now was my chance to share this special place with Anita. As it came into view, Anita raised my hopes of more revelations.

"Leave it to Pop to stir up something that is still talked about. He climbed to the summit with some of his pals and bet them that a horse had been to the top of the mighty volcano. It was such a rough climb no one believed it was possible, so they all took the bet. Pop was the first to get to the top and was soon yelling that he had found the proof he was looking for. His pals trailed behind him to find him pointing out a piece of horse manure on the rocky path. Of course Pop had smuggled it up in his pocket, but he won his bet."

We drove on to a lovely resort area with charming little cottages scattered along the edge of a gentle canyon. We got out and walked down to the river where we found ourselves in a dream of fern, tiger lilies, and violets. From there we headed on to Dunsmuir, which once had been called Shasta Springs and, before that, Sisson. Soon we pulled into the ranch that her grandfather had so proudly built but that held mixed memories for Anita. As a small child she remembered the mysteries surrounding her beautiful grandmother, Cleopatra, who had retired into a world of negligees, lace caps, lilac cologne, and laudanum in her private quarters.

I had seen pictures of Anita and my father and their father visiting the ranch alongside a young boy, Vernon Smith. Now he was an elderly man who, along with his wife, Cindy, ran the ranch and welcomed us back. Many years later I would share holidays with their family as I so enjoyed the magic and beauty of the countryside.

After a nice visit Anita announced it was time to pack.

"I think we've had it. Pop would say, 'It's time to call it quits.' It's a lovely country, but it brings back too many memories."

Anita paused for a most pregnant silence.

"Let's go home," she said. "No more memories."

Yet as I look back on that trip with Anita, I am particularly grateful to her for sharing with me those pages of her life that may well have remained closed if we had not had that time together.

One of the most emotional times I ever shared with my Aunt Anita was her last visit to California in 1979. New York had been her home for more than thirty years, and we had visited each other often, but now she said she wanted to return to spend time with her only remaining relatives, myself and my growing son, Edward. Most of the giants and the pygmies from the industry that had nurtured her were long gone, but there were a few friends she wanted to take the opportunity to visit with one more time.

She was now a frail little woman in her nineties, and I was a bit intimidated by the thought of her staying in my small home. She would have a room with a single bed and a dressing area, pretty and adequate, but a shadow of the wealth and elegance she had once known at her own stunning Neutra-designed beach house where the Pacific Ocean was her front yard. Life had been relatively smooth going with the help of Hallie Jenkins in the kitchen; Hallie's husband, George, who served as butler and chauffeur; and Anita's gifted secretary, Madge. Yet as Anita settled into my simple home in the Santa Monica Canyon with one maid-of-all-chores to help me tend to her needs and the needs of my son, she was obviously pleased to be there and happy with our small pool and overflowing garden.

Anita was incredibly feminine; I remember after having her coffee and putting away the notebook she still wrote in every morning, she sat at the dressing table in a negligee tying a ribbon at the nape of her neck. Her hair was longer now, so she could pin it into a neat bun; her shapely legs were crossed, and tiny marabou slippers covered her toes. She pouted slightly putting on her lipstick; she was ageless.

One change I noted was her dependence on Atavin to calm her nineties' nerves, but she reveled in watching Edward swim and in entertaining the friends who came to visit.

First came Eddie Albert and his wife, Margo, my closest friend, and they happily gossiped about what changes had occurred with all the people we knew in common. Edgar Bergen; his wife, Frances; and the future Murphy Brown, their daughter Candy, came by for a simple barbecue, as did our dear friend Jay Allen, the dean of literary promotion.

Anita also loved visiting the shops of Santa Monica, and in one children's store she found a middy blouse. Much to my surprise, she decided to buy it, proclaiming it a unique classic. "After all, even the Russian Czarist's daughters wore middy blouses."

"That didn't do them much good," I pointed out.

She waved her hand and said, "A classic is a classic. I'll take it."

The child's-size blouse fit her perfectly, and she was right; it suited her.

We drove along the Pacific Coast Highway and visited the Getty Museum. We passed her former home on the ocean front; she had been so lonely there that she only waved slightly as we passed, but she was very distressed to see that the sprawling mansion that William Randolph Hearst had shared with Marion Davies was being torn apart and turned into a beach club.

Since I had made a success with my novels, she was pleased I was no longer depending on the ever-changing film business, but she still wanted to see her friends from the industry that had been so important to her. George Cukor, who had directed *The Women,* one of her great MGM successes, and with whom she had stayed dear friends ever since, invited us to his house for lunch. George always served the most delicious yet low-fat meals, and I thought we had a very pleasant visit; but on the way home Anita took an Atavin, telling me her nerves were shot because she was so concerned that George was "slightly gaga."

Our next stop was the home of our old friend Allan Dwan. Allan had once directed the films Anita wrote for Douglas Fairbanks and had helped me early in my writing career by buying a *Liberty Magazine* story my writing partner, later my husband, Richard Sale, and I had written. Anita and I had both known Allan when he lived in a Brentwood estate, but now we headed to the San Fernando Valley, where he was sharing the home of his former housekeeper. That kind and gifted man had lost almost everything because of a wretched business manager, and now he and the housekeeper combined social security checks to get by. (When Anita intimated that the same thing could have happened to her, I had to bite my tongue not to say, "It did happen to you once, but because of a husband, not a manager, and you dug your way out.")

Allan was his old cheery self, surrounded by current magazines and books. We enjoyed a good long gossip over world-forgotten names and were every bit as comfortable as we would have been at his old estate. Allan was no longer a forgotten talent; the silent-film historian Kevin Brownlow had come to interview him several years before, and now Allan was basking in the joy of having his accomplishments respected once again and his memories valued as a contribution to history.

As was his custom, he walked us to the car and plucked several lemons from a tree in the front yard to give to us as a parting gift. After truly fond farewells we drove off, and Anita's handkerchief again attempted to absorb the emotion that had come upon her several times on this visit; but this time I knew she was relieved and happy that Allan had weathered the storm.

Now it was time to show her the phenomenon that my father, her brother, Clifford, had left. She certainly knew that after World War I he had founded a medical group with his partner Dr. Donald Ross and that this new approach to prepaid medicine had shot like a comet through the medical world. Decades before Kabat Kaiser came into existence, the Ross-Loos plan of monthly payments assuring the benefits of a socialized health plan had been controversial but so successful their small first clinic had grown into an enormous organization. Anita knew there were a few clinics, but she had no idea their plan had expanded into nineteen satellite offices and the huge hospital I was about to show her.

I planned my approach on the Hollywood freeway so that as we turned on to the off ramp, there in front of us was the seventeen-story behemoth of a building with the ROSS-LOOS insignia itself being several stories high.

The astonishment that took over her entire being was something to behold. "It's incredible," she said. "It's overwhelming. It's bigger than any billboard on Broadway!"

They were expecting us, and a small wheelchair was at the door to make her visit more comfortable. I insisted on doing the pushing, but when she was greeted by Dad's old partner, Dr. Ross, she jumped up to hug him.

"I had no idea that this . . . ," she waved her hand around, "would be so enormous."

"I guess Clifford and you were alike," Dr. Ross smiled. "You both thought big!" We visited several of the care areas and then Dr. Ross said, "Now I want you to meet the partners."

I wheeled her into the room where the partners were seated around a table, but when they saw Anita, they rose and applauded.

"Tell us," Dr. Ross asked in front of everyone, "Do you still think gentlemen prefer blondes?"

Anita smiled and lifted her hand and said, "Well, from what I have heard, today gentlemen prefer gentlemen."

A moment of startled silence was broken with loud laughter. Anita had charmed them again, and now cameras flashed as people gathered around her, shaking hands and asking for autographs.

It was only when we were back in the car and the adrenaline rush from the cheers and emotions died away that I could see how weary she was. It had been a great thrill to see what her beloved, belated brother had accomplished, and the joy of seeing it with her own eyes stayed with her. In fact, her parting words to me at the airport were, "I thought I was the family success. My God, my brother took care of hundreds of thousands of people's problems."

I gave that little woman a huge hug. "Anita, you made millions of people forget their problems with your pen."

In 1981 Anita was in her nineties and housebound, her vision and hearing failing. She required proper medical assistance, a skill more advanced than Gladys Turner, her housekeeper of forty years, could provide. Gladys had started as part of Anita's household in Santa Monica, advancing to a position of greater responsibility in New York, where her duties included acting as housekeeper, personal maid, chauffeur, and traveling companion. She also handled travel arrangements and household shopping, and she accompanied Anita to business meetings and rehearsals as her attendant.

Gladys would not accept the fact that Anita now needed more help, and Arnold Weisberger, Anita's longtime friend, adviser, and lawyer, grew concerned. He called me in California and suggested Anita might come live with me in Santa Monica, but within days of the call Arnold died suddenly. When I suggested the idea of Anita staying with me, Gladys rejected it vociferously and wouldn't let me get through to talk to my aunt. Avis Klein and Florence Weintraub, Anita's longtime secretaries, recognized her serious predicament when Anita gave them a letter to smuggle out, a written cry for help to her old friend Ruth Dubonnet. Ruth, also unable to get through to Anita, took the letter to Jay Harris, Weisberger's successor. He called me to come to New York, and I did so immediately. I was shocked to see Anita's physical state. Her weight was down to seventy-five pounds. With the help of Avis Klein I packed a few of Anita's things to take her to a hospital for tests. We ignored Gladys's resolute disapproval, ordered a car, and left.

I was staying with my dear friend Claire Trevor, who lived at the Hotel Pierre, and much to my surprise, Anita insisted on stopping for lunch at the Pierre before going to the hospital. Thinking that food was a good start, I hoped she would eat something. To my amazement she ordered spaghetti and wolfed it all down.

We then took her to the Doctors Hospital for tests, but as soon as she was comfortably settled in, she expressed anxiety about Gladys's welfare and worried that she wouldn't manage without her. It was the same pattern of concern she had showed for Emerson all over again. In fact, Anita would eventually bequeath to Gladys Turner a lifetime annuity, and Gladys lived until 2001.

Anita stayed in the hospital for five days and gained four pounds in that time. I visited every day, and Ruth happily augmented my vigils. When I arrived, Ruth would be sitting with a telephone and newspaper at hand and the two of them were laughing and gossiping, just as they had been doing for more than fifty years. I had to return home because my son was facing a difficult orthopedic operation, and when I stopped by the hospital on the way to the airport, Anita insisted on getting out of bed and into her marabou slippers to see me to the elevator. When I saw her start to return to her room arm in arm with Ruth, I was reassured she was with friends and would continue to improve.

When Anita was released from the hospital, it was with the assurance there would be full-time medical care for her. Gladys continued to block people from talking to her on the phone, but Ruth visited Anita often and assured me that her strength seemed to be returning and that she was eager to get back to writing.

On August 17 Anita rose from the chaise lounge where she wrote early in the morning and toppled over. The nurse called for an ambulance, and Anita was taken to Doctors Hospital. Ruth called and told me that Anita was in stable condition. I was able to call Anita, and she sounded fine, assuring me that there was no reason for me to come east and saying I should stay with Edward, who was recovering from his spinal operation. That morning I had received the galleys of my latest Bantam book, and I read her the dedication: "For Anita Loos: Aunt, Teacher and Friend. With love." She was pleased, of course, but most of all, I think, she was relieved that my success freed me from the unpredictable movie business.

Four hours later, Ruth Dubonnet called. Anita was gone.

Assured that Edward would be fine, I flew to New York immediately and went with Ruth to Campbell's Funeral Home to identify the dear, little body of Anita. She seemed so incredibly small and frail as she lay with a peaceful prettiness on her face.

I suppose you could say my last trip with Aunt Anita was to the family cemetery in the little town of Etna, just a few miles from the Smith ranch where she had been born. It had been one of her final wishes to be buried there. My son, Edward, along with a dear friend his age, Linda Bettinger, and I packed up the car in Santa Monica and once again headed north. We drove four hundred miles through the tall state of California, heading to Redding and then to the town of Yreka, once known as Rough and Ready. Thoughts of those days brought back all the tales of the forty-niners, the gold rush, and the success that came to my Great-grandfather Smith, giving him the means to start the still active cattle ranch that was our destination.

We were welcomed at the ranch to find friends gathering for a traditional potluck country celebration, very different from the New York memorial service held for Anita, but just as wonderful.

The next day we trekked to the Siskiyou County Masonic cemetery, passing simple markers to find the imposing marble tower bearing the names George and Cleopatra Smith. It seemed a bit strange to us for this to be Anita's final destination, yet there she would be surrounded by her parents, grandparents, and her brother. Breathing in the beauty of the cemetery, which was not a sad place at all, I almost heaved a sigh of relief as I gazed across the flower-filled field and scanned the names at my feet one more time.

Suddenly, I stopped and stared, not believing my eyes. There, next to the slab the men were preparing to move to create Anita's final resting place, was the name JOHN EMERSON. The man who had added his name to her work, had taken her wealth, and had in every way undermined her had somehow arranged to be next to his "Little Buggie" for all time.

Of course Anita must have known, must have even approved and made the arrangements, but she had never dared mention it to me, knowing full well what my reaction would have been. And I could just hear her saying, "Mr. E. is happy now."

Well, Anita was home again just as she wanted to be. On the long drive home through our beautiful California I felt proud to be a part of this unique and touching family and was comforted by the thought that someday I too would be in this lovely valley along with my beloved father and my darling Aunt Anita.

*Memorial Celebration
of Anita Loos's Life,
August 27, 1981*

Eulogies

Campbell Funeral Home, New York City. Eulogies by Richard Coe, Lillian Gish, Ruth Gordon, Morton Gottlieb, Helen Hayes, Leo Lerman, Josh Logan, Mary Anita Loos, and Jule Styne.

MORTON GOTTLIEB

I don't really need this (referring to a pad of notes). I'm making it all up as I go along. My name is Morton Gottlieb, and some of you I know very well, and I just want to tell you about the nature of our celebration for Anita Loos. Anita and I were talking about this fifteen years ago. It was very odd. Anita was helping to plan what was called the memorial service for Alexander Incze—who many of us knew—who was the publisher and the producer and a great pal of Anita's. Anita used to call him the King of Budapest. And Anita said—when she planned his memorial service with Peggy Incze—"Let's have it funny. Sandor was a funny man and let's only have people who will tell funny stories about Sandor Incze." And we had an hour of belly laughs in the theater, and afterward Anita said, "Oh boy, I hope some day when we get around to me, I hope we get the laughs we got for Sandor." And it made such a clear impression on me about Anita's life. And I think that if anybody has a smile or a laugh today, not to feel inhibited about the joy that we all know propelled Anita Loos.

Now some of us may have known her very well, and some of us might have known her only by reputation and her contribution to the mores of the world, the international world, because as we all know, she was one of the great philosophers of the mores; and if we didn't know, George Santayana told us that, but we all loved her, and she made a great contribution to our lives. Now I have about sixty-three stories to tell about Anita, many of which I've been warned by a group of people near to Anita Loos not to tell today, but I have known Anita since the spring of 1951, when I was Gilbert Miller's general manager and Gilbert Miller decided to do the play *Gigi*. And I got to know her instantly very well, and I'll tell you what the circumstances were in a second, but for most of every day for the last thirty years Anita and I talked at nine in the morning. Now I get up around then, but by the time nine o'clock came around, she had been up for four and a half hours. She had not only done four hours of work, and Gladys had not only fed her marvelously, but she had already gossiped with Ruth Dubonnet and Paulette Goddard and Dick Coe in Washington and the night before with Mary Anita, telling her everything that was happening; and I would start the day hearing all the news that was unfit to print, and let me tell you that what Anita gave to us is the sense of inspiration, an attitude of irony about reality, a sense of joy, a look into the future. This is what she always said, that it's an upward climb, that life can get better and if there's anything wrong that happens throughout the day, well, face everyone head-on, anyway. I face every day with her marvelous philosophy and her sense of joy.

And so today what we are doing, based on the phrase Anita said about Alexander Incze's, is a celebration and not a memorial service, a celebration of joy, and we are celebrating the life of Anita Loos, which we have all been privileged to have been part of.

Now one more thing about that first day that I met Anita Loos at Gilbert Miller's office. And we were talking for the first time about the play *Gigi.* And Gilbert said, "Anita, you know, you have some very, very funny things in this play." And she said, "Oh, Gilbert, don't worry. We can get rid of all those in Philadelphia."

Now the first person who is going to come up and really tell you something about Anita is her old, wonderful, great friend, and the star of her smash hit play *Happy Birthday* and coauthor with her of *Twice Over Lightly,* Helen Hayes.

HELEN HAYES

Before I launch myself on my memories and my thoughts of Anita, I want to tell you that I had a call from Ina Claire from San Francisco, and she sent a message, a typical message of Ina's and one that I am sure is apropos of what Morton said. He took the words right out of my mouth, talking about Anita's comments on Sandor Incze. Ina called up and said, "Oh this is terrible." She couldn't get here and she said, "Oh, my God, I loved Anita! She was funny." And then she said, "There are no more funny people left. Where have they all gone?"

Well, there are funny people left. We're all going to try our best.

My long, loving association with Anita got off on the wrong foot because a friend and an agent way back in the twenties tried to get me the leading role in the first Broadway production—it was a straight play then—of *Gentlemen Prefer Blondes.* It was going to be a big step for me to get the part of Lorelei Lee, and I was very excited about that and very much yearning for it, and Anita turned me down cold. She said to the agent, who repeated it to me, "She's too sweet and too naïve." I didn't know then, because I didn't know Anita very well then—I had only seen her around at parties—I didn't know then that those were the two worst things she could say about anybody.

It wasn't until I got connected with Charles MacArthur that my association with Anita really became more close. She had a choice of giving up Charlie or taking up with me. And she adored Charlie, so she took up with me. She did her best to make me worthy of Charlie and the kind of person she could feel happy with. She got me to go and buy clothes at Mainbocher. She took me in hand, and then finally she wrote a play in which I was tight for two acts. She did her best for me, God bless her. It's really funny that as our association went on, we found that we had one thing in common. We were both madly curious about life and what went on around us. And because we had this crazy curiosity, we were drawn so close together that we kind of left Charlie out in the cold. Marvelous things: she was a wonderful person to be around and have little adventures with. I remember we went to an auction in London because we had met the auctioneer, a man whose name I have forgotten; he was going to auction a great painting, and we sat through the whole auction wide-eyed, and a Van Dyke, a beautiful Van Dyke, went for very little money. I turned to Anita and said, "Dear goodness! You know this is Van Dyke and it went for such and such an amount. Crazy!" And she said, "Maybe it was by Frank Van Dyke."

In our book together I gave her the opportunity to choose the New York life she wanted to write about, and I picked the things I wanted to write about, like the Metropolitan Museum and Carnegie Hall and all those things. Anita came with a list—she had found a charm school in Harlem, a bartenders' school, a barbers' school. We spent a whole day at schools and they were really quite way out and great fun. And then, of course, I got in touch with the Moran tugboat people, and we had two choices. We could go and help bring in the *Queen Elizabeth* after one of her trips, or we could go off and collect garbage. You know Anita and which one she wanted—Anita chose the garbage, of course. There we were riding around on this beautiful sunny October day, and we had already got one great pile of garbage. We were out on the deck with this great mountain of garbage looking around, and there was this little white butterfly running over the garbage, just fluttering over it, and Anita said, "You know they only live for twenty-four hours, so wouldn't you think he'd find something better to do?"

I won't ever feel that I've lost Anita because I have a million such memories of her, so many. I just hope that she's as happy where she is as she's left us here. I just hope that when she gets to heaven, where she's bound to be, that she finds that heaven is chic. If it isn't chic, it will be hell to Anita.

MORTON GOTTLIEB

Now this is Leo Lerman, who is not only a neighbor of Anita's but a great friend and gossiper. He is also going to publish in *Vogue* an article Anita wrote very, very recently about Louise Brooks and herself being the resident brunettes at Paramount Pictures in the mid-twenties. Now we all know what a wonderful important talent Leo is, but Anita and I were wont to think of him as the assistant stage manager of *Behind Red Lights*.

LEO LERMAN

Anita Loos herself is a hard act to follow in any context. Miss Helen Hayes is an impossible act to follow. Anything I've prepared to say I can't possibly say now. I found myself today jotting—trying to write something down. There was so much to say about Anita, I never left my pad all morning long. I found myself jotting down isolated words. Now I want to tell you about Anita a little bit. And these are things you all know, I suspect. Number one, Anita was, to start, one of the tiniest people we know. She was absolutely enormous within that tininess. She was enormous in laughter, she was enormous in appreciation, she was even more enormous, as Helen said, in curiosity. There was a side of Anita that Helen touched on, and Ray and I had known her for a very long time before we found that side fully. We found ourselves in Philadelphia early in the '50s, and it was because of one of those Carol Channing things. We never, any of us, thought that Miss Channing, who we then knew as a very large girl, could be petite and thereby right for Lorelei. We had been known when we were staying in Middletown, New York, to come downtown at nine o'clock in the morning and read *Gentlemen Prefer Blondes* out loud, much to the consternation of the passengers who went that way. The conductor hated us. And we would roll in the aisles with laughter.

Ray and I found ourselves riding back on the train from Philadelphia rather late at night, and Anita talked and talked and talked. And what she talked about. . . . The first time she talked about some of her more intellectual friends, and there were a few well-chosen epithets. She talked about topics of all kinds, and then she really got going and she talked about gangsters. . . . She talked about their love lives worldwide, and she seemed to be their pet. She seemed to know them everywhere. And what she talked most about—Ray reminded me of that this morning—was gold diggers. She just loved gold diggers. She had an open eye for gold diggers. Now try to think about Dorothy and Lorelei. . . . We all know that Anita was really the Dorothy kind, always thinking of a good time. She knew the argot of these people, she knew how they talked in the twenties, she knew how they talked in the thirties, she followed their progress and she roared with laughter. Out of this tiny creature came some of the loudest and most informed laughter I've ever come across.

There's another thing. She simply loved young people, talented young people, and until last spring, which was the last time I spoke to her, she was always telling me about, oh do you know your Mr. So-and-So, some place in America, who knows where, who's written the . . . well, it isn't really a perfect play, dear, she'd say, but it's got some very good scenes in it. Or a composer or a poet. And everything was with an enormous sense of fun. That was what was so wonderful about her.

There's another side of Anita. Years ago when I was writing a book about the Metropolitan Museum of Art and I really had to get up at five o'clock in the morning, there were two who were awake that I knew about in those days, and one was Anita and one was Fanny Hurst. Fanny was out in Central Park walking those dogs who were as big as deer and Anita was at her typewriter. And occasionally, then quite a lot, I'd call early in the morning and Anita would say, "Do you know anything?" And what she meant was, had I heard gossip. . . . It could have been about King Tut for all she cared, just as long as it was gossip. But it also meant,

"Are you writing your book?" She was never a mother about that; she never said, "Are you writing your book?" But she gave you the energy to go on and on and on and on. And I think the energy she released in this world will go on and on and on and on as long as any of us are here. And that's one of the wonderful, wonderful legacies. I think, as Helen said, it's impossible to think Anita isn't here, because of course she is.

Now about her Lorelei side and her appreciation of gold diggers. One time she was reeling with laughter, and she told this story about one of her close friends, a famous star of screen. I cannot tell you the name. If you send me ten cents, no it has to be a twenty-five-cent stamp now, I might reveal it later. Apparently she and this great beauty were on a train platform somewhere, and it was so long ago a phone call cost a nickel; and they needed to make a phone call, and neither lady had a nickel. And just then a tramp appeared, and he wore broken clothes and broken shoes; and both ladies looked at the tramp, and then the screen beauty left Anita and had a little short talk with the tramp and then came back and held up a quarter. And Anita said, "Why did you take that poor man's quarter?" And the beauty said, "That's all he had!" And Anita adored that story. That's all I have to say right now.

MORTON GOTTLIEB

Now let me introduce you to one of the extras from *The New York Hat,* one of the first movie movies in the history of film. Before I go on, Anita once said, "Movies went downhill when we started calling them films."

LILLIAN GISH

Thank you. Yes I was an extra in *The New York Hat,* and my sister was too. And she should be here now because she got all the wit and comedy in our family, and they always said that I was about as funny as a baby's open brain ... [end of sentence obscured by laughter]. I never had the privilege of working with you. You wrote *The New York Hat* but didn't come into the company until a year or two later. We had never had anyone writing stories, and then in came this little thing with a brain like a man. I was frightened of her. I kept my mouth shut every time she was around, but I listened and at the time, having never gone to school, I was reading Spinoza, a great philosopher, and Shakespeare, if you remember, and her mind was so sharp that I called her Mrs. Spinoza, not to her but to other people. That became a kind of comic word for this little, dark-eyed pretty thing that had this very brilliant, comedic brain.

Anyway, pretty soon John Emerson came into the company, and he was directing my sister in *Old Heidelberg*. I think she was about fourteen, and she played it with her hair braided on each side and no makeup. In the love scene John Emerson told her she should kiss the prince. And she said, "We don't do that in this company," and he said, "Well, this is a love story and you're going to do it in this picture." Well, she got very cross and went in to see Daddy Woods. He was a white-haired man that we took all our troubles to when any arguments came up, and she said, "Mr. Emerson has asked me to kiss an actor and you know we're not allowed to kiss actors in this company. We don't kiss them because we might get a disease." So the whole company took sides for or against Mr. Emerson, and we had quite a battle. Finally Mr. Emerson had the principal's wife call my mother and say, "Your daughter is perfectly safe kissing my husband." So she lost the battle. That's one of the things that brought me here because, of course, Anita later married John Emerson. And when she wrote *Gentlemen Prefer Blondes,* oh, I wanted to get up the courage to ask, "Who were the gentlemen and who were the blondes?" Because I heard she had people in her mind, and I would have loved to know, but I never got up the courage to ask her. And Anita, I'd still like to know. Thank you.

MORTON GOTTLIEB

Now Jule Styne is going to tell us a few tidbits and play us a few songs and explain some of their pertinence to Anita.

JULE STYNE

(Jule Styne plays "I Haven't Got a Worry in the World," from *Happy Birthday,* then "Little Girl from Little Rock," from *Gentlemen Prefer Blondes.*) Anita was sophisticated about everything except music. You see, Anita loved saloon songs. This is the song Anita loved most from *Gentlemen Prefer Blondes.* (He plays "I Don't Want to Walk without You, Baby," which he had written for the 1942 movie *Sweater Girl.* Then he segues into "Diamonds Are a Girl's Best Friend.")

MORTON GOTTLIEB

As you all know, the Rodgers and Hammerstein song is from *Happy Birthday,* and Helen Hayes sang it, and afterward, for those who want to stay on, Helen is going to sing for all of us. The director of *Happy Birthday* is Josh Logan, and he's going to say a few words about [phrase drowned out by applause].

JOSH LOGAN

If he hadn't announced that Helen sang that song, I was going to say she not only sang it, she also danced to it, so that's what you'll see if you stay on. I was really a mistake as the director. It was planned for Rouben Mamoulian to do it for Rodgers and Hammerstein after *Oklahoma!,* and for some reason that didn't work out; so I was tried out. They sent me the script to see if I would do it. I couldn't imagine they'd want me even though I had just done *Annie Get Your Gun* for them. They were the producers. I still thought this was a very difficult problem because of Anita Loos and Helen Hayes and it being a fantasy. However, I relaxed after reading the first line Anita wrote in which she did the description of the set. She said it's a saloon and above the arch over the main part of the saloon are these letters: "Through these portals pass the nicest people in Newark." I just had to do it after that.

Anita was, as you have heard, always very strong and funny and cute and a little powerhouse. And we did *Happy Birthday,* and Helen and I went through some painful times because at first it didn't go. Anita had tried to give a very complicated character to Addie Bemis. She'd make a wisecrack, and then she did a nasty remark and then a wisecrack after that, all within a minute; and the audience didn't know whether she was mean or nice, and therefore they reserved their judgment and didn't comment at all. I remember in such agony hearing the audience saying nothing, not groaning, not puffing, nothing. And the silence before the actors . . . including Helen, who were saying the lines, Anita's lines, and some of them were surely funny, and finally at the end of the play, about five minutes beforehand, I went out in the back. I was just sick. I didn't know what to do. There was Oscar Hammerstein, and he was very quiet and leaning against the wall; and then I heard something like this, and I thought that must be someone applauding. It must be the end of the show. And that's all the applause it got, in fact, and then I heard the stumble and ruffle of people getting out of there, and pretty soon I knew the doors would open and they would be pouring out. The first two people who came out—and we were standing right in front of them— were Nunnally Johnson, who was in town with a show, and his composer, Arthur Schwartz, whom I had worked with. Arthur looked at me and said, "Hell, Josh, I just hated it!" That's the first thing I heard, the first comment on *Happy Birthday.* And I thought, oh poor Anita, that lovely Anita, she's . . . well, we've let her down, and Helen . . . she'll be desperate.

I walked home in front of Oscar Hammerstein because he was being talked to by his lawyer, who had suggestions. I listened to them all and kept walking, and finally we were to meet Anita, Dick, and Oscar up in Anita's suite at the Ritz-Carlton. And I thought, Oh, God! I hope they know how to produce, and I hope they keep the show running. . . . I don't know, they'd only done *Annie Get Your Gun.* Oscar opened the meeting by saying, "Let's fix it." And Dick said, "And by Monday." And I looked over at Anita Loos, and she winked at me; and I knew she felt great. I must say it was one of the most extraordinary experiences, and I'd like to go into more details, but there are other things to be said.

I'd just like to end my little talk here by remembering when I first discovered in my own heart Anita Loos. I was in school and I read *Gentlemen Prefer Blondes,* and here is the line I remember as best I can . . . the line that got me. Lorelei was describing Paris, and she became a kind of very chic travel book, and she said, "If you walk down the Champs-Elysées and put your back to the Arc de Triomphe and then look in front of you directly at the Place de la Concorde and then look over your shoulder, you'll see a great Big City sing." That's all. Anita Loos is a wonderful lady, wherever she is.

RUTH GORDON

Well, it's nice to have lived a long life because you've got a lot of memories, a lot of things to think about, and you know some of them are rotten, but then there are the nice ones, and one of the nice ones was early spring of 1925. I met Anita, and we became friends. I was in a play with the great Blanche Bates, a wonderful actress who was the star, and I played a supporting part, but it wasn't so supporting that I couldn't make a hell of a hit, and I did. And Anita and John Emerson sent me their new play, and it was called *The Fall of Eve,* and they offered me the part of Eve. I'd never played a starring part before, so, ah, I didn't fool around with reading the manuscript because on every page it said Eve. They gave me a contract that said that the first year that I played the play I'd get $450 [a week], the second year that I played the play I would get $750, and the third year that we played the play I would get $1,000. Well I was a member of a family where my father never got more than $37 a week, so this seemed like a hell of a good thing.

Well, we opened in Stamford for a week and that was all right, that was a decent place, and I was all right, nothing to write home about, and then John Emerson came in and gave me some notes—lose scene here, lose scene there, good line. . . . I said to Anita, "That's no good. Why don't you write them?" And she said, "Oh, no, John is wonderful and besides he's got technique." So we had plenty more technique in the play.

Anyway, we left Stamford, and we were going to open the new season in New York. Now the three of us met in Paris because we were going to pick out the clothes for me to wear in *Eve,* and you know Anita Loos could do a lot of things, but she could not pick out a bum dress. So we went to Lanvin, and there were the most beautiful clothes you ever saw in your life. They bought me one pink pasha coat, a wool coat, and it was lined with pink dyed ermine; you know they don't make stuff like that anymore. So we went back to Place Vendome, where Anita picked out her clothes, and I went with her, and a wonderful place called Chez Louis, a beautiful collection; and she picked out everything great, but there was one dress, just the last word, a black chiffon, little winking stars all over it, and she said, "I'll order that and I'll order it in navy blue." I said, "Why navy blue?" She said, "Mr. E. doesn't like me in black."

Okay, now we're back in New York, and we're going to go into rehearsal any minute. The play's entirely rewritten, and it's gone from pretty good to no good. And there's an actor playing in Asbury Park, and they think they'll drive down to see him. So they ask would I like to go, and I said yes, and they had a gorgeous car; I don't know what it was, it was like a chariot. So Anita sat in front, and John Emerson steered the car, and I sat in back. Well, we had dinner, we saw this actor, they didn't like him, but they did pick up a friend en route; so the friend sat back with me, and I sat there, Anita sat there, Mr. Emerson steered, and it was a pretty black night and the car was going faster and faster. All of a sudden the road took a turn, but John Emerson didn't take the turn and we swept right out into a field and there was corn coming in the windows. And there we all sat, and nobody said anything, and all of a sudden I hear that unforgettable voice of Anita's and she said, "Oh, Mr. E., you never think of anybody but yourself." It didn't seem to fit the situation but it covered a lot of ground. Mum's the word.

Well, we opened *The Fall of Eve* in the Booth Theatre, and the play got awful notices, and everybody in the cast got awful notices, and John

Emerson got awful notices, too. I think even the Booth Theatre got an awful notice, right down the line. And the next morning when the reviews had come out, they had a kind of batty secretary, and she came in, starry-eyed, and said, "Oh, isn't it wonderful? Aren't the reviews great?" And I said to Anita, "What does she mean?" And Anita said, "I think she thinks it's wonderful for Mr. E. and me to have our names in print."

Another time I remember Bill Blackwood staged a great event. It was welcoming the eighty-one members into the Hall of Fame, the Theatre Hall of Fame. And Carol Channing had been elected and little Anita stood in for her. So in the Uris Theatre, way in the back, way in the dim background, the little figure of Anita came along, her hands like a Dresden doll, and she came out in the bright light, looking terrific in a long black dress. She said, "I'm standing in for Carol Channing. She is tall, she is blonde, she is beautiful. I'm not any one of those things, but in this life you have to take what you can get." (loud laughs) Wait for the punch line. "And you are stuck with me."

I wish we were all stuck with Anita. I wish that we all were. She had more friends than anybody I knew from 1925 until right now. She had more friends, and you know something, I never knew a friend of hers who was a bore. Can we all take a bow?

MORTON GOTTLIEB

Richard Coe of the *Washington Post,* who's just flown up from Washington, I must tell you, used to speak to Anita almost as often as I did, not quite as often as Ruth Dubonnet. But he'll tell us a few secrets about his many, many years of being a close friend of Anita's.

RICHARD COE

Weren't we all lucky to know such a joyful person! It was typical of our Anita that I didn't meet her through such mutual theatrical friends as Helen or Carol or Mortie. No, I met her through a sportsman, George

Marshall, the late, very effervescent, irascible George of the Washington Redskins, a gambling man, just the sort of rogue male Anita always preferred. George called me one afternoon to meet Anita in what we called the Belle Watling Room of the Willard Hotel in Washington. That setting was so right for Anita, who shined with the purity of one of those diamonds Lorelei so adored. What a surprise she was. No affected accent, no verbal la-di-da, but her voice had the sound of a sensible Iowa farmwife who might have evaluated pigs and then chuckled as she cleaned up the manure. She didn't mind manure. She took it along with everything else that makes you alive, but she just didn't want any on her own elegant self. In time she would remark on how gambling men treated her, how Wilson Mizner was probably the love of her life, and how she turned him into the gambler Clark Gable had played in *San Francisco*. And remarking that she had married one. Anita was never down, sharing the news that the money her husband took from her over the years would be used to support the final eighteen years of his life in an asylum. Her wit came from a holy, piercing, democratic honesty, a truly rare trait.

After an evening out one night, we walked home via Eighth Avenue. An aging friend waved to her. Anita stopped to ask, "How's business?" They exchanged small talk. After we resumed walking, Anita explained that her friend was a prostitute. Anita didn't live by theories; she lived by her acts.

Carol Channing and Charles Lowe can't be here today because they were indeed very heartily warned that if, through the controller's strike or the weather, they missed this evening's performance of *Hello, Dolly!* in Cleveland by being here this afternoon, the management would sue them for tonight's gross of $350,000. Anita, I told them, will never forgive you for coming or for letting down a sold-out house. Give them a good show, Anita would always say, and they'll always come back. While Carol was playing Lorelei at the Palace, Anita would take her friends from all over the world, and when Carol would introduce them, the house would rise in salute and with some surprise, such a youthful air about her, everyone remarked about her.

But if I choose for you a story about Anita, it happened one night when my Christine and I took her to a Washington party. One of the guests was President Nixon. As we drifted within a few feet of the president, I murmured, "Would you like to meet the president?" Anita answered, "Not particularly." And she drifted away.

MORTON GOTTLIEB

I just want to read you a few sentences that Carol Channing dictated. As Dick Coe said, she cannot come East because of the various plane schedules to get her here and back from Cleveland. She asked me to read you this: "Anita Loos gave me her most precious assignment, Miss Lorelei, the little girl from Little Rock. Anita did this when I was an unknown. Through the years as I grew to know Anita, she became a spiritual mother. As Anita Loos had Lorelei proclaim, diamonds are a girl's best friend. Today, dear Anita, you are our diamond, and we are all your best friends."

Anita's niece, Mary Anita Loos, was lucky enough to have known Anita Loos every moment of her life.

MARY ANITA LOOS

The audacity of following all these beautiful and famous people who shared Anita's professional life is only because I was there from the beginning. I knew her before you did, and I was privileged enough to know some of the marvelous analyses she made of current events and one-liners about people. It went back mostly to when Anita came back from New York, after John Emerson had bought German marks with which they could have wallpapered this room. And she had to go back to work again, and so she went to work at Paramount Studios, and I was a kind of a gangly kid, as tall as I am now; and when I really got to know this petite, adorable woman, I felt I had more knees and knuckles and elbows than anybody in the history of the world. But she took charge of me and she said, "Now the first thing we have to do is pull your eyebrows because one brow is not in." Well, I had the privilege of having Anita get me started in getting away from childhood and being a girl and a young woman, and she was very good at it and awfully tough. And the first thing she did was warn me about men. She said if they're attractive, let them hang around, but watch out. As time went on and I became a writer, I became terribly obsessed with the fact that I was following Anita, and finally one day I said, "Nobody can follow Anita. Whatever she does is her thing, and whatever I do is my thing, so I'll just have to forget about it and just love her for what she is and not be overwhelmed by her talent."

She had such a marvelous way of categorizing people, and she had such generosity of spirit. I think some of you were in her house on Sundays when she had such a marvelous collection of people around her, and through this I was privileged to start knowing people like Aldous Huxley and Helen Hayes, people like Ruth Gordon and Garson Kanin, and people who came to her house. I remember one particular day, and I think Gladys does too because Gladys was usually shuffling up wonderful food for these wonderful people. I think Stokowski was there and Garbo and Aldous Huxley, and I was there and my father, her older brother, Dr. Loos, and we were all sitting having a magnificent discussion when Anita got up and looked out the window next door. And she came back and sat down and everybody was wondering what was going on, and she said, "I don't like to disturb this conversation, but Lena Horne is out there taking a sunbath." So we all immediately got up and looked out the window.

Now another time, when she was doing *San Francisco,* and maybe I shouldn't tell this story, but I think I will because I think everybody probably knew Mr. Gable had a little crockery in his mouth. And one time Anita said, "I love that man. He's so wonderful, and I'm not completely devoted to actors, but I love him." I said, "Why do you, Anita?" And she said, "Because the other day I was on the lot and he had his teeth out and he was washing them in the drinking fountain. And he saw me and he put them back in and he looked at me and said, 'Anita sweet, I'm America's Sweetheart.' From that day on, I loved that man."

She had marvelous one-liners. One time my former husband and I were working in London, and we were working for Alex Korda, who was about to do *Around the World in Eighty Days,* and Korda sold it to Mike Todd, and we were a little disturbed because we were nervous about Mike Todd. We didn't do it; instead, we bought her sequel to *Gentlemen Prefer Blondes* and made an absolutely dreadful movie out of it. But anyway, I said, "Well Anita, what do you think about Mike Todd?" She said, "I think he's terrific." And I said, "Why do you think so?" She said, "He's like a diamond in a dirty shirt."

And when she did *Gentlemen Prefer Blondes,* I said, "Anita, it seems so marvelous to me that you had the audacity to take a great big, beautiful creature like Carol Channing and have her be that delicate Lorelei Lee." And she said, "Well, I'll tell you why I really did it. Carol Channing is a Great Dane who thinks she's a Pekinese."

That's the sort of background that my aunt bequeathed to me. She was generous of spirit, she was talented of mind, and she was absolutely beautiful. About two years ago she came out to visit me in California and she was sitting at a dressing table and she had on a ruffly negligee and her hair was falling on her shoulder and one of her absolutely exquisite little feet and a leg were leaning out, and I looked at her and she was the epitome of feminine beauty. It didn't have anything to do with age. And she never did have anything to do with age. There was a wonderful article in the *Los Angeles Times,* and she said, I can repeat it because it was published, "Anita thought the two most boring people she knew in her life because they talked about age all the time were Elsie Mendl and Maurice Chevalier."

When I heard about Anita passing on, I happened to be at King Vidor's ranch working on a book. I was quite upset, and he said, "You mustn't be upset; you're going to New York to celebrate her life." And I thought that was one of the most wonderful things. That's why we're all here. We're here to love her wonderful spirit and talent, and she doesn't really need us because the whole world loves her and her spirit; her works will continue to inspire students as well as people who knew her.

One last story I must tell about her. She was devoted to Irving Thalberg, and he equally thought she was a wonderful talent. He used to call her quite often into his conference room, and she would sit in the outer office, and she could never be idle; she was always crocheting. I remember one time I got a washcloth from her for Christmas and I thought, "What's this?" She wrote, "The modern washcloths are too thick and lousy, you can't get them in your ears, so here's one you can get in your ears." Some of you might also have gotten them for Christmas; mine I'm going to frame.

But anyway, she knitted a scarf while she was waiting to talk to Irving Thalberg. She had a very good salary for that time, and finally Thalberg called her in after many of these waits, and he said, "Anita, what is that? What are you doing?" And she said, "Well, Irving, I think this is probably the most expensive gift you'll ever get, because I'm crocheting it for your Christmas present and so far it's cost MGM studios $20,000."

Anita was a joyous person. Whenever you had a sadness, she had a joke to make you forget. Our particular sadness today is that she isn't going to be on the telephone with us anymore. As Ruth Dubonnet said to me, "I think you remember most and love most the people who make you laugh, and Anita had that quality so I know she'll be with us."

NOTES

The principal source for this work is, of course, Anita herself and the papers and manuscripts she left to her niece, Mary Anita Loos. For our own writing, and for collaboration of certain facts, we depended on a variety of sources. First and foremost are Anita's own appointment books and her letters, ranging from 1912 through the 1970s.

We consulted various files and collections at the Margaret Herrick Library of the Academy of Motion Picture Arts and Sciences, including the George Cukor Collection, the Motion Picture Association of America/Production Code Administration files, the Hedda Hopper Collection, film production files, and files on Anita Loos. We also reviewed the collection of Anita's letters and files at the Museum of Modern Art.

Interviews quoted include those with Mary Lea Bandy, chief curator of the Museum of Modern Art; film historian and filmmaker Kevin Brownlow; Carol Channing; Peter Duchin; and James Frasher, longtime manager of Lillian Gish. We also depended on information provided by Booton Herndon and Patricia Eliot Tobias.

INTRODUCTION

1. Paul Gant, *Photoplay,* Dec. 1917.
2. Conversations with Mary Anita Loos.

3. Carol Channing, interview by Cari Beauchamp, 2002.

4. Karl Brown, *Adventures with D. W. Griffith* (New York: Farrar, Straus and Giroux, 1973), 100–101.

ANITA LOOS AND HER STORIES
FROM SAN DIEGO, 1888–1915

1. Records of Anita's sales of her film stories are from the Anita Loos Collection at MOMA.

2. Kevin Brownlow, *The Parade's Gone By* (New York: Alfred A. Knopf, 1969), 28.

3. Letters between Loos and Biograph are at MOMA and in her personal papers; Dougherty is discussed in Richard Schickel, *D. W. Griffith: An American Life* (New York: Simon and Schuster, 1984), 103.

4. Anita Loos, *A Girl like I* (New York: Viking, 1966), 73–74.

5. Anita Loos, quote as recalled by Mary Anita Loos in interview by Cari Beauchamp.

HOLLYWOOD SUCCESS
AND INTERNATIONAL FAME, 1915–1930

1. Loos, *A Girl like I*, 84–85.

2. Frances Marion, "Hollywood," 499, Cinema-Television Library, University of Southern California. This is a draft manuscript of what would be published as Frances Marion's *Off with Their Heads* (New York: Macmillan, 1972).

3. *Photoplay,* Feb. 1918; *Photoplay,* July 1918; *Motion Picture Magazine,* Apr. 1918.

4. Marion's "constipated brain" comment occurs in an interview she gave to Booton Herndon in 1971; Herndon was kind enough to send me his papers. Wedding details in *Photoplay,* Nov. 1919.

5. Bennett Cerf, *At Random* (New York: Random House, 1973), 44–49.

6. Quotes from "Anita's Dad Spills the Frijoles: Sensational Expose of Miss Loos' Early Life by the Father Who Prefers Brunettes," *Photoplay,* Aug. 1928.

7. Kevin Brownlow to Cari Beauchamp, Apr. 2002; and Brownlow, conversation with Beauchamp, London, Oct. 2002.

RETURN TO HOLLYWOOD, 1931–1944

1. Mary Anita Loos to Cari Beauchamp, personal correspondence.
2. Samuel Marx, *Mayer and Thalberg: The Make-Believe Saints* (New York: Random House, 1975), 182.
3. Anita Loos, *Kiss Hollywood Good-by* (New York: Viking, 1974), 34.
4. Ibid., 40.
5. Ibid., 40–41.
6. Anita Loos, quoted in *Women's Wear Daily,* Aug. 23, 1974.
7. Jason Joy to Irving Thalberg, Oct. 9, 1931, Motion Picture Association of America/Production Code Administration files (hereafter MPAA/PCA), Margaret Herrick Library (MHL), Academy of Motion Picture Arts and Sciences (AMPAS). Anita Loos's 1932 appointment book notes May 13 as the day of the preview of *Red-Headed Woman* at the Fox Uptown theater, with a conference immediately following at Bernie Hyman's apartment.
8. Irving Thalberg to Jason Joy, Oct. 10, 1931, MPAA/PCA, MHL, AMPAS.
9. Lamar Trotti to Irving Thalberg, May 16, 1932, MPAA/PCA, MHL, AMPAS.
10. Jason Joy to Will Hays, June 17, 1932, MPAA/PCA, MHL, AMPAS.
11. Mary Anita Loos, conversation with Cari Beauchamp.
12. Mary Anita Loos, conversation with Cari Beauchamp.
13. Loos, *Kiss Hollywood Good-by,* 135.
14. *Blondie of the Follies* production files, Cinema-Television Library, University of Southern California.
15. Anita Loos's appointment book. Unless otherwise noted, subsequent quotes attributed to Loos are from this source.
16. Anita Loos, quoted in *New York Sun,* Dec. 8, 1949.
17. Loos, *Women's Wear Daily.*
18. Anita Loos's appointment book.

NEW YORK AT LAST, 1944–1981

1. Frances Marion to Hedda Hopper, July 15, 1948, Hedda Hopper Collection, MPAA/PCA, MHL, AMPAS.
2. Carol Channing, *Just Lucky I Guess* (New York: Simon and Schuster, 2002), 78.
3. Carol Channing, interview by Cari Beauchamp, 2002.

4. Letters in the George Cukor Collection, MPAA/PCA, MHL, AMPAS.

5. Mary Anita Loos, conversation with Cari Beauchamp.

6. Mary Anita Loos, conversation with Cari Beauchamp.

7. Channing, interview.

8. Mary Lea Bandy, interview by Cari Beauchamp, 1998.

9. Jim Frasher, interview by Cari Beauchamp, 1999.

10. Peter Duchin, interview by Cari Beauchamp, 2002; see also Peter Duchin, with Charles Michener, *Ghost of a Chance: A Memoir* (New York: Random House, 1996).

11. *New York Times,* Mar. 7, 1974.

12. *New York Times,* Aug. 28, 1980.

WORKS BY ANITA LOOS

This filmography and list of books and plays by Anita Loos has been compiled from Anita Loos's records, her appointment books, letters to Anita Loos, and files of the Museum of Modern Art and the Margaret Herrick Library of the Academy of Motion Picture Arts and Sciences. They have been compared and cross-referenced with Gary Carey, "Written on the Screen," *Film Comment* (winter 1970–71); and Anita Loos, *Kiss Hollywood Good-by* (New York: Viking, 1974). Dates given for Anita's early titles are copyright and release dates (in that order).

FILMS
1912

The Earl and the Tomboy. Lubin. 1 reel. Mar. 3, 1912. Exact release date unknown.

The Road to Plaindale. Biograph. 1 reel. Apr. 11, 1912. Released Mar. 23, 1914.

The New York Hat. Biograph. 1 reel. Released Dec. 5, 1913.

He Was a College Boy. Biograph. ½ reel. Dec. 27, 1913. Exact release date unknown.

The Power of the Camera. Biograph. ½ reel. Dec. 27, 1912. Released Mar. 17, 1913.

1913

A Horse on Bill. Biograph. ½ reel. Jan. 27, 1913. Released Apr. 14, 1913.

A Hicksville Epicure. Biograph. ½ reel. Jan. 1913. Released Feb. 1913.

Highbrow Love. Biograph. ½ reel. Feb. 17, 1913. Released June 1913.

Unlucky Jim. Kornic. 1 reel. Apr. 9, 1913. Released May 25, 1913.

All on Account of a Cold. Kornic. 1 reel. Apr. 12, 1913. Exact release date unknown.

The Queen of the Carnival. Biograph. ½ reel. Apr. 16, 1913. Exact release date unknown.

The Mayor Elect. Biograph. ½ reel. May 6, 1913. Exact release date unknown.

Two Women. Kinscolor. 1 reel. May 12, 1913. Exact release date unknown.

A Hicksville Romance. Biograph. ½ reel. May 15, 1913. Released Aug. 5, 1913.

The Widow's Kids. Biograph. ½ reel. May 15, 1913. Released Aug. 1913.

A Fallen Hero. Biograph. ½ reel. June 12, 1913. Released Oct. 23, 1913.

The Wallflower. Lubin. 1 reel. June 14, 1913. Released May 12, 1913.

The Making of a Masher. Biograph. ½ reel. June 18, 1913. Exact release date unknown.

A Fireman's Love. Biograph. ½ reel. Sept. 8, 1913. Exact release date unknown.

A Cure for Suffragettes. Biograph. ½ reel. Sept. 15, 1913. Released Nov. 17, 1913.

Path of True Love. Biograph. ½ reel. Sept. 15, 1913. Exact release date unknown.

The Suicide Pact. Biograph. ½ reel. Sept. 15, 1913. Released Dec. 1913.

Binks Runs Away. Biograph. ½ reel. Oct. 16, 1913. Released Nov. 1913.

How the Day Was Saved. Biograph. ½ reel. Oct. 20, 1913. Released Nov. 1913.

When a Woman Guides. Biograph. 1 reel. Oct. 25, 1913. Released Apr. 12, 1914.

Fall of the Hicksville Finest. Biograph. ½ reel. Nov. 3, 1913. Released Apr. 10, 1914.

The Wedding Gown. Biograph. 1 reel. Nov. 6, 1913. Released Dec. 1913.

Yiddish Love. Biograph. ½ reel. Nov. 6, 1913. Released Dec. 1913.

A Girl like Mother. Biograph. ½ reel. Nov. 12, 1913. Exact release date unknown.

For Her Father's Sins. Reliance Mutual Corp. 1 reel. Nov. 19, 1913. Released Oct. 13, 1914 (starring Blanche Sweet).

The Mother. Biograph. 1 reel. Nov. 26, 1913. Exact release date unknown.

Gentlemen Thieves. Biograph. 1 reel. Nov. 26, 1913. Released Mar. 1914.

The Deacon's Whiskers. Mutual. 1 reel. Dec. 8, 1913. Released Mar. 1914.

His Awful Vengeance. Mutual. 1 reel. Dec. 8, 1913. Released Dec. 1913.

The Great Motor Race. Biograph. ½ reel. Dec. 13, 1913. Exact release date unknown.

A Bunch of Flowers. Biograph. 1 reel. Dec. 18, 1913. Released Mar. 2, 1914.

All for Mable, Man in the Couch. Mutual. 1 reel. Dec. 20, 1913. Released May 1914.

The Fatal Deception. Mutual. ½ reel. Dec. 20, 1913. Released 1914.

1914

The Deadly Glass of Beer. Mutual. ½ reel. Jan. 17, 1914. Exact release date unknown.

The Chieftain's Daughter, Some Bull's Daughter. Mutual. ½ reel. Jan. 17, 1914. Released Apr. 18, 1914.

The Stolen Masterpiece. Mutual. 1 reel. Jan. 17, 1914. Exact release date unknown.

The Fatal Dress Suit. Mutual. 1 reel. Jan. 17, 1914. Released Apr. 12, 1914.

The Girl in the Shack. Mutual. 1 reel. Jan. 17, 1914. Released May 15, 1914.

A No Bull Story. Biograph. ½ reel. Exact release date unknown.

The Meal Ticket. Biograph. 1 reel. Feb. 24, 1914. Released Aug. 16, 1914.

The Last Drink of Whiskey. Mutual. ½ reel. Mar. 2, 1914. Released June 7, 1914.

Nell's Eugenic Wedding. Mutual. ½ reel. Mar. 2, 1914. Exact release date unknown.

The Saving Presence. Biograph. Mar. 5, 1914. Released May 4, 1914.

A Balked Heredity. Biograph. Mar. 19, 1914. Exact release date unknown.

A Blasted Romance. Biograph. Mar. 21, 1914. Exact release date unknown.

Mortimer's Millions. Biograph. ½ reel. Mar. 31, 1914. Exact release date unknown.

The School of Acting. Mutual. 1 reel. Apr. 20, 1914. Exact release date unknown.

His Hated Rivals (A Corner in Hats). Mutual. 1 reel. May 1, 1914. Released Nov. 29, 1914.

Nearly a Burglar's Bride. Mutual. 1 reel. May 1, 1914. Exact release date unknown.

A Hicksville Reformer. Mutual. 1 reel. May 1, 1914. Exact release date unknown.

The White Slave Catchers. Mutual. 1/2 reel. May 1, 1914. Exact release date unknown.

The Style Accustomed. Mutual. 1/2 reel. May 1, 1914. Exact release date unknown.

He Went to the Dogs. Mutual. 1 reel. May 1, 1914. Exact release date unknown.

The Fatal Curve (Izzy and His Rival). Mutual. May 20, 1914. Released Aug. 1914.

The Million Dollar Bride. Mutual. 1 reel. Aug. 29, 1914. Released Oct. 4, 1914.

His Rival. American. 1/2 reel. Aug. 30, 1914. Exact release date unknown.

Where the Road Parts. American. 1/2 reel. Sept. 20, 1914. Exact release date unknown.

A Life and Death Affair. Biograph. 1/2 reel. Oct. 6, 1914. Exact release date unknown.

The Sensible Girl. Biograph. 1/2 reel. Oct. 6, 1914. Exact release date unknown.

The Suffering of Susan. Biograph. 1/2 reel. Oct. 21, 1914. Released Dec. 24, 1914.

At the Tunnel's End. Biograph. 1/2 reel. Oct. 26, 1914. Exact release date unknown.

The Old Oak Tree. Mutual. 1/2 reel. Nov. 3, 1914. Exact release date unknown.

A Flurry in Art. Mutual. 1/2 reel. Nov. 14, 1914. Released Dec. 24, 1914.

How They Met. Mutual. 1/2 reel. Nov. 14, 1914. Released Dec. 24, 1914.

Nellie, the Female Villain. Mutual. 1/2 reel. Nov. 25, 1914. Exact release date unknown.

1915

The Burlesquers. Mutual. 1/2 reel. Jan. 13, 1915. Exact release date unknown.

The Fatal Fourth. Mutual. 1/2 reel. Jan. 13, 1915. Exact release date unknown.

Sympathy Sal. Mutual. 1 reel. Jan. 13, 1915. Exact release date unknown.

Cost of a Bargain. Biograph. ½ reel. Feb. 1915. Exact release date unknown.

Mixed Values. Mutual. ½ reel. Feb. 1915. Released Mar. 30, 1915.

The Tear of a Page. Biograph. 1 reel. Mar. 15, 1915. Exact release date unknown.

How to Keep a Husband. Biograph. 1 reel. Mar. 1915. Exact release date unknown.

The Fatal Finger Prints. Mutual. Mar. 1915. Exact release date unknown.

Wards of Fate. Mutual. May 15, 1915. Exact release date unknown.

Pennington's Choice (adaptation). Metro. 5 reels. Released Nov. 8, 1915.

Mountain Bred. Mabel Normand Productions. Exact release date unknown.

1916

Macbeth. Lucky Film Producers. Dir. John Emerson. Writ. William Shakespeare and Anita Loos. Starring Sir Herbert Beerholm-Tree.

A Corner in Cotton. Quality Pictures/Metro. Dir. Fred J. Balshofer. Script by Anita Loos. Starring Marguerite Snow.

Wild Girl of the Sierra. Fine Arts/Triangle. Dir. Paul Powell. Script by Anita Loos and F. M. Pierson. Starring Mae Marsh, Bobby Harron, and Wilfred Lucas.

The Little Liar. Fine Arts. Dir. Lloyd Ingraham. Writ. Anita Loos. Starring Mae Marsh.

Calico Vampire. Fine Arts. Writ. Anita Loos. 2 reels. Starring Fay Tincher.

Laundry Liz. Fine Arts. Scenario by Anita Loos. 2 reels. Starring Fay Tincher.

French Milliner. Triangle. Writ. Anita Loos. 2 reels. Starring Fay Tincher.

The Wharf Rat. Fine Arts/Triangle. Dir. Chester Withey. Script by Anita Loos. Starring Mae Marsh and Bobby Harron.

Stranded. Fine Arts/Triangle. Dir. Lloyd Ingraham. Script by Anita Loos. Starring DeWolf Hopper and Bessie Love.

The Social Secretary. Fine Arts/Triangle. Dir. John Emerson. Script by John Emerson and Anita Loos. Starring Norma Talmadge and Erich von Stroheim.

His Picture in the Papers. Triangle Films. Dir. by John Emerson. Script by Anita Loos. Starring Douglas Fairbanks.

The Half-Breed. Fine Arts/Triangle. Dir. Allan Dwan. Script by Anita Loos, from Bret Harte's story, "In the Carquinez Woods." Starring Douglas Fairbanks and Alma Rubens.

American Aristocracy. Fine Arts/Triangle. Dir. Lloyd Ingraham. Script by Anita Loos. Starring Douglas Fairbanks.

The Matrimaniac. Triangle. Dir. Paul Powell. Script by Anita Loos and John Emerson, from a story by Octavus Roy Cohen and J. U. Giesy. Starring Douglas Fairbanks and Constance Talmadge.

Intolerance. Triangle. Writ. and dir. D. W. Griffith. Titles by Anita Loos.

1917

The Americano. Fine Arts/Triangle. Dir. John Emerson. Script by Anita Loos and John Emerson. Starring Douglas Fairbanks and Alma Rubens.

In Again, Out Again. Artcraft. Dir. John Emerson. Script by Anita Loos and John Emerson. Starring Douglas Fairbanks.

Wild and Woolly. Artcraft. Dir. John Emerson. Script by Anita Loos. Starring Douglas Fairbanks and Eileen Percy.

Reaching for the Moon. Artcraft. Dir. John Emerson. Script by Anita Loos. Starring Douglas Fairbanks and Eileen Percy.

Down to Earth. Artcraft. Dir. John Emerson. Scenario by Anita Loos and John Emerson. Starring Douglas Fairbanks.

Daughter of the Poor (a.k.a. *The Spitfire*). Fine Arts/Triangle. Dir. Edward Dillon. Scenario by Anita Loos. Starring Bessie Love.

1918

Let's Get a Divorce. Famous Players–Lasky. Dir. Charles Giblyn. Script by Anita Loos and John Emerson, from Victorien Sardou's play *Divorcons.* Starring Billie Burke.

Hit the Trail Holiday. Famous Players–Lasky. Dir. Marshall Neilan. Script by Anita Loos and John Emerson, from the play by George M. Cohan. Starring George M. Cohan.

Come on In. Famous Players–Lasky/Emerson Loos Production. Dir. John Emerson. Script by John Emerson and Anita Loos. Starring Ernest Truex.

Goodbye Bill. Famous Players–Lasky/Emerson Loos Production. Dir. John Emerson. Script by John Emerson and Anita Loos. Starring Shirley Mason and Ernest Truex.

1919

Under the Top. Famous Players–Lasky. Dir. Donald Crisp. Story by John Emerson and Anita Loos. Script by Gardner Hunting. Starring Fred Stone.

Oh, You Women! Famous Players–Lasky. Dir. John Emerson. Script and story by John Emerson and Anita Loos. Starring Ernest Truex and Louise Huff.

Getting Mary Married. Marion Davies Film Co. Dir. Allan Dwan. Script by John Emerson and Anita Loos. Starring Marion Davies.

A Temperamental Wife. Constance Talmadge Films Co. Dir. John Emerson. Script by John Emerson and Anita Loos. Starring Constance Talmadge.

The Isles of Conquest. Select Pictures. Dir. Edward Jose. Script by John Emerson and Anita Loos, from Arthur Hornblow's novel *By Right of Conquest.* Starring Norma Talmadge.

A Virtuous Vamp. Joseph M. Schenck. Dir. David Kirkland. Script by John Emerson and Anita Loos, from Clyde Fitch's play *The Bachelor.* Starring Constance Talmadge.

1920

Two Weeks. First National. Dir. Sidney Franklin. Script by John Emerson and Anita Loos, from Anthony Wharton's play *At the Barn.* Starring Constance Talmadge.

In Search of a Sinner. Joseph M. Schenck. Dir. David Kirkland. Script by Anita Loos and John Emerson. Starring Constance Talmadge.

The Love Expert. Joseph M. Schenck. Dir. David Kirkland. Script by Anita Loos and John Emerson. Starring Constance Talmadge.

The Perfect Woman. First National. Dir. David Kirkland. Script by Anita Loos and John Emerson. Starring Constance Talmadge.

The Branded Woman. Joseph M. Schenck. Dir. Albert Parker. Script by Anita Loos and John Emerson, from Oliver D. Bailey's play. Starring Norma Talmadge.

1921

Dangerous Business. First National. Dir. R. William Neill. Script by Anita Loos and John Emerson. Starring Constance Talmadge.

Mama's Affair. First National. Dir. Victor Fleming. Script by Anita Loos and John Emerson, from Rachel Barton Butler's play. Starring Constance Talmadge.

A Woman's Place. Joseph M. Schenck. Dir. Victor Fleming. Script by Anita Loos and John Emerson. Starring Constance Talmadge.

1922

Red Hot Romance. Joseph M. Schenck. Dir. Victor Fleming. Script by Anita Loos and John Emerson. Starring Basil Sydney and Mary Collins.

Polly of the Follies. First National. Dir. Joseph Plunkett. Story and script by Anita Loos and John Emerson. Starring Constance Talmadge.

1923

Dulcy. Joseph M. Schenck. Dir. Sidney Franklin. Script by John Emerson and Anita Loos, from the play by George Kaufman and Marc Connelly. Starring Constance Talmadge.

1924

Three Miles Out. Kenma. Dir. Irvin Willat. Story by Neysa McMein. Script by Anita Loos and John Emerson. Starring Madge Kennedy.

Learning to Love. First National. Dir. Sidney Franklin. Scenario by Anita Loos and John Emerson. Starring Constance Talmadge.

1927

Stranded. Sterling Pictures. Dir. Phil Rosen. Story by Anita Loos. Starring Shirley Mason and Buster Collier Jr.

Publicity Madness. Fox Film. Dir. Albert Ray. Scenario by Anita Loos. Starring Lois Moran and Edmund Lowe.

1928

Gentlemen Prefer Blondes. Paramount Famous Lasky. Dir. Malcolm St. Clair. Scenario by Anita Loos and John Emerson, from Loos's novel. Starring Ruth Taylor.

1931

The Struggle. D. W. Griffith. Dir. D. W. Griffith. Script by Anita Loos. Dialogue by Anita Loos, John Emerson, and D. W. Griffith. Starring Hal Skelly.

Ex-Bad Boy. Universal. Dir. Vin Moore. Script by Dale Van Every, from Anita Loos and John Emerson's play *The Whole Town's Talking.* Starring Robert Armstrong and Jean Arthur.

1932

Red-Headed Woman. MGM. Dir. Jack Conway. Script by Anita Loos, from Katharine Brush's novel. Starring Jean Harlow, Chester Morris, Una Merkel, and Charles Boyer.

1933

Hold Your Man. MGM. Dir. Sam Wood. Story by Anita Loos. Script by Anita Loos and Howard Emmett Rogers. Starring Jean Harlow and Clark Gable.

Midnight Mary. MGM. Dir. William Wellman. Story by Anita Loos. Script by Gene Markey and Kathryn Scola. Starring Loretta Young and Ricardo Cortez.

The Barbarian. MGM. Dir. Sam Wood. Story by Edgar Selwyn. Script by Anita Loos and Elmer Harris. Starring Ramon Novarro and Myrna Loy.

1934

The Social Register. Columbia. Dir. Marshall Neilan. Script by Clara Beranger, based on the play by Anita Loos and John Emerson. Starring Colleen Moore.

The Girl from Missouri. MGM. Dir. Jack Conway. Script by Anita Loos and John Emerson. Starring Jean Harlow and Franchot Tone.

Biography of a Bachelor Girl. MGM. Dir. Edward H. Griffith. Script by Anita Loos and Horace Jackson. Starring Ann Harding.

1935

Riff Raff. MGM. Dir. J. Walter Rubin. Story by Frances Marion. Script by Frances Marion and Anita Loos. Starring Jean Harlow and Spencer Tracy.

1936

San Francisco. MGM. Dir. W. S. Van Dyke. Story by Robert Hopkins. Script by Anita Loos. Starring Clark Gable, Spencer Tracy, and Jeanette MacDonald.

1937

Mama Steps Out. MGM. Dir. George B. Seltz. Script by Anita Loos. Starring Alice Brady and Guy Kibbee.

Saratoga. MGM. Dir. Jack Conway. Story and script by Anita Loos and Robert Hopkins. Starring Jean Harlow and Clark Gable.

1938

The Cowboy and the Lady. Samuel Goldwyn. Dir. H. C. Potter. Writing credited to Frank Adams, S. N. Behrman, and Sonya Levien, with story by Leo McCarey (Anita Loos and Dorothy Parker uncredited).

The Goldwyn Follies. Samuel Goldwyn. Dir. George Marshall. Script credited to Ben Hecht, Sam Perrin, and Arthur Phillips (Anita Loos uncredited).

Alaska (not produced).

The Great Canadian (not produced).

1939

The Women. MGM. Dir. George Cukor. Script by Anita Loos and Jane Murfin, from the play by Clare Boothe. Starring Norma Shearer.

Another Thin Man. MGM. Dir. W. S. Van Dyke. Script credited to Frances Goodrich and Albert Hackett (Anita Loos uncredited as script doctor). Starring William Powell and Myrna Loy.

1940

Susan and God. MGM. Dir. George Cukor. Script by Anita Loos, from Rachel Crothers's play. Starring Joan Crawford.

1941

They Met in Bombay. MGM. Dir. Clarence Brown. Script by Anita Loos, Edwin Justus Mayer, and Leon Gordon. Starring Clark Gable and Rosalind Russell.

When Ladies Meet. MGM. Dir. Robert Z. Leonard. Script by Anita Loos and S. K. Lauren, from the play by Rachel Crothers. Starring Joan Crawford and Greer Garson.

Blossoms in the Dust. MGM. Dir. Mervyn LeRoy. Story by Ralph Wheelwright. Script by Anita Loos. Starring Greer Garson.

1942

I Married an Angel. MGM. Dir. W. S. Van Dyke. Script by Anita Loos, from the musical by Vaszary Jones, Lorenz Hart, and Richard Rodgers. Starring Nelson Eddy and Jeanette MacDonald.

BOOKS
Fiction

Gentlemen Prefer Blondes. New York: Boni and Liveright, 1925.

But Gentlemen Marry Brunettes. New York: Boni and Liveright, 1928.

(with Jane Murfin) *The Women.* In *Twenty Best Film Plays,* ed. John Gassner and Dudley Nichols. New York: Crown, 1943.

A Mouse Is Born. New York: Doubleday, 1951.

(with D. W. Griffith) *Intolerance.* New York: n.p., 1955.

No Mother to Guide Her. New York: McGraw-Hill, 1961.

San Francisco. Ed. Matthew J. Bruccoli. Carbondale, Ill.: Southern Illinois University Press, 1979.

Nonfiction

(with John Emerson) *How to Write Photoplays* (includes the script *The Love Expert*). New York: James A. McCann, 1920.

(with John Emerson) *Breaking into the Movies* (includes the script *Red Hot Romance*). New York: James A. McCann, 1921.

A Girl like I. New York: Viking, 1966.

(with Helen Hayes) *Twice Over Lightly: New York Then and Now*. New York: Harcourt Brace, 1972.

Kiss Hollywood Good-by. New York: Viking, 1974.

A Cast of Thousands. New York: Grosset and Dunlap, 1977.

The Talmadge Girls (includes script of *The Virtuous Vamp*). New York: Viking, 1978.

Fate Keeps on Happening. Ed. Ray Pierre Corsini. New York: Dodd, Mead, 1984.

PLAYS
Produced

The Whole Town's Talking, with John Emerson. New York, 1923.

The Fall of Eve, with John Emerson. New York, 1925.

Gentlemen Prefer Blondes, with John Emerson. New York, 1926.

The Social Register, with John Emerson. New York, 1931.

Happy Birthday. New York, 1946.

White Nights. New York, 1947.

Gentlemen Prefer Blondes. New York, 1949.

Gigi. New York, 1951.

The Amazing Adele. Philadelphia, 1955.

Cheri. New York, 1959.

A King's Mare. London, 1967.

Unproduced

Every Girl Needs a Parlor, based on the book *The One I Loved the Best: Episodes from the Life of Lady Mendl (Elsie De Wolfe),* by Ludwig Bemelmans (New York: Viking, 1955).

The Gay Illiterate, a comedic takeoff on Louella Parsons's autobiography (New York: Doubleday, 1944) of the same name.

Hotbed of Roses, original drawing-room comedy set in Reno in 1949.

Old Buddha, based on an idea by Lionel Barrymore, about the last empress of China and her adventures with an American dentist.

Something about Anne, a version of *The King's Mare* as a musical with songs by Ralph Blane and James Gregory.

ACKNOWLEDGMENTS

Even an anthology requires many hands and eyes, to say nothing of arms for the occasional, much-needed hugs. For their expert advice, memory jogging, comfort, support, and every variety of assistance we are deeply indebted to Eddie Albert, Mary Lea Bandy, Jimmy Bangley, Ian Birnie, Kevin Brownlow, Carol Channing, Terry Christensen, Ned Comstock, Ray Corsini, Peter Duchin, Cahri Faulkner, Jim Frasher, Michelle Fuetsch, Morton Gottlieb, Barbara Hall, Jay Harris, Gene Hatcher, Belinda Vidor Holliday, Karen Johnson, Fay Kanin, Alva Klein, Brooke Kroeger, Jody Jacobs Leason, Madeline Matz, Bernice and Fred Meamber, Maggie Mosher, Joe and Carol Neal, Mona Onstead, Sue Vidor Perry, Maggie Renzi, Angela Shanahan, Charles Silver, Susy Smith, and Patricia Eliot Tobias.

We would also like to thank Charlene Woodcock and Eric Smoodin at the University of California for initiating this project and Kate Toll, Mary Francis, Rachel Berchten, and Sam Rosenthal for seeing it through to completion.

Particular appreciation must be given to our patient and industrious assistants, Gregory Archer, Virginia Brown, and Rebecca Fenning, and to our loving and supportive families: Catherine Beauchamp; Carl von Saltza and Tom Flynn; and Edward Sale, Teo Beauchamp, and Jake Flynn.

In addition, Mary Anita would like to acknowledge the friends who are no longer with us but crossed her path because of Anita: Jay Allen, Charlie Chaplin, Marion Davies, Ruth Dubonnet, Eddy Duchin, Allan Dwan, John Emerson, Clark Gable, Paulette Goddard, Jean Harlow, Helen Hayes, Audrey

Hepburn, Aldous Huxley, H. C. Loos, Minnie Loos, R. Beers Loos, Charlie MacArthur, Jeanette MacDonald, Frances Marion, Colleen Moore, Louella Parsons, Hunt Stromberg Sr., and King Vidor.

We apologize for anyone inadvertently not mentioned and, appreciating the help of so many, acknowledge that any mistakes are our own.

INDEX

MARY ANITA LOOS VON SALTZA is the third generation of her family to write for the motion picture industry. Her grandfather R. Beers Loos wrote silent-film titles for Famous Players–Lasky (now Paramount), and her aunt, Anita Loos, was the well-known screenwriter and author.

Mary Anita attended Stanford University, then divided her interests between archaeology—spending her summers excavating in the Southwest with the School of American Research—and travel, journeying on her own from Russia to Egypt in 1937. She witnessed the celebration of the North Pole Fliers in Moscow, saw the fear fall on Poland, watched Hitler and Mussolini drive by together in a car in Salzburg, and skied the sand dunes in Egypt.

She ran her own public relations firm in New York for several years before returning to her father's home in Santa Monica to write. She published a novel, *Return to the Vineyard* (Garden City, N.Y.: Doubleday, 1945), with Walter Duranty, the *New York Times* correspondent in Moscow.

Mary Anita joined the MGM publicity department, where she met the author Richard Sale, whom she later married. They became a writing team and wrote more than fifteen films together. As a screenwriter Mary Anita adapted and coproduced her aunt's book *Gentlemen Marry Brunettes,* which was filmed in Paris, London, and Monte Carlo and was released in 1955. Under contract to Twentieth Century Fox, Mary Anita wrote several films under the aegis of Daryl Zanuck; and at Howard Hughes's RKO she collaborated on *The French Line* (1954), starring Jane Russell.

Mary Anita also found success in television. Along with Sale she created, produced, and wrote the series *Yancy Derringer* for CBS. When her marriage to

Sale dissolved, she became a literary executive to M. J. Frankovich Productions at Columbia Studios. She resigned this position to write novels full time.

The Beggars Are Coming was selected by Bantam Books as the first book taken directly to paperback as a "super release" and was a huge success. *The Beggars Are Coming,* which was followed quickly by her novels *Belinda, The Barstow Legend,* and *A Pride of Lions,* sold millions.

After a lapse of fifty years Mary Anita serendipitously reconnected with her Stanford University sweetheart, Carl von Saltza. They married and had ten wonderful years together. She now lives in Monterey and is working on a novel and her memoirs.

CARI BEAUCHAMP is the award-winning author of *Without Lying Down: Frances Marion and the Powerful Women of Early Hollywood* (New York: Scribner, 1997), named Outstanding Book of the Year by the National Theater Library Association, a *New York Times* Notable Book of the Year, one of the One Hundred Best Books of the Year by the *Los Angeles Times,* and one of the Top Ten Biographies of the Year by Amazon.com.

Cari cowrote and coproduced the documentary film *Without Lying Down: Frances Marion and the Power of Women in Hollywood* (2002), based on her book. She was nominated for a Writers Guild Award for the documentary, which is narrated by Uma Thurman and features Kathy Bates as the voice of Frances Marion. The documentary is seen on Turner Broadcasting and on video from Milestone Films.

She also cowrote (with Henri Behar) the book *Hollywood on the Riviera: The Inside Story of the Cannes Film Festival* (New York: W. Morrow, 1992), in which she weaves more than one hundred interviews into a comprehensive and anecdotal history of the event that, for more than fifty years, has been the center of the international film industry for two weeks every year.

She has written on film and film history for a variety of publications, including the *New York Times, Vanity Fair,* the *Los Angeles Times, Architectural Digest, Written By, Classic Images,* and *Creative Screenwriting.* Her essays have appeared in anthologies including *Variety's History of Show Business, Great Women of Film,* and the *California Pop Up Book.* She has served as a judge for the *Los Angeles Times* Book Awards and is a frequent speaker at film festivals and on college campuses.

Cari has been a reporter and a private investigator, and she served as press secretary to Governor Jerry Brown of California. She lives in Los Angeles with her husband and two sons, Teo and Jake.

Indexer: Kristen Cashman
Text: 11/15 Granjon
Display: Granjon
Compositor: Integrated Composition Systems, Inc.
Printer and binder: Edwards Brothers, Inc.